The Colorblind Trilogy Book Two

Rose B. Mashal

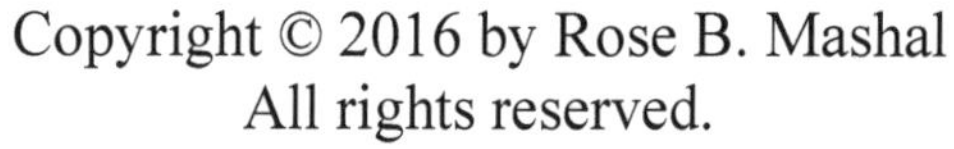

Editors:
Wennie Conedy
Kim Palacios

Proofreader:
Jaana Häkli

Cover Design by Jada D'Lee Designs

Formatted by Lindsey Gray

Dedication

To Sonia Delen, for being my rock and guardian angel.
I don't deserve you, but I'll love you forever.

Table of Contents

Preface

Love.

A four-letter word. Small. Simple. But strong, powerful, and – controlling.

Love gives you the strongest feelings, some happy, some joyful, some dreamy, some magical, and some sad. A terribly gut-wrenching, heart-crashing, and soul-burning kind of sad.

Love makes you smile. It makes you laugh. It makes you cry, and they are not always happy tears.

Love makes you act—with kindness, with compassion, with tenderness, and with care. But it also makes you act with rudeness, with disrespect, and out of fear.

Love makes you lie, but it makes you try. It makes you run in the wrong direction, because it comes to you without instructions.

Love is real, but it makes you terrified that it may become fake.

Love is wonderful, but sometimes it worries you that it may be all for appearance's sake.

Love is air.

Love is life.

Love is breathing deeply and smiling brightly.

Love is kissing wildly and hugging tightly.

Love is eating pancakes when it's night.

Love is kissing upside down that feels just right.

Love is leaving home to go home.

Love is going home to be with Love.

Love is wondering if being with Love is right.

Love is knowing that you're losing yourself.

Love is not wanting to be found.

Love is loving Love.

Love is having it tough.

Love is craving to be Love's only love.

Love is giving up your own life so that Love will stay … *safe*.

My name is Marie Grace Archer, and this is my story with Love.

One

Like a little bird, like a sparrow that just learned how to fly–that was how I felt.

No, maybe I was like a sparrow that had been trapped in a golden cage for far too long. That cage seemed like the perfect place to live, until the sparrow realized that there was a world outside it had never known. Or maybe it was just because the tiny thing *didn't want* to know it.

I wasn't physically imprisoned, but my mind was. It was caged with judgmental thoughts and doubts. But I thank God I'd found the keys to open the locks that had kept the doors closed tightly shut.

Right now, I felt like flying.

"Anita!" I called as I hurried down the stairs at my house. "Anita!"

When she didn't answer, I searched with my eyes

all around me, seeing that the door to the laundry room slightly agape, I hurried to it and called her name for the third time.

"Anita!"

"Yes, Ms. Archer?" she finally replied as she came out of the room.

"Pack my bags, I'm going home."

Telling Mazen that I wanted to stay with him, that I wanted our marriage, or whatever you call it, to work, wasn't something I could just blurt over the phone. Heck, I didn't even have his phone number.

This was something that had to be said face to face. I needed to look him in his eyes when I told him that I loved him. Oh, boy, how I loved him.

In the short car ride to Terri's house, I couldn't stop imagining Mazen's face as I confessed my feelings. I imagined him smiling until I could see his pearly whites. I imagined him taking me in his arms until our ribcages felt tangled, and kissing me until my lips swelled.

But I had doubts, and they couldn't be ignored.

I had doubts, and I had fears--so many fears.

I feared that he might tell me that it was too late, that he was over me. I feared I was no longer important to him, that I had been just a small blip on his radar and that he'd already forgotten about me. Two weeks wasn't that long, but it wasn't short either. At least it wasn't short for me.

I swallowed thickly, not knowing whether I should give in to those fears and call off everything I had planned. But, something inside me told me to keep going. I listened to it.

I was scared, remembering the reasons why I was back in my country again. Even after everything that had happened with Mazen and the fact that I realized I was in love with him, I was *still* scared. I thought about how he'd told me that I wasn't safe, and how he couldn't stay by my side 24/7 and all. But wasn't life about taking chances and facing difficulties? Well, that was the story of *my* life, anyway.

I wasn't going to stop now, not when every beat of my heart called his name; not when every breath I took pushed me to hurry up and be with him already, and certainly not when the sparkling happy tears in my eyes whispered to me that I was right, that I was choosing the right path.

But the thought of being close to his mother again, of living under the same roof as her, was truly disturbing. Maybe I had been able to get through the *incident* without being completely destroyed after what she'd wanted to put me through. But I couldn't deny that what she'd done left ugly scars on my soul.

For the past two weeks I had been too busy wallowing in my broken heart and in the pain of being away from Mazen to even think about what his mother had done. Now that I knew I was going back to where she was again, I couldn't help my heartbeat from racing at the mere possibility of being close to her and seeing her again.

But, I wasn't going to back away; I knew I would find a way to keep myself far from her. I knew that in the future I would find a way to protect myself.

If Mazen couldn't, his love would. His love would protect me.

"Marie! It's Sunday. If this is business related, I'm hanging up," Terri barked as she answered her phone.

I couldn't help the smile on my lips. "It *is* business related, and you can't hang up."

Terri let out a frustrated sound and then replied, *"True. What can I help you with, boss?"*

My smile grew, as she was in full business mode now. *Good girl,* I thought.

"I'll be at your place in five minutes. We're going to my office, so get ready."

"On it."

As I stood outside Terri's house waiting, I could easily hear screaming coming from inside. A woman was definitely upset with her about starting dinner before she had to go, and I assumed it was her mother-in-law.

"What's going on?" I asked with concern when I saw Terri's upset face, as Brad opened the car door for her.

"Nothing, just my monster-in-law being herself,"

she replied as she snapped her seatbelt in place.

"Let me guess, something terrible happened to her house again and she had to move in for a few days?" I asked, not hiding the sarcasm from my tone.

"Of course," Terri replied. "She found a spider in her bathroom and now she believes her house is under attack." She rolled her eyes.

I shook my head. "I have no idea why you put up with her!"

"Simple. I'm in love with her son, and he comes with a baggage." She shrugged her shoulders. I had to stare at her for a moment, replaying her words back in my head over and over again.

"Yeah, I know the feeling."

"I don't understand, boss," Terri frowned as she stood next to me in my office at Archer Enterprises. "Why are you showing me this? We already went through it three weeks ago, before you had to go to the Kingdom of Alfaidya."

I gazed at her with a knowing look, waiting for her to get it. And she did.

"Oh! You're going back!"

"I am. And now with Joseph no longer a part of the company, I need you to take care of the management, just as you did when both of us were away," I told her. "I have no idea when I'm going to come back."

Maybe in two days. The doubtful thought managed to find its way into my mind, causing me to imagine Mazen sending me back – again.

I willed the thought away and focused on the matter at hand, reassuring a very uncomfortable Terri.

Terri was the best of the best. Like all of my employees, she did her job exceptionally well. But that was what worried her. I was adding to her job, giving her the huge responsibility of watching and guiding the welfare of my company while I was away. She hated the pressure. She liked being my Chief Operating Officer, running the business and making sure everything worked with no problems. Making decisions was a big deal for her.

"You can always reach me whenever you want. We will call each other, chat or Skype whenever you need. I know it's a big deal, but I also know that you can do it, and everything will be just fine," I assured her. After all, any financial decisions or finalization of any contracts or agreements would still be run by me. I would be the decision maker and signatory, so I wasn't worried about anything being messed up while I was gone.

"Of course," she replied, not very happy.

I got up and took her hands in mine. Aside from being my Chief Operating Officer, Terri was also my best friend. And as my best friend, I needed her to understand why I was doing this.

"Terri, I'm sorry this has happened suddenly. I

should've given you more notice. But I have to be in the kingdom as soon as possible."

"Why, Marie?" she asked, tilting her head

"I miss Mazen," I replied with the most honest answer. "Terribly."

As we were flying to Alfaidya, my mind couldn't stop working. *Wouldn't* stop working. I'd taken care of everything related to the company and its branches, so everything would be fine while I was away, until I came back.

That wasn't what kept me restless, though.

What I was worried about was Mazen's reaction. There were so many *what if's* – thinking about how he might have spent the past two weeks, and with whom.

I feared that that cousin of his might've wrapped herself around him like a snake when I left. I wouldn't put it past her to take advantage that I was gone, while he was broken and hurt. She might have offered him a shoulder to cry on and the warmth of her bosom. That thought made my stomach twist in pain, the fear finding a willing companion forcing jealousy into my heart.

But, no – I wasn't going to let those thoughts stop me from following my instincts. If my heart was going to get broken by Mazen – I needed to hear it from him directly to be able to believe it. Because if I really wanted to fly, I had to toughen up and drop all of the weight that held me down. I needed to spread my wings of love and shake off the fear and bad feelings. Only then would I be able to fly.

An hour before we were due to land in King Qasem's airport, I got up and reached for the bag Anita packed for me, taking out the clothes I was going to wear for my first day back. I wanted to look as good as possible today, the day I was going to tell Mazen how my safety and comfort were only translated in the warmth of his presence and how much I needed him in my life. I needed his smile; needed his laugh. I needed his sense of humor; needed his wise words. I needed all of him, otherwise my life wouldn't be the same.

I put on the form-fitting baby blue dress that matched the color of my eyes. It reached below the knee with a small slit in the back. The ends of the sleeves touched my elbows, and the V-neck was modest, nothing too revealing.

I let my hair down in soft curls that danced over my shoulders and back, and then I grabbed the box that contained a decent amount of the jewelry that Mazen had gifted me on the day we got married. I made sure to put *all* of it on.

Finally, I took the tiara-like hair jewelry that the Queen Mother had given me and carefully put it over my hair, the diamond bangs easily falling into place, it completed the look of elegance that I was aiming for. Then I loosely tied a cream-colored scarf over the hair jewelry, careful to let it hide as little of the tiara as possible.

Perfect, I thought, with a smile on my light peach-glossed lips. In just a matter of minutes, I would be with Mazen again, standing on the same ground he was standing on, and breathing the same air he was breathing. I still couldn't believe it.

"Ms. Archer, please take a seat and put your seatbelt on. We're minutes away from landing," the flight attendant announced. My smile grew bigger.

When we landed, we were informed to wait until someone came for our passports and papers. It was something I'd expected. Through the window I saw three officers – or maybe they were guards – approach the jet and I rose from my seat then waited for them.

I took a deep breath and told myself that they weren't going to hurt me. The image of their thick beards and guns in their belt pockets would've sent the old Marie into a panic attack.

But not this one.

Two of the officers approached the pilot, his co-pilot and the two female flight attendants, and the third officer came directly to me. I could see that his eyes noticed the tiara on my head, and a look of confusion formed in his eyes before he nodded politely in greeting.

The officer reached for my passport, and I handed

it to him with a smile, waiting for him to read the name and hoping that the local news in the kingdom had mentioned my name when they announced the Crown Prince's marriage. Better yet, I hoped they had a picture of me, but I doubted that. That wasn't how things worked here. And even if they hadn't, I was sure that everything was going to be fine the minute I told him who I was married to.

As far as they know, anyway.

"Ms. Marie Archer?"

"That's right, officer. I'm Marie Archer, Prince Mazen's wife. The future queen," I said with my head held high. He quickly lowered his gaze, but not before his eyes slightly widened in shock.

"Forgive me, your highness," he said with a bit of a tremor in his voice. "Welcome back. I hope you are completely healed now, by the grace of God."

"Thank you. I really appreciate that. Would you please arrange for a car to take me to the palace?" I asked in a soft voice.

"Yes. Yes, of course, your highness, just give me a few minutes to inform the royal family and the royal guards of your arrival. Something must have gone wrong. We weren't informed or prepared for your arrival. If you will forgive and excuse me, your highness." He bowed his head, but before he could leave, I called to him.

"Officer …?"

"Ahmed. My name is Ahmed, your highness," he

said.

"Officer Ahmed, I would like to keep my arrival a secret, please. You can skip informing anyone for now," I said. Call me crazy, but I wanted to surprise Mazen.

"But I must have someone escort you to the palace, your highness." he protested. "Or else Prince Mazen will have my head cut off if your transport isn't secure."

I almost laughed; he sounded very serious. After what had happened with Jasem, Mazen issued clear orders for the guards to always protect me, no matter what. The alternative would result in someone losing their head, and I mean that literally. Of course, such action would necessitate in spreading a word of warning, and clearly, Officer Ahmed was well informed and warned, and it was the first thing he thought of.

"Um, … yeah. *That*." I shook my head, not able to keep the smile from showing; I may have even blushed a little. "How about you only inform Prince Fahd and tell him of my wish for my return to be kept secret for now? He will know what to do."

I trusted Prince Fahd, and I knew he would respect my wishes. He would send the car without telling Mazen. He was noble and loyal – of that I was sure.

It would have been easier I think, if Brad were with me. It wasn't easy to leave him behind. He had vociferously objected to the idea of me going back to the kingdom without protection, especially after everything that had happened with Joseph. I almost brought him with me, but he needed a visa to be allowed inside the country. It was going to take him a few days to secure one. I couldn't wait any longer. I was desperate to get to Mazen.

Half an hour later, I could see a limousine approaching from one of the small windows inside the jet, followed by an ambulance, and a police car. I wished silently that they would skip the fireworks this time, because that wouldn't be keeping my presence a secret.

My heart started thumping in anticipation as I saw the door of the limousine swing open. Someone in a *thawp* hopped out, not a royal guard as I'd expected. I swallowed thickly, thinking for a second that it might be Mazen. I prayed that it wasn't the case because I seriously wanted to surprise him. I wanted to see his face when he saw me without knowing that I was around, and him coming here would blow it all.

But as the man in question made his way towards the jet and got nearer, I was able to tell that it was Prince Fahd who'd come to meet me, and not just a guard.

"Princess Marie, what a pleasant surprise!" he said genuinely, with a hint of a smile on his lips, nodding his head.

"Thank you, Prince Fahd. It's good to see you," I greeted him back, offering him my hand, which he shook firmly. "May I speak with you privately, please?"

I asked.

"Of course, Princess," he said, and then nodded to the guards behind him, in a gesture that meant for them to back away, which they did within seconds. When he was positive we were out of their earshot, he turned back to look at me, waiting for me to speak.

"I – uh … I need to see Mazen. There are a lot of things I need to tell him, things that need to be said face to face and not over the phone. I was hoping that you could help me make this happen," I said. My voice was soft and my heart was racing.

He looked taken aback by my words for a second, but he quickly composed himself and replied, "I see. Honestly, when I was informed of your arrival, I thought that you had come back to check on the branch of your company, but hearing the real reason pleases me to no end." He smiled widely, the first real smile I'd ever seen from him, and if I wasn't mistaken, I think his eyes were glinting with joy. I could not help the blush that warmed my whole face.

"But," he said and my smile dropped, my heart following it to my stomach. "Prince Mazen is not in the kingdom."

What? My eyes widened. "Mazen is not in the kingdom?" I gasped.

Two

My head spun, my mind and thoughts whirling in every direction. Bad feelings twisted my stomach, and dark emotions closed my throat.

Mazen wasn't in the kingdom.

What did that even mean? Where was he? Why had he left? And for what? A million question bombarded my mind. *Did I come all this way for nothing? Why had he left, why? And, so soon?*

I swallowed thickly. "He's not?" I asked, hoping that maybe I'd heard him wrong. *Maybe I imagined it?* I wished.

Prince Fahd shook his head, "No."

My heart skipped a beat, for a disgusting thought violated my mind, the thought of his cousin … with him, together.

I sat down on the nearest seat, burying my head in

my hands, trying to even my breaths as I felt an approaching panic attack. "Where, then?" was my two-words question.

"London," Prince Fahd answered, and I frowned, searching in my mind for any answer I could come up with as to why he would be in London. I knew from what he'd told me just a day before I left that school wouldn't start for two months, and that he couldn't go there to start his training years even if he wished, because of his responsibilities.

"He left the same night you left. We've barely heard from him since," he added, causing my eyes to widen slightly.

"Oh!" I said, my heart settling the slightest bit as I figured he couldn't be with her; he'd left long before she could even return to the palace. And I suddenly remembered – there were *two* jets at the airport when we got out of the car. I had been too broken to pay attention as to why the other one was there. But now I knew – the other jet was for him, to go to London.

But – "Why?" I asked, confused.

"A Muslim husband can't leave his wife while she's sick. He couldn't stay here. People would've judged him," he explained.

I let out a breath I didn't know I was holding. It was because of me that he'd had to leave, not because of anything or *anyone* else. That thought was a little comforting. At least it meant he wasn't with her… right?

I truly had no idea why I was so full of jealousy – this feeling was all very new to me. But I was so desperate to see Mazen again, to have him take me back and agree to work things out – together. I was simply too afraid that something might have happened to blow up my dream. I was too afraid of losing him again before I'd even found him.

After a long pause, I asked – *begged* – "Would you please give me his address in London?" My eyes were pleading and my heart was aching.

Prince Fahd smiled, "Yes, I can do that." And my own smile returned.

"I'm going to London then," I nodded to myself.

"You mean now?" he asked, seemingly having heard me.

"Yes," I replied. "I mean, once they have the jet fueled and ready for the flight."

"But, Princess, that is not acceptable; it's insulting even, on so many levels," he said seriously.

"What? What do you mean?" I asked with shock, wondering what I said that could have insulted him.

"You've just had a long flight; you need a decent amount of time to rest. Your crew will also need to rest for at least 24 hours before they can fly again. Let me escort you to your wing and you can leave tomorrow, first thing in the morning."

My shoulders hunched forward. I knew that Arabs were known for their hospitality and generosity, but it wasn't a good night of sleep and a decent meal that I needed. What I needed was Mazen. I had to get to him as soon as fate would let me, but I couldn't decline Prince Fahd's offer. He'd already said it would be insulting.

But then, how could I go back to the palace? How could I be in the kingdom for a whole day and a night without Mazen? My blood ran cold just at the thought.

I guess my feelings showed on my face, because the next thing I heard was Prince Fahd's words, "You'll be perfectly safe. I promise."

It was like I'd heard them from the mouth of his brother, because the words sounded just like him, sounded like something he would tell me. It made the desire in my heart to see him again burn even more.

"Um … uh–" I couldn't find the words to explain my main concern. I knew that Prince Fahd knew more than the rest of the kingdom did, but I didn't know how far or how detailed that knowledge was. "Th-the queen," was all I could say, hoping that he would understand that it was her wicked actions I feared the most. My eyes were silently asking him if he could protect me from her.

Prince Fahd blew out a breath. "She wouldn't hurt you. Even if she wanted to." His eyes were honest, and his smile was assuring.

It was all I needed to hear.

In the jet, I waited for another half an hour, so Prince Fahd could oversee the arrangements of my arrival. When I disembarked from the plane, I found a woman in black waiting for me beside Prince Fahd. Weirdly enough, I knew right away that it was Princess Huda, even without seeing her face.

Over the past two weeks, we'd talked over the phone, but it was brief and I made sure that it was all business related. She would ask about my health and I would give the shortest of answers and end the conversation.

Huda was amazing as always, all smiling and easy to make small talk with. For some reason, I had the strong feeling that she knew more than she was giving away, because she didn't ask once why Mazen wasn't with me, or even hint at the fact that I'd arrived unannounced.

I was grateful for that.

Once inside the palace, I was confused. Something felt – *off*, and some things looked wrong. It was just – not the same. And if there was one thing I was sure of that was missing, it was the lack of incense in the palace. It didn't smell like musk and sandalwood anymore; the palace now was very ordinary.

As Huda and Prince Fahd escorted me to the wing, I was greeted with smiles or a nod of the head by whoever I met. It felt like I was seriously welcomed there, as if they were happy I'd come back. It was a nice thing to feel welcomed.

Once we hopped off the elevator, Prince Fahd told me to enjoy my stay and to have any of the guards send for him if I needed anything. He left us by the foyer, not entering any further, though Huda stayed with me.

My throat went dry as I entered the wing. My heart was racing, and my mind was fogged with memories. Mixed feelings of comfort, longing and sorrow consumed me.

The bedroom was pretty much the same, but oh, so different. Everything was in its place, but nothing looked like it had been. Something was missing in here, as well. Something big. The soul of the place.

Mazen.

Mazen wasn't there.

Before, I'd thought that dark memories would haunt me when I entered the wing. The memories of a gun pointed at my head, its cold steel warning me of how quickly death could come. I thought I would be assaulted with pictures of women pinning me down to the bed as another woman tried to rip my pants off. But that didn't happen at all.

Instead, it was sweet memories of the kindness with which Mazen had treated me, and the tenderness with which he'd held me. The memories were of us together, smiling, giggling, laughing, and memories of us crying in each other's arms.

It was memories of *love*.

And right then, I knew what the wing was missing most, and it wasn't only Mazen. It was life.

It was missing life.

I tried my very best to control the ache in my chest at the thought of spending a lonely night here without Mazen. I was successful in hiding my tears – to a point.

Huda took off her *niqab* and *abaya*, finally letting me see her face and also her gorgeous outfit. We chatted for a few minutes, and then she told me that my servant was on her way to the wing. I couldn't help my outburst when she said it was a new servant, someone named Donia.

"Why not Mona?" I asked in shock.

"Um, Mona is not a servant, Marie. She only spent that week with you for Prince Mazen's sake, after he requested it from her."

My shoulders dropped in disappointment. "Yeah. I understand." I'd forgotten for a second that the week was already over and so was Mona's kind service of staying with me, but – "I don't want her as a servant, I want her as a friend. Can't she come see me?" I asked Huda. I really wanted to see her, and even hoped that she would spend the night with me.

"I don't really know. I could call her, but it's up to her if she wants to come or not," Huda said.

"Come to the wing?" I asked, finding it really hard to believe that Mona could know that I was here and refuse to come; I knew she liked me.

"To the palace," she corrected. "She doesn't live here, didn't you know?"

"Oh, I see. I guess I never thought about it." But

even if she wasn't in the palace, I knew she would still come over. I hoped that her place wasn't too far away, like in another city or something.

Huda asked one of the female guards who was standing outside of the wing to inform Mona of my request. I took the time to find something to wear. I had told them to leave my bags as they were on the jet, and only took my carry-on with me to the palace.

Inside the walk-in closet, and once I'd turned on the lights, my legs took me to where Mazen's clothes were. My hands reached out to touch whatever I could touch of his *thawbs*, shirts, and every other thing. I brought a shirt to my face and inhaled deeply, then took another and hugged it tightly. A few tears of longing rolled down my cheeks. Longing for him.

By the time Huda returned, I had changed into pajamas and sat back down on the armchair like I was before, finishing my call with Brad. He'd asked me to call him once I landed and I'd forgotten. As crazy as it sounds, it felt a bit odd to have my cell phone with me inside the wing.

We heard a knock on the bedroom door, not long after, and my heart beat in excitement, thinking that it was probably Mona, the guards outside of the wing having let her in.

My guess was correct when I called, "Come in!" and I found Mona pushing the door open, her smile as wide as that time I'd told her I would be bringing Mazen his tea myself, only a day before I had to leave.

“Mona!” I cried as I stood up, my grin dominating my features. I met her halfway as she greeted me with a matching grin and open arms, an ‘‘Oh, *Benty*!” falling from her lips as we hugged. “I’ve missed you so much!”

“I missed you, too,” I told her, honesty dripping from my voice. When she smoothed my hair back in a motherly gesture, I couldn’t help the warmth that ran through me, or the feeling of how this day wouldn’t be as awful as I’d thought it would be.

In my eyes, thing were different. Everything was different. My feelings were unlike what I had felt before, and it made me see my stay in the palace in another light. I wasn’t that scared, sad and anxious girl anymore. No. I’d changed. I’d changed into someone better. There was a new light to the wing that I hadn’t seen before. A light that made everything look … prettier.

It was as if I’d had a black spot in my mind that made every nice gesture people in here had made before look like a game, some lame thing they were doing with hidden intention. They would serve me food and I would think it was probably poisoned, they would smile at me and I would think they were planning my death, they would bow their heads and I would think they were making fun of me.

Two weeks ago, I had felt as if they were my enemies.

But today as I sat with Mona and Huda, it was the complete opposite. All of the negative thoughts were like ghosts from the past. To me, the food they were serving me looked even better than before. I was aware of the fact that it was all Western dishes that had been cooked just for me, and I took it as an act of kindness. The smiles seemed so very genuine. And the bows were taken as a sign of the respect they had for me.

I'd changed.

And I was so happy about it. That black spot that had colored everything as sinister was gone. I was so grateful that I'd found my black keys. It made my heart feel so much lighter, and my shoulders weren't as heavy anymore.

I only wished that Mazen were here so I would be able to truly enjoy all of those wonderful feelings to the fullest. Because I knew that nothing would feel complete without him.

When Huda left a few hours later, it seemed like it wasn't only me who had been waiting for her to leave so I could speak freely. Because the moment the door clicked shut, Mona moved closer to me and asked with concern obvious in her voice, "How have you really been, *Benty*? Please, tell me honestly."

"Oh, Mona, it was – crazy. Things were just not the same," I told her, hoping that she would understand without me having to explain how miserable I'd been for the past two weeks.

She nodded. "It wasn't the same here either. The palace has been a mess since the day you left."

My eyes narrowed and I tilted my head to the left, trying to process what she was saying. I recalled how I'd felt when I entered the palace and how some things felt off. "What do you mean by a mess? What happened?" I asked.

A sigh left her mouth. "There are so many things that the queen does, I can't even count. Since she's absent, along with Princess Janna – no one is here to do those things. Princess Rosanna tried, but there's just so little she can do without leaving her bed," Mona explained, causing new questions to invade my mind.

I looked down at my hands in my lap. My chest tightened at the mention of *her*. And though I wondered what Mona could have meant by the queen's absence, I didn't want to ask. I didn't have the heart to speak about her, and also—I just didn't care. Maybe she'd left the country to do something important. Maybe she was sick. Maybe she was whatever. The most important thing was that she wasn't there to bother me, and to be honest and despite Prince Fahd's promise to keep me safe, it was still a relief to know that she was far away.

"Have you–" I paused, "Have you heard from Mazen?" My heart started thumping at the sound of his name falling from my lips, the same as it always did every time I thought of him. My question came out in a whisper as I dreaded the answer, knowing I would be jealous if she had heard his voice in a phone call while I hadn't.

Still, I wanted her to answer with a 'yes', because that meant that I would know something of how he'd spent the past two weeks, if Mona was kind enough to ease my worry and tell me.

Mona smiled sadly, and I knew the answer right away before she could verbalize it. "I'm afraid not, *Benty*," she said in a low voice. "He's the kind who suffers in silence."

Suffer. The word hurt my heart. But it gave me a little hope. It meant that Mona knew he was missing me, too, didn't it?

I couldn't say that I had a restless night, but it also wasn't the best. That night, I was seriously tired, and I did need to rest my body a bit. Mona sensed how tired I was when she saw me yawning, and excused herself with the promise that she would be here first thing in the morning before I had to leave for London.

I couldn't ask her to stay because I knew she probably had a home and a family of her own she needed to take care of. It was the first time I became aware of the fact that I knew very little about Mona, despite how much I liked her and loved her company. And I hoped that we would get the time someday for her to tell me more about herself, because all I knew was that she had a girl who was Mazen's age, and that was it.

I did feel lonely even with the knowledge that Donia was sleeping in the room where Mona used to sleep. She was a nice girl, no older than nineteen or twenty, with a smile plastered on her face and a blush that never faded – but she wasn't Mona, and sure as heck wasn't Mazen.

But the awareness that I was only one flight away from Mazen was enough to soothe me back to sleep every time I woke up in the middle of the night.

Tomorrow, I would be with him.

Morning finally came, and I was never happier to see the sun's rays as they made their way through the window to my right. I smiled brightly as I got out of bed, taking a quick shower and then getting dressed as Donia prepared breakfast for me. I wasn't up for eating, but I didn't want to disappoint her and make her think I didn't like the food, since it was the first meal she'd prepared for me. I took a bite or two with a cup of coffee as I waited for Prince Fahd to escort me back to the airport like we'd agreed yesterday.

Not long after, Donia informed me that Prince Fahd was waiting in the foyer. Before I left the wing, Mona came as she had promised to wish me good luck, telling me with a warm voice that she knew in her heart that things would only get better from this point on.

I believed her. Because it was what I wanted the most.

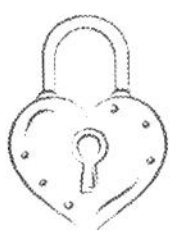

Reading people wasn't something that I was very good at. But knowing that Prince Fahd wasn't feeling very well wasn't that hard to notice. Something was bothering him greatly; I could easily see it in the frown that wouldn't leave his face. I could easily hear it in his voice that sounded somehow lower than normal.

As we made our way to the airport, I could tell that he was trying to be as polite as possible based on all of his questions about whether or not I'd had a restful night and if the food was okay and whatnot. However, every time he spoke, it confirmed more and more that there was something wrong.

I still said nothing about it. We weren't best friends – far from it – and it didn't seem fitting to ask what was going on; but when I was standing by the jet that was to take me to London and as we were about to say our goodbyes, I couldn't hold it in and had to ask him. "Is everything okay, Prince Fahd?" This man had never shown me anything but generosity and kindness; it was the least I could do to ask if he was doing well.

Prince Fahd looked taken aback by my question, but he recovered quickly, offering me a small smile as he replied with, "Yes, Princess Marie. Everything is okay."

But I wasn't satisfied; he looked far from okay.

A thought crossed my mind, and my eyes widened slightly before I asked another question, "Is Princess Rosanna okay?" My heart dropped at the thought of something bad happening to her or the baby; that would be devastating.

"Yes. She's fine, thank God." His tone spoke volumes of how much this man felt for his wife, and it was a heartwarming thing to hear. "Don't worry yourself, Princess. You have a long flight ahead."

I nodded, not very happy with the fact that I didn't know what was wrong, but thinking that if he didn't want to tell me, I really shouldn't push.

My persistent need to know what was going on didn't stop, however. As I was about to take the first step onto the plane's ladder, I had to turn around and ask yet another question, "Was it something I did?" because I couldn't help wondering if it was.

Prince Fahd smiled a smile that didn't reach his eyes, shaking his head, and then he took a step closer to me before he spoke. "We have a first family visiting us from a country that we've just started exchanging benefits with lately. It's important to keep up appearances in front of them, meaning they should feel as welcomed as possible," he started.

I wondered why it was such a big deal to have a meeting with a first family that it could be bothering him so much, but then he continued, "And since the queen is not around to take charge of arranging things, my wife has to do it. All of the arrangements needed for the visit, plus being there to welcome them personally and make sure they are as comfortable as possible. Those arrangements will require hours away from the bed that she should not leave, because the risk of losing our child would be so high, and I have absolutely no way of preventing it from happening other than praying."

Now I got it, the crease between his eyebrows was one of a caring husband and a concerned father, but he was pulling it together for the sake of his kingdom. But with a King who was too ill to do his duties, and an absent Crown Prince, he had all of those things on his shoulders to take care of. It was hard to understand how he was managing, because I couldn't imagine being in his place, having to choose between my family's wellbeing and the responsibilities I had for my people.

"Can't you tell them the truth? That she can't leave the bed?" I didn't see why it would be so hard to just apologize to them and get it over with.

"Not with these people, Princess. They'd take it as an act of rudeness. To tell them that everyone is sick or absent and they have to meet with the youngest of two princes to discuss a trade agreement, would be considered an affront and an insult. Since this president is accompanied by his wife, she'll have to be welcomed by a member of the royal family who is her equal, or someone close to it."

I closed my eyes, releasing a long breath; it was such a mess.

A moment or two passed as we stood there, both silent, each of us lost in our own thoughts, until I finally came to a decision.

I looked at the jet with longing, pressing on my lips together, then shaking my head before I spoke. "Princess Rosanna doesn't have to do it." Prince's Fahd frown deepened at the sound of my words. "I will."

Three

Honestly, I was terrified.

My steady breaths and calm demeanor could've fooled Prince Fahd in believing that I was confident in what I'd just said I would do, but I had a feeling that the sweat on my forehead gave away how I truly felt.

Inside me, there were mixed emotions. I was close, so close to being with Mazen again, and now I'd have to wait until this visit was over, because I just couldn't allow myself to leave while knowing that I could help. I went from being extra excited, to trying to convince my feelings to settle down a bit—to wait with me, wait until I'd be with Mazen again and could set them all free—not having to hide any feeling anymore.

But the terror and the fear of spending yet another day at the kingdom without Mazen had my heart in a firm grip, and for a split second I wished I could take back what I'd said. But, no. I couldn't do that. I wanted to help, and I was going to do it, no matter how much effort it would take to appear calm.

Prince Fahd's eyes widened at my words. "Pardon me, Princess?" he asked, wanting me to repeat what I'd said – presumably not able to believe it.

Well, I was no less shocked, and by my own words, no less.

I tilted my head to the side before taking a few steps away from the guards that were closest to us. Prince Fahd followed me, understanding that I wanted to be sure that our conversation would remain private, and then I spoke.

"Prince Fahd, legally I'm still married to Mazen, and everyone in the whole world knows that I'm the Crown Prince's wife. With all due respect, this places me in an even higher status than Princess Rosanna, isn't that right?" I asked, not really looking for an answer. We both knew that what I was saying was the truth.

"Yes, Princess," was Prince Fahd's response, confirming to me that he was already aware of that fact, especially since he'd only ever addressed me with my title, and called the wing 'mine.'

"I believe it would be much better, from many angles, if I met with the first family in question instead of Princes Rosanna, wouldn't you agree?"

"Of course, I would agree," he replied instantly, "But I can't ask that of you, Princess. I can sense that you're not very comfortable being here."

I was taken aback by the fact that he could tell I wasn't happy about my stay, even after I'd tried not to show it. I guess I wasn't good at hiding my feelings, after all. I didn't say anything about that, neither confirming or denying it, but instead, I asked him to let me do it.

"You haven't asked me to do anything, Prince Fahd. I am offering. Please, let me help. I would never forgive myself if – God forbid – something bad happened to the baby or your wife, knowing that I could've helped prevent it. I want to do this."

Prince Fahd looked deeply into my eyes, probably searching to see if I was being honest or at least trying to be honest. When he was satisfied with what he saw, the frown finally left his face, and a smile dominated his features. "Thank you, Princess Marie. For this, I'll owe you for the rest of my life."

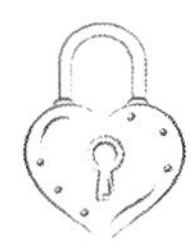

Goals.

Setting goals was my method for achieving everything I'd accomplished in my entire life. Through the years, I'd met with lots of difficulties, but the goals I would set for myself every now and then would help me overcome said difficulties.

In college, whenever studying hard had become too difficult, I had reminded myself of the goal I wanted to reach: being successful. Emotionally, I'd suffered deeply after my parents' deaths, but I had still managed to get on my feet and get Archer Enterprises running the same way as it had when my parents had managed it, because my goal was always in front of my eyes: to make them proud.

My goals were many; some were very big, and some were as small as taking a warm shower and drinking warm milk before going to bed, in order to get a very much needed good night of sleep – but they were always there.

And now my goal of meeting Mazen after all this time was the only thing that kept me going. And whatever it took to get me there, I would do it. Now, all I needed to do was to get all of these arrangements over with so that this state visit would pass peacefully – and then I would leave.

One would think I was being strong, but it wasn't strength that made me do all of this, to remain in the kingdom and fulfill my role as a royal family member.

It was hope.

I was stubborn. I was determined. And I promised myself that I would reach my goal. Because I knew that once I was through with all of these things, I would be with Mazen again. Finally. My hope for reaching my goal was what kept me standing, and that was it.

"The Future Queen" were the three magic words that Prince Fahd said, and suddenly everything was dropped on my shoulders when he announced I would be the one they should get back to for whatever responsibilities the Queen used to take care of, as long as I remained in the palace and until Queen Shams was back.

Later on, he told me that she wouldn't be back, apparently reading on my face how that announcement made me feel. I still didn't ask where she was.

One day in, and I was ready to quit. Well, almost.

There was so much to do, so many things to decide, and a thousand orders to carry out. I grew frustrated with the fact that I felt as if I were planning a wedding, not a simple ceremony for a friendly visit, as Prince Fahd had called it. I mean, why would it make any difference if they just went with whatever color for the roses in the vases where we would be seated? And if I couldn't choose yellow, why was it an option? And then again, if you know so much, why do you have to ask *me* to decide? It was seriously annoying. But – the goal was getting nearer, and to reach it, I was ready to do anything.

By nighttime, I was dead on my feet. Mona spent some time with me, going on and on about how noble my heart was. She continued to praise me for taking charge instead of letting Princess Rosanna worry about it, along with giving me advice on how things should be done, which I greatly appreciated.

Before she had to leave for the night, I couldn't help my answer when she asked me if there was anything I might need from her, because there was.

"Um … could you, like, get me a photo of Mazen, please?" The blush was heating up my cheeks as I made my request.

For the past two weeks, I'd slept with the photos I had printed of him from the internet, but I didn't have anything like that with me when I came here, and I was greedy enough to hope that Mona had a better quality photo for me.

Mona smiled sweetly at me, nodding before excusing herself to somewhere I didn't know, in order to find me one. As I waited for her to return, I took a shower and dressed, telling Donia that she could go to bed because I wouldn't need her to do anything for me, knowing that Mona would be allowed inside by the guards at the main door to the wing.

About fifteen minutes later, I called for whom I knew to be Mona to come in when I heard the knock on my bedroom door, my eyes brightening when I saw that she'd brought me a whole album. I prayed silently for it to be all of Mazen.

And it was.

For what felt like hours, through frozen memories captured in pictures, I watched most of Mazen's life with my own eyes. I saw him grow up from an adorable baby to a handsome teenager and then to a strikingly attractive, fully grown man. It was absolutely fascinating.

My smile lived on my lips until my cheeks hurt, and the tears I spilled because of so much sweetness streamed down my face. I just … I loved him more than I'd thought it was possible for me to love anyone.

My beautiful prince's pictures with Thunder were some of my favorites, but I couldn't decide if I loved them more than the ones of him as a toddler wearing a tiny *thawb* that made him cute enough to eat.

His pictures with Janna were proof enough of how much he adored her, from the first one when he was just a little boy holding an infant in his hands and smiling big at the camera with his two front teeth missing, to the last one which was only a year or two old, where he carried her piggyback style while she stuck her tongue out at whomever took the photo.

Prince Fahd was very serious in most of the pictures. Mazen was serious in some, but not all. You could see his playful nature and his easygoing personality in others. You could see it in his smile, the peace sign he flashed at the camera in certain photos, the bunny ears that he constantly made behind Prince Fahd's head. He was just full of life and amazingly wonderful. I think seeing that album made me fall in love with him even more.

Before I knew it, next day came, and I found myself at the airport standing by Prince Fahd's side. We were surrounded by a heck of a lot of guards as we waited for the president of Republic of Naria and his wife's arrival. I was grateful that this visit was friendly and wouldn't be recorded on TV or anything like that, as Prince Fahd had told me. I didn't want Mazen to know I was in the kingdom. I was sure he would be as confused as ever if he turned on the TV and saw me in King Qasem's airport meeting with a first family.

I didn't want him to know that I had come back because I still wanted to see the look on his face in the instant he realized I had returned. I knew the look he would give me would be enough to show me whether I was doing the right thing by going back to him—that it would only confirm how right I was. Or so I hoped.

Prince Fahd had explained to me that this visit was only to test the waters, to tentatively explore their options with respect to trade. I tried to understand as much as possible, but to be honest, I couldn't wait for the visit to be over with so I could put it behind me and leave.

The First Couple were lovely. They didn't speak English – or Arabic for that matter – but we had interpreters helping us translate every word.

They seemed pleased with everything that was arranged, and Prince Fahd's eyes gleamed with gratitude every time they would catch mine. It truly made me happy.

Later that afternoon and while we were speaking, the conversation took a turn, and I actually started listening with huge interest. I couldn't say much about it, though, not until I looked into the matter deeper. I took the chance during one of the breaks we had during the day, and went straight to the wing. I was tailed by two royal guards who didn't leave me until the door to the foyer was closed shut.

Once I sat down, I opened my laptop and did some research; I'd had my doubts, but my digging confirmed that I was right. For a second, I wished I could call Joseph, he knew much more about the kingdom than I did. After all, he was the one managing everything related to what I was trying to figure out right now.

Only after twenty-five minutes of research, and a long phone call with Terri, had I come up with a plan that I knew I should share with Prince Fahd.

When we met outside where our guests were seated, I took Prince Fahd to the side and started explaining what I discovered, along with my proposed strategy.

"I'm afraid I don't understand, Princess Marie," he said, and I took a deep breath, determined to make him understand my point.

"Prince Fahd, their country's industries are wholly dependent on oil. They will have to import it, no matter what, as they have no deep oil reserves of their own. And they know that partnering with the Kingdom is the best strategic move for them. The kingdom has deep oil reserves, is their closest neighbor, and that means that the cost of importing oil from here will mean fewer transport costs for them. "You don't need to take something you don't need from them in exchange for the oil!" I told him.

"You mean I don't have to structure the deal this way?" he caught on.

"Yes! Let them know that their proposal falls short of

creating enough reciprocal value for the kingdom. That will get them to rethink what they bring to the deal. It'll take some time to negotiate a beneficial agreement for the Kingdom, but I promise you that you will get a better outcome. We have the upper hand here. The Kingdom is rich in oil, and that's exactly what they need."

"Hmm!" Prince Fahd looked deep in thought, trying to process everything I'd said. "I didn't think about the transport charges."

"One more thing. For the sake of keeping the lines of communication and negotiation going between the two countries, you do need to import something from them. But don't position it as a need. Position it as a benefit for both countries. You first wanted to import wheat, which is perfect. Their country has the best environment for growing wheat, unlike the kingdom – it barely rains once a year here. We import wheat from them, and in exchange, offer them something of equal value that we could export to them."

"What is that?" he asked.

"Gold. And the kingdom has it. Plenty of it."

"Oh, I think I've started to get your point!"

"My point is not to put wheat face to face with oil – it's kind of insulting! There's no comparison between the two, not in value and not in the amounts needed. But you have gold to do that with. And this way, you'll be exporting two kinds of goods to their country, not only one. Structure a separate deal for oil."

"Oh, dear lord!" he exclaimed. "This is brilliant! How do you know all of these things?"

I had to smile. "Prince Fahd, I'm the CEO of one of the biggest import/export companies in the United States, remember? This is my playground. My game. I have a pretty good idea what I'm doing," I said with pride to his amused face.

"I'm very grateful that you stayed, more than I can say. Thank you very much, Princess Marie," he said sincerely.

"Don't mention it," I smiled. "Now, don't say wheat until their team comes to finish the deal for the oil. And then after that, you can bring up the gold."

"Got it, Princess." His smile was genuine, and it was enough of a reward for me.

I couldn't wait until the morning to leave. I requested to depart that night just an hour after the visit with the first family was over. I couldn't let anything else delay my meeting with Mazen.

But Prince Fahd had one more request to ask.

"Would you mind paying my wife a short visit? She really wants to meet with you." And I couldn't deny him that; I also wanted to see her.

Princess Rosanna's and Prince Fahd's wing was on the same floor, across from Mazen's and mine. And by the look of the foyer and the way the closed doors were positioned, I realized that their wing was almost a replica of ours, minus the colors and the furniture. All in all, it was lovely, warm and cozy.

Prince Fahd escorted me inside, asking who I assumed was her maid to inform Princess Rosanna of my presence, and a few minutes later we were invited to go in.

Sitting on the bed, there was a beautiful young woman whom I knew right away to be Princess Rosanna. Her welcoming smile brightened her whole face, exposing two dimples that made her even prettier.

Prince Fahd walked towards the bed while I stood a few steps away. He then bent down and kissed her forehead, causing her smile to grow even bigger, and one to grow on my lips at the sweet sight. And then he introduced us to each other, as if we didn't already know who was who.

"Princess Rosanna, this is Princess Marie," he smiled. "Princess Marie, this Princess Rosanna, my wife."

"Hello! Pleasure to meet you," I said politely.

"Princess Marie," she said happily. "The pleasure is all mine. Please, come, have a seat." She pointed to an armchair that was next to the bed, and I smiled as I took her offer and sat on it.

Princess Rosanna was so friendly, even more than Huda, believe it or not. She didn't have green eyes like her sister, or her aunt, the Queen; her eyes were brown like Janna's and Prince Fahd's, telling me that she probably got them from her father. Her dark hair was thick and long, framing her pale face beautifully. Her bangs covered her forehead, and her blush covered her cheeks.

Her smile remained as she touched my hand. "Thank you so much for all you've done for us, Princess Marie. We owe you like no other," she said.

"You owe me nothing. Anyone in my place would've done the same thing," I told her, but she insisted on making it a big deal that I had stayed and delayed my flight to take her place – or the queen's, or whatever.

"How's the baby doing?" I tried to make small talk.

"He or she is doing just fine. I just hope the baby likes it in there long enough to have a better chance of surviving ," she said, and my smile turned into a sad one.

"I'll keep you in my prayers," I promised, and she placed her hand over mine and squeezed, uttering a 'thank you.'

"I have your wedding gift, and I wish I could give it to you now, but I want to do it the proper way. I want to wait until I'm allowed to walk freely – I hope you'll forgive me."

"There is nothing to forgive, Princess Rosanna. This is very kind of you, but you don't have to," I told her.

"Of course, I will. And please, call me Rosanna." She smiled.

"Rosanna," I nodded, smiling back at her.

Soon, but not soon enough, I was standing yet again on the tarmac, in front of the jet that would take me to London. I was only hours away from Mazen and I couldn't be happier.

I said my goodbyes to Prince Fahd and got on the plane. When I was seated and we began our take-off, I held my diamond cross that my love had gifted to me and prayed.

When I opened my eyes, I was already in the sky. I couldn't help my smile, or the speeding of my heartbeat.

Mazen, here I come.

Four

Thoughts. Memories. Fantasies. All invaded my mind in the sweetest way.

I would think of him, his smile and his look, and my chest would swell. I would remember him, his hugs and his kisses, and my body would tingle. I would fantasize about him, the heat of his kisses, the desire in his touches, and my world would spin.

I just … I missed him, so, so much. I couldn't wait until this plane landed and I would be closer to being with him, looking into his eyes, burying myself in his arms and inhaling his scent.

But the doubt … oh, God, the doubt. My anxiety was hitting the roof, and my worries about Mazen not wanting me back, not wanting to try – were the damper to the joy I felt over finally making the journey to where he was.

My fear of his refusal to work things out was so strong, it was killing the smile on my lips and urging my tears to fall. But I wouldn't let them. I wouldn't let those bad thoughts take the happiness I was feeling away from me. Mazan and I were too good, and it would be a crime against myself to let my worries get to me.

I already knew that I wanted Mazen; I loved him, more than I could say. And if I didn't try to work things out between us, I would always wonder what it would be like if I *did* try.

Love was powerful, and from it, I got my strength to kick those thoughts away and leave a space in my mind only for dreams of upside down kisses and lopsided smiles. For soft chuckles and teasing words that made me laugh. A space only for gentle touches and bone-crushing hugs. For happiness and joy.

A space only for Mazen and loving him.

Many times while on the plane, my fingertips touched my lips at the memory of his own pressed into them. I placed my hand over my chest and begged my heart to slow down. It was beating so fast as I remembered the heat of his body and the way it was pressed to mine. I sighed at the thought of how his firm, warm chest felt as I rested my head on it each time he carried me bridal style. I closed my eyes and bit my lip as I recalled the sound of his heartbeats when we touched.

Throughout the entire flight, I was drowning in

thoughts of Mazen and my longing for him.

It was noon when the jet landed at Heathrow Airport. Prince Fahd hadn't given me the address. Instead, he'd taken care of everything I would need upon arrival, and for me to get to where Mazen was, while still keeping my presence a secret as I wanted it to be. I was so grateful for that most of all.

When I hopped off the plane, there was already a limousine waiting for me. The driver's British accent alone made my heart thump in my chest, for it gave me a hint as to how close I really was to Mazen.

The drive to Mazen's took about half an hour or perhaps a bit more. I spent most of it praying, because I knew that the more you pray, the less you worry. Boy, was I worried!

I knew that fretting wouldn't solve anything; it was a pointless feeling to have. All it did was drain me. It was fighting against the hope that was buried deep inside of my soul.

But I couldn't help it. I had done all of this, left my country, traveled to Alfaidya, then jetted to London, all to reach Mazen, when all I had was just a hope that things would be okay. A hope that we could be together again. A hope that was only there because of his words to me when he'd said he was falling hard for me. A hope that was there only because he'd promised he would never forget me. And I knew how well he kept his promises.

The car finally stopped by a massive gate. The

driver spoke into the monitor and then the gates slowly swung open, giving another reason for my heartbeats to race even faster.

We drove up a long driveway, lined on both sides by pine trees, with an extensive garden beyond them. The road ended at the front door of a mansion that surely was too big for just one person, but of course, a crown prince couldn't live anywhere less than a mansion, could he?

Once the car stopped, my door was opened by a man who appeared to be in his late forties or early fifties. He had pale skin and white hair that was combed neatly to the back of his head, not even one strand out of place. He was wearing a black suit with a tie that was the same color as his blue eyes.

He offered me his hand which I took, letting him help me out of the limousine. "Princess Marie, welcome," he said with a polite smile, and a French accent. "How was your flight?"

"It was nice, thank you …?" I said, asking silently for him to introduce himself.

"I am Philip, the house manager. I hope you'll enjoy your stay here," he said.

"Thanks, Philip," I replied, hoping for the same thing he'd just wished for me.

"This way, Princess." He pointed with an open hand, palm up, for me to go up the few stairs that lead to the main door. I nodded with another thank you, and followed his lead to the inside of the mansion.

My heels clicked on the white marble floor of the hallway that Philip led me to, and when a huge staircase came into view, Philip stopped and asked, "I am aware of your highness' desire to meet with Prince Mazen, but I was wondering if you would like a drink first? He's in the courtyard right now; perhaps you'd like to wait until he finishes his task and comes inside?"

Oh, please! I'd come this far, and I wasn't going to wait any longer. I felt that one more minute of not seeing him would bring me to my knees, for they were already shaking slightly just at the thought of being so close to him.

I shook my head. "No, thank you, Philip. I would really like to meet with the prince as soon as possible." *For my sanity ...*

"Of course, Princess," he smiled.

When I had imagined finally being in the same place as Mazen, I saw myself hurrying with my steps, I saw myself almost flying to be by his side– but that wasn't what happened.

The reality of it was that my legs felt heavier, and my steps became slower. My heartbeat went on full speed, and my throat went dry with my hitched breaths.

I was so excited, but my anxiety was taking all of the excitement away from me and replacing it with the fear of being rejected. But I still made my way to where Philip was leading me – home.

Once we stepped outside into the courtyard, Philip left me with a slight nod and a small smile. My nervousness didn't allow me to smile back, but I did nod in return.

There was nothing in me that was interested in admiring the swimming pool or how big it was. I couldn't take a moment to appreciate how beautiful the roses that surrounded the courtyard were. I didn't even notice what color the furniture in the corner was or how it looked. My eyes only scanned the place to find him, and when I did – I felt really close to fainting.

In a far corner, Mazen stood with his back towards me, in cut-off blue jeans and a white wife beater. In front of him was a large table with many tools on it, and from what I could see, there was some wooden piece in his hand that he was pushing a large chisel into with a small hammer, seemingly carving something into the piece.

The loud tap-tap-taping noises coming from the hammer were competing with the thumping of my heart inside my chest. I couldn't believe I was finally in the same place as him. I couldn't believe that I was finally able to see him. I couldn't believe that if I took only a few more steps and reached out with my hand – I would touch him.

I felt light-headed, my heart aching with so much passion and my chest swelling because of so many emotions. Goosebumps spread all over my bare legs and shoulders, not due to the slight wind that was ruffling my white sundress, but by imaging myself in his arms again, pressed tightly into his body.

The sun was making his messy hair appear a lighter shade of brown, and making the pale skin on the back of his shoulders appear even paler. Whatever he was doing made the muscles in his arms clench and unclench in the most fascinating way, showing how strong he was.

I swallowed thickly, willing my breaths to slow down, and my heartbeat to get back to normal. I willed the tears in my eyes to go away, willed the worry that was consuming me to just leave me alone, to let me enjoy this moment of finally reuniting with my love after what felt like ages of being away from each other.

Eventually, I willed my tongue to speak, willed my lips to utter his name, “Mazen.”

Mazen stopped what he was doing, and I prepared myself for the next moment when I knew he would turn around and face me – but he didn’t. Instead, he went back to what he was doing and continued hammering. I frowned, wondering if he’d heard me at all, so I tried again, “Mazen?”

He stopped, and once again I waited for him to turn, but he still wouldn’t. A moment or two passed while he stayed in his frozen state, and then he shook his head and started pounding on the wood again, harder this time, making my heart pound harder in my chest.

Why won’t he turn around? Why isn’t he acknowledging me? I wondered.

My vision started to blur, and my throat closed

from having my heart caught up in it. Doubt filled me and questions about whether or not I had done the right thing kept roaming in my head.

But, no, I hadn't traveled all this way only to walk away with nothing but him refusing to answer me. I needed to try harder, to call his name louder, to make him talk to me – no matter what.

"Mazen!" I called out loudly so I was sure that he would hear me clearly over all of the noise he was making. And that did it.

Mazen turned around and finally allowed my eyes to meet his. A tear escaped my eye and dropped down to my cheek, and the hammer escaped his hand and dropped down to the ground. My eyes were filled with hope, love and passion, and his were filled with shock and disbelief.

His lips parted in a soft gasp, and mine drew a soft smile. A smile that fell when I heard his voice for the first time since what felt like too long, because there were just too many emotions inside me at the sound of it to allow me to do anything other than take it in, embrace it, and keep it tucked tightly inside of my heart.

"Marie!" It was a whisper, a word that made me close my eyes, releasing a lone tear when I heard it coming out of his mouth. I savored the sweetness that I felt as I listened to him calling my name for the very first time ever, making me feel as if I had never been called by that name before, not even once, just by how beautiful it sounded coming out of his lips.

Opening my eyes again, I was welcomed with the green garden that was his eyes, still as disbelieving and shocked as they were a moment ago. His mouth was still agape, telling me how shocked by my presence he really was. It wasn't something that I read as a bad sign … or a good one, for that matter. He was just surprised that I was right there in front of him; after all, I had appeared to him out of nowhere.

We stood there, not moving, not speaking, not doing anything but staring at each other. He blinked his eyes a few times, making me think that he was doubting that I was real, and was just making sure that I was truly there and his eyes weren't deceiving him. I took the time to fill my eyes with the beautiful features that I had missed so much, feeding my insides with the feeling of safety that I'd only ever felt with him.

He was as handsome as he'd always been, but there were slightly dark circles under his eyes. I wondered if his nights were as restless as mine, and if it was because of me or because of something else. His beard was slightly longer than what I was used to seeing, just some scruff and the start of a mustache. And there was no doubt that he looked … tired, maybe even more than I was.

Silence surrounded us as I tried to calm myself down, to get all of my emotions to settle down a bit before I had to tell him what I wanted to say. However, when my breaths were somewhat back to normal – I found out that I'd forgotten everything I wanted to say.

All of the time I'd dreamed of this moment of seeing him again, and now that it was here, I found myself speechless. I pushed myself to just say everything inside me; he needed to hear it all – my feelings, my thoughts – and he needed to hear of my hopes and wishes.

"So …" I started, "Turns out I couldn't live without you." I smiled through my tears, unable to tell if they were happy ones or if I was just too emotional not to shed a few tears, lest I explode with all of the passion that was in my heart for this man.

Mazen didn't reply, he just stared at me, still frozen in place, so I went on with my speech, not waiting for him to say something first.

"I went back to my country just like you wanted me to do. And when I got back , nothing was the same. Nothing was right. I missed you, I missed you so much. But I tried to go on. I tried to pretend that nothing had happened, to leave it all behind me. But I couldn't," I told him. "Things happened, and I realized that I hadn't been a very good person, but I've changed. I've changed so much, I promise. I've found my black keys," I chuckled half-heartedly, disliking the fact that I could see no expression on his face that could tell me what he was feeling – only nothing. He showed me *nothing*.

"I went home like you wanted me to, but then I realized that home wasn't there. Home is with you,

Mazen. Only with you. Because – I love you," I said fervently, honestly, telling him my true feelings. I knew I had to tell him; he had to know how much he meant to me.

It was only then that Mazen started to show me something other than just being frozen. He sucked in a sharp breath at the sound of my words, and I could've sworn that I saw his eyes glistening with unshed tears.

He shook his head, and my heart dropped to my stomach. *He isn't rejecting me, is he?* I couldn't help the worry inside of me. And then he spoke the words that didn't do anything to ease my anxiety.

"You're not safe with me."

I blinked away a tear. "I'm *only* safe with you, Mazen." Because that was how I truly felt.

He shook his head again, pressed on his lips hard, and my heart only sank more. My whole world was spinning; I couldn't accept that he could be saying 'No' to us being together again. I wouldn't handle the pain if that was the case. It would kill my soul.

"We've already been through this. I can't always be with you. At some point, I'll have to go somewhere and I won't be able to protect you. If something bad happens to you, I would never be able to forgive myself. Hell, I wouldn't even be able to *live* with myself. You're safer in your country, away from me," he said, his voice cracking towards the end. It didn't make me sad like I thought it would, it made me – mad. At him.

"Shut up! Shut up, Mazen, you need to shut up!" I said in frustration, seeing his eyes widen at my outburst. I was probably the first one to ever tell him to shut up or talk to him that way, but I was too freaking mad at him for denying us this. I *knew* in my heart that he felt something for me, and it was so unfair to let his worries and fears block us from something that was so good, like being back in each other's arms.

"You don't know that. You can't convince me that you can see the future. You can't convince me that what you're thinking is the right thing, you know why, Mazen? Because I did as you told me to do, I went home. You told me that I would be better off without you, and you were wrong. Horribly wrong. I wasn't even slightly better. I was lost, sad and depressed," I said, disliking the tears in my eyes and the shake in my voice.

"You say you won't be able to protect me all of the time. Well, guess what? I don't need your protection. I didn't need it the past two weeks, and I stayed in one piece. But without you, my heart is not safe. It's slowly dying, it's shattering to pieces. Don't you get it? How many times do you want me to tell you that I can't live without you?" I was hurt, and I couldn't believe that I was almost begging him to take me back. It wasn't me; that was never something I'd thought I would do. But I loved him, and love makes you try.

"You're not safe in the kingdom; it was proven many times! Have you forgotten?" he asked. The frown on his face and the cracking in his voice were saying so many things other than the words he was speaking.

"You're wrong!" I exclaimed. "I haven't forgotten, but I was only in danger because of our families, and their need to get things the way they wanted – not from your people."

"You can't know if anyone else wants to hurt you," he said.

"The same as you can't know it!" I deadpanned. "I was in the kingdom without you. I arranged a ceremony and met up with the first family of Naria. You *weren't* there to protect me, and yet here I am, standing in front of you, safe and sound. So, what is your point exactly?" More tears rolled down from my eyes, watching as his filled with more disbelief.

"You were in the kingdom?" he asked in shock.

"I was. For the past three days. Alone." I insisted on pointing out that he wasn't there, for he believed that without him the earth might open up and swallow me whole, or some messed-up thing like that. "How do you think I showed up here?"

A few minutes passed in silence before he spoke. "You don't know what you're getting yourself into," he breathed out.

"I know exactly what I'm doing, Mazen. I want you. And you just come with baggage; I would take it for you," I whispered. "If you'd let me."

More silence filled the space around us, and to be honest, I started to lose hope, but I decided to try one more time. With my shoulders hunched down, and a throat drier than an abandoned desert, I asked,

"What do you say? Do you want to try and work things out between us?"

Mazen narrowed his eyes, his lips going to the inside of his mouth for a moment as he pressed on them, and then a small crooked smile played on his lips before he sighed.

"Are you asking me if I want my soul returned to me, Princess?"

It took me a moment to register what his words meant, but when I did – I couldn't help my legs as they ran the few steps that separated us. I launched myself into his arms as he met me halfway and lifted me off the ground, hugging me tightly to his body.

Our lips met, and the whole world around us disappeared, leaving only the sound of our tangled breaths, and the thumping of speeding heartbeats. Arms hugged, and hands buried deep into soft brown hair. Aching hearts finally started to beat as one. Leaving only the feeling of familiarity, of passion and adoration and I'm-only-ever-safe-in-your-arms.

Our lips met, and my world became whole.

Our lips met, and I felt complete. I finally felt home.

Home.

Five

He kissed me. Long and hard. The kiss wasn't like anything I'd expected. Because when I fantasized about this moment in my head over the past few days, I'd thought it would be one of those smacking, sloppy and wet kisses, with tongues and all. Maybe even with music playing in the background. But it wasn't like that.

It was much better.

Our lips were pressed tightly to each other's, making promises that could not have been made with words. The kiss was sweet, soft, and oh, so passionate. It was the type of kiss where the only thing that could pause it was that fact that I had to smile into it every two seconds. I was flying, flying high and free. The singing of nearby birds made a sweet melody that was better than any other background music.

That kiss was a memory that I knew would last forever. I would keep it in my heart, if not in my mind.

Mazen set me back gently on my feet, his eyes not leaving mine, when we broke the kiss. His eyes were glistening with so many feelings that I wanted to hug and cherish each and every one of them. They were so pure and so tender, and I knew they were all toward me. *For* me.

My smile wouldn't leave my lips, and the butterflies in my stomach wouldn't stop flying. I loved how he was looking at me so much. I didn't want to blink, not wanting to lose this magnificent sight for a mere second. It was just too good to waste by closing my eyes, no matter how briefly.

His own eyes studied me as if he were memorizing my features, and then his hand came up to my face. His fingertips started touching my skin softly, grazing gently at my cheek, my jawbone, and my lips. "You're real," he whispered to himself.

I couldn't help the soft chuckle that escaped my lips. "Of course, I'm real," I told him. "You're touching me."

He shook his head slightly, "You have no idea how many times I imagined you being here. How many times I thought I heard your voice calling my name." He moved a wayward hair out of my face and put it behind my ear.

This is why he didn't respond when I first called him. He thought he was imagining it! That thought didn't really help to diminish my smile that already didn't want to fade; it now grew even bigger. And my heart was drowning in the sweetness that was pouring out of him.

"I never stopped thinking about you," I admitted.

Mazen hugged me back to his body, my head resting on his chest where I could hear his heartbeat, which was beating so fast.

My favorite place...

"Neither did I, Princess." He hugged me even more tightly to his chest and then kissed the top of my head.

Our sighs matched as we enjoyed this moment that I'd been waiting for since what seemed like forever. And my smile remained on my lips as I closed my eyes and savored every minute that fate would allow me to stay in Mazen's arms. Where I belonged.

The darkening sky was the only thing that told me exactly how long I had stayed in Mazen's arms, pressed tightly against his body as he kissed my hair repeatedly every now and then and I kissed his chest – just above his heart – in exchange.

My legs were aching, but I still didn't want to let go. I'd already done it once, and I'd only gotten a broken heart out of it. A heart that was being restored from its shattered pieces just from being close to him.

The feeling of being with him was nothing that I

could describe with words; it was too good for words. It was magic. Like a fantasy, something you read about in fairytales. Something that was too great for me to know how to describe.

It was as if I were starving and finally got something to eat. It was as if I were thirsty and finally got to drink. It was as if I were dying and, just before slipping away, found the nectar of immortality.

I found it all in Mazen's arms. My love. My safety and my comfort.

"You came all the way from the kingdom straight to here?" Mazen asked into my hair.

I nodded into his chest, snuggling my head more into him if that was possible, inhaling deeply the sweet scent that was all him and his warmth.

"You must be so tired," he said. "And starving."

Not for food, I thought.

"I feel fine," I told him, but the truth was, I was even more than fine. I was in heaven.

"It's not possible," he stated, and took a step back away from me. I almost cried for him to come back again, but his thumb and forefinger as they held my chin to make me look up at him were enough of a comfort. "Let's get you something to eat, okay?"

I nodded with a smile.

Mazen took my hand in his, tangling our fingers together before leading me back into the mansion. "You actually met with the First Family of Naria?" he asked as we made our way to the hallway, and I had to chuckle.

"I did," I replied with a grin dominating my face.

"You never cease to surprise me, Princess," he said with a matching grin, stopping in his tracks when we got closer to where Philip was standing as if he were waiting for orders to do something.

"Philip, please prepare us something to eat, whatever the Princess fancies for dinner," he said, smiling my way.

I smiled back, looking at Philip when he asked, "Anything you prefer, Princess?"

Shaking my head, I replied, "No, anything would be fine. Thanks."

"Yes, Princess." He nodded his head before he turned to Mazen and asked, "Your Highness, where should I put Princess Marie's luggage?"

Mazen paused for a moment. "Um … any of the main rooms that she chooses," he said awkwardly.

Why couldn't I sleep in his room? I wondered, trying to suppress the pout that I wanted to make.

"Uh, … " I didn't even know what I wanted to say.

"I'll take you on a tour if you're up to it, Princess," Mazen offered.

"Not tonight, maybe later," I muttered. "Any room close to yours would be perfect."

Mazen's answering grin was infectious, and I couldn't help but return it, even if the fact that I was going to be sleeping in another room was bothering me.

I knew that by the 'normal' standards I shouldn't

be living with him now; after all, I'd only known him for a short time. But what was normal for us? Our relationship has never been normal. Far from it.

We were married two weeks ago, and by the law and what everyone else knew – we were *still* married. But I also knew that his religion considered us not married, because I was forced, as he'd said. But that was between the two of us. *God!* I didn't know where that would leave us, or where we stood now.

Could it be that we would start over? From the very beginning, like getting to know each other and dates and all that cheesy stuff? That wouldn't work for us. I was already in love with him. We had already shared a room for six days, shared laughter and tears. I'd just bared my soul to him, admitted that I couldn't live without him. It couldn't be that we needed time to get along or whatever.

But at the same time, and when I really thought about it, I knew that we couldn't simply go on and live our lives as if we were newlyweds – we did need time. And I thought it would be for the best, even if I didn't like it. Not a little bit.

While Philip prepared us dinner, we talked. A little bit. We spent more time smiling at one another than talking, our eyes saying so much of what our tongues failed to say. I couldn't contain the joy in my heart that appeared on my lips, and I could tell that Mazen was just as happy as I was with our reunion.

And when the food was served, it sent warmth to my heart at how the simple act of eating with him seemed and felt so familiar, proving to me once again how familiarity and safety meant nothing if it didn't include him.

My grandmother was right; it's the people we love who make a home, not buildings and lands. Because though we were in a different setting from when we last ate together – a different place and even a different country – the feeling was the same. Comfort and peace. And it just proved to me even more how it was Mazen that was home for me, and I believed he would always be.

But then, too soon, our time was up, and Mazen spoke.

"You must be so tired, my princess," he said, brushing his knuckles down my cheek, sending shivers down my spine.

I smiled and then bit my bottom lip, shaking my head slightly, not saying anything.

"What?" he wondered with a smile in his eyes.

I sighed, "I don't know what I like more, you calling me by my name, or calling me your princess."

Mazen's smile grew, his eyes watching his touch on my face. We were sitting on a couch in the living room that had room for more than three people, but we had chosen to sit close while we waited for the food to be served. And since then and even after we ate, we still stayed in our place. I didn't even know for how long.

"I have a hard time calling you by your name," he admitted in a whisper, his eyes finally looking at mine.

I frowned in confusion, "Why?" I couldn't understand why it would be so hard for him to call me by my name. Was it somehow offensive to his religion or something? I didn't get it.

Mazen's thumb caressed my jawline softly, and I leaned into his touch, blinking lazily as I waited for him to explain, my frown already gone just because of his gentle touch.

It took him a moment to reply, but before he did, he took my right hand with his left, the one that wasn't touching my face, and put it on his chest, so my palm was flat right above where his heart was.

"Because every time I think about you, think about your name, my heart beats so fast that I feel like it's going to explode. And that's only thinking about it, let alone actually saying it," he explained softly. "Can you feel it, *Marie*?"

I nodded, sensing the strong thump of his heart. I stared into his eyes with so much passion inside of me that I was hoping showed in my eyes. But – "It's just a name, Mazen," I told him, smiling slightly.

"You're so precious to me. All of you. Even your name. I don't think I can explain it."

I couldn't help it, I had to kiss him. Because when he said things like that … *oh, God! Help me*.

Our lips were soft against each other, but the kiss was hard. Like, pressed-tightly-and-never-wanting-to-stop kind of hard. My hand that was on his chest moved up to the back of his neck, burying my fingers in his soft hair, my other hand coming to join it as I pulled him even closer to me, not wanting him to back away ever.

I couldn't stop thinking about how much I'd missed this. Having him so close, yet it still didn't feel like he was close enough. Being able to touch him, yet still feeling like it was too little. But I was grateful, *very* grateful for whatever I could get of him. Because for the past two weeks – almost three now – all I could think about was how I craved just one touch, one kiss, one hug. Now that I've had them all, and though it still felt like too little, I was just going to take whatever he would give me.

I wanted more, so much more, especially when his arms surrounded me and pulled me closer to him. But when tongues got involved in our beautiful kiss, it took everything in me to back away.

"We … I, uh …" I panted, not being able to form a sentence, my head still spinning from the sweetness of kissing him. "It's forbidden in your religion to … uh, …"

Mazen shook his head. "I know," he said, out of breath, "But I'm not a saint." And then he started kissing me again, with even more passion this time, and I have no idea where I got the strength to pull away from him.

"I don't want you to do anything that you might regret later," I told him. It was so ironic, because that line should be said the other way around, from him to me, not me to him. But I knew Mazen and how he felt about disobeying God. I knew from the last time we had been together and things went a little too far that he didn't like to break laws – not the ones that his religion commanded, anyway. And I didn't want him to be upset.

Mazen froze, his eyes swimming between mine for a minute before he backed away, and then he nodded, pressing on both of his lips. "You're right," he murmured. "I shouldn't ha–"

"Hey," I interrupted him, "It's okay." I patted his hand and then held it in mine.

Another minute passed in silence, and then I decided to break it, "Would you show me where my room is? I need to take a shower and get to bed."

Mazen nodded, then got up, with my hand still in his, leading the way up the stairs to the second floor.

My hand stayed tangled with Mazen's as we climbed the stairs. We exchanged smiles and soft looks on our way to what would be my room.

As we stepped inside the room, I took a minute to look around at my surroundings. The furniture was elegant, the golden color giving it a luxurious and opulent look. The walls were pale gold, and the huge chandelier above the bed went so well with the coffered ceiling. The bed was dressed with crisp white linens, and a white chaise lounge was positioned at the end of the bed. Between the art on the wall I could see a golden door which I assumed led to the bathroom, or the walk-in closet, or maybe both. On the opposite wall, there was a beautiful dresser with a round mirror surrounded by more art on the wall, and the wooden floor was accentuated by a rose-shaped white carpet. I liked the room, a lot.

"What do you think?" Mazen asked.

I smiled, "It's lovely."

But what will I do with all the space? I thought, for the room already felt too lonely, despite how warm and cozy it seemed to be.

When I chose my penthouse in New York, the wide space was what I loved the most. But now, all of the space seemed to make it feel somehow colder, and I wanted to tell him to stay, but I knew I couldn't, so I didn't.

"Um, I guess I'll leave you now to get some rest," Mazen said.

"Yeah," I nodded, twisting my lips to the side.

Neither of us moved from our spots for a few moments that we spent just standing there awkwardly, staring at everything around us but each other. Eventually, Mazen took a few steps toward me until he was standing right in front of me.

I looked up at him and he smiled. His hand touched my arm as he kissed my forehead with a long, loving kiss that was tenderer than butterfly wings and sweeter than honey.

"Goodnight, Princess," he said softly, and then he was gone, closing the door behind him.

I let out a long breath that I'd been holding since his lips touched my skin. My hand came up to above my head and I fisted my hair in frustration. I didn't know what was going on. Things looked a lot different, or better yet – complicated, all of a sudden. Or maybe it was that I hadn't really thought much about it.

I huffed, then decided to take a quick shower and head to bed, and that was exactly what I did. It took me a while to get everything I needed from my bags, and the round white tub in the bathroom was calling to me, but I was too tired to even do that, wanting to just get in bed already.

After my shower, I dressed in simple shorts and a tank top, then got under the covers. But once my head hit the pillow, I was suddenly wide awake.

What have I done? Was the thought that wouldn't leave my mind. Now, I was so sure of my love for Mazen and how important he was to me. There was no doubt in my heart that he was The One. I loved him with everything in me. Loved him to the core. But – was I too fast in what I'd done? I couldn't tell.

I knew that being with Mazen was what I wanted

the most. And so I acted to make it happen. I'd traveled all the way to the kingdom, then to London, just to be with him. But – what about *my* life? What was I thinking?

In my desperate need to be with Mazen again, I hadn't thought of my company or what was I going to do with it, especially with Joseph out of the picture. I couldn't just leave it to my assistants! I needed a better manager if I was going to be away.

My grandmother.

Oh, God! I guess I always had her in my heart and thoughts. In the back of my mind, I knew I could always visit her every now and then, at least every couple of months. It wasn't like she would notice my absence anyway. But still … I hadn't thought this through.

Lastly, Mazen. Now that I was here with him, he was a few yards away, but that was it. He was still *away*. Things had gotten all awkward, and I had no idea where we stood now. I had no idea how long I would be in one room while he stayed in the other. I wanted him closer, but at the same time – I had no clue if I was even ready to have sex without marriage, myself. Something I knew with no doubt Mazen wouldn't do.

So, what were we going to do? Live together like best friends in love, or what.

I didn't know. I didn't know anything.

I closed my eyes, willing my thoughts to settle down while wishing for sleep to come over me. Maybe tomorrow would bring me some answers.

Six

London's sun was a shy one, but today it peeked bravely through the grey clouds, giving us a perfect day. There was a shining light from warm rays and a cool wind that was just right.

I closed my eyes and faced the sky, enjoying the feel of the gentle wind that ruffled my hair and caressed my cheeks. I smiled and exhaled deeply.

Everything looked so good in my eyes, and everything felt so perfect in my heart.

Love was responsible for that. Mazen was. Oh, well, Mazen was Love.

I opened my eyes, and continued my walk through the gardens that surrounded the mansion. The green color of the grass created a perfect rhythm with the red and yellow colors of the flowers.

Even that was perfect. Love made it this way. And

my heart was filled with it. Filled with love.

My hand reached out and touched one of the sunflowers that were in one corner by the fence. They were so tall, almost my height, and I loved that so much, because that too was so beautiful in my eyes. Everything was.

"You like the sunfollowers?" A memory of Mazen asking me that question – the other day when we took a walk together here – surfaced, and my smile only grew bigger.

"Followers? It's flowers, not followers. Sunflowers," I'd corrected him. *"And, yes, I like them."*

"Oh, no. It's sunfollowers, that's what we call it in Arabic. Because they follow the sun wherever ..." he'd explained, sounding serious.

"Okay ... but they're called sunflowers, and we're speaking in English now, so don't confuse me," I'd replied with a funny expression on my face.

"Arabic or English, it's sunfollowers, they follow the sun."

"Don't make up your own language," I'd frowned playfully at him.

"But they do follow the sun!" he'd protested.

"If you say 'follow the sun' *one more time, Mazen ..."*

"What, what? You'll kiss me?" I remembered seeing the smile shining in his eyes, along with that teasing look he had in them whenever he was trying to make me laugh.

"Maybe." I'd bit on my bottom lip, trying to hide my smile.

"Follow the sun, follow the sun, follow the sun!"

I'd laughed out loud. *"Someone could mistake you for a twelve-year-old sometimes, I swear."*

Mazen actually had pouted at that. *"Oh, I'm sorry. I meant one would mistake you for a two-year-old,"* I'd told him, and then ran before he started chasing me.

It was always like that – fun and laughs, love and smiles. Everything was good and perfect. My heart was living in heaven, and my spirit was flying up in the sky. Mazen was making everything beautiful.

I sat down on the wooden bench near the sunflowers, right where Mazen and I sat a few days ago. It was where we'd talked for hours and hours. About everything and some more.

I'd asked him about Salma and Thunder, and it was obvious that he didn't like the fact that they weren't here with him in the UK, but he'd said that he hadn't even had time to think about them when everything happened.

I hoped that he would bring them soon – they already had a small stable at the back of the gardens – but I didn't say anything about it. Believe it or not, now after nearly two weeks of being in London with Mazen, I still had no idea where life was taking us.

I knew Mazen would have to go back to the kingdom one day soon; I knew I wouldn't mind going there with him. But – where would that put me? I knew that in people's eyes, and the law's eyes, we were married, but both of us knew we really weren't. I still didn't know if that was the next step in our relationship or what.

There was only one thing that was bothering me, and I couldn't stop thinking about it: Mazen had yet to tell me that he was in love with me.

Everything was all roses and sunshine, but that was the only thing that hurt my heart whenever I thought about it, so I tried not to.

Because I could see it. I could see that he loved me each time he looked at me. I could feel it in my heart each time he called my name. It was enough for me, but I couldn't help but want to hear it from his mouth as well.

I would wait for him to say it after every nice moment we had, or after a sweet kiss we shared. I would wait for it after a certain look in his eyes and a certain smile on his lips that he would give me every now and then – but it never came.

I wondered if it was as hard for him to declare his feelings as it was for him to apologize or say my name. My name that whenever he said it, he made it sound like something sacred, as if I was someone of huge value.

I wondered, a lot. I tried to understand. But I still waited. Because I knew that when he would say the words I longed to hear, my heart would feel no drop of sadness after that. Forever.

It was like I was in some kind of trance, but instead of everything feeling numb and blank, in my case everything was happiness and love. I was high, drunk, even. High on loving him, and drunk on his sweetness and the tender emotions I felt whenever I was with him.

Every day I found that I loved him more than I did the day before.

I was in a love trance, and all of the voices, concerns and worries in my head that tried to take away my happiness, I blocked them all, because I couldn't let go. Seriously, how could you choose not to be so in love, having day after day that was filled with nothing but joy? How could you let go? I knew I never wanted to.

I leaned back on the bench, and pulled my phone out of my jeans pocket when I felt it vibrating. When I checked, the alert wasn't what I hoped for; it was only an e-mail from Terri about work. It wasn't anything urgent, so I made a mental note to reply to it later, maybe when I woke up from my La La land at some point later tonight.

What I was hoping for, though, was for the alert to announce a text message from Mazen, or better yet – a call. As crazy as it seemed, we had only just exchanged our phone numbers that morning. How insane was that? We were living together, I was so in love with him, and it was only today that I'd gotten his phone number.

But then again, I could barely name anything that wasn't crazy about my relationship with Mazen.

Everything was crazy. Beautifully crazy.

I thought about sending him a text, but didn't know if it was a good time for him or not. I didn't want to bother him. He had a meeting with one of his professors. They were going to talk about his specialization, and that was the first time that we hadn't been in the same place together since I'd come to London. He'd asked me whether I wanted to go with him and maybe wait for him inside until he was finished with his meeting, but I declined. I regretted it now, though. Because if I was there, at least I would be closer to him.

Yes, I was that much madly in love, I couldn't even stand a few hours away from him.

Over the past two weeks, Mazen had shown me around London. He took me everywhere. We went out every day and every night. From long walks in London's streets to the fanciest restaurants to a tour by bus. We went to museums and watched Shakespeare in Love at the theater. We ate chocolate that tasted like heaven and ice cream that I could never forget. I'd had the best days of my life since the day I came here.

It wasn't because all of the activities we did were amazingly wonderful, no – it was all about the company. Having Mazen with me was the best part about everything.

Last week, I thought I might take a chance and check on the London branch of Archer Enterprises. I was already worried about the reports I was receiving, and I thought an in person visit would be much better than any exchange of emails or video chats.

After telling him of my plans for the day, Mazen asked if I wanted him to go with me. I loved the idea of him being there.

My few visits to the company were productive; I managed to close several contracts, establish guidelines, and straighten out personnel issues. However, Mazen's presence was highly distracting. He would give me that smile that made the butterflies in my stomach go nuts, and I would always ask whoever was speaking to me at the time to repeat themselves.

Every day with Mazen was like that fifth day after our wedding, that day when we kissed upside down and made pancakes, the day when I couldn't stop smiling or fill my heart enough with his closeness even when he was on top of me, bare-chested.

I sighed at the memory and felt the heat creeping up my cheeks as I thought of his touch and his kisses, and all of the looks in his eyes that could bring me to my knees begging for more. Mazen was simply consuming my whole being with the love I had for him in my heart.

I shook my head slightly as another memory came playing in my mind. It was about four or five days ago, and my lips tingled with my ever-present smile.

"We should've waited, Mazen," I said with a disappointed voice.

"Yeah, I guess so," he said sheepishly, looking

down.

I narrowed my eyes at him. "I should've never listened to you, but you knew I wouldn't be able to say no to all of the begging."

"Oh, c'mon! Don't put all of the blame on me, you told me to take it out," he protested.

"Well, you begged," I told him, "But it was too soon."

"It smelled so good, I couldn't resist."

"It did." I looked down at what we'd done. "What are we going to do now?"

"We can feed it to Philip," Mazen shrugged, and I had to laugh and punch him playfully on the shoulder.

"That's lame! I should feed it to you*, you ruined it. I've never made a cake that bad. It needed more time in the oven," I sighed.*

"I'm really bad at this whole cooking and baking thing," Mazen stated.

"You think?" I tried to give him my best glare, but soon I was laughing at him and at the situation with our ruined cake, turning the events to yet another beautiful memory with him.

It was just like a honeymoon, with how we barely left each other's sides and how we spent our days doing nothing more than loving and laughing and living. I couldn't imagine life could get any better.

It *was* just like a honeymoon – but one without sex.

Another buzz from my phone that was now lying on the bench beside me made me look at it as it moved a little with the vibrations. I knew it was probably another work e-mail, but despite how I still wanted to stay in my Mazen-filled haze, I knew that I couldn't ignore it.

Picking up my phone with a huff, I found out that I was wrong again. It was a text message from Mazen.

My heartbeat sped up just seeing the name on the screen: *'Prince Charming'* – Mazen was the one who had entered his name into my phone like that, another way to tease me about my slip the other day when I told him that I'd called him that in my mind once, or maybe ten times…

I was like a teenager all over again, so eager to open the message that the split second it took for the phone to show it felt like three hundred years and two days.

By the time I opened and read the message, I was now smiling like a kid on Christmas morning.

'I miss you' his message read, and my heart was about to burst out of my chest.

His voice rang in my ears over and over again, it saying those three words that meant so much to me, even more than I could explain. I had no idea how many times I read that one simple message, over and over again. When I finally stopped, I realized that time had passed while I was staring at the screen.

He missed me. I wondered if it was as much as I was missing him, because if it was – it meant that he was missing me so freaking much. The thought warmed my heart.

'A long, tight hug would be perfect right now, you know?' I typed, meaning every word, and then I clicked 'Send.'

Waiting for his response anxiously, I decided to move on with my walk. I got up and my legs took me to another part of the garden where we'd spent many hours just lying on the grass, with Mazen sitting cross-legged, and my head on his lap, as I lay on my back.

He was playing sweetly with my hair while I closed my eyes and enjoyed the moment, peaceful silence surrounding us. My left hand reached to touch his that was resting on my shoulder, because I wanted to be even closer to him.

His response was to take that hand up to his mouth and kiss it tenderly, making me smile and causing my insides to tingle. After he kissed it, he didn't put it back, instead he swept his thumb over my wedding rings. That made me open my eyes and look up at him.

Mazen studied the rings for a moment, and then he looked back at me, a look I couldn't read in his eyes, "You're still wearing them," he stated, maybe to himself and not to me.

I nodded slowly.

"I've never taken them off since you put them on," I admitted to him, and his answering smile was so sweet before he leaned down and pressed his lips to mine in another upside down kiss for us to share and remember. It was the best part of that day.

In my heart, I knew that maybe the only reason why Mazen had yet to reply to my message was because he was busy, but I couldn't help but feel disappointed as the time passed with no response. I thought about sending him another message, but I knew I shouldn't do that … for some reason.

My legs kept moving me here and there in the wide garden, and I stopped when I was standing right by the pool outdoors. Not the one that was in the courtyard; this one was much bigger, shaped like an egg.

I sat down and dipped my fingers in it, playing lazily with the water, remembering with a smile all of the times I'd watched Mazen slicing through the water like a pro; he treated it as a sport more than pleasure.

The pleasure was all mine, though.

I couldn't settle on what I loved to see most – Mazen in the water, his arms parting the waters to propel him forward, the strength of his legs kicking him towards his goal, or watching him get out of the pool in nothing but a swimsuit, wet body, and damp hair. From where I sat, during that particular hour in the morning, the sun was in his eyes, causing them to squint slightly, just the way I liked.

My bottom lip made it inside of my mouth as I remembered how many times I almost lost it whenever I saw him that way. It was his daily routine to swim every morning, and it became mine to sit nearby and stare.

With a sigh, I stood up once again and walked

slowly around the pool, stopping once or twice to sniff a rose or touch another. Without warning, my vision turned pitch black as I felt two hands of someone who'd come up behind me covering my eyes.

I was surprised because I hadn't heard anyone approaching, but the smile on my face didn't disappear for a second. I knew immediately who it was. My heart knew before my mind.

"Guess who," he whispered.

"Um … Peter?" I questioned, saying the name of our gardener.

"Oh, no. I'm not him, you two are not that close," he chuckled. "Try again."

"I don't know … Philip, maybe?" I said, the smile apparent in my voice. "Oh, wait! I know. Anita!"

My vision became clear again and he turned me around to face him, his beautiful green eyes tightening with a playful glare. "Anita? Seriously, Princess?"

I laughed out loud. "Well, I was running out of people who should be home now." I paused, looking down at my phone screen to be able to tell the time. "You're early." He wasn't supposed to come back for at least another hour. Not that I was complaining …

Mazen smirked. "Someone said something about a long, tight hug."

My insides warmed and my cheeks blushed, but that didn't stop me from throwing myself into Mazen's arms, taking all he had to offer of the peace and security that I would forever feel whenever we were touching.

His arms surrounded my body and mine came around his neck as I stood on my tiptoes to be able to rest my chin on his shoulder. I closed my eyes, enjoying being pressed tightly to his body; the long moment we spent in silence still felt too short. My stomach did a flip or two when his lips touched my bare shoulder where my sleeveless shirt didn't cover it, and then it just dropped down when I heard the same words that had rung in my ear so many times since I read them in his text, "I miss you."

He didn't say it in the past tense, and I knew exactly what he meant. Because despite the fact that he was hugging me and I thought I couldn't possibly get any closer to him, I was still missing him. I missed him even while staring right into his eyes. It was just how much I loved him. I knew my heart would always ache for him, no matter how close he was to me and no matter how long we were together.

With a half step back, I was able to look into his eyes again, without actually leaving his arms. My smile was no longer there, but it didn't mean I was any less happy, quite the contrary, but the emotions inside me were too intense in that moment to allow me to smile – could you imagine?

There was no hesitation in my hands when they pulled his neck down so I could let my lips meet his. When I kissed him, my lips told him in another way other than words exactly how much I missed him in return. The squeeze he gave me as his lips pulled my bottom one inside of his mouth told *me* exactly how missing me wasn't the only feeling he had for me.

I still wanted to hear *those three words*, though.

When we pulled back, his fingers brushed my hair out of my face and touched my cheek. I leaned back into his touch and then turned my head slightly to kiss the inside of his hand while my own covered it, watching his smile that was even more beautiful than watching the sunrise.

"Would you go out to dinner with me tonight?" he asked, which was silly. He didn't have to ask; he knew I'd never objected before, how could I?

I nodded and he smiled. "Great. I have a surprise for you."

Seven

The surprise wasn't actually that he had a surprise for me; Mazen made sure to surprise me with something or other every single day. It would be a new magical place, or a new kind of food. It would be his way of talking or learning something new about him, like the fact that he played the guitar. It would be a 'Marie' coming out of his lips so easily in one of our conversations, but still making it sound so precious.

Sometimes it would just be the way he picked up so fast and so well on how I liked certain things.

Like, the way I loved to rest my head over the left side of his chest more than the right side, because there I could better hear his heartbeat. That was always where he placed my head whenever we embraced and he would hug my head to his chest, and how he would set me on his lap or carry me bridal style to my bedroom after falling asleep while watching a movie together.

Or like the way I liked my coffee and what I preferred to eat in the morning, he would ask Philip beforehand to make for me. Or like things as simple as reminding me to shut down my laptop instead of just closing the lid, because he knew I'd always forget to do that.

Today's surprise was a beautiful thing that he bought for me to wear to wherever we were going tonight. It was a semi-sheer, floor length, one-shoulder red dress that hugged my curves just the right way when I put it on. I liked it a lot, and couldn't wait for him to see me in it.

"Bring me my black heels, please," I asked Anita after I finished putting on my matching red lipstick.

"Right away, Miss Arch–Princess," Anita replied awkwardly, causing me to snort internally while I checked myself in the mirror. She was still not used to calling me 'Princess,' even though I hadn't actually asked her to call me that. I guess she thought she should call me by the same title that everyone else was using, even my dear 'husband.'

Anita had come all the way from the States last week at my request for her services here in London instead of New York, in exchange for a very nice raise. Philip was doing a great job taking care of the mansion, but it felt weird to have him wash my clothes for me – don't ask me why. I wasn't very comfortable with the idea of him seeing my underwear.

After I spoke to Mazen about it and asked if I could bring her over, he'd welcomed the idea and even said that he was going to ask me if I needed to hire any other help from London instead, but I preferred to have someone I already knew.

I won't lie and say that I knew everything about Anita, but I knew enough to trust that she was the best, after so many years spent working for me. She literally had no family, and was really bad at socializing. The longest conversations we had were no more than a handful of words, but she always understood what I needed and did it perfectly.

Her conversations with Philip, though, were something else. They were always arguing and fighting about who should do what. Their arguments would always be a mix of English with a bit of French and Spanish words – and a large number of glares. Mazen and I decided to let them manage their business on their own and not step in, as long as there were no flying dishes or broken vases. Thankfully there hadn't been any. Yet.

At first, I'd been concerned about her asking why I wasn't sleeping in the same room as Mazen, but she never spoke of it. I couldn't decide if it was the fact that she didn't care, or if she thought it was just some sleeping habit such as one of us preferring to sleep alone. Whatever it was, I was grateful that it was never mentioned. None of my conversations with her was ever personal, anyway.

There was a knock on the door right as I was finishing putting my heels on. "Come in," I called, and Philip entered the room.

"Pardon, Princess. Prince Mazen asked me to inform you that he will be waiting for you downstairs whenever you're ready to go," he said.

"Thank you, Philip. I'll be right behind you," I told him, taking one final look at myself in the mirror before leaving the room.

Going down the stairs carefully with a part of my dress being held in my hand while the other hand touched the wooden railing, Mazen came into view with each new step I took. His back was turned to me, but I guess that the clicking of my heels alerted him to my presence and he turned around to face me. The view of him in a tux nearly made me trip.

Very *Titanic* style, his eyes shone with a look that went straight to my heart, and then his hand reached out to help me down the last few steps. He didn't say anything, he only stared deeply into my eyes with adoration and then without warning, his lips caught mine in a streaming-hot kiss.

His arms grabbed me tightly and even closer to his body, while his lips kissed mine passionately, not leaving mine until I was almost out of breath.

I half-panted, half-chuckled, "I guess you like the dress."

Mazen grinned. "You look absolutely stunning, my princess."

His words made me blush, as I looked at him with smiling eyes and smiling lips. “Thank you.”

‘‘Ready?” he asked, offering me his arm, which I clutched with my hand right away.

“Wait,” I said, and took out his silky pocket square, then wiped the lipstick smudge on his mouth with it. Then I nodded, “I’m ready now,”

“Let’s go,” his grin mirrored my own.

“Are we taking any guards with us?” I wondered, because it was different every time we went out. We didn’t want to bring attention to ourselves, but most of the time, we had at least one tailing behind us.

“Only Fawaz,” Mazen replied. *Of course*, I thought. Fawaz was a royal guard who reminded me a lot of Brad. He would go nuts whenever Mazen would say we were going out alone, but Mazen never listened to him or had to beg like I did with Brad whenever I wanted to be left alone.

Thankfully, Mazen always knew what he was doing and we were always perfectly safe every time we went out without security.

The ride to our destination – which was still unknown to me – was quite long, something I knew I wouldn’t be feeling if Mazen was actually talking to me. But he wasn’t.

Being quiet for so long has never been our thing. We’ve always found something to talk about, anything. Yes, sometimes we’d be silent, just enjoying each other’s company when he would place a kiss on my forehead or play with my hair while I read something. Or when I watched him working on that wooden piece that he's been working on for weeks now. But that was a comfortable silence; this one though … it wasn't. It was awkward, and I wondered what was wrong.

Last night when I went to wish him a good night in his office, after he had disappeared for an hour or more, I saw something that made me frown a bit, but I didn't comment on it, and neither did he. By the morning, I wasn't really thinking about it, but now, I knew that there was something seriously bothering Mazen.

He'd told me before about his habit of writing down his thoughts when there were too many and he wanted to sort them out. Last night, I saw him burning some papers, which I immediately knew had something important written on them – whether it was something related to the kingdom and its security, or his thoughts.

I was only ever interested in the latter. But I still said nothing, because I figured that if he wanted to involve me in said thoughts, he would speak to me about it. I wasn't going to push him.

Now I was seeing that it was physically affecting him. He was sitting right beside me, glancing my way every few minutes and offering me a sweet smile, but his mind was somewhere else, which wasn't like Mazen at all. He was always in control of his expression and showed no emotions, even if a war was going on inside of his head. But the foot tapping he was doing told of how nervous he was. I disliked the fact that he wasn't including me in his problems, wondering if he knew yet that he could trust me with them.

The thought saddened me. Because everything about Mazen and me wasn't about how long or how often. Normal wasn't something you could say about anything related to our relationship, so I couldn't say that it was too soon for him to trust me. What our hearts had felt in the past few weeks, since the first time we saw each other, could easily equal the emotions of two people in love for a lifetime. I knew that even with the fact that he had yet to confess his love to me.

Because our love was something else.

"Are you okay, Mazen?" I had to ask. He was looking out the window, completely lost in his thoughts so that I had to call him once again. "Mazen?"

"Huh? Did you say something, Princess?" he asked, not even aware of what I'd asked him.

"Yeah, I asked if you were okay. You look nervous,'' I told him quietly, starting to get upset that I knew nothing about what was going on with him.

"No, no. I'm all right," he replied quickly, taking my hand, kissing it, then putting our joined hands on his lap. "Don't worry about it."

Disappointed, I offered him a small smile and then looked out of my own window, hoping that we would get to our destination soon. I thought that maybe then Mazen would go back to being his usual self, or maybe even tell me about what was bothering him – because I knew that there was something, even if he said otherwise.

Ever the perfect gentleman, Mazen opened the door for me and took my hand as I stepped out of the car. With a smile, I looked at my surroundings as Mazen guided me to no less than a yacht that was waiting for us in the water of the River Thames.

My smile grew once I saw it, completely touched by his choice of how to spend the night: being surrounded by the beautiful sight of dark water sparkling with all of the different lights that hugged the river from both sides, and the dark sky sparkling with shining stars.

Happiness reflected on Mazen's face when I looked at him with gratitude and excitement filling my eyes. All of the thoughts about him not sharing his concerns with me fell away, because I decided that I was going to enjoy this magical night that Love planned for us to spend peacefully together.

Everything about being on the yacht was touching, from his choice of the string quartet playing soft music which started the second I set foot inside the yacht, to the delicious Italian food that he'd arranged to be cooked for us right here on the yacht.

Our server was such a nice guy, polite smile, polite small talk and everything, but I couldn't help but try really hard to hide my laughter every time he addressed Mazen. He made it sound more like: *Prince Maizon*, and it just sounded so funny in my head, because I had no idea where he got the 'O' from.

Once we finished our dessert and the server had left us, Mazen asked me with a smile about the reason behind my hidden snickers. I'd made sure that to the server, they were only evidence of how much I was enjoying my time and not actually laughing at him.

"It's just – he says your name in a pretty funny way. I'm sorry I just can't help it," I chuckled, to which Mazen grinned.

"Yeah, I get that a lot from non-Arabs. I guess he's never heard my name pronounced in front of him before, only read it." He shrugged.

"Yeah, could be." My smile was evident until what Mazen had just said registered in my mind. "Wait a second, you get that a lot from non-Arabs?" I asked in shock, my smile falling.

"Aha," was Mazen's reply.

"But – I pronounce your name correctly, right?" The thought that I'd been saying his name the wrong way all of this time was kind of terrifying.

Mazen's eyes tightened, and he pressed on his lips as if he was trying to stifle a laugh himself. My eyes widened.

"Are you kidding me? I pronounce your name the wrong way?" I freaked out.

"Calm down, Princess. I think it's – uh, cute the way you say it."

"Cute?" I almost yelled. "I had no idea I was saying it wrong. I thought it was the same way your family pronounced it!"

"It's not wrong, it's just that – you say it with a slight accent, is all," he said with a smile.

"God! I can't believe it." Could it be that I was pronouncing it the same as the server I'd just been making fun of in my head? Oh, how I wished I could curl into a ball and disappear.

"Relax, Marie," he said softly, reaching for my hand to hold it. "I love the way you say my name." He smiled, and it was like magic, because though I still felt bad about it, his touch, his smile and the way he said my name while telling me to relax sent calmness over me, and I did relax in my chair.

Smiling, I told him, "I love the way you say my name, as well," earning myself a grin that made him even more beautiful in my eyes than he already was, if that was possible.

After a pause, I asked, "What does it mean, anyway? Your name, I mean." I was curious.

"It means Rainy Clouds," he said.

"What? Like clouds that have rain in them that has yet to fall? Ones that appear in the sky right before it rains?" I wondered. I couldn't get why anyone would give their kid such a name. Though it sounded lovely, it still meant something gloomy.

"Yes, that's it," he smiled.

I thought it was weird, and wondered if the other names were just as gloomy. "How about Fahd?"

"Leopard."

"Leopard? Seriously?"

“Yes, it gives you the feeling of strength and power,” he explained.

“Well, that’s true.” I didn’t think about it that way. “Mona?”

“Wishes.”

“Fawaz?”

“Winner,” he translated.

“Oh. What about Huda?”

“Faith.”

“Why does everyone have a strong or cheerful name and yours is gloomy?” I blurted out my question before thinking about how it might hurt his feelings. But it wasn’t really fair how his parents had named him, no matter how beautiful his name sounded.

“Gloomy? It’s not gloomy, Princess. What are you talking about?” He looked confused.

“Well, maybe to people who like the rain …” I trailed off.

“Marie, when you googled for products my country needs the most, what did you find?” he asked. I frowned in confusion; what did that have to do with what we were talking about?

I replied anyway, “Food production, wheat mostly.”

“And why is that?” he asked, but I had a feeling he already knew the answer.

“Because wheat needs a significant amount of water, and you don’t have any pure water source other than rain,” I said, and then it hit me. “Oh! You don’t have any pure water source other than rain," I repeated, finally understanding how important rain was in countries like his, most of all. Rain was the only pure water they had, and even that happened rarely since it was a desert land.

Mazen smiled, knowing that now I understood why his parents had named him that – a rainy cloud told of goodness to come.

"What a beautiful and meaningful name you have," I said honestly.

"Thank you, Princess," his smile wrapped his voice.

He never failed to amaze me – with his knowledge, his manners, his intelligence, his beautiful soul – in and out. He even amazed me with the meaning of his name.

Towards the end of the evening, we found ourselves standing by the railing, watching the beautiful sky – well, I was looking at the heavens. Mazen was hugging me from behind, his head buried in the side of my hair that was falling down past my shoulders. He would inhale deeply every once in a while as he took in my scent. I would feel his soft lips on the spot behind my ear, sometimes kissing it and other times just touching it with his lips. It made my eyes roll to the back of my head.

He was swaying us lazily, and though we were mostly silent, I couldn't help but think how being this close to him, feeling his warmth and tenderness, made me feel. My heart was flying up high in the air and my soft smile stayed on my lips without any effort from me to keep it there.

I was so happy. Happier than ever. I couldn't believe I could be any happier. But Mazen decided that in this very moment he would interrupt my thoughts and prove me wrong.

"You know," he whispered, "From the moment I saw you for the first time at the airport, I knew that my life wouldn't be the same. I was extraordinarily attracted to you, and I knew that your smile would be buried in my head for my entire life."

I smiled and hugged his arms that were hugging me right over my stomach. He was just too sweet.

"The next day I promised in front of all men, in front of God, that I will cherish you, and respect you for the rest of my life. And I truly meant that," he said, warming my heart and causing my smile to widen. "I was so happy with the unexpected gift from God that was you, someone I learned had a great heart, just by knowing that a big cut of her earnings went to charity, monthly. Someone who'd also saved my sister's life, the most precious person to me. Someone I wanted to learn more about, and see more of her smiles."

My breaths hitched at the sweetness of his words, and I couldn't help but want to hear more, so I said nothing, just rested my head back even more on his chest.

"Things happened, and my thoughts were, *'Well, it was too good to be true.'*" He sighed softly, and I followed him, letting out a long breath that still didn't help the thumping in my heart, nor did swallowing down my hitched breaths after it.

"But I still couldn't let go of the hope of making things work between us. I had a feeling that we could be something really good, that we could be really happy together, and then – I had to let you go." His voice dropped, and it was as if he was trying to control his emotions, because it was affecting the way he sounded. Something told me that remembering our painful separation wasn't his intention.

"Letting you go was the hardest thing I've ever done in my whole life," he said with pain and honesty dripping from his voice. "Because despite the fact that I knew I had strong feelings for you, I still didn't know that it was love."

I stopped breathing.

"I'm so in love with you, Marie," he whispered right in my ear, sending shivers down my spine, and warmth spread over my soul. He covered my hands with his and hugged me even more to his body.

I thought that my heart probably skipped a beat.

My eyes couldn't not want – need – to see him in that moment. I had to turn around, had to look right into his beautiful green eyes with my teary ones, and when I looked into them – I could've sworn that I saw right into his soul.

Pureness and clarity. And love.

"I've lived the worst days of my life while you

were away from me, Princess," he said softly. "You were in my every thought, never leaving my mind for a second. I dreamed about you, your smile and your touch. I yearned to hold you in my arms just one more time. I was breaking inside."

I swallowed thickly, my eyes traveling between his as his hand stroked my face, and his other held me close to him.

"But then you came back to me." He smiled softly. "And I knew right then that I will do anything in my power to protect you, to keep you safe, and to keep you in my life, forever."

Mazen paused for a moment, his eyes staring into my own, a plea written in them that I couldn't hear very well, but saw so clearly. I had no idea what he was begging me silently for.

I only knew that whatever he wanted, whatever he needed from me – I would do it in a heartbeat.

His hands left me as he took a step back, and it almost hurt not to have him close. He never broke his gaze as he reached into his pocket while getting down on one knee.

My eyes widened, knowing exactly what he was about to do, but not believing it was happening at the same time.

One of my hands covered my mouth to muffle the huge gasp that I wanted to let out, while the other settled over my chest, willing my heartbeat to slow down a bit, because it felt like my heart was going to burst out of my chest.

Mazen help up a tiny box in his hand, which held an amazingly stunning diamond band inside it. With love shining in his eyes and adoration filling his voice, he asked, "Marie Grace Archer, you make my life bright. Would you marry me?"

My thrilled smile got mixed with my happy tears, but the joy didn't prevent me from replying to his question, to end his misery, because it looked like he was holding his breath until I gave him the answer.

"Oh, my God! Yes! Yes, of course I will marry you," I said in excitement. That was his cue for drawing a beautiful smile on his lips that made it look like I'd given him life, not just an answer to his question.

It all happened so fast, one second I was looking at him on his knee, and the next second he was on his feet, hugging me so tightly and then sweeping me off the floor and spinning us in a circle. Our laughs of happiness and relief flew through the air, with new promises of more bliss to come over us.

Sadly, back then I didn't know that it was only the start of more heartache and misery.

Eight

There was an undeniable tightening in my chest right after I hung up with him. I tried to let it go, didn't want to dwell on it, but I couldn't help the horrible feeling that settled in my heart for being denied something like that.

I won't lie and say that I hadn't expected it, because I did. I knew this might be his answer, but I still hoped, and the fact that I had that hope in me was why I was hurting now. I was on the edge of a panic attack, and I didn't want that to happen.

Inhaling through my nose and letting go of my breath slowly through my mouth, I willed my anxiety to go. It didn't help. His words rang in my ears over and over again. Painful and agonizing. It was so unfair of him to say so, but still – I'd expected it.

When I knew that there was no denying what was

to come, I reached for my phone and typed *'Need u,'* then sent it as a text message. It was all I could manage to do; I could barely see through the tears that had started to fall heavily.

It was only a few moments before Mazen was knocking on my door, but it felt like ages and ages. I couldn't reply to him, I was choking. All I could do was put my head between my knees as I sat on the edge of my bed, trying my hardest to even my breaths.

When Mazen heard no response, he opened the door slowly. "Prin– …" was all he said before I heard his rushed steps and saw him as he kneeled down in front of me.

"Hey, hey, it's okay. You're okay," he said as he smoothed my hair out of my face, trying to get me to look at him. I wanted to keep my head down, and I wanted to raise my head up and face him at the same time. Also, I really didn't know what I wanted to do.

I cried, hard. It became ugly crying when my sobs started echo in the room. His touch was soothing, and his voice and words were comforting, but I couldn't stop my shallow breaths or control them. I felt light headed, and I knew I could possibly faint.

"Marie," Mazen said, "I'm here. I'm right here, I'm not going anywhere. You're so strong, you know that, right? You know that, Princess," he assured me, taking me in his arms so I was now hugging him and crying over his shoulder, fisting his shirt tightly, as if I was afraid he would disappear.

"Shhh … it's okay, Princess," he whispered right into my ear. "I love you. I love you so much." And it was like magic. His words came out of his mouth, and my breaths started to slow down, very slowly, but surely.

He loves me. He really loves me, I reminded myself. *That's all that matters.*

"Hi," Mazen said with a small smile when I finally looked him in the eyes, my tears still streaming down my cheeks, but less heavy and further between. My breaths were much more even and somewhat controlled.

His hands wiped my tears away, and then they stayed on my face, hugging it, comforting me with the tender touch and the passion that was pouring out of him for me.

His eyes betrayed him, though. I knew he didn't want to show me how concerned he was, but I could so easily see the worry reflecting in them. His lips found their way to my forehead, and he pressed them to it in a long, loving kiss. I closed my eyes and sighed, resting my head back over his shoulder as we hugged.

We stayed this way for quite a while, long enough for my tears to dry and for me to calm down and be able to speak normally again without gushing or choking on my words.

"They don't want us together." The words were heavy, on my tongue and on my heart.

There was a pause before he spoke, and I felt his

hands tightening around me a little more when he heard what I'd said.

"Who?"

I wondered if he thought I was talking about his mother. I wasn't.

As a matter of fact, we'd never spoken about her at all, not once. I believed Mazen was giving me time, thinking that I might talk to him about her later, in one way or another. But the truth was – I never wanted to speak about her now or ever. It was like, if I didn't mention her, she just wouldn't exist.

"I just– … " I was about to tell him, but my tears started falling again and I couldn't speak.

"It's okay, Princess," Mazen soothed. "You don't have to say anything about it now."

I nodded into his shoulder, taking a few more minutes to control my emotions a little before I tried to speak again. In the back of my mind, I imagined he was feeling uncomfortable kneeling like that all of this time, but my selfish self wouldn't let me tell him to get up. I needed him to hold me in his arms forever, couldn't bear the thought of him moving away even an inch.

"I just called my priest, I wanted him to marry us. He refused when I told him you were a Muslim. I can't believe he did this," I sobbed into his shoulder.

Mazen's hand – the one that was smoothing my hair slowly – stopped its movement, and he didn't say anything. I had no idea if it was because he was shocked, or if it was because he was hurt. But in both cases, I knew that he was upset, for me if not for what was upsetting me.

"It's okay," he whispered eventually, his words holding sadness in them.

I had to back away to look him in the eyes, to see if I could tell why the sadness was there, if I'd hurt his feelings by telling him that. Maybe I hadn't thoroughly thought it through before speaking, but it was the truth. Father Hart had said the church would never allow it, and it killed me. I'd seen Catholics marrying Jewish men, and even atheists before, so why couldn't I marry a Muslim? It wasn't fair; that was not how God had told us to be, and I'd learned that the hard way.

I saw in his eyes the sadness that I'd heard in his voice, and I imagined my eyes matched his. I thought it was better to explain to him to make him understand my point.

"You don't understand, this is very important to me. I wanted him to marry us the same way he'd married my parents. He was the one I went to confess to my entire life. I wanted to fly him over and have it all like I wanted, but it's not possible. Now it's not only about a dream being denied. He said no priest would ever do it, The Church won't allow it."

It was easy to see that Mazen was simply speechless, something that was very unlike him. He only looked at me deep in the eyes, but something told me that he had taken off to another place and wasn't here with me with his mind.

"We can do it my way; it's the same thing, Marie," he finally said. "There will be someone to marry us, there will be witnesses, and we both agree. It's what marriage in both of our religions is all about."

"Yes, but I wanted it *my* way. You should feel for me, it's just like you don't want to live in sin, neither do I," I told him, my voice cracking at the end.

"You won't be living in sin, Princess, you won't," he assured me, "We will make our vows and promises in front of the God we both believe in. Isn't that what really matters?" he asked, his eyes pleading with me to see it the way he saw it.

I didn't reply, I only looked away.

Mazen's hands came once again to my face as he hugged it, making me look him in the eye. "Do you have any idea how much it hurts to know that you want something that I can't give you?" he asked. "I can't even tell you how bad I feel right now. I just want to do anything to make you happy. I *will* do anything to make you happy. I honestly just don't know how."

"Being with you makes me happy," I told the ultimate truth.

Mazen's smile, though small, was genuine. It brightened his sad eyes and sent a wave of calmness over me.

"Being with you makes me happy, as well, my princess," he whispered. "Let's do just that. My way, your way, it doesn't matter. It's for God only, and we both are believers in Him."

I pressed on both of my lips hard, a tear escaping my eyes before I nodded and offered him a small smile. "It's all that matters," I assured him, but the words were assuring to me, as well. It was all that mattered: our love.

Once again we were hugging, and once again he was soothing me. "It's going to be okay, Marie. We'll figure it out. We love each other, that's all that matters," he repeated my words.

As he repeated the words, I realized that I was already convinced.

Staring at my wedding band, I couldn't help the smile on my lips as all of the beautiful memories and all of the promised ones for the future filled my thoughts. But the memories weren't the only beautiful thing, there was the wedding band itself, as well. My new wedding band.

Rings weren't a part of weddings ceremonies in Mazen's culture. They wore them, yes. But it wasn't a must. So, it didn't matter if it was presented before or after the wedding. I knew I was never going to take mine off, either way.

My smile grew, remembering how Mazen was about to put it on right after I said 'Yes,' but found no space left on my left hand. I already had two rings and a wedding band there on my engagement finger. The confusion on his face as he stood there for a moment not knowing what to do was just too adorable. Insanely, I loved seeing how nervous he really was, even after we'd hugged and kissed in silent promises of a happily ever after.

I'd chuckled and decided to end his pain, giving him my right hand to place the band on my right ring finger instead. I knew it wasn't the traditional way, but who cares? I simply couldn't find the heart to take off my other rings and band; they meant a lot to me.

Maybe I would get lots of questioning looks whenever someone saw it, but I seriously didn't care. *Let them wonder*, I thought.

The beautiful design of the band told me before Mazen could tell me himself that he'd been the one to design it, like he'd done with my diamond cross. The band was made of tiny diamond hearts. It was so simple, but the meaning behind it was so far from simple, that when I really thought of it – it brought tears to my eyes.

Every heart in the band was upside down to the two other hearts on either side of it. Upside down. Like our favorite kisses, like our relationship: married, then fell in love. Like how our lives had turned since we met each other. And now, like I wore it on my right hand and not the left.

Everything around us was upside down, but that was us – we didn't do usual.

"What are you smiling at, Princess?" Mazen's

voice interrupted my thoughts.

I looked up at him from my spot where my head was resting on his lap. We were supposed to be watching a movie, but I wasn't watching anything other than my wedding band and fantasizing about our life together. From the looks of it, Mazen wasn't paying much attention either, since whenever I looked at him he would be looking at me or his hand's movement over my hair.

"Us," I simply replied.

That earned me a sweet smile from him. "What about 'us'?" he asked.

"I'm very happy with you, and I can only imagine myself being even happier ten years from now – completely in love, telling our kids about that love and praying that they'll find the same. I'm dreaming of a long, happy life with you," I confessed with all honesty.

"Oh, Marie," he breathed, sounding in awe of what I'd just said, before he bent down and kissed my forehead. "I can never tell you how much this makes me happy."

I smiled, watching as he hugged my hand with his then raised it up to kiss the back of it. A moment of comfortable silence went by before Mazen spoke again. "There's … uh," he paused to clear his throat, "There's something that I wanted to talk to you about."

"Sure," I said as I got up, turning on the couch to face him as I sat with my legs folded underneath me. I wondered why he'd put on his blank mask that he wore often in front of other people. It was only the two of us, after all.

"Are you using any method of birth control?" Mazen asked, to which I blushed deeply and bit my bottom lip. The thoughts about why I would need birth control were too many and so intense that I got lost in them and didn't reply.

"C'mon, we're both adults, and this is an important thing to discuss," he offered me a small smile.

"Uh … yes, of course," I said. "No, I'm not on any birth control." I was one of those lucky girls who didn't experience any pain during that time of the month, and my period was never late, never early, so I couldn't find a reason why I would use birth control.

"Oh. Okay. Would you like to set up an appointment with a gynecologist? I can recommend one or two," Mazen said, blank expression still on. Now I could understand why he'd put on that mask on the first place.

"Um … no, it won't be necessary. Why do you think I need birth control?" I asked in confusion, and for a second – Mazen appeared confused as well, nervous even.

"We're – uh, we're going to get married very soon and, uh … we're – you know…I mean, if you want to…"

I bit my bottom lip again, but this time it was to hold in my laughter, finding a nervous Mazen to be very adorable and just plain cute. I couldn't just sit there and watch him be that uncomfortable, I had to interrupt him, "I know we're going to *'you know.'* " I made air quotes to which he smiled shyly, narrowing his eyes playfully, "But I don't need birth control – not now, anyway."

"But, princess," Mazen started, "That means that you could get pre–"

"Of course I know what that means," I interrupted him yet again, "And I want it."

Mazen's eyes shot up to his hairline in shock, seemingly in disbelief. "Oh," was all he said before he got lost in his thoughts.

I couldn't help my smile as I moved even closer to him and held his hand in mine. "I want to have kids. With you," I told him, the smile not leaving my lips.

Mazen's face broke into a wide smile and he brought our hands up to his lips to kiss the back of my hand. "This makes me happier than you can imagine, Princess," he said. I squeezed his hand in response, but after a short pause, he cleared his throat and started speaking again. "But I don't want you to do that for my sake – it's not fair."

I frowned. I knew that Mazen needed an heir as soon as possible, but that wasn't the reason why I wanted to have kids, and I told him just that.

"It's not like that, Mazen. I've always wanted to have a family, always wanted to have kids. I've got to admit that I didn't expect it to be so soon, but I wanted them with a husband who I love more than anything in the whole world. And that's you, Mazen. I love you, and I can't wait to start a family. With you." My voice was dripping with honesty.

"Oh, Marie," Mazen sighed, kissing my hand once again. "I keep thanking God for gifting me with you, and I don't think I will ever stop."

I grinned, "Same here."

"I want the same, I want to start a family of my own, but I know that your culture is different from mine, so I had my doubts that you'd want the same thing I do," he explained. I was sure by now that he'd put his mask on so I wouldn't be able to tell what he wanted. He wanted me to state my own opinion, not based on his needs. Could he be any sweeter?

"I know. But don't forget that I'm Catholic. I wouldn't use any birth control anyway unless it was for making a space between kids, or because pregnancy would affect my health somehow," I said.

"I see," he smiled, "And how many kids do you want?"

I had to chuckle and shake my head at his playfulness. "As many as we can afford to give the best life to."

Mazen leaned in and kissed me chastely on the lips. "That's a lot of kids, Princess." He grinned.

"I know. Do you want fewer?" I asked, already knowing the answer.

"No, no. I want as many kids as God will grant us with," he said, his lips still so close to mine. "Plus, I've heard that it's really fun to make babies." And suddenly I was on my back as he attacked my neck with kisses where he knew I was ticklish, at the same time as his hand tickled my sides.

I was laughing hard and begging him to stop while I actually didn't want him to, thinking of how I really couldn't wait to know how fun it would be to make those babies of ours.

Nine

Before I knew it, it was my wedding day. I was in a simple white dress that was exactly what I'd wanted my wedding dress to be. My best friend and assistant – Terri – was with me and had helped me as much as she could with preparations. She came all the way from the States to join me on my big day. Being my best friend, she didn't ask many questions after I told her enough about everything that had happened to me in the kingdom. She was exactly who I wanted by my side as I married the love of my life.

There were only four people in our wedding party, including Mazen and me. Terri was my bridesmaid, and Fawaz was his best-man. I'd always wanted a small wedding, my groom, myself and only six guests. But I guess you can't get everything you wish for, right? It wasn't a big deal, though; I was marrying the man I loved more than life, and that was the only important thing.

The walk to the altar that Mazen had insisted on building just for me was short but memorable. It still left a heavy ache in my heart to be walking it alone. I'd always dreamt of my father, or at least my brother walking me to my groom – giving me away. That was another thing that I couldn't have, but decided not to dwell on. I was supposed to be happy, and only happy on this day, and I was going to be. Today, and hopefully the days to come – for the rest of our lives.

What I couldn't get out of my mind, though, was the fact that it wasn't a priest who was marrying us – it was a Sheikh. I tried my best not to think so much about it, but how could I help it? It was near impossible. It wasn't just another detail to complete the wedding day, and it wasn't something like the color of flowers or how high my shoes should be. It was very, very important to me; it was my faith and what I'd believed in my whole life, and not being able to get married in a Catholic Church wasn't that easy to accept.

But I let it go.

Not because I'd stopped thinking about it, but because I knew that there was nothing else we could do. If there was, I knew that Mazen wouldn't hesitate in finding it and getting it done.

By the end of my walk to the altar, my eyes were locked tightly with the green ones of the man who'd captured my heart with his wisdom and kindness, more than he had with his captivating looks and his charming self.

The promise that he held in his eyes – which I could hear loudly in my ears without his mouth speaking it – was enough to remove any doubt from my heart that I was doing the right thing, given the fact that I'd let go of something as important as marrying as a devoted Catholic would.

Sitting by a round table near the end of the altar, the Sheikh asked us pretty much the same things a priest would in a Christian wedding ceremony. The difference was that there was a lot to ask Mazen to promise about protecting me and treating me with care, more than I was asked to do for him, which was actually a nice thing to hear.

When I said *'I do'* my heart was so filled with happiness that there was no place in it for sadness or heartache. Everything in my eyes was just so wonderful – even better than my dreams.

The emotions inside me were almost enough to get me high. No, not almost, I *was* high on joy and … love.

This time, we didn't sign any papers, which Mazen had already explained to me. I was actually surprised that I hadn't figured it out on my own before, and instead needed him to explain it so I could understand how things worked.

We were already married in the eyes of law, given the contracts that I'd signed on that day in the kingdom, but because I was forced back then it was not considered to be a truthful contract in the eyes of God.

Mazen had explained to me how important it was for both of us to accept marrying each other, to have witnesses, to promise to take care of each other in sickness and in health, to respect each other and to never deceive one another. And that was what today's ceremony about. The legal papers were the same since we'd never gone through a divorce beyond the two words he'd said to me.

I remembered asking Mazen about how it was so easy to get a divorce in an Islamic culture, and he'd replied, *"It wasn't slightly easy on me, Princess."*

"I know," I smiled. "I meant in general, you just say two words and that's it?"

"Well, it's pretty complicated, and about the two words, don't forget that when you get married you say only two words, as well. It's all about what's in your heart and what you promise in front of God. Papers are to satisfy legal matters, not spiritual, and it takes months to get that done in Arabian countries, just like any other place."

"Huh," I said. "How complicated?"

"Let's see, you have three months and ten days after saying the two words to work things out, and you won't need a new marriage contract then, up to two times. The third is final, unless the wife marries another guy and they divorce or he dies, then they can get married again if they want to."

"Wow! That's complicated." I said, earning myself

a sweet smile from him.

At the end of the ceremony, Mazen took my hand and led the way to yet another altar. I was confused for a few seconds until my confusion was replaced by shock. At the end of the altar stood a bishop in all of his glory. I was so freaking surprised that I literally stopped in my tracks and gasped.

"He's here to bless our marriage," Mazen said with a soft smile. I could see the unsure look in his eyes, as if he was afraid he'd done something wrong. "It's the best I could do."

"It's perfect," I said in a rush, ending his suffering. "Thank you so much," I thanked him as a tear slipped down my cheek. A happy tear.

The bishop asked me the questions I knew he would ask, and I replied honestly, then he asked Mazen if he would promise to never force his faith on me. Mazen replied with a, "Yes, sir."

The third time is the charm they say, and it was with the bishop that I said my third 'I do' to marrying Mazen. He then blessed our marriage and I couldn't have been happier. Everything was just plain perfect.

Mazen's bedroom –the main bedroom in the mansion – now became our bedroom. Once we stepped inside and Mazen locked the door behind us, I couldn't help how nervous I suddenly became.

He'd wanted to take me to Paris for our honeymoon, but I didn't feel like we needed to. We'd already been living the best honeymoon since I came from the States, and all that mattered was being with him, so I didn't see the need to go to another country for a week or two.

After all, it was only Mazen's closeness that I wanted the most. It didn't matter where we were as long as we were together – same room, if possible. He was all I needed.

Plus, I knew if I went to Paris, I'd have to visit the branch we have there, and I would be buried with the amount of work that would surely be offered to me, and I didn't want that.

I smiled nervously when Mazen offered me his hand. When I took it, he pulled me into his arms, hugging me tightly. He sighed into my hair, "Finally!" and I had to smile at the relief that was mixed with all of the nice emotions of love and care in his voice.

"Finally," I replied with a sigh of my own into his shoulder, hugging him just as tightly if not even more. He had to know that I'd wanted this for a long time, and that I'd wanted to be with him forever even before I knew it myself. I loved him, so much, and I was willing to show him in every possible way how much he really meant to me.

We kissed sweetly, tenderly. But what was sweet and tender quickly turned to one of those hungry and wild kisses where hands would be everywhere all at once and tongues fought for dominance. We kissed until we were out of breath, with flushed cheeks and lips that were the darkest shade of pink, lips that smiled in shyness and fingertips that shook with the sweetness of touching one another.

I wanted a moment to collect myself and I started to take a step away from him – I was a mess. But, oh, what a mess it was! Mazen caught my hand and stopped me.

"We don't have to do anything tonight, you know that, right?" he said.

I wasn't having any of that. "I know, but I want to," I said boldly. My eyes were playful and with a bite to my bottom lip and a smirk, I let go of his hand and walked to the dresser, leaving him with a shocked expression at my words.

Standing in front of the big round mirror, I started taking off my jewelry. Mazen then came to help, unlocking the clasp on my necklace while I took off my earrings. When his hand came to the middle of my back where the zipper of the dress started, I stopped breathing.

His eyes were locked with mine in the mirror as he stood behind me, but not really touching me, The look of hunger in his eyes said everything, those same eyes that were silently asking my permission to continue unzipping the dress.

With a lazy blink of my eyes he got his 'yes' and slowly he drew the zipper down until the end. My dress fell to my feet, leaving me only in my white strapless bra and thong.

His lips were on that spot behind my ear, then he left wet kisses up and down along my neck, driving me crazy with lust. Once I felt his erection pressing on my lower back – I knew I was a goner.

Mazen's hands were on my hips, then they were on my sides, then back on my hips– they felt like they were everywhere. I was trying my hardest not to sound so needy with all of the moans I wanted to let out, but when his hand softly kneaded my backside, I couldn't help but moan loudly and ask for more.

Mazen's hand returned to the middle of my back, but this time it was to unhook my bra, removing it and leaving me topless in front of him, wearing nothing but my sorry excuse for panties.

Something about watching what he was doing to me in the mirror was just so erotic that my blush was burning my cheeks, but it wasn't only my cheeks that were burning. His touch felt as if it set every inch of my skin in flames from its hotness. Suddenly, it was all too much, and I had to cover my breasts with my arms.

"Don't," he breathed into my ear, his breath all hot and his voice all gruff, "Don't hide from me, beautiful princess."

He gently pried my arms away, and covered my breasts with his hands. Trapped in his hands, he started to squeeze and press with enough pressure to drive me wild with lust.

His fingertips captured my nipples and he pinched them. "Oh, God!" I gasped loudly, earning myself a groan from him, and another grind of his hardness into my lower back.

"You feel so good, Marie," he whispered, "So good." His hands were fondling my breasts so heavily that my knees buckled and I could no longer carry my weight properly; my legs had turned into jelly.

His hands left me just for a second to shrug the jacket of his tux away, and then they were back on my skin, touching, gripping, squeezing and pinching. His eyes were giving me lustful looks through our reflections in the mirror. They were enough to get me dizzy; I had to throw my head back onto his shoulder and Mazen had to tighten his grip on my body to keep me from falling.

Suddenly, Mazen's hands turned me around and lifted me off the floor. He carried me to what had now become *our* bed. I warped my legs around him all the way to our destination, enjoying the feel of his erection right on my center. And from the sound of his groan, he was enjoying it as well.

Mazen laid me on my back softly, and I started unbuttoning his dress shirt, his hands helping me getting rid of it even faster. When he was shirtless in front of me, I all but moaned at the sight, all tight muscles and well-defined abs.

I licked my lips and Mazen's reaction was to kiss those lips hungrily, as if the motion had turned him on even more. He then started placing soft kisses all over my chest, making me moan wildly when he caught my left nipple with his mouth.

"Oh, Mazen," I breathed, begging him silently with my moans to do even more, urging him with my hand on the back of his neck, pulling him down to suck even more on my tender nipple.

He didn't disappoint.

I don't know how long his assault lasted, but I know that by the time he was done with my breasts I was nothing but a limp noodle in his hands.

Mazen wasn't nearly finished with me. He hooked his pointer fingers on both sides of my thong, pausing for a second to ask my permission to take it off.

"Is this okay, princess?"

With a shy smile, I nodded. I was actually embarrassed by how wet I was.

Mazen covered my sex with wet kisses, and through the rush of lust I felt, I didn't feel anymore shyness or anything like that. I was in heaven.

"Mazen!" I gasped as I felt the tip his tongue over my clit, licking me just the right way, in all of the right places, holding my legs apart as I was unconsciously closing them on his head. Maybe I wanted to keep him there in place, afraid that he would let go.

He stayed where he was, licking and sucking my sensitive flesh for God only knows how long. By the time he gently inserted one of his fingers inside of me, I screamed loudly at the sudden feeling.

He stopped immediately, maybe thinking he had hurt me. But I couldn't bear not having his tongue working me again.

"Please, please, please!" I begged, and it was all he needed.

His teeth scraped over my clit while his finger worked in and out, touching a certain spot inside of me that had me writhing. When he slowly added a second finger it was my undoing.

I came loudly, screaming his name and pulling on his hair as I pushed my hips forward, wanting even more from him.

It was like I passed out for a moment or two from the power of my orgasm, because the next thing I knew was the feeling of him as he started to push himself slowly inside of me.

With each slow push, I felt some pain, and when he reached my barrier, he paused, looked at me, and with a nod, I encouraged him to go on. With one deliberate push, he took what I so willingly gave him. I couldn't help but wince at the pinching feeling that though not extremely agonizing, still didn't feel like a piece of cake.

It *was* painful, but when he stopped and asked, "Are you okay, Marie?" I nodded and told him to, "Go on."

Mazen kept looking at me to make sure I was okay before he slowly, but surely made his way inside of me. I gasped at the feeling of him filling me this way.

With every moan of discomfort I let out, he hushed me with sweet kisses and tender touches over my hair, and he didn't start moving until I told him to do so.

"Shhh, it's okay." He said breathlessly, "You feel so good, *hayaty,*"

His pants in my ear and his whispered words of a language I couldn't understand as he lost himself inside of me were enough to make me forget the pinching feeling for a while.

Skin to skin. Soul to soul. We were one.

I watched his face as he came, panting my name, and I knew then that everything in my life was complete. I knew that whatever happened from now on, I wouldn't care as long as I had Mazen beside me.

Ten

Warmth surrounded me – not the kind of warmth that I craved and grew to love each day more than the day before. Not Mazen's warmth, but the kind that you get from letting warm water seep into your bones.

Standing under the showerhead, I hummed as the spray touched my skin. The water was a bit more than warm and actually scalded just the tiniest bit, but I welcomed the feeling as it relaxed my tense muscles. Mazen had worn me out last night (the past four weeks was more like it).

I was so caught up in my thoughts of Mazen, and in enjoying the water, that I didn't hear movement behind me. I only felt hands grabbing my hips from behind, out of nowhere. Gasping was the first thing I did, but not because I didn't know who was touching me – I'd recognize those hands anywhere. It was because the touch was so sudden.

"Princess," my Prince Charming of a husband whispered in my ear.

"Mazen," I breathed. "You're awake."

"Mmm-hmm. And guess what I woke up to?" he asked, his tone playful and his touches cool against my warm skin.

"What?" I smiled.

"I woke up to the sound of my wife moaning under the shower," he said, pretending to be offended.

"Oh!" was my smart reply, "But I wasn't moaning, I was humming."

"Humming? Let's see." Before I could respond, his lips were on the side of my neck, and his naked chest was pressed flat to my back.

I moaned.

"Yes, exactly. It doesn't sound like humming to me," Mazen said, his breath fanning the tender spot behind my ear. My eyes rolled to the back of my head.

"No …" I said half-heartedly, not able to form thoughts or in the mood to argue. I was in the mood for being with him, though. This way and every other way possible.

"Yes," he said, pressing his erection into my back, making me feel how hard he was for me.

"Yes!" I gasped.

"Good girl." The smile was evident in his voice.

His hands snuck up to my breasts and he cupped them, proving even more that this part of my body was his favorite to touch, just as the past days and nights had taught me.

And I knew in that moment that I was in for more amazingly good lovemaking with him. I would never complain about that.

With a kiss, I left Mazen to take his shower and wrapped myself in a towel, my body still tingling from the orgasm I had during the shower sex. After I blow dried my hair, I left the bathroom and went into the walk-in closet.

Half an hour later, I was dressed in a black pencil skirt and a grey blouse. When I walked into the room, I found Mazen with a towel wrapped around his waist. He looked so good with his hair wet and body glistening with a few drops of water, I felt like eating him.

His smiling face dropped when he saw what I was wearing. "You're going to work again?" he almost whined.

"Yep!" I replied.

"But you were there yesterday!" he complained.

"Well, that's the funny thing about work: you go five days a week. Eight days a week when you're the CEO," I told him, grinning in an attempt to lighten the air, since he really didn't want me to go. He wanted me to stay and play House all day and all night long. God!

He was like a machine.

"We're still on our honeymoon, Princess," he said. I was almost waiting for him to stomp his foot like a little child who didn't want Mommy to go.

I went to him and wrapped my arms around his neck, not caring if I got wet from his damp hair. "We've been on a honeymoon since I got here almost two months ago, angel," I reminded him.

He smiled, "I love it when you call me that," and kissed my lips. I smiled into the kiss, knowing that I'd gotten him again. "Can I at least come by later so we can have some sexy librarian fun again? You look so hot right now."

I smiled and shook my head. "You never get enough, do you?" I bit my bottom lip and blushed at the memory of what we did at work a few days ago.

"No." He sounded serious.

"No, you can't. You have to study, remember?" I reminded him, then kissed his pout away. He was going to be the death of me with all of his handsomeness and sweetness. I swear.

Truly, everything had become better. Life was all roses and sprawling gardens. I saw heaven every time I looked into his eyes. My own version of Prince Charming. A version with dark hair and green, mysterious eyes. Mysterious but dreamy. A version who spoke erotically in Arabic when he lost himself inside me. A version that was perfectly well-mannered, full of kindness and sweetness, full of passion and love. And all of it was for me. To me. All was mine.

The smile didn't leave my lips as I entered the building, greeting everyone and whomever, not caring if I didn't know who they were. The people who knew me were sure that I was in a love coma. One that I didn't ever intend to wake up from.

At the office, I was running the companies better than I had ever had since my parents had passed away. Everything was going very smoothly since I'd sent the manager of London's branch to the States, where he'd always wanted to be, beside his family. And now everyone was happy. More than happy, if you ask about me.

The branch in Alfaidya was doing well under Princess Huda's management. Now, I just needed to pay a short visit to Paris to look at the branch there from up close to see for myself how things were going. Other than that – everything was just perfect.

A dreamy sigh left my mouth as I ran through the files on my desk, our memories together never leaving my mind as I worked, as I ate, as I dressed, as I did whatever. Mazen was always on my mind. And I knew I was always on his. He'd told me so himself.

A knock on my door interrupted my musings, my assistant stepped inside after I called for her to come in. "Ms. Archer, can we speak about the shipment from

China now?" She had asked earlier and I'd delayed it, but I knew it couldn't wait any longer.

"Yes, sure. Sit down, please," I said, and right then the phone rang. "Let me just get this," I told her and she nodded with a smile.

"Marie Archer speaking," I replied into the phone.

"Hmm … I would like to hear her moaning, though. Just like this morning under the shower, and last night under me."

Startled, I abruptly hung up. But not a second later, I heard it ringing again. Smiling politely to my assistant as much as I could manage, I picked it up again.

"Hello!" I choked out.

"Did you just hang up on me, Ms. Archer?" Mazen asked, a devilish grin in his tone.

"Uh, yes, sir." I swallowed thickly. "I guess I did."

"Oh! Sir? That's hot," he said and I had to clutch the phone tightly, afraid I would drop it. "You need some punishment, though."

My breath was held in my throat. "Sir?"

"Yes, Ms. Archer. Probably some spanking on that tight little–"

My legs clenched together and I coughed, interrupting him. "Yes, sir. See, my assistant is right here and we're about to discuss an important shipment to China. Can we speak about your… ahem, *business* later?"

"Oh, she's right there?" he asked wickedly. "Well, tell me, wouldn't it have been easier if you'd allowed me to come with you? I would've hidden under your desk; no one would notice."

"Y-yes, sir," I stuttered, thinking of the possibility.

"I know you'd like it, because I would've kept myself busy down there. I would've buried my face between those beautiful, long legs of yours," he told me, and I squeezed my eyes tightly shut. "Would you be up for that, Ms. Archer?"

"Yes, sir. I would," I replied quickly, honestly.

I heard him chuckling lightly. "Good girl, we'll see about that when you get home. And I won't forget about the spanking." Then he hung up.

Darn it, I could kill him right now!

Life was all roses and sprawling gardens. Everything was running smoothly and the day was going so well. Aside from a complication or two which I faced at work – it was all perfect.

Life was all roses and sprawling gardens until I felt it later that day – a cramp.

It had been almost a month since we got married and started having sex. The idea of having a baby wasn't something I wanted – it was something I craved. I even dared to think I wanted a child more than Mazen did.

It wasn't like I was obsessed with the idea or anything, no – I was more than that. I didn't know if it was my hormones or the way I'd been raised, being a Catholic and all, but I'd always wanted to be a mother.

I loved babies more than I should at my young age, and had always wanted one – or a dozen. But of course I knew it'd come after marriage, not before that.

Now that I was married, the thought wouldn't leave my mind. Almost every time I had sex with Mazen, I kept thinking of the possibility of it being the time when we would make a baby together.

The fact that I was so in love with Mazen also didn't help that much. I wanted a baby that looked just like him, a little boy like the baby I'd seen in photos back in the kingdom. I wanted that little kid with dark brown hair and green eyes, with the same mysterious look and mesmerizing smile of my angel.

I wanted a baby so badly that it wasn't healthy, but I didn't dare to speak about it to anyone else – they would've thought I was just being crazy – I didn't even speak about it to Mazen. It was kind of embarrassing how much I wanted a little one that smelled so good and was just so small, with those little fingers and oh so very tiny toes. God! Was I insane?

For the past month, I kept having those thoughts of how I could really be pregnant. Lots of people got pregnant on their first try; I could be one of those people, right? Or so I'd hoped.

But all of those hopes went out the window when I felt that darn cramp that was exactly like the ones I always got right before my period.

The thing was, I was four days late, and that had never happened before. My period was always so perfectly timed, you could set a clock by it, and suddenly after I became sexually active I was late. I had all of the hope in the world that I was pregnant, but this cramp made me think twice. Maybe it was just late because of the changes my body had gone through.

Sighing, I closed the lid of my laptop and stood up before my fingers ran to Google and I started searching about the symptoms of pregnancy – I was crazy that way.

On my way home, I thought about our horses – Faith and Hope, Thunder and Salma – and I wondered if I could ask Mazen to bring them to our mansion. We had a place for them, though I had yet to visit it since it was empty. I thought the stable was large enough to handle four horses, so why not just bring them here?

Things were going so well in London, and I could see myself settling here, at least for the two years left of Mazen's studies. To be honest, I'd rather live in London than in the kingdom. But then again, the kingdom held one of the best memories of my life. It was there where I'd met the love of my life, after all.

But, I could see myself living here forever.

Wanting Faith and Hope maybe had something to do with all of the motherly hormones that were going crazy inside me, but I didn't care. I still wanted them here for one reason or another. And I knew Mazen would love it if Thunder and Salma were here as well.

Once I stepped inside the mansion, I felt something odd, because it was only Philip who'd greeted me by the door. I was used to Mazen waiting for me by the main door every time I came back home, but he wasn't this time.

My first thought was that maybe he was in a playful mood and wanted to search for him. So I did just that.

Easily, I found him in his office, the first place I'd searched for him. Mazen wasn't sitting by his desk or on his favorite armchair, like he often did in that room, with a book in his hand. He was standing by the window, seemingly lost in thought, and like always – the weight of the world was heavy on his shoulders.

Closing the gap that separated us, I nudged him with my finger on that shoulder that carried the worry of the world. Mazen turned to look at me with a frown on his face, then the frown was gone once he saw me and a small smile appeared on his beautiful lips. "Princess, you're home." He took me in his arms and hugged me tightly, tighter than I'd thought he would and longer than just enough.

I let him hug me for all it was worth it. I loved it in his arms, but something just felt wrong. Wrong.

So I backed away a few inches and asked, "What's wrong?" because I had to know. I was so worried.

He shook his head. "Nothing is wrong, Marie. As long as you're in my arms – nothing could ever feel wrong," he assured me.

A smile lifted my lips as I heard his words, but the unease was still living inside my heart at his tone and the sadness in his eyes – something had happened. I mean, he'd called me and was all fun and games, and now that I was home – it was like he had lost a dear one. Oh! Wait …

"Mazen, is everything okay? Your family? The horses?" I asked, concern filling my voice.

He nodded slowly, then he attempted to smile. "C'mon, let's go eat something, you must be starving."

"Mazen! Tell me right now what's going on! I'm not going anywhere," I demanded, to which he sighed.

"It's my brother and Princess Rosanna," he said in a low voice, and in that moment, I knew what he was going to say. "They lost the baby."

Our grief for the loss of the unborn child lasted for days. I understood Mazen's concern about his brother and his cousin and the possibility of them never having a child together – it was the sixth time, after all. But also, I understood his concern for the kingdom. The repercussions of his family not having any heirs were enormous.

It was easy to understand that if his father died without Mazen or his brother having an heir, the crown would go to his uncle, and then to Jasem – and nobody wanted that, not even me.

Mazen wasn't worried about the title going to his brother. He was only worried about it going to Jasem if his father didn't make it until we had a boy child.

I really wanted to tell him that my period was late, that I might be pregnant, but I couldn't make him hope for something that might not be true after all. I couldn't do that to him, not with everything that was going on with his brother and Rosanna. He had had enough.

Life was all roses and sprawling gardens until we received a call from the kingdom. The king requested Mazen to come home immediately because there was something important he wanted him for.

Life was all roses and sprawling gardens until … well, until it wasn't.

Eleven

Tender, soft kisses were placed all over my cheek and jawline, and I opened my eyes lazily to be met with warm green ones.

"Hey," he smiled, and nuzzling his short beard was my only reply. "We're landing in an hour. I thought you might want some time to freshen up."

"Mmm-hmm," I hummed my approval, still too cozy and comfortable to find it in me to wake up.

I heard Mazen's soft chuckle and then felt his lips on my forehead before he moved away a bit, as if he was about to leave. I pulled him by his shirt that I had fisted in my hand.

"Stay," I whispered.

He didn't make me ask him twice before he got back in bed with me, wrapping his arms around me and kissing my lips softly before laying back. I rested my head on his chest, enjoying the feeling of him as he moved his hand through my hair.

"How long was I asleep?"

"Um, about six hours," Mazen replied.

"Wow!" I gushed. "That's so long. I can't remember the last time I've been so comfortable on a plane. Heck, I don't even get up to pee unless we stop for fuel."

It still amazed me how safe Mazen made me feel whenever he was around, and I thought I should tell him exactly that.

"Your closeness comforts me."

Mazen hugged me more into him. "I still remember the first time you said those very words to me, Princess. I can't be more grateful that you feel this way."

I knew exactly which time he was referring to. I was sitting on his lap right after we'd shared our first upside-down kiss, that day when I was so in love with him but still too stupid to even realize it. I couldn't believe how much we'd gone through since that night.

My hand that was on his chest came up to his neck and I pulled him to me as I looked up at him, forcing his lips gently to meet my own. I kissed him with passion and love and he kissed me back with even more feelings; it was almost too much for my heart to bear.

All of his kisses left me speechless.

When we broke the kiss, I looked up into his eyes and we shared a warm look before he spoke. "I'm sorry for not being myself the past couple of days."

A soft, sad smile found its way to my lips and I shook my head slightly. "You don't need to apologize for that, angel. It's only made me see even more how kind and loving you are; to have all of those feelings for your family and your concerns for the kingdom … you're a wonderful human being and I'm so lucky to have met someone like you," I told him honestly.

Mazen had been feeling really down since we'd gotten the news about Rosanna's miscarriage. He'd been praying more than usual, and his conversations were limited to him being polite to me and his attempts not to sound rude. I understood him, though – he was the kind who suffered in silence and he needed his time to get over it. I could only imagine what his brother and his wife were feeling, and it made my heart ache for them just thinking about it.

He pecked me on my lips and smiled, then told me that he loved me so much, knowing very well that I could never get tired of hearing him say that.

With a modest dress and a scarf tied loosely over my hair, I waited with Mazen by the door of the jet. We stood there doing nothing for over ten minutes.

Growing impatient, I finally asked, "Um, Mazen? What are we waiting for?"

"Preparations for our arrival," Mazen shrugged, as if that gave me all of the answers.

"What kind of preparations?" I asked, but didn't wait for him to reply. I walked back to the middle of the jet and looked out one of the windows. "You've got to be kidding me!"

"What?"

"There is a whole number of people out there, and I see some of them rolling out a red carpet!"

"So?"

"Is this going to happen every time we leave the country then come back? Because with the amount of traveling I'm going to do every month from now on, this is going to be nothing but a waste of money and time!"

Mazen offered me a small smile. "I believe you're aware we can never worry about money even if we tried, Princess."

"Mazen, that's not the point. This is just a waste. Red carpets, roses and dozens of cars – and supposedly three are family members waiting outside? They have jobs to do that I'm sure are more important than waiting for us, to welcome us to our own home. And please don't make me start on how many other better ways this money could be spent."

"You're making a very good point, but we have to keep up appearances. The whole kingdom has been waiting to hear good news about your health. They knew you left because you were sick, so this is just a celebration in your honor, Princess. It won't happen every time. Well, not this big," he explained.

"Oh, no! Celebration in *my* honor? And what do you mean by 'this big'? Are you telling me there's more that I can't see? No way, Mazen. Call everything off," I demanded.

"What? Why?" Mazen looked confused.

"We can't celebrate anything, angel. Not with everything going on. How do you think Rosanna would feel about that?"

Mazen's eyes were locked with mine for a moment before a warm smile touched his lips. He took the few steps that separated us and hugged my face with his hands before kissing me.

"You say you're lucky you've met someone like me, but every day you prove to me that I'm the luckiest person on earth to have someone like you whom I can call a wife," he whispered, to which my heart warmed just hearing the sincerity in his voice. "Bless your kind heart, my princess."

Inside our wing, things felt weirdly normal, but the truth was – everything was different. I could see the same feeling in Mazen's eyes as he looked around our bedroom. I could almost see the memories he was recalling as he looked at the bed, the couch, the armchair, and the door to the sunroom. I could see it all. And those memories invaded me at the same time.

Servants were bustling all around us, busy

unpacking our bags and putting away our things, but it felt like it was just the two of us standing in the middle of the room.

I continued to watch Mazen and his expressions, remembering doing the very same thing when I first came back to him two months ago, after the two weeks it took me to realize my true feelings towards Mazen back in the States.

Mazen's eyes caught the spot where we'd stood together and cried our souls out while saying our goodbyes, and I could see it on his face that the memory pained him just like an old wound being cut open again. That was when I had to interrupt his thoughts, as I couldn't bear the thought of him hurting.

One of my hands touched his, and the other pulled him by the neck down to me until our foreheads touched. Mazen's arms wrapped around me and he took a deep breath then let it go, his eyes closed and his shoulders hunched down – something he hardly ever did. He always stood tall and steady with broad shoulders, which told me just how much he was feeling right now.

"What are you thinking, angel?" I whispered my question.

Mazen only shook his head slightly, but his arms hugged me into him a little bit tighter.

"You know you can tell me anything. I'm your wife, and I love you more than life."

"You're my wife," he said, almost to himself, and

after a long pause, he spoke again. “It really was the hardest thing I’d ever done my entire life.”

I already knew what he was referring to be ‘*it*’, he didn’t have to explain.

My heart ached, and a small, sad smile formed on my lips. “I’m here now.”

“Don’t ever walk away from me again, Marie,” he whispered his plea. “I don’t know if I could take it.”

“Don’t ever let me go again, Mazen,” I whispered back, unshed tears glistening in my eyes. “I *know* that I could never take it.”

“Never.”

“Never.”

Hours later when we’d finally been left alone for the night, the memories still continued to haunt the both of us – memories of the six days we spent together in this wing, where we laughed and cried – where we fell in love.

We were lying on our sides on the bed, facing each other while holding hands, totally spent from the long flight and then the sweet lovemaking that we’d just had. A smile crept onto my face as I realized something. Mazen caught it right away and asked what I was smiling about, so I told him, “It’s the first time we’ve shared this bed together – do you realize that?”

“Oh! Yes, I guess so. I fell asleep beside you once

before, though. When you had a fever. I didn't mean to, but it happened."

My smile dropped as I remembered exactly what he was talking about. I remembered waking up to him, my first feelings towards him slowly blossoming as I saw his angelic face while he slept peacefully. I remembered wondering what it would be like to wake up to his face every morning. But I also remembered what I'd told him afterwards, and how I'd accused him of raping me.

"I'm sorry," I found myself saying, ashamed that it had taken me all of this time to finally apologize for that.

Mazen offered me a small smile and his hand squeezed mine, he knew exactly what I was apologizing for. "There's no need to apologize, Princess. You were scared, and you had every right to be – I get it."

I shook my head, then I got up on my elbow, raising myself a bit from the pillow and looking closely at him, while holding the sheets up to cover my naked chest. "How do you do it? How can you be so very understanding? So forgiving?"

He only shrugged one shoulder in response.

"I mean, you didn't have feelings for me back then – not strong feelings anyway. I kept on being mean to you, saying hurtful things, never apologizing, and you still treated me so kindly. I just don't get it!"

Mazen turned onto his back and sighed, looking up at the ceiling for a moment before he turned his gaze back to me as he spoke. "One day when I was little, my father took Fahd and me on a safari in South Africa. While we were walking and exploring, we found a cat that had fallen into a small lake. It was clutching to a tree branch which was the only thing preventing it from drowning, but you could tell it couldn't last forever and it would drown at some point."

I nodded my head, listening to him carefully – confused as heck as to why he was telling me that story, but still interested to learn the rest of it.

"My father's first reaction was to go to the cat and try to save it. He asked the guards to step away because they were scaring it, but the cat scratched my father's hand when he reached out for it, so he had to take a step back.

"A moment later, my father reached for the cat with his other hand, and the cat scratched it as well, refusing to let my father come closer. I felt sorry for the cat, thinking that there was no way to save it since it wouldn't let anyone touch it. But that wasn't the case.

"When we saw our father reaching for the cat for a third time, Fahd screamed at him to just let it go, the cat would only hurt him more, but my father didn't listen, and in one swift move he was able to save the cat."

I smiled widely, happy that the king was able to save the cat, but still not understanding why Mazen was telling me this story instead of actually replying to my question.

"My father then came to Fahd and told him, don't

let others' actions affect the way you feel in your heart. If what's in your heart is kindness, what good would it do if you can't use it to save someone or make them feel better? How would you feel if the cat had died just because you didn't try hard enough? Don't allow others force you to act any differently from what's in your heart, no matter what they do to you."

"Wow!" was all I said; his father was a really wise man.

"I've never forgotten that lesson, Princess. And it's how I've treated people my whole life. I've treated them with what's in my heart, not based on how they've treated me. And my heart was always telling me to treat you better than you were treating me. You weren't feeling safe, you were locked up with a complete stranger, and you had just been betrayed by the closest person to your heart – of course you would act that way. But if I treated you the same way you were treating me – what would be my excuse? I couldn't live with myself if I'd hurt you."

I bent down and kissed him on the lips. "Whenever I think I couldn't possibly love you more, you prove me wrong. Always."

"Same here, beautiful princess." He pulled me to him and kissed my lips. What I thought was only going to be a small peck, turned into a heated kiss with tongues and even teeth involved. I was so lost in the kiss that I didn't even realize that Mazen had turned me onto my back and was now on top of me.

His lips were on my neck, then on my collarbone, and then I felt his tongue on my nipple. A gasp left my parted lips and I smiled, "You're insatiable, do you know that?"

Mazen chuckled into my stomach. "I'm satiable all right; I just can't get enough of the woman I love – is that a crime?"

"You won't find me complaining," I giggled, following it with a moan when I felt him sucking on the skin of my hipbone.

This guy would be the death of me, I just knew it.

The next morning, I heard Mazen as he took his shower and then watched him while he prayed after getting dressed. I got up from the bed and put a robe on as I watched him tie his shoes.

He looked up at me and smiled, "Good morning."

"Morning, angel." I went and placed a kiss on his cheek. "Are you going to meet the king now?"

"Yes. Fahd is waiting for me outside; my father wants to meet us both together."

"You still have no idea what this is about?"

"No. But we'll find out soon." He got up and went to the dresser, applying cologne to his neck and pulse points. The scent itself gave me the sweetest feelings because it was very him, though still not as good as when I smelled it off his skin. I went to him, giving his neck a light kiss then hugged him.

Mazen kissed my hair. “Are you going to be okay? I don’t know how long it’s going to take.”

“I’ll be fine, don’t worry,” I assured him, hating that I might not see him for the rest of the day.

“Do you have plans for the day?”

“Um, I don’t know. I might go visit the Queen Mother, and I wanted to visit Rosanna, as well. Do you think that’s okay?”

“Of course, it’s okay, I know they’ll both love it,” he smiled. “But don’t you want to go check on the branch first?”

“Nah, I already Skyped with Huda two days ago, and everything is fine. I’ll go tomorrow.”

“All right. Would you like to go to see the horses tonight?”

My eyes brightened. “I’d love that!”

“Okay then.” He kissed my lips. “I’m going to miss you.”

“I miss you already, angel.”

Donia informed the Queen Mother of my request to visit and I was told right away that she was expecting me. I asked Donia to also inform Rosanna I would like to pay her a visit later today and was told that I was more than welcome.

On my way out of the wing, I found Fawaz

standing outside. It was odd.

"Why are you here? Why aren't you with Prince Mazen?"

"Prince Mazen asked me to escort you for the day, your highness."

Of course he did, I thought.

Nodding my head, I told him I'd go to the Queen Mother's wing first, and with a gesture of his hand and an, "After you, your highness," I headed to the elevator.

"*Marhaba!*" I greeted the Queen Mother with a huge grin, using one of the few Arabic words that Mazen had taught me over the past couple of months.

"Oh, *benty*." She reached for me with both hands and a warm smile spread all over her kind features. I hugged her then kissed her forehead like I had seen Mazen do before, surprising myself when I didn't find it any kind of strange to do something like that.

Donia played our translator for this visit. I stayed with her until she did the same thing she'd done with me the first time we met – saying verses from her holy book to protect me from the evil eye while she smoothed my hair back, warming my heart with her kindness and gentle nature.

Later, during my visit with Rosanna, my heart broke seeing how she was trying to keep a smile on her face, while her eyes held the sadness of the world. She was so kind, but her smiles were forced. I held her hand and told her that I could never express how sorry I was for what had happened.

It was then that she broke into tears, and it brought my own tears to my eyes when I saw her break down. I couldn't imagine what she was going through, and it was my undoing when she told me how she had no ounce of hope left in her.

Though I knew no amount of reassurance would do her any good, I still tried my best, and was rewarded with a hug that told me of an upcoming strong friendship between the two of us – I just knew it.

We had dinner together since the meeting with the king had lasted the entire day and we hadn't heard anything from our husbands. It wasn't until Prince Fahd came back to his and Rosanna's wing that I got up to leave, feeling as if my legs couldn't take me fast enough to my wing so I could be with Mazen again.

I was dying to know what the long meeting was about. I searched Prince Fahd's features for answers, but just like his brother – he was a master in offering a blank face.

Surprisingly, Mazen wasn't in our wing when I got back, and I was completely confused as to why he wasn't, since his brother had already come back from the meeting.

With a sigh, I changed for bed and then checked my e-mails, answering the most important ones and leaving the rest for tomorrow. I really hated when I didn't know what was going on; the wait was killing me.

Hours later, Mazen finally came back. I got up and

greeted him with a hug, and if it was possible, the weight on his shoulders looked even heavier in that moment.

I touched his face and looked into his eyes. "Tell me," was all I said, and with a deep sigh he responded.

"My father is changing the law."

Twelve

My lips were parted as I listened to Mazen tell me how the meeting had gone with his father. I couldn't believe my ears as he told me how things had gone—every decision that had been made was confusing to me.

"Say something, Marie, please!"

The problem was, I had no idea what to say.

"Uh, I'm sorry, Mazen. I just don't understand. Could you explain further? Please?"

Mazen drew in a deep breath then let it out. "My father is passing me the title while he's still alive."

"Is that even possible? You don't even have an heir – yet."

Unconsciously, my hand touched my stomach, and the thought of how I could already be pregnant came to my mind. I really wanted to tell him how late I was, but I still didn't want him to get his hopes up for nothing. I wanted to be sure first.

"He's changing the law."

"I get that, but what will the rest of the royal family think? Don't they have a say in that?" I wondered.

"They do. But eventually, it's up to my father to make the final decision."

"Your uncle and his son are not going to be pleased with this."

"They are not, but my father made sure that his change in the law is fair enough for my uncle to get the title if things come to a head."

"What do you mean?"

"I'll become the king while my father lives, according to his orders. However, because the original law gives my uncle the right to the title if my father passes away before he has a grandson from either of his two sons, my father added to the law a two-year period after his death before the title would go to my uncle. That's plenty of time for one of us to have a son, if God wills it, but still gives a chance for my uncle to eventually be the king."

"Huh. I guess I understand now. But – why now? What brought it up?"

"Princess Rosanna's miscarriage."

"What? Why is that?"

"After everything that happened with Janna, my father's heart condition worsened. The doctor suggested a heart transplant. He'd been delaying it until Princess Rosanna gave birth, hoping it would be a boy and Fahd would become the king in case my father died while in surgery. But now, there's no point in waiting. The new law gives my father assurances that if he dies on the operating table, the kingdom would be safe."

"Mazen, with all due respect, why do I feel like your father is trying so hard for the title not to go to your uncle?"

"It's true, Princess. He doesn't want that. Nobody in the kingdom does. My uncle being the king only means that a few years later Jasem would be the king, and then his son after him. Nobody wants that."

"Not even me," I sighed.

"You should see the princedom he's been ruling for the past two years – it's all messed up. We try our best to keep it on its feet, but still."

"That's upsetting. So what's going to happen now?"

"The coronation ceremony is the day after tomorrow."

"What?" I said, a bit louder than I intended to. "It's final? That soon?"

"Yes. My father was already working on it before we got here. He just needed to confirm it with the rest of the family before making the announcement."

"Wow! I don't even know what to say. How do you feel about it?" I touched his hand. Mazen looked even more nervous than he'd been when he proposed to me. His eyes were filled with worry and concern, the two emotions that seemed to never leave him.

"Honestly? I'm not ready for this. I'm just… God!"

"Hey!" I pulled his face to me, but he wouldn't look me in the eyes. It was the first time I'd ever seen Mazen this way; the first time I'd seen him unsure and maybe even confused. "Hey, look at me." He finally did, and my chest tightened when I saw the look in his eyes.

"Of course you're ready. You knew that someday you were going to be the king. You've been preparing for it your entire life, Mazen. I know you have other dreams, but your kingdom needs you, your people need you. It's only that God wants you even earlier than you'd thought. You always wanted to help people, and now it's time.

"Being King means you will have a lot of responsibilities, I get that, but would you rather *someone else* do it? Someone you couldn't even trust to rule a princedom, let alone the whole kingdom?"

Mazen shook his head slowly.

"There you go, angel. This is your destiny, and you have to accept it. I know in my heart that you'll be the best king this kingdom has ever known – trust me on this."

Mazen's arms wrapped around me and he hugged me close to him as we sat on the couch. "I don't know what I would do without you, Marie."

"You would still do great, it's all you – I have nothing to do with it. You're noble, kind and loyal. The kingdom will be best with you ruling it."

"With you by my side as my queen," he said, and it was like someone had just doused me with an ice bucket. My eyes widened and my body tensed. Mazen must've felt it because the next thing he did was pull away from our embrace to look at my face.

"Hey, are you okay? You look like you've just seen a ghost!"

"I, uh, … I'm going to be a queen," I stated, as if I wanted to hear myself saying it for it to register better in my head.

"Yes …?"

"Oh, my God! I know that this is how things go, but – I, uh, I hadn't really thought about it." I'd been called Future Queen several times, and I knew that it was going to happen eventually, but I didn't think it would happen so soon. Oh, God! There was a lot to think about.

"Hey, don't freak out on me now," Mazen actually chuckled.

"I'm not freaking out!" I touched my forehead, feeling lightheaded. I *was* freaking out.

"You're going to be the best thing that has ever happened to this kingdom – trust me on this," Mazen repeated my words, and I had to be in his arms again, seeking comfort. The truth was, it was more than just me freaking out, it was a heavy weight that I didn't think I was ready for. Something in me told me that I could never be ready for this. Ever.

The next morning, Mazen had to leave early. He told me that Fawaz would escort me to the company branch, and I only nodded in response. I didn't tell him how I felt, and I was sad that I was hiding things from him, hiding what I truly felt, but I couldn't be honest with him. It would only hurt him, nothing more.

I knew that Mazen trusted Fawaz the most, which was why he had left him with me instead of having Fawaz accompany him for the day, or even yesterday. Though I liked Fawaz and knew him better than the rest of royal guards, I still didn't feel like him being with me would help me turn off how I was really feeling.

I ended up staying at the wing, working from home. I had meetings later that day with the palace staff regards to the preparations for the ceremony tomorrow. I thought it'd be better if I finished my work as quickly as possible, since things would get even busier from now on.

Donia interrupted my work briefly to ask whether I wanted something specific for dinner that night, and I asked her to do whatever she thought Mazen would like. I'd never been a picky eater, but that wasn't the only reason I couldn't care less about food – there was a lot more.

"Donia, can I ask you to do something for me?" I asked when she was about to leave.

"Of course, Princess, whatever you need."

"Can you manage to inform Mona that I would like to see her?"

"Yes, Princess. I can do that. I'll get right on it."

"Thank you," I said with a smile, ending the conversation with her and then looking back at my laptop.

I spent the next hour on the phone with Terri, then called London to get updates on the projects I'd left before I came to the kingdom. Another hour passed while I was doing nothing but addressing problems with the projects, and issuing more orders on how things should be done.

I felt that my presence was really needed there if I wasn't going to hire a manager soon to oversee the office and run it properly. Because right now it seemed like things were slipping through my fingers again. I didn't want that to happen. I never would.

Yes, I knew that I'd go back to the kingdom eventually, that I couldn't stay in London forever, but I still couldn't help but dream that things could've stayed the way they were, therefore I didn't make future plans for that branch.

New York's and Paris's branches were doing well, the kingdom branch had yet to be operational, but Huda was taking very good care of things so far. It was now London's branch that was worrying me, it wasn't stable, and I had to find a solution for it. As soon as possible.

For a split second, I thought about how things would've been much easier if Joseph was still managing things with me, but I dismissed the thought right away. He'd gotten what he deserved, and I regretted nothing.

My fears and worries didn't stop, not for a second. Though I tried to work as quickly and as efficiently as possible, I still couldn't help the sinking feeling in my stomach as I thought of what lay ahead for me from now on, and how things would grow even more complicated tomorrow.

When Mona arrived, I was so happy to see her, just as she appeared to be happy to see me. We hugged and chatted for a bit, and she was very eager to hear details about our small wedding and how things had been going for us in London. She seemed genuinely happy for us – not that I had expected any less from her.

"I, uh, I really need to ask you to do me a favor," I said, feeling the blush as it crawled up my cheeks.

"Of course, *benty*, I'd do anything for you."

"Thank you, it really means a lot to me," I smiled nervously. "It's just, you're the only one I trust around here and I – uh, I know you won't tell anyone, so– …"

"Whatever you need, just say it, Princess. I swear it'll never go further than the two of us," she assured me. I shook my head at her calling me by my title, no matter how many times I had told her to call me by my name.

"I know." I took a deep breath. "I want you to buy

me a pregnancy test."

Mona's eyes widened. "What? Oh, my God, you're pregnant?" she exclaimed.

"Shh," I shushed her quickly. "I don't know if I'm pregnant, that's why I want the pregnancy test. I'm just late."

"Oh, dear God! I'm so happy!" I saw tears in her eyes as she gushed, and though it warmed my heart, it was exactly why I didn't want to tell Mazen. Nothing was confirmed, yet. And I was so afraid that after he got all excited about it, he would be disappointed and even heartbroken if it turned out that I wasn't pregnant after all.

I smiled. "I knew you would be, but nothing is certain yet, and I want to make sure before I tell Mazen."

"Oh, dear, how late are you?"

"Nine days today," I answered.

"Wow! Why have you waited so long to take a test? Has it ever been this late?"

"No. Never. It's always pretty much on time. But don't you need to be like, ten days late before you take a test?" I thought I'd heard something like that somewhere.

"Of course, you're pregnant! And you don't have to wait ten days. Some tests can even tell you before you're a day late," she told me.

"Seriously? Oh, my God!" I couldn't help my shocked grin, but I tried my best to contain myself. I still needed to be sure first before I let my heart go flying into the air out of joy.

"Yes! I'll go get it for you right away," she said as she got up from the couch we were sitting on, in my living room.

Looking at the time, I pursed my lips. "I don't think we have enough time right now. My meeting with the coronation ceremony planners is in half an hour; I have to get ready."

"I see. I'll bring it to you in the morning then, before you have to go. I have to be here anyway."

"All right, that would be great, thank you."

"It's my pleasure, Princess. I am honored you trust me with your confidence. I won't let a soul know. Congratulations again, you'll make a great queen for our country," she smiled, and I really hoped that her words would become true.

Mazen came back very late that night. He had already called and apologized for not being able to make to dinner, leaving me to eat without him yet again. I wondered if this would be the case from now on. The thought was unsettling.

We had barely eaten together since we'd arrived here. I knew it was out of his hands, but it wasn't so easy on me to accept the idea of us being far away from each other for the entire day, every day.

When he lay in bed with me, he told me about his busy, tiring day and all of the things he had to do, then he asked me about my day and why I hadn't gone to the company as planned. The fact that he knew my whereabouts made me think of the possibility that he'd called Fawaz to check on things. He'd done that before when I was in London and hadn't wanted to disturb me by calling me directly.

It still made my heart tingle to know that I was always on his mind, just like he was always on mine.

I told him that I hadn't found it necessary to go and that I'd taken care of things from home. I hated the fact that I was lying to him about the real reason why I hadn't left, but still couldn't find it in me to tell him the truth.

We made love long and sweet that night. I was exhausted by the time we were finished and I could tell that Mazen felt the same. My eyelids were so heavy as he took me in his arms, as I lay on my side facing away from him so we were spooning. I was finally able to relax, because in his arms, I found what I was looking for, just like I knew I would. Just like he was always able to give me safety and comfort.

His sleepy voice came and whispered in my ear, "Sleep tight, my princess. Tomorrow you're going to be a queen."

Suddenly, I was wide awake.

Thirteen

We were awakened at the ungodly hour of four in the morning on the day of the coronation; I'd barely gotten any sleep. My mind just wouldn't shut down and let me rest. I kept thinking about everything that lay ahead of me, the possible pregnancy, my marriage, my companies and all of my new responsibilities as a queen for a foreign country.

It was all too much, and I was overwhelmed. That, and things were soon to start getting even heavier, busier and messier.

Self-doubt filled me, and I started thinking that I could never manage all of those things. I hated that I was such a mess from the inside, but there was nothing I could do other than to try my best and give all I had for everything to work out.

I owed a continued success of the companies to my

parents, owed a success as a queen to Mazen, and owed a success as a woman and a good human being to myself and before all to my God. I wanted to be a mother, I wanted to be a good wife and daughter, but I also wanted to be someone I could be proud of.

So, I was determined to try to be all of that. Try even harder.

It didn't escape my mind that this was exactly how I'd felt when I'd realized I had to take on my parents' load and manage the main office in New York. Maybe the new responsibility of being a queen was scaring me, but I knew in my heart that it was much more than that.

Still, I gave myself the pep talk I needed, hugged Mazen once he'd stepped out of the shower – drawing all of the courage and encouragement I needed from his embrace – and decided that I was going to do it, and do it well. I was going to be strong and handle whatever life threw at me. Because I was born a fighter, and I knew that there was so little in this life that I couldn't do. I just had to push myself a little and believe in it.

"Are you going to be okay?" Mazen asked in a low voice, his arms still holding me to him.

"I think so."

"I'll be in the next room the whole time, okay?" he said. I wondered if it was because he sensed how nervous I was, despite all of my attempts to hide it.

"I know. It's going to be okay," I assured myself more than him. "Next time I see you, you're going to be a king." I hoped that my smile would tell him that I was fine; I hated to make him worry about me.

Mazen's smile was beautiful as he backed away to look into my eyes. "Next time I see you, I'll be more in love with you than I am now." His lips touched mine as he gave me a tender, warm kiss. He'd always told me that his love for me grew a little more every second, but this time I'd needed to hear it more than ever, because from his love, I got my strength.

The second I got out of the shower, everything was happening so fast. Suddenly, there were too many people in the room, and everyone was doing something to get me ready for the ceremony. But I wasn't very comfortable, to be honest.

Mazen had already left while I was still in the shower, and Donia wasn't always around. I kind of felt alone in the crowded room, and the negative emotions I'd had before about not seeing a familiar face were coming back again.

I was quiet most of the time as they dressed me in a seriously heavy dress; it was the darkest shade of red with golden decorations all over it. It looked like one of those dresses that you see on rich families' daughters in classic movies. It was all kinds of beautiful, but the heat I felt once I was put in it wasn't at all welcomed.

The dress was a little loose and needed to be tightened a bit in the waist area. I could feel how nervous the designer was due to the lack of time we had, but she managed to get it fitted quickly – I was impressed.

Apparently, the crown was designed to be worn on top of a thick veil, so the hair stylist had to leave my hair loose with small waves at the bottom. It looked good and I liked it, but it wasn't how I'd expected it to look.

What annoyed me the most was the fact that I wasn't allowed more than half a glass of orange juice for breakfast. I had no clue why anyone would tell me what to eat or drink. But I wasn't going to complain like a little brat and demand the rest of my orange juice, so I let it go. Sort of.

I grabbed my cell phone and fired off a text, *'Can you come to my wing once you're in the palace, please?'*

'Sure. I'll be there in five minutes,' was the instant reply.

The designer was still working with something on the dress, but I didn't even know what the problem was – it looked fine to me. I didn't say anything, though, and just let her do her job.

"Princess Huda is here, your highness," Donia informed me.

"Let her in, please!" I almost rolled my eyes. With all of the people who I didn't know that were in the room, she had to ask my permission first for Huda to come in? It was silly.

"Good morning," Huda said cheerfully, her ever-present smile brightening her face. "Oh, my God! You look so beautiful!"

"Hey! Thanks. You're here early."

"Yeah, I was at the gates when I got your text. It's very crowded outside; it's a miracle I made it here. That's why I left early, I knew it'd be like that," she explained. My smile dropped, realizing right away that it was why Mona still hadn't shown up. I knew that if she arrived any later, I wouldn't have time to take the test.

"Is everything okay?" Huda asked, bringing my attention back to her.

"Yes," I said, then motioned for her to come closer so I could speak in a lower voice. "I, uh, I'm really nervous and I needed a friend with me," I told her honestly. My first thought was to text Rosanna, but I didn't know how active the doctors were allowing her to be.

"Aww!" Huda spread her arms, ready to give me a hug, but I guess she thought better of it; maybe she didn't want to mess up my hair or something, because she lowered them right away.

"That makes me so happy," she said, then her eyes widened, realizing how that might have sounded. "that you thought of me, not that you're nervous." She giggled and I smiled, shaking my head.

"Of course I think of you this way. Are you kidding? You've been helping me non-stop since the day I met you. I owe you a lot."

"Ah! You owe me nothing, I'm so glad to help."

"Can you help me find out why I wasn't allowed more than half a glass of orange juice?" Yeah, I was still not over it.

Huda stepped even closer and whispered in my ear, "Um, so you won't have the need to pee during the ceremony."

My eyes widened, and suddenly it all made sense, but it also made me realize that from now on, everything would be counted and planned for me. Even my bathroom breaks.

After asking for permission, Huda changed her clothes in one of the rooms in the wing. I told her that was such a crazy question, of course she could. Then right before I left for where the ceremony was being held, Mona arrived.

"Princess, I am so sorry for being late. It was very difficult to navigate through the crowds and traffic to get here earlier."

"It's okay, Mona. I understand. We will do it later, don't worry." I whispered, offering her a small smile.

"I slipped it in the first drawer of your nightstand, *benty*," she whispered back.

I nodded.

With a deep breath, I left the wing, trailed by Huda,

Mona, Donia and some other servants. When I got inside the elevator, only Huda and two female guards got in with me. I held the door open and with confused expression I asked Mona, "Aren't you coming in?"

"No, Princess. I can't. Only royal family is allowed where you're going. I'll be at the ceremony, though, with the rest of the audience." She smiled sweetly.

My mouth fell open. "Why not? There'll be people from all over the kingdom in the room!"

"Yes, I'll be with them. I promise."

"Mona, please, come with me." To be honest, I felt like Mona was a mother to Mazen more than Queen Shams was – or maybe that was just me.

Mona looked hesitant.

"Come on, Mona. It's the Future Queen's request," Huda encouraged.

A smile was painted on Mona's lips. "It's such an honor, your highness." She finally got into the elevator with us. Although Mona and Huda's presence gave me a sense a comfort, my heart sank even more as the elevator descended.

A sense of déjà vu came rushing to me when the doors of the elevator opened to the very same room where I had waited with the princesses on my wedding day.

The fact that half of the faces in there were exactly the same princesses who'd waited with me before the wedding ceremony started didn't help the rushing memories.

When I heard Huda clear her throat, I knew that I had taken too long to step out of the elevator, so I squared my shoulders, and took one step into the room. I kept my smile plastered on my face as I saw all of the smiling faces in matching beautiful dresses with tiaras above their heads, and started walking towards them. I was guided by one of the ceremony planners that I had met with yesterday.

I nodded my head and thanked everyone who congratulated me as I walked past them. Many of them were people I could remember from the wedding. When I came to one of the main doors of the room, I was politely asked to wait in my spot while the princesses formed a line behind me.

At nine o'clock sharp, the doors opened. I heard the rhythmic beat of drums while a declaration in Arabic was loudly spoken into a microphone. All I could understand was my name before I walked through the doors.

I swallowed thickly as I saw the gathering in front of me; there were so many women, hundreds and hundreds of them. Not that I didn't know that would be the case – people came from all over the kingdom just to be present for the celebration. But I had no idea there would be this many – and they were only the royal family and their families.

With a smile, I took my place in the middle of the stage, while once again, all of the princesses took their spots behind me. I imagined it to be such a great sight, but I didn't know if I could look behind me or not.

The planners had answered all of my questions yesterday and told me how things would go, in detail, but I still felt like I wasn't prepared enough. I was nervous as heck that I would do something wrong and not follow protocol.

The drums stopped, and there was a moment of silence before I heard the voice speaking again. This time, the voice droned on and on for a long time and I didn't understand one word. That made my throat tighten even more, but I managed to stand still and keep my face blank. As I listened, I heard my name mentioned more than once, it was all I recognized in the whole speech beside Mazen's name.

The drums started again, and I heard it, "Al-Ameera Rosanna bent Hamed Alfaidy."

The doors located at the back of the rows of chairs opened and all eyes turned to look at Rosanna as she made her way to the stage with steady steps, holding what looked like a very thick book in her hands.

She offered me a very sweet and genuine smile when she neared, and I smiled back, really happy to see her there. She took her place to my right and I got a look at the book in her hands – it was the Bible.

Once again, the drums started and the voice announced, "Al-Maleka Al-Om Shams bent Salem Alfaidy." And my heart dropped to my feet.

She was here? In the same room where I was? What was she doing here? Would she hurt me? What did she want? My head started spinning with all of the questions, fear creeping into my heart just at the sound of her name. It took every ounce of strength in me not to leave the stage right then and there and simply run away.

Once she stepped into the room, I couldn't look at her. My head turned to the left and my eyes caught Mona's where she was standing at the far end of the stage. She nodded to me with her head once, the look in her eyes telling me silently that I could do it, and I tried my best to take the encouragement from just that look.

When I looked back ahead of me, the Queen was now closer. I decided to be strong and look straight into her eyes. Strangely, they weren't as hard as I remembered them, and if I was being honest, I could swear I saw joy filling them, even without a smile on her lips.

The greenish in her eyes reminded me of another set of green eyes, ones that belonged to the man I loved, the one I was doing all of this for, and that was all it took to convince myself that I could do this.

She got up on the stage and stood right in front of me. I didn't doubt that both Rosanna and the Queen could hear the racing thumping of my heart.

A microphone was held between the two of us when Rosanna spoke quietly, "Place your right hand on your holy book, your highness, please." Her tone and her words were very formal despite the fact that her voice was just above a whisper.

As requested, I put my right hand on the Bible and raised my left one like the planner had told me to do yesterday. I swallowed around the lump in my throat and waited with anxious eyes for what was to come next.

The Queen spoke, her voice steady and strong, "Princess Marie Grace, daughter of Luke Archer, and wife of King Mazen, son of his royal highness Qasem Alfaidy," My heart was beating even faster as I heard her saying King instead of Crown Prince. "Do you swear in front of God Almighty and all people that you will obey the laws of the kingdom of Alfaidya, respect the rules and people, and use all of the powers provided to you as Queen of the kingdom to protect its people and lands and keep them safe and in peace?"

"I swear," I said with a small nod of my head.

A hint of a smile crept onto Queen Shams' lips, and she nodded her head. Rosanna lowered her hands that were holding the Bible a bit, and I took the cue to drop my own hands back to my sides.

Queen Shams raised her hands to her head and took off the magnificent crown she was wearing – which I'd been too nervous to ogle before – and slowly put it on top of my head, as I lowered it the slightest to make it easier for her to put it on.

Boy, was it heavy!

The next thing she did was to take off the red sash she was wearing and drop it over my shoulder, then she took the small golden brooch shaped like a crown from her dress and pinned it very carefully to my dress, right above my heart.

"I now announce you as the new queen of the Kingdom of Alfaidya."

Fourteen

It was such an odd thing to happen. I really couldn't understand my feelings, but I was actually happy about it. I was happy about being a queen. I admit that it was so hard to believe. A few months ago, I would've never believed I could come to this country and actually spend any time in it, not even for a short visit, and today I found myself crowned as the new queen of said country. How was that even possible? I still couldn't understand it.

My feelings were a mix of joy, concern and some more joy. The power I felt as people stood and applauded was so overwhelming that the queen's presence wasn't even that annoying anymore. Queen Mother, I mean. *I* was the queen.

Holy! It was hard to comprehend.

A grin dominated my features as I stood and

looked at the faces around me. I couldn't see a sad or disgruntled face. Everyone was smiling while clapping their hands, and all I could do was press my hand to the middle of my chest in an attempt to make my heart settle down a bit, to stop it from beating so fast. I felt as if it was ready to burst out of my chest.

A few minutes later, I was guided to one of the rooms on the first floor of the palace for a quick break. I was really looking forward to said break after standing on my feet for so long.

The fact that Mazen was already there in that room took me by surprise, but it was such a wonderful surprise. After the door was closed behind me, I didn't move, but Mazen. who was looking out one of the windows, turned around to look at me.

When our eyes met, my smile remained as I took in the piece of jewelry on his chest. It looked like some sort of thick necklace that had been dropped over his shoulders with the middle piece of the necklace resting over his broad chest.

His smile widened as he took me in, the look in his eyes warm and full of love. "Look at you!" he said, his eyes looking me up and down as he seemed to take his time appreciating every inch of me with his gaze.

"Well, look at *you*," I replied, "King Mazen."

In one second, I was in his arms as he hugged me tightly to his body. His lips pressed onto mine in a tender kiss that held so much more passion than words could describe.

"You look so beautiful in that royal crown, your majesty," he smiled, his hand cupping my jaw while the other rested on the small of my back.

I had to chuckle at that. "With how heavy it is, it should make me look beautiful."

"Yes, I've heard it's heavy. But trust me when I say that it's not as heavy as the responsibilities that come with wearing it."

I sighed, "I know."

"We can do it together. I know that as long as we're close – we can do anything. We could even rule the whole world, not only a kingdom. Don't you agree, Marie?"

I nodded. "We can do it, Mazen. With God's will, we can do it." I needed to hear myself saying it even more than I needed to tell him those words.

Mazen hugged me again and I let go of a heavy breath. "With God's will." I felt him nodding.

We stood there for a few minutes, hugging and taking comfort from each other, because if I was not mistaken, it seemed like Mazen needed this embrace as much as I needed it.

"Where's your crown, though?" I asked into his chest and heard him chuckling.

"Kings don't wear crowns in this kingdom, princess."

I frowned. Was that piece of jewelry over his chest all there was?

"You guys are weird," I told him.

Mazen laughed and moved my head up with his hand to peck me on the lips. "You're so cute, princess."

"Hey! I'm a queen now, if you didn't notice," I joked, tightening my arms around him.

He looked deep into my eyes with his mesmerizing ones. "You'll always be my princess."

After our brief reunion, we were separated again. Two guards – one male and one female – came to guide us out of the room and into other reception rooms. Before we parted, assistants appeared to refresh our appearances, and when one started wiping a smudge of red lipstick off of Mazen's mouth, I turned the same shade of a tomato, though Mazen only smirked. *Cheeky jerk!*

In the other room, Rosanna stood to my right and introduced every female member of the royal family to me – Every. Single. One – as they lined up and passed me with nods of their heads and a kiss to the crown above my head. It was their way of showing respect and telling me that I had been accepted by them as their queen, or so I was told.

"Princess Hager Alfaidy," Rosanna said as one young girl came to me with a smile and nod. I smiled back and lowered my head for her to reach the crown.

"Princess Sana Alfaidy,'' Rosanna said as another young girl did the same as the two and a half million before her. Or maybe it was just a hundred, I didn't know – it felt like much more.

"Princess Alia Alfaidy."

"Princess Eman Alfaidy."

"Princess Shahd Alfaidy."

My legs were about to give out from standing for too long, and my cheeks hurt from too much smiling. By the time we were close to the end of that part of the ceremony, I was ready to take off my heels and sit down on the floor, waving my hand to whomever passed by me from then on.

Dreams!

"Princess Kareen Alfaidy."

"Princess Talia Alfaidy," Rosanna announced and my eyes widened as I heard her name. I knew that name – oh, I knew it *so* well.

I watched the one with the angelic face as she approached me with a devilish smile painted on her lips. My heart thumped hard in my chest as the words she'd spoken to me the only time I'd ever met her before sounded in my head:

"And you should be aware that when he needs an heir, it's my stomach that will bear his child, not yours. His seed will only get someone royal-born like me pregnant, not some commoner like you who only got the title four days ago."

Just like the time I'd heard those words, my throat tightened as I remembered them, and my chest hurt. But I kept my face blank. I wasn't going to show her how much she affected me, because it shouldn't be the case. *I* was the one who was married to Mazen. *I* shared his bed. *I* got his love and his attention – this girl had nothing on me.

Or so I tried to convince myself.

Talia nodded her head once. Her smile looked more like a sneer than a smile. Her green eyes were colder than ice and the look in them spoke volumes as to how much she wished I would vanish from planet Earth.

When she came closer she paused, but I never felt her as she placed that kiss she should've put on the crown. Instead, I found out it was just for her to whisper, "It doesn't end here, just so you know."

My blood boiled in my veins and I clenched my teeth hard; she was doing it again with her nonsense talk. But I refused to stay silent like last time. It wasn't the same anymore. *I* wasn't the frightened shaking mess that she'd met before. I was the queen of this kingdom. *Her* queen.

Before she could back away, I grabbed her forearm and stopped her. Her eyes were filled with shock as she looked down at my hand gripping her arm then looked up into my eyes. It was then that I spoke.

"Dream on, *princess*," I said, emphasizing the last word so she would remember well what her position was and what mine was.

It only took her a moment to recover, and then the devilish smile was back on her lips again.

"Oh, I intend to do just that, *your majesty.* For my dreams *always* come true."

Minx!

Next, I stood with Mazen in the main foyer of the palace, ready for our first appearance as the king and queen of the kingdom of Alfaidia.

An announcement was made in Arabic. Again, all I could get was Mazen's and my names, before Mazen smiled at me, taking my hand and walking us out of the palace. Guards stood on both sides of us in unbelievable numbers. They could easily form an army, and thinking about it, they could really *be* the army.

We were ushered into a ridiculously long limousine, where we stood to be seen through the sunroof of the unmoving car.

"Are you ready?" Mazen asked.

"Yea– … oh, wait!" I toed the back of my shoes and took them both off, disliking the fact that I became shorter without them, but I really couldn't handle one more minute wearing them. "I'm ready," I smiled at him.

Mazen nodded to one of the guards standing beside the limousine, and he called something, then the car started moving slowly. There were six horses with guards on their backs surrounding the car, then there were about eight cars surrounding them in such a beautiful way.

"Where's Thunder?" I leaned in to ask Mazen.

"He doesn't let anyone other than me ride on his back," he answered near my ear.

As the limousine neared, the main gates of the palace slowly opened wide as I heard our names ringing loudly all around us. We heard cheers and gunfire, lots and lots of it.

Once my vision focused on what was outside of the gates, my eyes widened in shock. There were so many people, standing on both sides of the road covered by a huge red carpet that seemed to go on forever.

My right hand gripped Mazen's where nobody could see, and I took deep breaths so as not to freak out at the sight in front of me. It seemed like the whole country was gathered in front of the palace.

Mazen squeezed my hand, his thumb making soft touches over the back of it. That was all the assurance I needed, even if I didn't get to see him looking me in the eye while he did it.

Once the car made it through the gates, the cheers became even louder and I found myself smiling as we both started waving at the people around us.

"Oh, my God!" I gushed.

"What is it?" Mazen asked, not looking at me as he continued waving.

"I just realized that I've only ever seen the palace and the airport!" I kept my smile on as I waved at people who started throwing roses at us. We were too far from the crowd for any of the roses to reach us. They were all dropped on the guards who walked around the procession that was surrounding us.

I could barely hear Mazen as he chuckled softly, "I'm sure you'll get to see plenty of it soon enough."

My mind still couldn't get over the fact that I'd become a queen of a country I knew so little about, that I'd become a queen just because I was married to the king, even though I wasn't even carrying his last name.

I had actually been worried about the whole last name thing when we first got married, and was thinking of ways to let me get away with it, in a way that didn't upset Mazen. I was surprised to find out that in his – our – country and most Arabian countries, the wife forever had her father's name and not her husband's.

In the royal family, they had the same last name, anyway. Because almost everyone was married to his cousin.

I shook the thought out of my head. I wouldn't let the thought of 'cousins' lead me to think of a certain cousin of my husband who was apparently obsessed with him.

"And I actually showed you a very nice part of the desert, my princess – have you forgotten?" Mazen said. Nothing in him gave away that he was telling me something like that. He still stood tall and firm while he waved at people, his smile on his face as his left hand squeezed mine once again.

My grin was wide as I took in his words. Of course

I hadn't forgotten – how could I forget the place where we'd shared our first kiss and started falling for each other, under the dark sky with a full moon and sparkling little stars? It was out of the question.

I squeezed his hand back. "Not in a million years, angel."

After that there was a military parade, then military aerobatics, and eventually we had a separated dinner with the royal family, with me sitting at the head of the table of female family members.

I was grateful for no Talia or evil mother-in-law more than I was grateful for actually finally getting something to eat. The apple I'd gotten to eat when we took our first break wasn't that satisfying.

It was my first day as a queen and I was starving – how crazy was that?

The food was amazing, except the guava juice that was a bit sour. But I was too hungry to be picky and was polite enough to eat a decent amount of everything that was placed in front of me.

By the time I got back to my wing, I was dead on my feet and ready to crash. I asked Donia to prepare a hot bath for me, hoping that by the time I finished bathing, Mazen would be home so we could call it a day.

My muscles were relaxing slowly but surely as I

spent a good half an hour in the round tub. The oils Donia had put in the water smelled so good, and the salt was working wonders on my skin. I could literally feel the tension of the day easing with every passing minute.

When I hopped out of the tub, I wrapped myself with a towel and headed straight to the walk-in closet. I had already told Donia that I wouldn't be needing her help getting dressed and that I would call when the king needed something.

The king!

A naughty thought crossed my mind and I found myself biting my pointer finger as I realized I really wanted to do it. My lips formed a grin and my cheeks heated at all of the images flashing inside my head.

On the couch that was placed in front of the main door of the bedroom, I waited for Mazen, wearing only a sexy gown that left little to the imagination – and the royal crown. My smile didn't leave my face as I imagined the look in his eyes when he saw me, ready and waiting for him.

Not too long after, the door opened and Mazen entered the room, his eyes finding me immediately. The way he looked at me made my insides tingle; it was exactly like I'd imagined it. Even better.

His eyes darkened with desire as they roamed all over my body, and a sweet smile was drawn on his slightly parted lips. He closed the door behind him, but didn't make any other move, so I decided to make a move myself.

I stood up and took a few steps closer to him. "See something you like, your majesty?" I bit my lip, giving him the most innocent look I could muster.

"Not really," he answered, and I gave him a questioning look. "I'm seeing something that I love."

A small laugh escaped my mouth and I took the rest of the steps separating us, until I was standing right in front of him. "Are you going to do something about it?" I dropped my hands over his shoulders, right where the royal necklace was.

His hands touched my hips. "Oh, I plan to do something about it," he nodded, his eyes not leaving mine. "Lots of things, actually." His lips crashed my own as he gave me a steamy kiss that knocked the air out of my lungs and left me breathless.

His lips left my mouth and hungrily kissed all over my jawline and neck. I moaned and squeezed his shoulders in response. "Oh, Mazen!" I breathed.

"You have no idea how much I've wanted to do this all day long." he panted into the tender skin behind my ear, sending shivers down my spine, his hands touching wherever he could reach and his erection grinding into my hip.

He was placing kisses all over my face when he suddenly stopped. My vision was clouded with the lust I was feeling when I looked at him questioningly, my eyes widening at the look of distaste on his face. "What? What's wrong?" I asked in confusion.

"Uh, … "

"What is it? Tell me."

"It's, uh, the crown," was all he said.

"The crown? What about it?"

"Um, my mother used to wear that thing, so …"

"What do you mea– … oh! Ooh!" I said as I finally got his point, and it was my turn to mirror the same look that was on his face.

Mazen laughed at how fast I took the crown off, walking to the dresser beside the window and placing it there. I gave him a look that made him shake his head at me as he started taking his clothes off.

"Did you know that she was going to be in the ceremony?" I asked him when he came to stand next to me, as he placed the necklace beside the crown.

"Of course I knew. That's why I asked if you were going to be okay!" he replied, frowning. "Wait! You didn't know?"

I shook my head.

"I thought that one of the ceremony planners had told you about all of the details of the ceremony!"

"She did. She said the *'Queen Mother will do this, and the Queen Mother will do that.'* I thought she meant your grandmother; I didn't realize she was talking about your mother. I get it now, though."

Mazen shook his head. "I'm sorry about that, princess."

"Hey, it's okay. I'm fine. I promise," I told him. "The ceremony was magical and everything went okay."

"Yeah, it was," he smiled.

"Will I ever get to see your side of the ceremony? I really dislike the fact that I wasn't there while it happened."

"Me too, I wish you could've been there. And of course you can see it. You can google it," he winked. "It wouldn't be the first time you've googled my name."

"You and your smart mouth!" I narrowed my eyes at him, and my answer was said mouth being pressed to mine in another steamy kiss.

"Hey, Mazen?" I breathed when he broke our kiss to work his way down my neck.

"Hmm?"

"I need to learn Arabic soon. Like, yesterday."

Fifteen

Later that night, I was still confused about Mazen's mother and her actions. My confusion led to me telling him about how his mother had acted during the ceremony – how she'd looked like a different person and how she'd looked genuinely happy while giving me the crown. She wasn't even close to happy on our wedding day.

Mazen explained it in a few words, and it was so easy for me to understand when he said, "My mother wanted me to be a king, Princess. It's all she's ever wanted, and today she got her wish. I bet she wasn't even showing how happy she truly was."

Since we were actually talking about her now, I thought I might ask more questions, maybe to just feed my curiosity.

"Where has she been all this time?" She'd

obviously been elsewhere; she hadn't been taking care of the palace or any of the things she usually managed around the kingdom. Prince Fahd had told me that she couldn't hurt me even if she wanted to, and I always wondered what that meant, but had been too skittish about bringing her up to actually ask.

Mazen told me that his mother had been punished by his father for her actions. There was a small, private trial where she'd been judged guilty for humiliating and attempting to hurt the Queen Mother– her punishment was to not leave her room for the next five years. She was only allowed by the king to do her part in the ceremony, and that was all.

To be honest, I found myself a little mad that her punishment was only for what she'd done to the Mother Queen, and not for what she'd done to me. But sadly, there was no law against Common Deflowering, even if none of the women in the kingdom accepted it and most men didn't really find it necessary.

Either way, I was glad she wouldn't be a bother for me anymore.

"Mazen, does that mean that she won't be able to accompany the King to Germany for his surgery?"

"Yes."

"But the King will be all alone in a foreign land. It's already going to be difficult for him, being so far away without any family." The king was such a nice man, and I disliked the fact that he wouldn't be surrounded by his loved ones during this hard time.

"Fahd will be with him for the entire time, for his surgery and through his recovery and treatment. Janna will also be meeting them there to help take care of him." Mazen assured, and I was actually happy to hear that.

That night we fell asleep very late despite the fact that we were both exhausted from the long day. We made love and talked for hours; I was so happy in Mazen's arms that I couldn't believe anything could take away from our happiness.

I was wrong.

A few hours later, I was awakened by a sharp pain in my lower stomach. For the past several days, I'd had cramps on and off, but none of them were as sharp as the pain I was feeling right then. Heck, it wasn't like any pain I'd ever felt before.

I stayed in bed for a while, hoping that the pain would go away, but a few minutes later, the pain was so unbearable that I had to get up and go to the bathroom, trying my best not to disturb Mazen, for I knew what a light sleeper he was.

In the bathroom, I was devastated to see the blood on my panties – not because it was too much, but rather because I'd really thought that I wouldn't see it for a long time.

A lone tear escaped my eye at the disappointment I felt when I realized I wasn't pregnant, then the tear found companions when other tears followed, streaming down my face.

It was stupid, I shouldn't have been that upset, knowing that I'd tried all this time to convince myself that I might not be pregnant. I guess the hope was still alive in me despite all of my attempts not to let it be.

I spent God only knows how long in the bathroom, crying my eyes out and internally cursing myself for being so upset about something that didn't happen, but I really couldn't help how I felt.

A knock on the door startled me and then I heard Mazen's voice that was laced with concern, "Marie, are you okay? You've been in there a long time."

I should've known better than to think I'd been successful in not waking him up when I'd left the bed, but it was really sweet to think that he'd stayed up waiting for me to come back to bed.

I wiped my tears with the back of my hand before answering, "Just a minute," then got up and searched the cabinets for some pads or even a tampon. I found one cabinet that was packed with many options that I could use; I had no idea if it was Janna's doing, since she'd been the one to prepare everything in the wing, or someone else's. But I was grateful.

When I came out of the bathroom, Mazen was waiting right outside, his smile disappearing when he saw the look on my face that I couldn't tame.

"Hey, are you okay? What's wrong?" he asked, taking me in his arms for a second and then backing away to look into my eyes the next.

"Um, yeah," I replied. "I, uh, I got my period." I

waited to see a look of disappointment in his eyes. I waited to see sadness, but it was concern that I was met with.

"Oh." He paused, and I would've paid anything to know what he was thinking in that moment. "Are you in pain?"

"Yes, horrible cramps," I said honestly, not able to control the tears that left my eyes.

Mazen thought it was from pain, and it was, but it was the pain in my heart, not the pain he thought it was.

"Oh, princess. Come here." He took me in his arms again, hugging me tightly, and I closed my eyes, inhaling his scent, knowing very well the kind of effect it had on me. "I'm sorry about that. Do you use a specific painkiller, or do you want me to get you something?"

"Anything strong would be good. Thank you," I said in a low voice.

Mazen carried me to bed and tucked me in, placing a tender kiss on my forehead and telling me he would be right back before he put a shirt and sweatpants on since he was only in his boxers, and then left the room.

I took the time he was gone to curl into a ball and cry some more, wondering if Mazen was actually upset because I'd gotten my period and was just hiding it from me, or if he really didn't care.

For some reason, I couldn't decide on the latter, and told myself that he just didn't want to show me how sad he was that I wasn't pregnant.

Thankfully, the pills that Mazen gave me made me drift into a deep sleep just fifteen minutes later, while he smoothed my hair above my head and wiped my tears away.

The pain wasn't as horrible over the next few days, but my period lasted longer than ever and I'd never had it that heavy before. I just thought it was because of how late it was and didn't think much of it.

Mazen was incredibly sweet and took good care of me whenever he was around, but there were days when he had to attend to the affairs of the kingdom and be gone for the whole day. When that happened, he called as much as he could and always sent a text saying that he loved me. His messages always came at a time when I really needed to hear it. He even made sure I had chocolate beside me all the time.

For over a week, I didn't leave my wing, not for work and not to do my duties as queen. I took advantage of everyone who was willing to help me – Rosanna and Huda, even Mona took care of things for me and offered me all of the help I needed.

When my decisions were needed, I made them from inside the wing and did everything possible not to leave it while Mazen wasn't with me.

Mazen thought it was only because I was sick. And I let him believe it.

It wasn't easy to accept that change in my life, but I tried all I could to make all of the adjustments needed to make it feel normal. I knew my not leaving my place wasn't normal, but I hoped that one day soon I could do it. One step at a time, I told myself.

One of the letters I received during the week was from Janna. She was congratulating me on the coronation and apologizing for not being able to be there, telling me that her appearance prevented her from attending the ceremony.

A smile found my lips as I read her words, realizing that she meant she was showing more than she should be, as far as everyone knew. The thought of my nephew or niece doing well in her stomach made my insides warm, imagining what my parents would've felt about that.

'Would you like to visit the horses with me tonight? We never made it that night after all,' Mazen texted.

'Sure. What time?' was my instant reply.

'I'm not sure yet, but I'll do my best to come back early tonight. I love you.'

'Can't wait. I love you back.'

I made sure to finish most of the work during the day. I really was looking forward to a night with Mazen; it felt like it had been so long since we'd been intimate. I wasn't feeling well most of the time and had as little conversation with him as possible.

He hadn't pushed me to talk, only hugged me and kissed my lips, pouring all of his love for me into those hugs and kisses and kind words. I didn't know what I would've done without him.

When Mazen finally made it home, I was dressed

in jeans and a t-shirt, knowing that we probably wouldn't be seen in public which would require me to dress in something more formal. Mazen also changed into casual clothes and then asked if I was ready.

I was a little confused when we didn't use the secret tunnels, but didn't question it. And then I was surprised to see that two cars were leaving with us when we started moving. Both were full of royal guards, of course.

"Is that necessary?" I asked Mazen, pointing to the cars. "I mean, we have Fawaz and that other guy's name I can't pronounce."

Mazen chuckled, "Mo'taz, Princess. His name is Mo'taz."

"Right, that one."

"Of course it's necessary. Our safety is more important than ever now; we have millions of people depending on us."

I nodded my head in understanding. I didn't say anything when we went to the stable while eight guards protected our every step. It wasn't comfortable, but I didn't argue. Mazen was right, our purpose in life went beyond our own personal goals now – it involved other people as well.

We had a good time with the horses. Faith and Hope looked so much bigger than the last time I'd seen them over three months ago. God! It seemed like forever. Too much had happened since then.

Mazen took me by surprise when he suggested that

we go to *our* mountain. I was all for it, but didn't think it would be as good as last time, given that we wouldn't be alone.

"How come I can ride Thunder if he only allows you on his back?" I asked Mazen as he helped me to hop on like he had last time.

"Because it's me who's helping you onto his back. You wouldn't be able to do it alone," he replied as he got on behind me.

I made myself comfortable and got ready for the wonderful ride I knew was to come. My grin was already planted on my lips and my heart was already thumping hard in excitement. I didn't know that Mazen was planning to leave me breathless with the next words he whispered in my ears.

"You know, the last time we did this, Princess? You were panting and screaming, *'faster, faster.'* You gave me the most painful hard-on right then and there. I imagined you saying those words in a much different setting – those words rang in my ears for a long time."

Oh, my God! I'd had no idea! But thinking about it, it just clicked in my mind that this was the reason why he'd hopped off Thunder so abruptly last time. I don't know how I hadn't realized it then.

"You're such a pervert," I chuckled, trying to hide my blush.

"Am I?" he asked, not really waiting for an answer as he tightened his left arm around me then pulled the rope around his right hand, causing Thunder to run faster and put more excitement in me than anything else.

The ride was as amazing as I'd imagined it to be – even better. I may have had said 'faster' once or twice just to tease Mazen, enjoying the sound of his groan as I panted the word, and laughed when he said, "You're playing with fire, Marie."

For his sanity, I decided to stop with my teasing. Thunder stopped when we reached our destination, as did the eight horses with the guards behind us. Four of them went up on the mountain to scout the area while the rest waited with us.

After a few moments, Fawaz came back saying, "Everything is clear, your majesty," to Mazen, and then we made our way up, very grateful that we would be left alone up there.

In the spot behind the telescope, a thick carpet had been placed and a few pillows were draped over it. I almost rolled my eyes when I saw it – of course they would do that, lest we scratch our skin sitting on the rocks or something silly like that.

"Did you arrange that?" I asked when I sat down on the carpet.

"Well, I told Fawaz of our destination and plans for the night; he took care of the rest," Mazen smiled as he sat down beside me.

"It's nice."

Memories invaded my mind while we sat there and talked – good memories. I couldn't believe how different a person I was then – much different. Maybe some of my worries and my fears were still living some place in my heart, but I liked to believe that I was a better person, that I was more understanding and accepting than I had been.

After all, I knew that I couldn't love Mazen more than I already did, and I knew that loving him would get me anywhere I wanted to be – it would help me go on.

"So, are you ever going to tell me why you've been acting off the past few days?" Mazen asked while I lay in his arms.

I sucked in a deep breath then let it go, not knowing what to tell him.

"You know you can tell me anything, don't you, Marie?"

I knew I couldn't. Some things I just didn't want him to know, for one reason or another – maybe to not hurt his feelings, or maybe to not create a problem out of nothing. Other times I just didn't want to worry him. But I also knew it was unfair to stay silent yet still show my off mood.

I nodded slowly.

"I know you were PMSing, but I have a feeling it's more than that. Please tell me what's going on in that pretty head of yours."

"It's just – I'm really upset that I got my period, that I wasn't pregnant. I'd kind of hoped that I was," I said honestly.

Mazen eyebrows shot up to his head. “Are you serious?”

I nodded again.

“Oh, my crazy princess.” Mazen shook his head, taking me in his arms, “You’re being so silly. We’ve only been married for a month and a half – it’s too soon to worry about that!”

I sighed into his chest, “I know, but still. Sometimes it only takes one try.” Our siblings were living proof of that.

“And sometimes it takes longer. It’s God’s will, not our choice,” he said. “C’mon, Marie, we still have the rest of our lives to try.”

We didn’t. We had only a limited time. He needed a boy child, and who knew how long it would take me to provide him with one. Plus, I really wanted to be a mother.

“Yeah. You’re really not upset about it?” I wished he’d tell me the truth.

“Well, to be honest, I would’ve been the happiest man on earth if you were pregnant,” he said and my heart dropped, “but I’m not miserable because you’re not either, you know? It’s mostly because I want a baby with you more than anything. But, you make me really happy just by being there. God knows I might not be so thrilled about sharing you with a baby, after all.” He smiled, moving a lock of hair behind my ear.

A small smile found its place on my lips. “I want a baby with you more than anything else, as well,’’ I told him.

"Leave it in God's hands, Marie. We'll do our thing and when God wills, there's no stopping that, okay?"

"Yeah," I nodded, his words really sending calmness over my soul and easing my worries. "True."

"Plus, we can try as much as we want. Just to know that we gave it our best shot," he winked.

"You think?" I chuckled.

"Aha. I plan on trying at least twice tonight once we get back home."

"At least?" I gasped, then bit my smiling lip.

"Yes. I'll try. Hard."

Sixteen

They say that honesty is the key to any successful relationship. I agree with that, in principle, but sometimes, it was hard to follow.

There were lots of things that I couldn't tell Mazen, and I didn't know if I ever could.

One night after Mazen got back home, we were talking and I decided to bring up the subject of my travel to him, not knowing how he'd feel about it. When we'd talked about it before, I was only a princess, and didn't bear the responsibilities as Queen.

"Um, I'm going to the States in two days."

"In two days?" Mazen looked surprised, because I hadn't discussed it with him before.

"Yes."

"Is everything okay with the company?" he asked.

I could've lied to him and said that something

needed my personal attention, but I couldn't.

"Yes, the company is doing well. It's just … I really miss my grandmother, and I want to check on her." That wasn't all a lie. That was the truth, at least partially. "Of course. But can you delay it for a few days? The official opening of Al-Eman hospital is in two days. We've talked about that."

I'd really hoped that he wouldn't bring that up, but I was crazy to wish that he wouldn't remember that one particular detail.

"Can't you do it?" I already knew he couldn't – he wouldn't even be in the country that day – but I was stalling.

"Marie, you already know that I can't," he replied, "And you know that Fahd is in Germany with our father."

The tone of his voice and his last words told me that he'd become suspicious of my motives, of what I was avoiding – I was trying to get out of attending the opening of the hospital.

I looked down and fidgeted with the hem of my gown. I didn't know what to say, so I just stayed silent.

"You can't delay your trip for one day?" he asked, and I kept my head down. "Okay. Can you leave right after the opening?"

It was important for one of us to be in attendance for the hospital opening. It's been under construction for the last three years, the biggest hospital in the Middle East. The presence of a member of the Royal

Family was very important. One of us had to be there to officially open the hospital. And Mazen had a meeting in Cairo, Egypt, that he couldn't miss.

"All right." Mazen moved so that he was completely facing me while we sat on the bed. "How about you tell me what's going on?"

It took me a moment or two before I replied to him. "I'm not feeling comfortable with doing that," I told him honestly, still not looking at him.

"You won't feel comfortable? Why is that?"

"There will be so many … *people*. An official ceremony and gathering – I don't think I can do it."

"Why not?"

"I, uh, I don't feel safe."

Mazen's eyes stared at mine for a long moment, his expression not giving away any of his feelings about what he just heard.

"What?"

"I don't feel safe around people I don't know, Mazen."

I saw his jaw clenching as his eyes stared at me. Then he spoke, "Any kind of people? Because if I remember correctly, you didn't feel this way in London."

"Don't go there. Sometimes I feel like this even in New York."

"Why do I feel like you're not telling me the truth?" He narrowed his eyes slightly, tilting his head to the side.

"I AM telling you the truth. I don't feel like I could go there alone and not show how scared I am."

"Scared of what?" he asked, and I didn't reply. "I can't believe this, Marie. Where are all of your promises from when you first got to London? This is what I've feared the most, but you convinced me that it wasn't how you felt anymore."

"I know. And I'm sorry. I meant every word of what I said in London. I thought I could do it. I have been working up the courage to go, to fulfill my duties as your wife and Queen. But each time I think about it, I get close to a panic attack." I cried.

Mazen shook his head before burying it in his hands, no words leaving his mouth for a few minutes.

"Listen, I'm going to go to see my therapist while I'm in the States, and hopefully he can help me through it. It'll be fine. I think I just need time to adjust," I tried.

Mazen then raised his head and looked at me. "You're going to your therapist? So this is why you're really going there – it's not about your grandmother, is it?"

I could hear his tone changing, and that hurt my heart. I was upsetting him, and I hated it.

"It's just that I thought…"

"It's all right, Marie." He got up and left the bed. "I don't know how we can ever communicate the right way, if you keep holding how you feel back from me."

I looked down again, he was right. I wasn't honest with him about how I felt. I kept hiding my thoughts from him, even convincing him of the opposite, that I was all right and that I could do it. It wasn't right.

"All of this time, you've barely left the wing, and I thought you were just tired or busy. I didn't think much of it or worry that it was something else. Because I thought, you would come and tell me if it was more than that, if something was bothering you. But you hid your fears from me. You didn't tell me that you were uncomfortable or not feeling safe. You didn't give me the chance to fix it, and I just– ..." He shook his head, not looking at me.

"I – I'm sorry, Mazen."

"You shouldn't feel sorry about how you feel." He let go of a long breath. "I need some time to think. I'm going out. Don't wait up for me."

That night was such a long night. I eventually fell asleep waiting for Mazen. Donia woke me up the next morning because the palace managers were coming to discuss matters that would need decisions for the upcoming week.

Donia informed me that Mazen had already left for the day, and I couldn't be more upset about it. I wasn't aware that he returned, or felt him when he got up this morning and took his shower. I felt sure that he was avoiding me. I hated it.

After I had breakfast and went through the

decisions needed for the day, I started going through my e-mails and messages, sending one e-mail to Terri to tell her that I wasn't sure yet if I could make it to New York tomorrow, but to keep my appointments the same, just in case. I still didn't know if I could get away from the hospital opening without upsetting Mazen, just as I didn't know if I could force myself to do it in the first place.

'When are you coming home?' I texted Mazen. I wasn't used to not hearing from him all day like that, he always called or texted just to check on me.

It was so long before I got a reply that I'd lost hope that he would reply to me at all, thinking that he was giving me the silent treatment, but eventually he replied, *'In a couple of hours, everything okay?'*

'Yes. Can we have dinner together tonight?' I hoped he would manage to come home for dinner, but it wasn't an easy task, I knew that.

'I'll try my best. But I can't promise,' he texted. It was something anyway, better than nothing.

'I'll wait for you,' I replied, and a moment later I sent another text, *'I love you.'*

'I love you, too, Princess. Always.'

The smile returned to my lips.

When Mazen got back home, we had dinner and a light conversation about his day. The tension was thick between us, and I didn't know how to ease it or what to do to get things back on the right track. I didn't like this awkwardness between us.

To my relief, Mazen decided to address the elephant in the room.

"I'm going to do the hospital opening tomorrow," he said.

"Oh. What about your meeting in Cairo? You can't miss that."

"I managed to have it delayed for a few hours until I'm finished here, then I'll fly to Egypt right after. It's only a two hour flight," he answered.

The guilt that settled in my chest felt like a ton when I heard his words. He was going to go through all of this trouble for me; because I couldn't find the courage to pull up my big girl pants and act like his partner, his queen. I hated to put him through all of this when he'd already had so much to think about and do.

"You don't have to do that. I'll do the opening like I'm supposed to," I said, my heart thumping hard at just the thought of doing it.

"I'm not going to let you do anything that makes you uncomfortable. And it's already been arranged, don't worry about it."

I looked down at my hands on my lap, feeling so small. I disappointed him and was shirking from my responsibilities. I knew that nothing I could say could change Mazen's mind. He knew and felt that I wouldn't be comfortable going to the opening by myself, even if

I said I would.

"I'm really sorry, Mazen. I've been through a lot, and I'm trying my best to be better at accepting my new life, but it's not a piece of cake." I whispered, tears prickled in my eyes and my voice cracked at my last words.

Mazen sighed, "I know that, Princess, and I'm trying to be understanding, but I can't help but think what if you never manage to get over your fears? You can't spend the rest of your life inside the palace – it's not right."

"I have a hope that I can do it, but I just need more time." My tears finally made it down my cheeks and I quickly wiped them away.

"Hey, don't cry, Princess. You know how much I hate it when you cry." Mazen moved closer to me and touched my cheek, wiping new tears away with his thumb.

"And I hate to think that you're mad at me."

"I'm not. I'm not mad at you, Marie," he argued. "I'm just sad that you kept something like that from me, and I'm seriously upset that you're even feeling this way. But I'm willing to do anything that will help you through it. Anything you want me to do, anything you name – it's yours. But I don't read minds, Princess. How will I know how to do the right thing with you if you keep hiding what you truly feel from me?"

"I only wanted to avoid upsetting you," I sobbed.

"Did it work?"

I shook my head slowly.

"Promise me you won't do it again, please. Or I'll always keep wondering if what you're telling me is the truth or not. It's not a good way to live, you know?"

"I promise," I said, nodding.

Mazen bent down and kissed my forehead, wiping more tears from my face. "That's good. Now tell me, what do you think would make you feel safer, more at ease? Additional royal guards?"

I shook my head. "I, uh, I don't think so."

"Okay, you said it had happened sometimes before in America – how did you manage to get over it then?"

"I don't know – Brad was always with me, and I – I trust him." I bit my lower lip, looking down.

"Brad, your bodyguard?"

"Yes. I've known him for many years."

Mazen looked deep in thought for a few minutes, then he spoke, "Do you think Brad would agree to relocate?"

My eyes widened. "You mean I can bring him here?"

"If he agrees, I don't see why not, but it won't be easy. We'll have to do a deep background check on him first, and he'll have to go through a lot of training with the royal guards. It'll take him a long time to get used to things here and the complicated design of the palace. I suppose he's been well trained, but he'll have to go through some tests here, as well. It's the Queen of Alfaidya's safety we're talking about here." A hint of a smile touched his face and I jumped up and threw myself into his arms.

"Thank you so much, this changes a lot." I hugged him tightly, my eyes closing as a wonderful sensation of safety went through me.

"I'm glad. But– ..." Mazen paused and I sat back and looked at him, waiting for whatever he had to say. "He'll have to learn about our culture and follow it, Princess. As you know, it's very different from yours, and I don't want the media speaking about him and his actions. He won't be wearing the army's uniform and he'll be getting a lot of attention."

"What do you mean?"

"Well, he's not allowed inside the wing, just like the rest of the royal male guards. He can't put his hands on like guiding you to a place or something of that sort. The only time he can do that is when he is protecting you. He can't be alone with you in a room with the door closed. The things that all of the royal guards are not allowed to do, Princess."

"Huh!" I said, not knowing what to think of all that.

"Listen, I trust you like I could never trust anyone else, and I would never doubt your loyalty – it's just how my culture is. I'm an Arab and this is how we were raised. I don't want people talking or making up stories about you; you know what it's like around here."

"I understand, Mazen."

In the early morning I was seated in one of the jets that the royal family owned, and once we were in the air I felt how different flying alone, without Mazen, was.

I had insisted on not taking any royal guards with me, telling Mazen that Brad would be waiting for me at the airport and it wouldn't be necessary. He wasn't happy about it. I reasoned with him as much as I could and eventually he still didn't agree. I'd let him know that I wasn't actually happy about it. He wouldn't even let me go without three servants with me.

"Hey, I just landed," I said into the phone. Mazen had made me promise that I would call once I landed safely.

"*Alhamdulilah.* I'm glad to hear that, Princess."

"I know it's late, so I won't keep you u–Holy!" I gasped as I looked out the window.

"What is it, are you okay?"

"Mazen, there's a red carpet and a half dozen cars out there – did you do this?"

I heard him chuckling. "I had nothing to do with it. You just have to realize the fact that you're a queen now, Marie, and you're visiting another country – what did you expect?"

"Oh, God!" I groaned. I was annoyed by this very thing happening in the kingdom, and to find out that they were doing this in my own country as well wasn't so pleasant.

"Good luck, your majesty."

Just like I'd expected, my grandmother hadn't even noticed that I'd been gone for so long. But I sure as heck had missed her. I visited with her for hours and hours, talking with her about anything and everything. I still wished she could remember me, but I wasn't that lucky. Like always, she thought I was my mom.

I told her about Mazen and she instantly fell in love with him. I knew she wouldn't remember him the next time I visited, but I had no problem talking about him over and over again.

My visit with my Mama lifted my spirits, and I was determined that I wouldn't take that long to visit her again. I would try to at least come once a month or once every three weeks.

Since Brad had already offered last time to come with me to the kingdom, I knew that it wouldn't be hard to convince him, he would agree to come with me this time. He really didn't have much family, only his father who lived in Indiana, and he hardly ever visited, so things wouldn't be much different for him.

I went through what Mazen had told me with him, and he seemed very accepting of everything. He took it as an honor when I told him that I trusted him with my life more than I did the royal guards, and he promised to not let me down.

It was all I needed.

My therapist agreed to a home visit, since he was aware of my new position and how every step I took was now scrutinized. God forbid that the public became aware that the queen was human and needed to consult with a therapist! Unlike my visit with my grandmother earlier that day, which was light, happy and full of smiles and laughter, this visit was heavy and full of tears and heartache.

I told him everything that had happened since the day Joseph had told me he was marrying a princess, up to the moment I'd left the palace two days before. He listened patiently, interjecting only to ask questions about details that I hadn't viewed as significant but that must have been important for him to know.

"I have a feeling you're more comfortable around women there, am I correct?"

"That's true, Dr. Walker. I'm not bothered when the gathering is all women, even if Mazen isn't there. And I have no problem going around the palace with the royal guards' company. But then when I think of leaving the palace, or meeting with strangers, I just freak out," I admitted what I couldn't tell Mazen.

You'd think that with what had almost happened to me because of a bunch of women, I would fear them, too. But I didn't, though I had no idea why. I could only hope that one day I would feel the same about men, as well.

"I see. Does the king know of your fears?"

"To a point. I promised him that I'll be okay, that I'm going to be safe even when he's not around, but here I am, not able to keep my own feelings at bay."

"Why are you not telling him the truth?"

"I told him the truth. Well, part of it. I just didn't want to hurt his feelings. I don't want him to still think of me as the judgmental girl I was, because I've changed. It's just like – I'm not familiar with the people and customs there, and I always feel like I'll do something wrong, so I just sit there and don't do anything."

"What are you afraid of the most?" he asked.

"I don't even know – so many things."

"Name one."

I only shook my head.

"Are you afraid of the people in the kingdom?"

"I think so."

"Is it because of their religion?" he pushed, and I had to take a moment before I replied.

"No. No, Dr. Walker, it's not." I said with confidence. I'd changed. For the better. "I know that they weren't the ones who killed my grandfather."

"Then why are you afraid of them?"

"I'm afraid I won't be able to be the perfect Queen to them, that they won't accept me. I'm afraid that I will mess something up because I don't know everything I need to know. I'm afraid that Mazen will think I'm not an appropriate wife for him." My eyes widened as I heard the words falling from my mouth.

I'm afraid that Mazen will leave me because I'm not good enough.

"Why do you think your husband would do that?"

"Everyone I ever loved left me. Why wouldn't he?" Tears filled my eyes as I looked down. My grandfather died, my parents died, my grandmother doesn't even remember me. My own brother betrayed me and held me at gunpoint.

"Do you believe that all people are the same? Do they all think alike? Act alike?"

"No."

"You need to take a few steps to reach a safe zone in your mind. You need to take a step forward to start getting rid of your insecurities. What do you think the first step should be?"

"Uh, I need to learn more about their culture and protocols," it was the first thing I could think of, I didn't want to do something that would embarrass Mazen.

"But before that, you need to acknowledge your new life. You need to accept your new position. With that, your anxiety will disappear, you'll realize you're the right person for your partner. Can you do that?"

I hesitantly nodded.

"You fell in love with him, not his family and not

his position. It's okay that it is taking you time to feel comfortable in this new role, which is a big role and which was thrust upon you suddenly and unwillingly."

"Yes."

"I believe that time heals all wounds, Marie. You just need to get used to it – but most importantly, you really need to believe deep in your heart that you can do it, that you will accept it, and with time – you will. You'll learn that those people will eventually become your own people, not strangers."

I nodded my head slowly. I knew I wanted to feel normal. I wanted it so badly, and for that, I was willing to push myself harder, but – I had no clue how much time that would take, and if Mazen would still keep up with me if it took longer than he could bear.

Seventeen

His hands on my hips were driving me insane, as he kept me in place while he thrust upwards inside of me. I wanted to meet him halfway, but he wouldn't let me. I wanted to set the pace, but he was completely in control, even though I was the one riding him.

"Oh, Mazen," I moaned his name when he pressed on my hips, pinning me down as his thrusts become even harder and faster. He sat up a little and I felt his tongue on my left nipple, which made me moan even louder as he sucked on it.

My head was thrown back and my hands were gripping his hair. I used the time as he got busy on my breasts to start pushing myself up and down his length, taking control.

He groaned into my breast and bit down on my nipple, the sensation going straight to my clit. In that moment, I felt as if time had stopped. I felt as if the whole room was spinning. I felt as if we were the only two people in the entire world. And for a second, I forgot my name.

"Marie," he breathed as his lips worked their way up my neck.

Yes, that's the one, I thought.

"You feel so damn good."

"I'm – oh, God, I'm so close!" I gasped, going even faster, but he had other plans for me. Mazen flipped me over so that I was on my back and he was on top of me, without breaking our connection, and then he started thrusting harder inside of me.

I moaned when he started panting in Arabic into my ear as his thrusts become even faster. I knew it meant he was close too and he was completely losing himself as he felt my walls starting to tighten around him.

By now, I had started to understand some of the words he was always whispering in my ears before he came – he was calling me his soul, his love and his sweetheart. It filled me with so many good emotions to know that he'd been calling me those things for so long, even when he knew I couldn't understand them.

Mazen was bracing himself on one hand while the other traveled between us and reached just above where we were connected, touching my most sensitive spot and rubbing it just the right way, driving me even faster to the edge.

"Oh, Mazen, please, please, please," I begged, not really knowing what exactly I was begging for exactly, if it was more of his hand or more of his thrusts or more of his tongue over my neck. I just wanted more.

"Yes, Princess, that's it! Let me feel you coming all over me." Mazen pressed harder on my clit, causing me to close my eyes tightly shut until I saw stars dancing behind my eyelids as a powerful orgasm shocked my whole body. Mazen followed just a moment later with a loud groan.

A few minutes passed in silence; the only noises you could hear were our pants as we tried to catch our breaths that had been lost because of the mind-blowing sex.

"I've missed you so much!" Mazen said into my hair as I rested my head on his chest, then I felt him place a soft kiss on it.

"I missed you, too. More than so much." I smiled, then pressed my lips on his bare chest and kissed just above his heart.

"Don't go away for so long again."

"Hey! You were the one who wasn't here when I came back," I pouted, though I knew he couldn't see it. I'd spent four days in the States, going through so many new projects and a few new clients with some issues that required my personal attention.

When I'd come back, Mazen had already left for a conference in Turkey, and he had just returned after three days. It had been the longest time we'd spent away from each other since the day we got married.

"If you'd just come home one day earlier," Mazen sighed.

"I know." It was my turn to sigh. "I really miss spending time with you."

"Me too," he said. "It's been too long."

It really had been too long – for months all we'd both done was work and perform our duties as king and a queen of this kingdom. I'd traveled to the States every three weeks, and Mazen was always away for something or another.

It was becoming even busier since the new branch in the kingdom had started operating, with me managing it. We only met at night and we were mostly too exhausted to stay up for too long.

One day we'd decided to go to the beach mansion for a couple of days, but then some things came up and we couldn't go. Now with winter and all, I didn't think we could do it until next summer.

"I'm going to Italy next month – how about you come with me? We can spend some time there together, just the two of us." He smoothed my hair down my back.

"I don't know, it'll probably be the same as here. You'll be away most of the day, and we'll only have the nighttime."

"Yes, probably."

I sighed, "I don't want something fancy. I just want to spend a day with you – talking, laughing, just enjoying each other's company." Mazen had managed to take me to some places here, but all of the security and all of the attention we were getting took away from the intimacy of the experience, so I'd rather we stayed home. "Do you remember that day we spent talking for hours then watched the sunset, then I made us pancakes for dinner?"

"Are you serious? It was one of the best days of my life."

"Mine too." I looked up at him and saw the smile on his lips that matched my own. "I want a repeat of that."

"That's all?"

"That's all."

"We can do that," he said and I got so excited.

"Really?"

"Of course! Anything for you, Princess."

"Okay, but later at night you have to promise to go all the way and not leave me hanging. That's one part that I don't want a repeat of," I teased.

Mazen chuckled. "Never again, Marie. You're my wife now, my other half. I love you."

"I love you, too, angel."

Kisses were placed all over my neck and collarbone, so soft and tender. It was the second best thing to wake up to. The best thing ever was waking up to his handsome face every morning. Just one look at him and I would know that my day would stay bright no matter what, because all I needed was him.

"Princess?" Mazen whispered near my ear, trying to wake me up.

"Hmm?" My eyes stayed close, too comfortable to open them.

"I have to leave for a few minutes," he said and I was wide awake.

"What?" I sat up on the bed, looking at him as he sat beside me, with his legs hanging over the side of the bed. "But you said we'd have the whole day to ourselves," I whined.

"I know, I'm sorry. I won't take long. I just need to check on my father. Fahd just texted me that he didn't have a very good night last night, and I need to see him."

"Oh."

"I'll be here before you finish your shower, I promise." He caressed my cheek.

"Will you be here for breakfast?"

"Wouldn't miss it for the world, Princess." He smiled, causing a smile to appear on my lips.

"You'd better." I kissed his lips back when he leaned in to kiss me goodbye – or see you later.

With a sigh, I watched him leave and close the door behind him. I stretched in bed and yawned, hearing a knock on the door just a minute after Mazen had left.

"*Come in*," I called in Arabic. Mazen had told me it would be best if I used the language more so I didn't forget what I'd learned and to help me improve my accent. I had learned a lot in the past few months and could almost have a full conversation in Arabic with his grandmother without needing a translator. She was even sweeter when I understood what she was saying directly.

"Good morning, your majesty," Donia smiled, taking my robe off the hanger and handing it to me. I guess she could tell I was naked under the sheets I was holding to my chest since she didn't wait for me to get up then drop the robe over my shoulders like she usually did.

"Morning, Donia."

"Your bath will be ready in a minute," she said, and when I nodded she went to the bathroom to prepare things for me. I got up and put the robe on, checking on my phone quickly to see if I had anything urgent I needed to reply to. I'd promised Mazen I'd turn my phone off for the day and he'd promised to do the same. We didn't need any interruptions – not today. It was only ours, and we were determined to keep it that way.

"All ready, your majesty," Donia said once she came out of the bathroom. "It's a lovely day, would you like to have breakfast in the sunroom?" she suggested.

"Yeah, that would be perfect," I told her with a smile. "The king will be here for breakfast, so make sure it's breakfast for two."

"Of course, your majesty. Anything else?"

"No, thank you, I'll call you if I needed something else." I'd already discussed with her last night what to tell the palace managers, and had given Brad the day off, so it was all good.

After I finished my shower and blow dried my hair, I went to the walk-in closet, only to find Mazen in there as he was going through one of his shelves, wearing only his boxers.

"You're back," I smiled.

"I promised I would." He smirked.

"How's your father?" I asked. Since he'd come back from Germany after over a month and a half there, he was doing even worse than he had been before. His heart was no longer the problem; his new one was working just fine. But unfortunately the amount of antibiotics that had been given to him after the surgery had caused his kidneys to fail. It had been awful since then. I was really sad for him – life wasn't treating him well.

"He's seen better days," was all that Mazen said, and I didn't push for a longer answer. I knew it was upsetting to him and he didn't like to talk about it.

"He's always in my prayers."

"You're so sweet, my princess. I really appreciate it." He smiled and went on looking at the shelves.

"What are you searching for?"

"Something comfortable to wear."

I walked to stand next him and ran my eyes

through his shirts, picking out an olive-colored t-shirt and black sweatpants. I liked how his eyes looked when he wore that color; it made the green in them even more piercing.

"Here."

"Thanks," he said as he took them from my hands and started putting them on.

My answer was a smile before I went to my own shelves and picked myself a blue tank top that had a question mark in yellow drawn on the middle of it and aqua-colored sweatpants. I was excited that I was finally going to relax for the day and wouldn't have to be in my high heels all day long.

When I turned around Mazen was still standing there. "Do you still need something?"

"No," he said, folding his arms in front of his chest and leaning against the wall.

"Um … I'm just going to put these on. Why don't you go ahead and wait for me in the sunroom?"

"I'd rather stay here for a bit," he smirked. I couldn't help my smile that was obvious even while I bit on both of my lips not to show it.

I narrowed my eyes. "Is that so?" He nodded. "Okay, then." Slowly, I took off my bathrobe, letting it fall to the floor with a light thud, my eyes watching him as his raked all over my body and the smirk disappeared from his lips that parted slightly once my robe hit the floor.

I chose a black thong and bra, then started putting

the thong on. I could swear I heard him gasping as he watched me very carefully.

When I was about to put my bra on, I heard him clearing his throat. “What?” I asked, standing still as I waited for him to answer.

“Are you sure you want to wear that?” He raised his eyebrows.

My bashful smile returned and I bit on my bottom lip. I shook my head no and put it back in its place, meeting his smile as he continued to watch me as I put on my clothes. He then walked over and pressed his lips to mine, taking my hand in his as we made our way to the sunroom.

Winter in the kingdom was so nice, far better than in New York, and I was really grateful for that fact since I didn’t like so much heat. The sun was warm and we ate our breakfast peacefully while having small talk about whatever.

Hours passed and the day was going just as I’d hoped for it to be – maybe even better than I’d thought it would be. The few times we got interrupted were when Donia was bringing food or taking back empty plates after we’d eaten.

We talked a lot, about work, about our families. Mazen told me some stories from his childhood, and I told him whatever I could remember from my own.

We made out and touched, not getting dirty but rather saying with our mouths and hands how much we couldn’t stay away from each other and how much we wanted to stay close.

Everything was going so wonderfully. Just half an hour before sunset, Mazen asked if I wanted to go to the roof of the palace to watch it like I'd told him I'd wanted to do.

I draped one of the cloaks that I had in my closet over my clothes because I assumed it would be cold outside – and to be honest, I didn't want the guards up there to see their queen in her pajamas. It'd be weird.

Strangely, there weren't any guards around. Only at the far ends of the roof, I could see a few with their backs turned to us. They seemed unaware of our presence, which was seriously odd. I didn't think much of it, figuring maybe they'd known we were coming through communicating with the other guards or something and had cleared the area for us.

The sight was beautiful, just like I knew it would be. It felt much better than last time. I was so much in love and I was having a wonderful day – things couldn't get much better.

"You're not watching the sunset," I told Mazen as he placed a soft kiss on my neck while he hugged me from behind.

He inhaled deeply into my hair and whispered, "I'd rather watch you."

"Now you're distracting me, as well." My voice dropped low, and my eyelids grew heavy as his warm breaths fanned over my skin.

"I'm aware."

"Mazen," his name came out of my mouth in a sigh as I dropped my head back onto his broad chest, enjoying the feel of his warmth surrounding me.

"My beautiful princess," he breathed. The next thing I knew, both of us were startled by some noises behind us.

At first, I thought it was one of the guards, but when a moment too long passed and we heard nothing, Mazen had to call, *"Who's there?"* His question was in Arabic, and it was directed to whoever was behind the big water tank from where we'd heard the sound coming.

My heart started thumping hard as another moment passed with no movement. Mazen let go of me and took a few steps forward, presumably to check what had caused the sound.

I grabbed his hand and with wide eyes I shook my head, telling him silently not to go. I pointed with my other hand to the guards behind us and then held his wrist to pull him back again, because I thought it'd be best if we called them to check for us.

Before Mazen could reply, a woman fully dressed in black came out from behind the water tank, her steps steady and sure. I wondered if she was one of the female guards, but the jewelry on her hands and the lack of a green badge on her arm told me that she was probably one of the princesses who'd been visiting Mazen's father regularly. One look at the bottom of her peach-colored dress that was peeking from under her black clothes and I knew exactly which princess she was.

"It's me, your majesty," she replied with the softest of voices, "Talia."

"Talia!" Her name came out of his lips in a gasp, and it was like someone had put their hands on my throat and started pressing on it, choking me.

Now, I could handle hearing my husband talk to other women. It wasn't something that bothered me – it would be crazy to be annoyed by it. However, the way he said her name sent a sharp pain down my stomach, and the fact that he hadn't used her title before her name made the sting even more painful.

Mazen had never spoken about Rosanna without saying Princess before her name – not even once. It was the same for Huda and for any other princesses that came up, so why was she different?

I tried to convince myself that it was because he had just heard her say her name and was echoing it, nothing more. He hadn't meant anything by it, or so I wanted to believe.

"What are you doing here?" he asked her. His voice wasn't as shocked as before, but it was gentle, and the fact that he wasn't averting his eyes from hers was driving me crazy.

"Uh ... I just wanted to be here for a few minutes. I hope you don't mind, your majesty." There was a look in her eyes that I couldn't tell what it meant, but I knew what it felt like – it was choking me even more. It was

like there was a conversation going back and forth between them that I couldn't read, and I was almost ready to scream my head off out of frustration just to cut it off.

"And what were you doing behind the water tank, exactly?" I decided to interrupt. I could've spoken in the language they were speaking, but I didn't want her to make fun of my accent, even in her mind. I wasn't that good. Yet.

Her eyes were on me as I asked her the question, but then they went to Mazen's as she replied, "Memories. Pleasurable memories connect me with this place. I wanted to refresh them, is all."

I swallowed thickly, feeling Mazen's hand as it tightened on mine. My other hand that was on his wrist sensed how his heartbeat sped up at the sound of her words. It was all of the confirmation I needed for the doubts that were running through my mind.

Memories.

Eighteen

My throat was closing up and I felt a little dizzy. The whole place was spinning around me, and I didn't know if I wanted to just run away and escape this girl's company – maybe curl up into a ball and cry my eyes out – or take a few steps in her direction and rip her throat out.

Everything in me wanted to do the latter.

Eventually, and after inhaling a long breath, I decided to do neither. What I decided, though, was to defend what belonged to me. "Great!" I managed the best smile I could offer, knowing very well that it looked more like a sneer than anything else. "Next time, though – you'll need to get permission from *me* before doing that. I don't like *people* roaming around *my* house without my knowledge."

Mazen's gaze dropped to the floor. I didn't know if

he'd finally remembered his manners or if it was because of what I'd said. Either way, I dared him to say anything about what I'd just told her, because if he did, things wouldn't be pretty.

Finally, it looked like I'd said something to make that stupid girl shut up for once, because her eyes were frozen on mine. Fire was dancing behind the green as she stared. A moment passed and I still didn't hear her reply, so I decided to push it.

"Am I understood, Princess Talia?" I raised an eyebrow.

Her eyes went back to Mazen as if she were waiting for him to say something, and when she realized that wasn't going to happen, she spoke, "Of course, your majesty." Her voice was low, not holding the same confidence it had just two minutes before.

"Good. It was *nice* to see you. You're dismissed."

Those green eyes of her widened at my words, then looked at Mazen once more. This time there was more of a desperation for him to say something, but that didn't go as she'd hoped – Mazen stayed silent.

"Your majesties." She nodded her head and then went on her way, and out of our sights.

I let go of a long breath and released Mazen's hand from mine. My hand came to my forehead as I rubbed it firmly, willing the spinning sensation to stop. Once I felt more collected, I left him standing there and went to the secret door we'd come from earlier.

"Hey, where are you going? The sun is about to

set."

"Look who finally remembered how to speak English!" I turned for a second to look at him, threw my hands in the air in frustration, then went through the secret door, making my way to our wing and to the bedroom.

When I took off my cloak, I stood in the middle of the room, not quite sure of what to do with myself. I was angry, and it was mostly because of what I had seen and the thoughts running through my head, and I didn't like that the conclusions I was coming to.

"Are you mad at me or something?" Mazen asked from behind me.

"No, I'm thrilled with you, can't you tell?" I faced him with a mocking expression, then quickly replaced it with a furious stare.

Mazen sighed, "I'm sorry I didn't ask her what she was doing there in English, but it's not like you couldn't understand it, Marie. You knew what I was saying."

He was right, I knew what they were saying. I knew lots of Arabic words and I could manage to make light conversation. But he knew that there were even more words that I still couldn't understand, even though the professor who came every two days to teach me was only teaching me how to speak it and understand it, at my request. I hadn't started learning how to write it or read it, yet.

When I didn't reply, Mazen stepped closer to me.

"Please, don't be mad," he said in a low voice. "If I knew it would upset you, I wouldn't have done it. You know that."

It wasn't like the whole Arabic thing was what was making me mad – it was more, but I didn't know how to bring it up. There were things I needed to know, but I didn't know how to start this conversation.

There was a pause before I nodded, then I turned around and faced him. "There's something I need to know."

Mazen swallowed and he looked hesitant, as if he knew what I was going to say, and that only managed to feed the fire that was already smoldering inside me.

"Talia was the one you were supposed to marry, correct?" I asked, already knowing the answer, but still dreading it.

I watched as he pursed his lips before he nodded slowly, and I felt my blood start to boil, as if I hadn't already expected that answer.

"Okay. What I know is that the engagement was never official. You were only promised to each other by the 'unspoken rule' or whatever," I said, the words tasting bitter in my mouth. "My question now is – how often did you speak about it? The both of you. Together."

The community in the kingdom was very tight knit. Women were overly protected – even from a male's gazes, not just their hands or actions. I could only assume that since they were only allowed to see their sisters and mother and so he hadn't even seen Talia's face as a grown-up – unless it had happened "accidentally", like that time he'd entered the room in his father's quarters while she was there, not all covered up.

That meant that if they'd actually talked together, it would've been in private, away from people's gazes, because meetings between a man and a woman were simply *not* allowed. The thought made my blood boil even more.

"A few times." He couldn't meet my eyes as he replied with his three-word answer.

"You met her in private?" I choked out my question.

Mazen didn't lie. In fact, he was a terrible liar. When he attempted to fib about an insignificant thing, like if he said he wanted the lights on because he knew I wanted them on when he actually wanted to turn them off; or if he wanted to stay up to chat, when he really needed was to put his head on a pillow and fall asleep

But when the lie was meant to save lives, or prevent a huge problem from happening – he did it very well. You could easily believe him and never doubt him for a second. And that was what I feared the most.

"Yes."

I inhaled a sharp breath. The fact that he wasn't looking into my eyes made everything feel even more awful than it actually was. "Just talking?" I could feel the tightening in my throat returning; it was a miracle that I was still standing on my feet and breathing.

"Don't lie to me." My voice was shaking, and though I wanted to know the truth, I actually wished he'd lie to me, so I would have some peace of mind if the true answer came out to be a 'No.'

"Why are you asking that, Marie? It's not important." He tried to avoid answering my question.

"It's important to me," I said. "Please answer."

"You're not supposed to talk about your sins." This wasn't actually a straight answer, but it was clear enough to answer my question.

"So, there *were* sins," I stated, tears prickling in my eyes. "With her."

"I, uh, I repented," he tried, but the words had no effect on me whatsoever – they didn't take the pain away.

"How far did you go with her?" I knew that Mazen was a virgin before me, but all of the thoughts I'd had about how a good kisser he was, how his hands and tongue belonged to an expert, and how he knew how to open the zippers in my dresses – which I didn't even know were there – came rushing back. The image of them together, kissing and touching, was painful enough to knock the breath out of my lungs. I was so close to fainting.

"Princess, why would you want to know that? It happened in the past, and it's all over with now. It was all over the minute I knew I was to marry you. There's no need to talk about it."

"C'mon, Mazen." I folded my arms in front of my chest, trying to look as casual as possible, though it was actually to protect myself from what was to come – a knowledge that would only hurt me, yet I couldn't stop myself from wanting to know. I just had to know. I had no doubt that the tears rolling down my cheeks were giving away how I was truly feeling about that, though. "We've never actually had the talk about our pasts. You've never asked how many guys I kissed before you."

Mazen's eyes burned into mine and his lips turned up in an angry sneer. "I don't need to know that." His voice was strong, and his tone was warning. His fists clenched tightly on both of his sides.

"Really? You've never wondered about it?"

"I was your first, just like you were mine. That's all I need to know, and I suggest ending this conversation right now."

"Why? Because you don't want me to know about your past?"

"It *is* my past, not my present. My present is *you.* Only you, Marie, and *us* is the only important thing."

"Fair enough. But I want to know – where did the two of you used to meet up?"

"Why are you even asking that?"

"No reason." I shrugged one shoulder, thinking of how many places I would have to burn down.

"Some places around the palace, here and there." He rubbed the back of his neck and huffed, going back to not meeting my gaze.

"Was the roof one of them?"

"Yes."

My boiling blood turned ice cold in my veins, and my breath caught in my throat. My eyes searched his for a few long moments, disbelieving and shocked.

"How could you take me there?" My voice was disgusted and I felt the undeniable need to break something. "Did you want to relive old memories?"

"What are you talking about?" Mazen defended. "Of course not! It's a nice place to watch the sunset, nothing more."

"Yes, of course. A nice place with 'pleasurable memories'." I made air quotes, my tears rolling down my face uncontrolled.

"What? Marie, the first time I took you there we weren't allowed out of the wing. It was the only place I could think of other than the stable, which we had already gone to. And today you were the one to ask for it."

"Because it held a good memory for me. I didn't know it was tainted by traces of you with her all over it! How could you do this to me?"

"Are you listening to yourself right now? You're so mad at me for something I did long ago. It wasn't actually as if I were cheating on you. It was all before you, Marie. You're not being fair."

I knew in my heart that he was right, that I was being crazy. But I hated that he'd given that girl a piece of himself. I hated that she got his firsts – his first kiss and his first touches. And those thoughts were driving me mad, driving me insane. Only because it was her. Though I didn't know if I would have the same reaction if it were another girl. *Wait...*

"It was only her, right?" Please, say yes.

"Yes, Marie. Only her."

"Don't say 'only her'," I said through clenched teeth.

"You asked!"

"Still."

"She is my *past*, you are my present. I keep telling you this, but you don't seem to get it!"

"So, I'm stupid now, huh?"

Mazen huffed, shook his head and then spoke in a quieter voice, "It seems that whatever I say will only manage to get you more upset with me. This is why I suggested ending the conversation before, but you didn't want to, and look at what's happened now – you were mad before and now you're mad *and* hurt. I understand your feelings, but I don't think you're being fair, judging me for something I did before you, and for another thing I did with no hidden intention other than to make you happy.

"So, I'm sorry to say that I'm not going to answer any more questions, because anything I say – you'll manage to find a way to make it sound like something I didn't mean for it to be. I'm sorry this conversation happened, and I'm not going to collaborate in continuing it."

Again, he was right, but I couldn't seem to get a hold on my feelings. The fact that this girl kept hinting that they were still going to be something more was making me that crazy. It sounded like she still wasn't over him. It even seemed like she believed they would get together again somehow. And that was why I was so mad about the whole thing.

At first, I'd thought she was only bitter about the fact that she was going to marry him and then she didn't – I couldn't blame her. Mazen was all kinds of the perfect husband – loyal, honest and incredibly sweet and kind. That, and he was the most handsome guy I'd ever seen in my life; of course she couldn't get over him.

However, I'd thought it was all in her head, that there was nothing Mazen had done to make her want him more or feel more for him. I'd thought it was only an unofficial arrangement that had been broken with our marriage. But to find out there had been more? That they had broken rules for one another? That they were once close enough that they'd actually met up, kissed and touched? It was more than I could bear.

Talia wasn't someone I'd thought I should worry about before, but now – I did. I worried a lot. The look in her eyes, her threats and the way she'd spoken about Mazen being her fiancé even after we were married – it was enough to make me realize that she was more than just a bitter girl who'd been dumped for nothing she'd actually done, but rather because of what fate had put on all of us.

With that in mind, I was determined that I wouldn't let her speak that way about my husband again, and that if she showed any other interest in him or spoke that way to me again, I would stop her in her tracks.

I was her queen, and she was only a princess. Respect and obedience were needed on her part.

I was his wife, and she was merely his ex – or whatever thing she could be labeled as. It could never be something close to being his life partner like I was.

Mazen was right. She was his past, and I was his present, and I was willing to remind myself of that often. Because when it came to love, the past is only old memories and the present is when we make new ones.

That night, it was the first night we'd ever gone to bed while we were actually mad at each other. It didn't mean that I loved him any less, and I was sure it was the same for him. But I thought that maybe sleeping on it would help us get over it, and tomorrow I would have a clearer mind to react the right way regarding everything I'd learned today.

Our backs faced each other as we went to sleep, but when we woke up, I was nestled comfortably with my head on his chest and our arms around each other. I knew then that the worst had passed, and that the Talia thing wouldn't affect our relationship whatsoever.

I was wrong.

Nineteen

The need to stay a bit longer in his arms compelled me to stay still with my eyes closed even after I had awoken. Sadly, just a minute later, I felt Mazen as he carefully slipped away from me and got out of bed.

Now that I was much calmer than yesterday, I realized that I had truly been unfair to him by going all crazy jealous just because I knew he had a history with that thing called Talia. But that didn't mean he had the right to be mad at *me*. I wasn't yet over the fact that he'd taken me to that place the first time. Even if I believed him when he said that it wasn't the reason why we'd gone there. I just couldn't help my feelings, that was all.

I listened as he took his shower, and when he came out and went straight to the closet, I went straight into the bathroom, hating that I couldn't say 'Good morning' to him. I wanted to hug him and never let go, yet I couldn't even say a word to him. Was that even sane?

Things were awkward between us, and I wanted to save myself from the hurt I'd feel if he gave me the silent treatment. And to be honest, I didn't know if I wanted to talk to him just yet, anyway.

When I came out of the bathroom, I was startled when I saw him standing fully dressed by the window that was near my side of the bed. He was looking out of it, seemingly lost in thoughts that were interrupted by the sound of the bathroom door closing behind me.

"Hey!" Mazen greeted with a small smile when he turned in my direction.

"Hey, good morning," I offered him a tight smile, meeting him halfway as he took the few steps that separated us to stand right in front of me. His eyes searched mine for a moment before he bent down and kissed me lightly on my lips.

"Can we talk for a minute?" he asked, and I hesitated. I wasn't expecting him to talk to me so soon, and I wasn't sure whether I was prepared for a serious conversation this early. I wanted to ask him to wait until I got dressed, but I knew he was already running late by waiting for me to get out of the shower. He always woke up before me and left while I was still in bed, after placing kisses all over my face to wake me up before leaving.

My lips were pursed when I nodded my head, and

Mazen pointed with an open palm towards the couch. I sat down, tightening my bathrobe over my body, and waited for him to speak.

"I'm sorry about the way I ended our conversation last night, but it was the only way I could think of so you wouldn't get more upset with me," he started. "I can tell you anything you want to know, but you have to promise to stay calm, because if you're going to be as livid as you were yesterday, then we'll only get into another argument. You know what I mean, Marie?"

I looked down at my lap, paused for a second, then nodded.

"I swear to God that it wasn't my intention to take you there because it was where I used to meet her. It hadn't even crossed my mind."

After I inhaled a long breath then let it go, I nodded. "I believe you," I said, "But it hurts."

Mazen sat closer to me and took my hand in his. "Do you know when you eat something bitter and the taste is awful in your mouth, so you eat something sweet to get rid of the bitterness on your tongue?"

I frowned at his question, but nodded anyway.

"Maybe that was what I was doing, unconsciously," he said. "Maybe my mind was just trying to erase the old taste and get a better taste instead, one that would last forever and wipe the traces of the first one out of my memory. Maybe I wanted to claim this place as ours. New memories. Better ones. Sweeter."

I looked up at him and tried to understand what he was saying. My heart wanted to believe him, but my jealousy was burning me up from the inside. I couldn't deny that his words had eased the hurt I was feeling, though. A lot.

"It's only you in my heart, only you in my mind, Marie. Constantly," he promised.

"The image of you being with her is just–" I couldn't finish my thought. It was too difficult.

"Don't. Don't think of it, Marie. It's gone," he started. "That thing with her is what I regret the most—I regret ever doing it. I always felt guilty about it, but I convinced myself that since she was to be my wife, to just keep doing the wrong thing, to keep sinning. I knew deep down that marrying her one day still wouldn't make it right, but I did it anyway.

"When I learned about Janna's pregnancy, I knew it was karma. Someone did with my sister what I'd almost done with another. Do you know where they first met?"

I nodded, Joseph had told me before.

"I felt as if Janna were paying for my mistakes. And it made me hate what I'd done even more," he said. "When I think about them now, Marie, it's never pleasurable memories. It's guilt and shame I feel for myself."

My tongue darted out to wet my lips before I chewed on my bottom one for a second. "Did you … were you in love with her?" I asked after a pause, my heart sinking just thinking about it.

Mazen looked down, and I felt a tightening in my throat. It was the same question I'd asked him the morning that followed our first wedding ceremony. He didn't reply to me then, and I knew that if he didn't reply to me now – I'd get the answer just by him refusing to say it.

"For a long time, I thought I was," he said, and I thought that my heart stopped beating for a second. "I'd known she was to be my wife since I was a little boy. You could say I got used to the idea of her, and I cared for her. To a point." My nostrils flared and my eyes started to sting with unshed tears.

"But then, there was you." His eyes looked deep into my own. "And I finally understood the connection that God mentioned in his book. What I felt for you the moment I saw you was beyond what I'd felt for her in all the years I had known her. And then when I fell in love with you – I knew that you were my first love, my only love, my true love."

I swallowed thickly.

"Only you, Marie. There's only you in my heart. I never knew what love was like until my heart would flutter at the mention of your name and just the thought of you. I've only ever been in love with you, and there's nothing that could change that. Please, believe me."

His eyes were pleading with me to believe him, begging for me to understand. And I did.

I let go of his hand that was holding mine and I could see the panic in his eyes, thinking that I was going to get up and leave him. But I assured him right the next second that it wasn't the case, as I surrounded his neck with my arms and hugged him tightly. "I love you, too, angel," I told him. "It has only ever been you."

His arms wrapped around my body, and he inhaled deeply into my hair, saying nothing. But he didn't need to say anything more – I knew what he was feeling. It was relief.

"I'm sorry for what I said last night." And I meant it.

A groan left my mouth once I turned on my phone and heard the constant beeping of incoming messages and e-mails. The woman who was doing my hair froze in her place, apparently thinking she'd done something wrong. I looked at her through the mirror, wiping away the look of horror on her face with a smile of my own and a nod for her to go on.

This is going to take a while, I thought when I realized I had more than forty emails and text messages needing a reply.

I started typing furiously on the screen of my phone while my hairstylist continued doing my hair and another put shoes on my feet that I didn't even have time to glance at. *Whatever,* was all I could think – I knew it would be a long day.

"Your majesty," Brad greeted with a nod of his head as I walked out of the wing.

"Good morning," I said with a smile, glancing around and seeing my four royal guards standing ready and waiting for me to get into the elevator.

Once inside, I was followed by Brad and one royal guard as well as my private secretary, who I could see wanted to start talking from the moment she saw me leaving the wing, but I'd silenced her with a wave of my hand. I was still trying to reply to e-mails.

When I got out of the elevator, my other three guards were already waiting for me there, and all of them together escorted me to my office on the first floor of the palace, from where I conducted most of my daily duties.

After the coronation ceremony, we had been offered Mazen's parents' quarters – because it made things easier, they said. But I didn't want to switch our wing for another. I liked it there, and it wasn't like the offices and the great meeting rooms were a mile away; they were just downstairs from where our wing was. Nothing too complicated.

"Darn it!" I groaned again once I was seated on my chair behind the desk. The e-mail I'd just opened was from Kareem – my assistant for the kingdom branch. It was about some legal issues regarding one of the shipments we'd ordered from France. I really didn't need to deal with this above all. Not after a day off and a million things to do.

This was one e-mail I couldn't reply to; I had to go to the branch office and have a face to face meeting about it. So I asked one of my private secretaries to call Kareem and arrange a meeting at the company later today.

Almost two hours later, when I had finished replying to all of the e-mails and messages, I finally got the time to look up at all of the faces waiting for me to give them my attention.

"Okay." I took a deep breath and let it go. "Manar, you go first."

Manar was one of my private secretaries. She was originally from Lebanon and though she was always wearing a headscarf, she never covered her face. It was a refreshing thing, to be honest. Almost all of the women I worked with had their faces covered, and I mostly recognized them by their voices.

"Whom do I have to meet with today?" I asked.

"Only the Prime Minister, Prince Fahd, at six o'clock, your majesty," she answered.

"One meeting?" I asked in shock. I usually had three official meetings, at the very least. It was tiring and stressful sometimes, but I'd gotten used to it.

"Yes, your majesty."

"I knew I liked you for a reason," I smiled, then I turned my attention to another private secretary and then another, going through what needed to be done for the day.

A few hours later, one of the guards entered the office before speaking, "Your Highness, Princess Rosanna is outside, requesting for a few minutes of your time."

"Oh please, send her in."

This was one of the few times I'd seen her with her black clothes and face cover. We mostly met up in the privacy of our wings, or during all-female gatherings.

"*Marhaba*," she greeted; the smile could be heard in her voice.

"*Marhaba* to you!" I said. "What a pleasant surprise."

"*What did we say about the language*?" she scolded playfully in Arabic. She sided with Mazen on how I should speak Arabic more often. She tried her best to keep a decent part of our conversations in Arabic just for me to get better at it.

"How about, *'You're such a pain'*?"

"Not so bad," she giggled, and I pointed for her to sit down on one of the chairs located in front of my desk.

"Have a seat," I said. "To what do I owe the pleasure?"

"It's been weeks since we last ate together, and it's time for lunch." Her voice was smiling.

"Sure thing. There's just one thing I need to go through, and then I'm yours. Erm, for half an hour."

She rolled her chocolate-brown eyes at me and

nodded; she knew my time was ridiculously limited and she understood that. Our friendship had grown stronger as the days had passed. She was one of the sweetest people I'd ever met, and almost every time we met she taught me a thing or two about the culture and being a queen.

Rosanna never hesitated to give me advice whenever I asked for it. I was already meeting three times a week with a lady who taught me much of what I didn't know about the royal protocol and such, but things were much simpler and easier to understand when they were explained by my sister-in-law.

I dismissed the men in the room so that Rosanna would be able to take off her face cover and feel more comfortable until I was finished with the last one of the palace managers for the day.

She was showing me new designs for the female royal guards' uniforms. Before, I'd thought they were just black clothes, just like any other cloak that women wore around here, but it was more than that.

The designs were different, easier to walk in, with more arm mobility than regular cloaks. I went through them all as the designer explained the differences between each of them, and I chose the one that looked more comfortable than the others.

While I talked to the designer for a bit, I noticed that Rosanna had taken the file and was looking through it with pursed lips. I didn't give it much attention until we were out in the gardens, heading for a gazebo to have lunch there. That was when Rosanna brought it up.

"If you don't mind, your majesty, I have a small comment about the design you chose," she started, and I knew she meant business when she didn't use my name.

"Of course, what is it?"

"The design is the most comfortable with regards to the mobility of the guards wearing it, but the face cover that comes with it is not the best choice."

"How's that?"

"It needs to be tied from behind, and face covers like that sometimes press on the nose and makes breathing a bit more difficult," she explained. "The face cover that comes with design number four is better. It's attached from the top of the head mostly, and would make breathing much easier. Therefore, it won't be a bother for them, and they need to be comfortable in their clothes so as not to be distracted by them."

"Oh."

"If I may, I suggest that you tell the designer to put that face cover with your design, instead. But it's your choice if you wish to keep it the original way. And forgive me if I'm overstepping." She offered me a small smile that I could see in her eyes rather than on her lips.

It didn't escape my notice that despite our friendship, she still respected my position and was so proper in every situation. She was so polite and hadn't wanted to embarrass me by pointing it out earlier when the designer was there in the office. Rosanna was just that noble.

It was just another day where it was proven that there was a lot left to learn about … everything.

My time spent at company headquarters that afternoon taught me more than I ever wanted to know about mundane trade regulations. For some baffling reason, the French government had not only rendered it illegal to import things from certain regions. Its position was counter to every other state in the European Union. Not only had our shipment been delayed for two days, caught up in some customs warehouse they'd shipped it to. It had issued us an official warning and was threatening to hold our inventory until we paid a rather large fine.

I couldn't say that it was anyone's fault, but I really should've known that something like that could happen. My excuse to myself was that everything was a bit too much and of course something like that would come up.

Eventually, we were able to find a solution to avoid the legal issue. But I didn't go back to the palace right away, I had to stay at the company a bit longer to look at a new project that Kareem needed me to approve first before they could proceed.

"Wait, wait … you're telling me that the kingdom has been importing incense burners since forever?" I asked Kareem in shock.

"Yes, your majesty. It's a very successful business."

"No kidding!" I reviewed the papers in my hands, looked closely at the numbers and all of the details of the process. It really looked like a very successful business, but I already knew it would be just by the mention of the name of the commodity.

I kept shaking my head at what I was reading. I couldn't believe that this was actually happening. Why hadn't anybody thought of this before?

An hour later, I had gotten all of the facts straight and an idea was planted in my mind which I had no intention of letting go.

My meeting with Prince Fahd took longer than expected, because after we went through the discussions that were planned for this meeting, I had to talk to him about the idea to import incense burners. The results of my conversation with him were satisfying, but I still had some things to do before I went back to my wing.

It was close to eleven when I was greeted by Donia, who informed me that King Mazen was already inside and waiting for me in the living room.

I groaned as I took off my shoes, it was such a long day. I went straight to where I knew Mazen was. A smile touched my lips when I found him lying on the couch with one leg stretched out in front of him, and the other dangling off of it as he watched one of the news channels.

When I took a closer look at him, he was sleeping peacefully and I felt so much guilt for keeping him waiting like that – and even more guilt when I realized I had to wake him up.

I knelt in front of him, and then moved my hand through his brown locks, waking him up with a soft touch and then a soft kiss on that cheekbone of his that I could kiss forever.

"Hey, angel," I whispered with a smile when I saw his sleepy green eyes opening slowly and gazing at me.

"Hey." His hand reached for mine over his jaw and he turned his head slightly to kiss my palm, making my heart melt with his sweetness. "Long day, huh?"

"Yeah, I'm sorry for keeping you waiting."

"It's fine. Were you able to solve the problem at the company?" he asked as he sat up, helping me off the floor.

I didn't ask who'd told him, because I knew he often had his assistant ask mine about my whereabouts when he knew I couldn't return his calls or texts, and I imagined they'd told him about it.

"Yeah, I have something to discuss with you, though," I said as I sat on the couch beside him.

"Sure, about what?"

"It's about a commodity that the kingdom has been

importing from Japan, and–" I was interrupted by the sound of Mazen's groan. "What?"

"Work, Princess? Can't it wait until tomorrow?"

I could tell that Mazen was exhausted, maybe even more than me, but I was so excited about the whole thing and I just couldn't wait. Eventually, I realized that tomorrow wasn't that far.

"Yeah, no problem." I offered him a small smile.

"Have you had dinner?" Mazen asked with a yawn.

"Um … now that you mention it, I just remembered that I didn't."

He shook his head and shot me a disapproving look. "C'mon, let's put some food in you."

"Will you eat with me?"

"I could eat." He smiled and I leaned down and kissed his cheek.

Over dinner, we had a light conversation. It was almost impossible to hold my tongue about everything that I wanted to discuss with him. And later when we were in bed, my mind couldn't stop thinking about it, even when his lips were on my neck and his hands were fidgeting with my clothes.

He was kissing behind my ear when he abruptly stopped and sat up, reaching for the button on his nightstand and flicking the lights on.

"Okay, what is it?" Mazen asked.

"Uh, … what?"

"We both know you won't stop thinking about it until you've said what you have to say, so just say it.

I'm listening."

I sat up excitedly and I could swear he almost rolled his eyes, but I couldn't care less. I was finally going to tell him about everything I'd been working on since four PM.

"The kingdom has been importing incense burners from Japan for a long time," I said.

"Okay …?"

"Well, I believe it's a big mistake for such an important commodity in this culture to be imported. We should have our own local factories to make them here," I told him.

"I'm not sure. It's no big deal, importing is much easier."

"It is a big deal, Mazen. Those kinds of things are not important in my culture or in Europe," I told him. Heck, the first time I'd ever seen one was here, when Mona had asked me what I thought about the scent. "But here, it's something that is used every single day in every home. It's such a shame that we're not making it!"

I kept going on and on about how it would help the economy of the country even more, and how building factories here would provide more job opportunities for youths. The commodity would even be much cheaper if it was made locally.

Mazen was concerned about the materials and such, and that it would lead us to import something else. I told him that I'd already done my research, and we could make the clay and wooden ones instead of the metal – we had plenty of those materials.

"Hmm … well, I think it's a great idea," Mazen said, I couldn't help smiling from ear to ear. "But are you aware that importing goods means more money for your company?"

I looked at him for a moment. "Yes. It does. But I'm looking at the bigger picture. It might benefit my business, but this way it will benefit the kingdom and its people a lot more." I was taken aback by my own words. Was that what my therapist was telling me about? Had I started to see them as my own people instead of strangers? The thought made my heart beat faster.

Mazen's smile was soft. "When I think I can't love you more …" was all he said before placing a soft kiss on my lips.

"So, you agree? We can start working on the factories?" I asked excitedly.

"It's not so simple, Princess. You need to talk to Fahd about it first and see– …"

"I already did, but he said it's your decision. He agrees, though. We studied most of the things about it in our meeting tonight."

Mazen shook his head. "When you're after something, there's no stopping you," he said as a matter of fact.

I grinned. "Would you sign the papers?"

"Now?"

"Um … I guess it could wait until the morning."

"Oh, thank God!"

"Thank you, thank you, thank you," I said as I peppered his face with kisses. I couldn't help but feel that I'd managed a huge accomplishment in a matter of hours. Just getting Mazen's approval was something big. I was proud of myself.

The feeling was amazing, but just thinking about the power I had to make things happen, and how I could manage to make so many changes by really wanting them, then simply convincing Mazen to do it – the thrill inside me was indescribable.

In that moment, a few words that my mother-in-law had said to me months ago came rushing back into my mind and kept ringing in my ears.

"Queens rule!" she'd said to me, and it was then that the thought stuck in my mind.

I could change laws.

Twenty

There's a fine line between jealousy and doubt. I was very aware of that fact. I was so jealous of that cousin of his when I learned about their history together, but that was something I could get over. It was difficult, but I managed to control my feelings eventually so as not to lose my mind.

But when he came back home with a bright pink lipstick smudge on his blinding-white *thwab*, doubt filled my heart and mind. Doubt. I questioned my husband's faithfulness right then and there.

It was a dark February night when I heard the noise caused by the vibration of his phone as it lay on top of his nightstand. I was half awake as I felt him reach out for it, then the next moment he was getting out of bed and going into the bathroom.

I briefly wondered who would be texting him so late at night, but my drowsiness took over me and I fell asleep with the knowledge that he was in the bathroom and would come back to bed soon.

I had no idea how long I dozed off, but when I turned over in bed and reached out to touch him – I found his spot empty and cold.

My eyes were suddenly wide open and a frown of confusion rested between my eyebrows. I wondered if he was still in the bathroom, but when I took a look at the bathroom door from my spot, I found it pitch black. He couldn't be in there.

Sitting up on the bed, I looked closely at the big clock on the side wall, which read 4:26 AM. Where could he be?

Worry filled my insides, along with confusion. I couldn't imagine a place he could be at such a late hour. And the first prayer of the day wouldn't be for at least another half an hour.

The first thing I did was reach for my phone and call his. But I was only met with the sound of it vibrating next to me on Mazen's nightstand. He'd left it.

I got up and stood in the middle of the room, not knowing what to do with myself. Although it wasn't likely that he'd be in any room other than his praying corner which he didn't use that much – since he prayed anywhere – or his home office, I still searched most of the rooms for him, which took me a good twenty minutes. I knew Donia was probably asleep, so I didn't want to disturb her to ask if she knew what was going on.

It was times like this that all of my disaggregated doubts united and formed themselves into a behemoth of uneasy questions. I had absolutely no control over the thoughts that popped into my head and the feelings consuming my heart – questions about his safety and wellbeing, and questions about his whereabouts and why I didn't know of them.

He was the king, after all; maybe some urgent matter of state had drawn him out of bed, I tried to tell myself. Maybe his father's health had taken a turn for the worse. I knew deep down that I was overreacting, maybe because I'd been abruptly awakened or maybe because my lack of sleep made me vulnerable, but I couldn't help the lone tear that rolled down my cheek.

My hand was holding my cross tightly over my chest, and I imagined that worry was evident on my features when the bedroom's main door began to open.

My heart was pounding hard in my chest for the short moment it took me to make sure that Mazen had been the one to open it. And when my eyes caught his, I couldn't help my legs as they raced to get to him.

I threw myself into his arms and my tears continued to flow. I was embarrassed by how emotional I was. And for nothing. He was in my arms, safe and sound. So why was I making it such a big deal? What was with all of drama I was forcing myself to live in?

But I couldn't help it. It was like having a bad dream, a very bad one, and waking up while still feeling whatever you felt in that dream. It was like fighting with someone in your dream and waking up actually mad at them for something they hadn't actually done.

In my case, my dreams were my thoughts. I was worried about him because of the pictures my head drew of ugly scenarios of him not being safe.

"Hey, what's going on? Why are you crying? What happened?" Mazen asked, tightening his arms around me, then kissing my hair.

I chuckled through my tears, "It's really stupid. Nothing." And it really was. Stupid, and nothing. Having him close brought my senses back to me, because, of course it could have been any number of things. Yes, maybe his father. Or maybe Thunder had gotten out of control and they needed him there to tame him – it had happened before.

Mazen smoothed my hair, and I wiped my tears, my vision clearing when no new ones appeared out of my eyes. I smiled into his chest, touching my cheek to my favorite spot above his heart. And that was when I saw it.

There, right above his chest pocket, was a bright pink smudge. A color I knew I'd never really used. And I was sure that neither his father nor Thunder ever wore it, as well.

I swallowed thickly, taking a step back and untangling our arms, a look of shock and disbelief dominating my features. My eyes finally looked up at him after staring for far too long at that smudge that though small, still had a huge impact on my heart.

It was his turn to have a frown of confusion on his face. "Are you sure you're okay?"

I wanted to believe it was his mother's, but I knew she only lined her eyes and that was about it for her usage of make-up. And other than his mother and grandmother, there was no other woman besides me in the whole palace that his religion allowed him to touch.

So – I knew right then that Mazen hadn't been faithful to me.

"You cheated on me?" I choked out my question.

"What?"

My thoughts were frantic again; it all made sense now. His sudden leaving and me not knowing of it. It all made sense. "Oh, my God! You're cheating on me!" I stated. My hand flew to cover my mouth as my voice cracked on my last words.

"Marie! What the hell are you talking about?" He sounded a bit angry, which I wanted to laugh at. How dare he be angry?

The room was spinning and I felt dizzy – two very familiar feelings that seemed to enjoy my company a bit too often lately. I couldn't believe Mazen would do that to me. He was too noble to do something like that. But here it was, staring me right in the eyes: the evidence of his unfaithfulness.

"This is what I'm talking about!" I pointed to his

chest, too shocked for my tears to actually fall out of my eyes now, though it was what I wanted to do the most, to just curl into a ball and cry my eyes out.

Mazen looked down to where I was pointing, and his frown deepened as he held his clothes up to take a closer look at the awful thing on his chest. I watched as his frown deepened, he paused for a moment, then he shook his head.

I wondered if he was plotting a lie, and for a moment I wondered what he could come up with.

"It's Janna's."

Janna's. That was the very same name he'd told me before while we stood pretty much in the same spot we were standing in now. The same name he'd said as a response when I asked whose blood was on his arm. I imagined that back then my face held the same the look I had now. I was horrified and shocked.

Janna's. A simple word that made everything clearer. And every doubt in me was gone. It was replaced by shame and embarrassment.

"You really thought I would cheat on you, Marie?" His eyes narrowed, and his lips formed a sad smile.

"I … I– …" I was speechless and I couldn't form words. "I didn't know that Janna was here." It was all I could come up with.

"It was a surprise visit," he said, his voice just above a whisper. He wasn't angry. He was hurt.

"Mazen, I'm sorry, I don't know what came over me." It was the truth, I acted unreasonably. I should've asked him first before accusing him of cheating, but once again – my emotions were simply out of control.

He didn't respond. The air in the room felt heavy. My heart was gripped in shame. There was a long moment while we looked at each other, me, silently begging for his forgiveness; he, unsure, hurt, and pained. He didn't say anything. He didn't make a sound. Instead, he went straight to the bathroom, leaving me standing there.

My apology was not accepted.

Mazen's parents' quarters weren't my favorite place in the palace. Their walls held awful memories. And they meant that I most likely would be met with awful people. Or one awful person in particular.

One crazy thing about the culture in the kingdom was that people made a huge deal about reuniting. It was their first priority to visit each other in sickness, or simply when someone came back from a trip. That trip could be years, or mere days. It was treated as duty to let a returned relative know very clearly that he or she had been missed.

If you delayed visiting for no apparent reason – you would be considered rude. No questions asked.

That was why my private secretary cleared my first hour of the morning right after breakfast for a meeting with Janna to welcome her back to the palace. Because, technically, she was in my house now, and I, as Queen had to make her feel welcomed.

It was ridiculous, in my opinion. It was the house she'd grown up in. Of course, she was welcome anytime. Her rooms before and after our marriages had stayed the same, untouched. Rooms that no matter how many visitors we entertained in the palace, we would never actually need. We had more rooms than I cared to know the exact number of.

But, of course, she would stay in her father's quarters until I told her otherwise.

Ridiculous, I say.

As I made my way to Mazen's parents' room, I kept thinking about what the reason could be for the 'surprise visit.' I didn't even know if it was safe for her to travel for such a long time when she was about to have a baby. I didn't know how far along she was, but I knew she was nearing the end of her third trimester.

Maybe she wants the baby to be born here, I thought.

Moments later, I was entering the bedroom escorted by two female guards. I figured Janna had been with her father since she'd arrived at the palace.

To my surprise, I found Prince Fahd standing by his father's bed; Rosanna was there as well, standing beside her husband. I could only tell that she was Rosanna because of Prince Fahd's hand that was resting on her shoulder.

I was confused for a minute as to why she was

fully dressed and covering her face – only her husband and uncle were in the room. I didn't think much about it, and my eyes drifted to the girl sitting on the edge of the bed with her back turned to me as she faced the man lying on the bed.

Just seeing her beautiful dark hair, I was able to tell that it was Janna. A smile was born on my lips when she turned her face and looked at me with her own cheerful smile. A smile that I remembered seeing the very first time we met. Or at least – close to it.

Though her smile was broad and spoke of joy, her eyes held sadness and maybe even misery inside them. I found myself wishing I could take that sadness away, to get her back to the girl she used to be before … before my brother happened.

I greeted everyone with a "Good morning," then turned to Janna, who stood up and came to me. "Janna." My arms opened and we hugged. "It's so good to see you."

"Thank you, your majesty. I'm so happy to be here," she smiled. "There's someone I would like for you to meet."

I watched as Janna walked to the far corner of the room, and my eyes were met by Mother Queen Shams' hard gaze. I offered her a tight smile just to be polite, but we both knew that I couldn't stand her no matter what, or no matter how much time had passed since the *incident*.

Next to her on a chair sat Mazen. I was shocked to

see him there; I absolutely had no clue. It explained why Rosanna was covered up, though.

My tight smile turned into a genuine one at the sight of him, though he wasn't looking at me. He was looking at the tiny baby in his arms with the warmest of smiles on his lips, and a look of longing in his eyes.

My hands flew to my mouth to cover the gasp that wanted to escape at the sight of the baby as Janna took it carefully from Mazen's hands and walked towards me. "Oh, my God!" I gushed.

"Say *'Hi'* to your niece!" Janna smiled as she offered me the baby in pink.

"Oh, my God!" was all I could say, not able to hold it together to actually take the baby from her hands.

It took me a moment too long before I was able to take my hands away from my mouth and reach for the tiny little girl and take her from Janna's hands. My tears were dropping from my eyes uncontrollably. A different kind of tears than the ones from earlier.

The feeling of having my niece in my arms was something I couldn't put into words. I was overwhelmed with so many feelings, rushing to my heart all at once.

Joy, happiness, adoring, loving and … and longing.

"Oh, my God!" I said for the third time, a lot lower this time. The sweetness in my arms looked up at me as she sucked on her thumb in the cutest way. "She looks just like Joseph."

Her eyes were bright blue, and it looked like she

was completely bald, but I could see a few blonde hairs. Her tiny lips were the most beautiful shade of pink, and her cheeks appeared rosy against her pale skin.

"She does," Janna agreed.

It felt as if the whole world disappeared as I looked into the little girl's eyes and studied her soft features. "She's so beautiful," I commented, not really saying it to anyone, but expressing my thoughts. "What did you name her?" I asked Janna without moving my eyes away from the angel in my arms.

"Marie."

"Yes?" I responded, my eyes still looking at my niece's.

"Marie," Janna said again, and I had to look up at her so she would know she had my attention and didn't have to call my name again.

"Yes, Janna?"

"Marie. We named her Marie, your majesty," Janna smiled brightly, and my tears grew heavier. Happy, grateful and overwhelmed kind of tears.

Apparently, baby showers in Arabian countries happened after the baby was born, not before it. I found it a bit odd given the fact that they made bedrooms for the kids even before marriage. But I wasn't going to complain; anything that was related to little Marie only managed to make me happy, even hearing her burp.

Baby showers happened on the seventh day after the baby's birth. So, two days after Janna's arrival, we were in her wing waiting for the party to start.

The baby shower was limited to close family members only. And so far, it didn't seem like Talia was close to Janna – she wasn't there. And I couldn't have been happier or more relieved.

What bothered me was that my seat was in a very special spot, making me stand out among the rest of the guests. I really didn't want to be the center of attention – little Marie was. I wanted to sit with the others and have fun watching the beautiful things they were doing, but there were things we simply shouldn't argue about.

It was the first time I'd met the newest generation of young princes and princesses, since it was the first gathering that included a baby. The baby shower was unlike anything I'd ever seen before. It was chaotic and very loud with all of the kids around, but so beautiful.

It looked like a fun indoor birthday party in America, minus the cake. There was a crazy amount of sweets being given to the kids and a special box that was shaped like a baby bottle, and a very large candle.

The kids were so happy and eager to open the box. There was some popcorn and candies inside it, and when they ate everything inside, they held the candle in their hands, formed a line and waited.

"What are they waiting for?" I leaned in a bit to ask Rosanna, who was sitting on a chair beside me.

"For Marie to show up," Rosanna smiled, though

there was something in her eyes that I couldn't figure out. It seemed like sadness to me, but I knew that she was happy with little Marie almost as much as I was, so I didn't know if it was truly sadness that I was seeing in her eyes.

Suddenly, the kids cheered and there was Janna, looking as beautiful as always. She was holding a small bed, decorated ridiculously with shiny stuff, and little Marie was in it.

Janna stood back, all smiles and grins as the kids circled her. Nora – Janna's servant – started to light the candles for the kids and they began singing such a beautiful song as they moved around Janna while she held the baby.

They went on like that for some time, and then the grownups joined in. I couldn't just stand there and had to get up and join them, though I didn't know what they were doing, but I was happy with it.

Little Marie was then placed on Mazen's grandmother's lap and she started shaking her little bed heartily. My eyes widened as I watched the scene in front of me, and I almost ran to take the baby away, but Rosanna held me back, laughing.

"What is she doing to the baby?"

"Relax, she's not hurting her."

"But – you're not supposed to shake a baby that way!"

"She's going to be fine, trust me," Rosanna laughed again.

I watched for a minute more, but then couldn't as the shaking became harder and I had to take a step back. "Is that in Islam?" I asked Rosanna.

"No, it's a culture thing. She's going to be fine, I promise. We all went through this, even King Mazen." She winked.

I listened to Mazen's grandmother's words as she shook little Marie. Her words were so funny that I actually chuckled hearing them, despite my worry. She was telling her not to listen to anyone but her because she was the oldest, and if her mother was hard on her to come to granny's arms straight away. Then she told her something embarrassing, like how Janna used to wet her bed until she was four, and to use that information against her if she didn't treat her well.

I had no idea why things like that were being said, but the way she said it made it funny. And Janna was actually laughing really hard as she listened to her grandmother's jokes.

A while later, things seemed to settle down, and the kids weren't as loud as before. Only grownup princesses were standing up, and then Nora gave a silky white cloth that was folded neatly to Janna.

"What are they doing now?" I whispered my question to Rosanna.

"Another tradition. For the sake of the next baby in the family."

I frowned, watching as Janna came closer with a soft smile on her lips, then stood in front of Rosanna and unfolded the cloth, which turned out to be a cloak.

Rosanna stood up and when Janna was about to put it over her head, Rosanna stopped her. Then she took the cloak from her hand and stood in front of me.

"Your majesty, please accept this instead of me. There's nothing that could make the whole kingdom happier than for you to bear King Mazen's child," she said and I swallowed thickly.

The fact that Janna had gone to her first signaled to me that this practice was for women who were yet to have a child; of course since Rosanna had been married for years, Janna offered it to her.

My throat tightened just thinking of Rosanna doing this for me instead of accepting it for herself. The practice most likely was nothing real, but I still felt highly overwhelmed to be offered something like that.

Standing up, I nodded, knowing that the sparkling unshed tears in Rosanna's eyes matched my own. Janna took the cloak from Rosanna's hands as she offered it to her and then started putting it on me.

The grandmother's wheelchair was pushed closer as she held the baby, and then she gave little Marie to Janna. Janna then took the baby from her hands, kissed her forehead, then offered her for me to do the same – which I did with trembling lips.

Janna carefully held the baby up over my neck, and then Rosanna reached for the cloak's neckline and stretched it for Janna to put little Marie inside it. More princesses came and helped as Janna started lowering the baby slowly to my chest then to my stomach and held it there for a few moments.

I bit my lips hard, trying to swallow back my tears as I felt the baby this close to me, right above my stomach – as if I was actually pregnant with her. Janna's and the princesses' hands held her there as her grandmother started a prayer with everyone saying *'Amen'* to everything she was saying. A prayer for mine and Mazen's happiness, and for God to bless us with a child sooner rather than later.

My heart was beating really hard as they carefully lowered the baby further until they got her out from underneath the cloak, as if I'd just given birth to her. The cheers and noises they made with their tongues whenever there was something to celebrate filled the air around us.

In that moment, and when they put her over my chest – outside of the cloak this time – and told me to hold her, it seemed like I didn't care if they saw their queen crying.

Twenty-one

There was nothing worse than accusing a Muslim husband of cheating, Rosanna told me. In Islam, cheating on your spouse is punishable by death, she added.

Three days had passed since the last time Mazen and I spoke. Three days. It was the longest I'd gone without talking to him since we were reunited almost seven months ago.

The first day he refused to speak to me, even after I'd apologized. And by the second day, I knew I must have done something horrible, because it wasn't like Mazen to be so cold. I'd never been treated this way by him before. Never.

On the third day, when he got up and left before I even woke up – the same as he'd done the two days before – I knew it was going to be another day without him speaking to me.

What killed me the most was that his back now faced me while we slept, and not once did he allow his hand to touch me. That hurt, most of all.

I craved hearing his voice as he spoke to me. Craved it. I wanted to tell him about what had happened at the baby shower. I wanted to talk to him about what I was feeling and why I had acted that way. I just wanted to talk to him. But we didn't spend any time together. He'd wake up and leave before I got out of bed, then come back at night and go straight to bed without even glancing my way.

I'd freaked out, I know. But I wanted him to forgive me.

"He'll speak to you today," Rosanna had assured me. Her declaration made me frown – how could she know something like that?

"Muslims can't cease to speak to another person for more than three days, and you're his wife," she'd said. Her smile was kind, and what she said sparked hope in my heart. I really missed him.

Opening up to Rosanna was something I couldn't regret. I needed a friend to talk to, and Terri couldn't be that friend for one reason or another. She might just say he was a jerk in order to please me and that would be it. But that wasn't what I wanted. I wanted someone to understand. I'd obviously hurt him, and I didn't know why it was so bad this time. Mazen already knew I mostly had no control over my emotions, and he was always forever patient and understanding with me. I wanted to understand why it was different this time.

Rosanna listened, explained and assured. It was all I needed, and I couldn't have asked for more.

The night to this day couldn't come fast enough. I counted the minutes until I could return to my wing again and see if he'd speak to me. I'd like for him to speak to me because he missed me, not because he was forced by an Islamic rule. But I wasn't going to complain. I just wanted to talk to him.

It was like I'd been choking and someone pumped air into my lungs again when my phone vibrated with a text from my 'Prince Charming.' I couldn't open my inbox fast enough, or read his question any faster – would I like to go out for dinner with him tonight. My one-word response took less time than actually opening the message.

'No,' I texted back, a smile plastered on my face. Not a minute later, my phone started ringing, and my smile turned into a grin.

"Hello!" I answered after I'd dismissed everyone in the office.

"Listen, I know it's not something to discuss over the phone, and you're probably busy right now, but I– ... uh, I just want to ..." I listened to the love of my life as he stumbled over his words. The forever calm and collected speaker who always knew the right thing to say was not able to form a sentence, because I'd said

'No' to his offer of going out for dinner, and it made me grin even wider.

I wasn't waiting for him to apologize for the three days of silent treatment. I knew I'd hurt him, and though I wished he had spoken to me earlier – I understood he needed his time. I was only enjoying his voice a bit too much; that was why I didn't interrupt him as he spoke.

"Marie ..." he breathed, *"Please, let's go out tonight. It feels like years since we– ..."* I heard him huffing, and I was evil enough to enjoy hearing him struggling for words, thinking I was mad at him for not speaking to me or something.

The thing was, I knew he wasn't talking to me because he was upset and hurt, but I'd never doubted his love for me. I knew that right now he was worried sick that I would give him a hard time before I spoke to him again, and I wouldn't let him suffer any more.

"Your majesty," I started, "Going out would prevent me from hugging you and kissing your lips the way I want. I would like to have dinner with you in the intimacy of our home."

His sigh of relief was followed by a soft chuckle, and it felt like I couldn't love him more in that moment.

Mazen was hurt mostly because I had doubted his faithfulness to me. It wasn't about doubting how good of a Muslim he was, as much as doubting how good of a husband he was to me.

"Marie, I'm in love with you. The thought of touching another woman makes me sick. How could you think I would do that?" he'd said, and it made me feel awful. Putting myself in his shoes, I would be beyond mad if he accused me of cheating, and I wouldn't be as collected as he was – I'd be a mess.

With time, Mazen was slowly teaching me how to be a better person. He didn't say it out loud. He was always telling me that I was the best thing that had ever happened to him. That life without me was nothing but pure torture. He told me he was in love with everything that was me, from my laugh to my stubbornness, and even my toes. But deep inside I knew, he was turning me into a much better person.

With time, I learned to be more considerate, more patient. I learned to wait, ask and learn before I judged or made a decision. Most importantly, I started to learn how to control my feelings.

I wasn't as good as Mazen in that aspect, not even close. But I was getting better at showing my poker face and holding back my tears. I became more measured and trusting, not jumping to conclusions right then and there in every little thing.

Mazen taught me. But not in a 'Do this, don't do that' kind of way. He taught me through living with him, watching him act and interacting with him. He taught me through our fights and how he dealt with them, through our arguments and how he kept them at bay. He taught me how to be a better person through his unconditional love for me.

With time, I learned to ask him or someone else I trusted to explain things I didn't understand. I learned to ask for help and to admit to being wrong. I learned how to deal with emotionally charged situations much better than I used to.

Months passed, and I felt myself growing, maturing. My love for Mazen was even stronger, and his love for me was indescribable.

May arrived, and on the thirteenth, we celebrated my birthday. A chapel built just for me inside our wing was one of my birthday gifts. This was a gift that I couldn't put value on, or describe in words the amount of happiness it gave me.

The old Marie would've felt awful because Mazen's birthday was in November and I hadn't even known. I wasn't even there in the kingdom that day. But the new Marie knew that things like that didn't matter. Mazen taught me that every day of our lives together was worthy of celebrating. The new me made him feel even more special than he already was every single day by just telling him and showing him how much my world revolved around him.

He was my everything. Simple as that.

The new me shared with Mazen her deepest thoughts, concerns and worries – things I'd always kept hidden away, tucked away safely in my heart and mind, heavy on my shoulders. I learned that speaking of them to Mazen and how we dealt with them together made everything brighter, lighter and easier.

Things weren't as hard once I shared them with him.

On my birthday night, he woke up to find me crying next to him. He simply took me in his arms and kissed my forehead repeatedly. He let me cry, and then he stayed silent as I poured my soul out to him about things that were bothering me.

I'd turned twenty-three, and my life was nothing like I had planned. I didn't mean to sound ungrateful, and Mazen knew that wasn't the case. But sometimes, life happened and I felt like I wasn't what I'd always wanted to be.

I'd never wanted to be a CEO. Before my parents' deaths, I absolutely knew nothing about running a company. I'd forced myself to learn, because Archer Enterprises was the result of my parents' hard work and I didn't want it to fade away along with their bodies. I wanted their memories to last forever.

Months were spent learning about things I'd never cared to know about before – importing and exporting, managing and organizing. Things I didn't really feel passionate about. But I'd done it for my parents.

And then there was you, I told him. I trusted our love enough not to fear that my next words would damage it. I knew Mazen would understand. And I knew I had to tell him, to feel at ease I had to tell him.

Because sharing my worries with him made things much better, and I wanted to feel better.

I told him how I found myself facing a new challenge with my life – I had to learn how to be a queen, a ruler. To people from a different culture and religion, no less. I told him how I was always afraid I would mess up somehow, that I would embarrass him, or cause trouble.

I told him how hard it had been, and how hard it was to keep going, that it was a struggle. And with both – the company and my duties as a queen – things weren't at all easy and were forever stressful.

"When I look at my life now and reflect on what I've accomplished for myself and my own dreams – I find nothing, Mazen. Zero," I said. "I'm trying my best and more, but it's all for others, because of what was put upon me, not what I chose."

Like always, he made me see things differently. He made me see that I *did* choose. Getting the company back on its feet was my own choice, not even Joseph's. And going back to Mazen was for sure my choice, the best choice I'd ever made.

He made me see that my own dreams were still there, and I was actually living them – just maybe not the same as I'd wanted. But still … they were there.

Worries became lighter and easier, and things looked brighter. Just like I knew they would.

I felt better, but deep inside me, I knew I would rather have lived with Mazen in a much smaller house, having much fewer duties and many more children.

The last part was the only worrisome topic that I couldn't speak to Mazen about. Because just speaking of it hurt me beyond words. Heck, just thinking of it caused a new round of tears that I couldn't explain to him. And he always let these kinds of talks be on my own terms. No pushing.

Ramadan came, the Muslims' holy month. They fasted starting from sunrise until sunset every day until the end of the month. I asked many questions about it, and was always welcomed with open arms and given patient answers – from Mazen, Rosanna or even Mona.

I knew they didn't eat a single thing or drink a drop of water in that period. Mazen had explained it was to feel the hunger and thirst of the poor, to value what we have and donate money and whatever we could to make their struggles less painful.

It was a very inspiring thing to learn about. And to a point, I fasted with them, just to be respectful. I made sure not to eat or drink in front of anyone while they fasted. But it wasn't just that – Mazen had fasted with me every time I did, and even in the Big Fast before Easter, he didn't eat anything I didn't eat; I thought it was only fair to do the same for him, or at least try to.

With a few sips of water here and there and one quick snack during one of my breaks, I managed to pass the days without the concern of offending anyone or being disrespectful by eating in front of them while they starved.

Mazen had told me it was okay and that they wouldn't be offended or anything, but still, I wanted to be considerate of others' feelings. I wanted to support my husband.

One day during Ramadan, I happened to be awake before Mazen had to leave for the day. He kissed my forehead and hugged me, but I couldn't let go just yet. I had to kiss his mouth, and I was enjoying it too much to realize how Mazen's body stiffened suddenly. When the kiss deepened, he abruptly pulled away, his hands on my shoulders as he pushed me slightly back, while saying "No."

The old me would've been hurt, would've walked away all upset and maybe even mad. But the new me swallowed the hurt of feeling kind of rejected, and asked what was going on.

It turned out that during fasting, a wife and husband couldn't touch in any sexual way, just light kisses or something like that. Nothing deep enough to turn you on. I was confused – what did sex have to do with fasting?

"When we fast, we leave food and drinks and even lust behind our backs in order to please God. I could eat and drink and even touch myself while I'm alone, where nobody can see, and only God would know. So it's between me and Him, and I'm rewarded for it in the afterlife." He offered me a soft smile as he explained.

"Oh, I get it now," I said. "But everything aside, can I tell you that the thought of you touching yourself is so hot? Or should I keep that until after sunset?" I loved to tease him more than anything.

I had to laugh when I heard his groan. "You'll pay for that later," he said before he left.

Insanely, I found that teasing Mazen about this was the best thing about the whole fasting practice. He always had a kind heart about it and didn't seem offended whatsoever; he even seemed to like to prove how much strength he had in holding back.

June marked a year to the first day I had ever stepped foot in the kingdom. We didn't celebrate it as the day before our wedding anniversary, but as the day we first met.

Janna was still in the palace; she never went back to the States. To be honest, it broke my heart that my brother never got to spend any time with his child.

Mazen had told me that we couldn't make her feel uncomfortable staying here, so we never mentioned anything about it. Not that I was going to ask her about him or anything – it was unspeakable between the two of us. It didn't take a genius to know things weren't working out between them, though.

Every now and then, whenever I could, I spent hours with little Marie, and I didn't know how I would feel when and if she left. I knew Janna and Joseph weren't divorced, but they weren't any better than a divorced couple anyway.

With all of my heart, I wished they would make up – it had been a whole year. I wished they could get back together, for their daughter's sake, and for Janna's as well. I knew she loved him, still. I could see it in her eyes every time someone mentioned how their daughter looked a lot like him. She loved hearing it. But there was nothing I could do, really.

One day, I had a long, long meeting with the Foreign Affairs Minister, and I ended up coming back to the wing after ten that night. Once I set foot inside, I knew there was something wrong. It could've been the frightened look on Donia's face as she stood shaking in the foyer. Or it could've been the sound of glass shattering that made me realize something was off.

"What is it?" I asked with wide eyes as I handed her my purse, my legs taking me quickly towards the source of the sound.

"I don't know, your majesty," Donia replied, her voice shaking just like her hands. "His majesty seems to be really angry."

Once I made it into the bedroom, I closed the door behind me. I took a deep breath to collect my nerves, but it did little towards calming me. I was worried sick about Mazen.

It was only once before that I'd heard him this mad – the night when he realized he had to let me go. I couldn't think of any reason why he would be like that again. The last text from him said that he would go to see his father, as he'd requested, before going to our wing – what could possibly have set him off this way?

I knew that breaking things was Mazen's way of letting his anger out. I knew that Mona had advised me before to let him be and he would come around, but I simply couldn't stand there and listen to him being that upset without doing anything to calm him down. He was my husband, and his wellbeing meant my heart's safety.

Without giving it much thought, I went to the living room where I knew Mazen was, using one of the secret doors. My eyes scanned the room before landing on him as he held an ashtray in his hand and threw it towards the wall with all of his might, causing it to break into a million pieces and drop to the floor.

I flinched all the way to him as I watched him taking one object after another and doing the same thing with them that he had with the ashtray, the question of what had made him this mad repeating loudly in my head.

"Mazen!" I called to get his attention, but he didn't hear me until I had to yell it, "Mazen!" He stopped mid-throw to look back at me.

"Get out!" he yelled, continuing with his throw, maybe even harder than before.

"Mazen, what are you doing?" It wasn't actually a question that needed an answer, for it was already happening before my eyes, but it was more of a scolding for him to wake up from whatever had gotten to him and stop.

"I said, get out!" he shouted, throwing some crystal antique into the opposite wall.

Mazen had never, ever yelled at me this way. Heck, he'd never yelled at me at all. And it only made my heart swell to realize he was so upset that he couldn't control himself.

I clenched my teeth and took one step forward followed by another until I was standing right next to him. I let him throw one more thing before I caught his hand and held it firmly in mine. "No!" I said.

Mazen started to pull his hand away, but I wouldn't let go. He tried to pull himself free but I was clutching it so hard that I had to take another step forward to keep my balance and not fall flat on my face. "Stop it!"

"Get out of here, Marie," he said again. This time he wasn't yelling as much as before, but his voice was broken and he sounded hurt. "I don't want you to see me like this."

What the heck had happened?

"No!" I said again, more forcibly this time. "Stop it!" I moved to stand in front of him, my heels making my eyes almost at the same level of his bloodshot ones.

He wasn't angry, he was furious, and his eyes wouldn't meet mine, but his face was screaming with the many sad emotions that were going through him. I knew I would do anything to take it all away. Anything.

"Look at me!" I said, and when he made no effort to do so, I let go of his hand and reached with both hands to his face, forcing his eyes to look into mine. "Look at me, Mazen."

Eventually, he did. And my heart broke a little as I saw the look in his eyes. He was panting hard, his eyes telling me everything his mouth wouldn't speak of. But it wasn't loud enough for me to understand it. I only wished I could.

"What's wrong, angel?"

Suddenly, his lips crashed into mine; he kissed me so hard that our teeth knocked into each other. I was taken aback by surprise at first and didn't actually return the kiss until a moment later.

His hands found their way to my hips and he pulled my body to his, his hands squeezing hard as he held me firmly to him. The next thing I knew, he was pushing me against the nearest wall, pressing his body to my own so that I could feel his erection rubbing over my hip.

Whoa! Well, that was something I hadn't expected, but it certainly wasn't something I would complain about.

Mazen's lips left me breathless, and he didn't waste any time moving down my jawline and then down my neck. My hands pushed his head more into me because I just loved the feel of his lips and tongue over my skin.

His hands roamed all over my body in such a frenzy that they felt everywhere all at the same time. And before I knew it, he was unbuttoning my suit jacket, moving it off of my shoulders, and then dropping it to the floor. All the while his lips never left my neck, and his erection never stopped grinding over my hip.

"Mazen," I gasped when he squeezed my left breast over my blouse, finding my body responding fast to his touches and kisses, wanting him right then and there.

Without a warning, I felt him pushing my pencil skirt up and over my hips, and in one swift movement, he ripped off my panties as if they were made of paper.

A moan escaped my lips, caused by the sweet friction the panties made over my most sensitive spot when Mazen pulled to rip them off. And Mazen groaned at the sound of my moan.

I pulled at his pants, helping him get rid of them, but only managed to get his fly open before Mazen took a step back and then turned me around so I was facing the wall.

A moment later, he was pulling my hip with one hand and positioning himself at my entrance with the other. His foot pushed mine to the side, making me open my legs further, which caused me to bend over a bit more. It made my backside press even more against him, and I couldn't have loved the sensation more.

With one hard push, he was inside of me. And he started moving fast, leaving no time for me to catch my breath as one of his hands pulled on the top of my blouse, ripping it open so that buttons flew everywhere.

He pulled on my bra along with it, baring one breast for his hand to squeeze and fondle from behind.

"Oh, god! Mazen!" I gasped as he pushed himself harder into me, his one hand tightening over my hip so hard that I was sure he would leave bruises, and the other clutching my breast for dear life.

All you could hear was the sound of my moans and his groans mixed with our pants and my gasps, along with the slipping and slapping of our skin as we made contact with each other over and over again.

When his thrusts became even faster, I knew he was close. I was already tightening around him, but not quite there yet. Mazen – forever the amazing lover he was – couldn't let go before I did. His hitched breaths were fanning over that delicate spot behind my ear, sending shivers down my spine, while the hand over my hip moved south to where we were connected, and he started rubbing circles over my sensitive spot.

"Mazen, please! Oh, yes! Yes!"

"*C'mon!*" he groaned into my ear in Arabic, losing himself in the sensation, and making me lose it when he bit down on that spot where my neck met my shoulder. And it was like he had pressed a button because the next thing I knew, I was coming hard all over him, feeling him as he released inside of me just a split second later.

That night, Mazen carried me to bed, for my legs felt like Jell-O and I simply couldn't walk. Later on, he held me close all night long, like he'd never done before. It was like he was afraid I'd simply disappear if his arms weren't wrapped tight enough around me.

There were no words spoken between us, but he was calm enough to breathe evenly and stop being so frantic. That was all that mattered. But the look of sadness that I could easily read in his eyes made me wish he had stayed mad so I wouldn't see him that broken.

Though I was dying to know what happened to make him so mad and sad, I didn't ask any questions that night. I knew he would tell me whenever he was ready. I just wished he wouldn't take long, because I didn't know if I could take the agony I saw in his eyes. It would kill me to see him even more fractured than he already was, even if it was just for one more day.

Twenty-two

Mazen never told me what had gotten to him that night, and I didn't ask. I really wanted to know what it was, but I understood that there were things we couldn't share. I was upset that he didn't tell me, and I wondered who he would talk to about what was bothering him, if not his wife.

But then again, there were a few things that I couldn't share with him, either. My feelings about my brother, and my thoughts on the pregnancy that wouldn't happen, for example.

There were times when I truly missed Joseph, and other times when I actually *needed* him. But I never spoke about those feelings to anyone, not even to Mazen. Heck, it was hard enough to admit it to myself.

It wasn't like I didn't trust Mazen or didn't want

him to know. It was that some things hurt when you simply think about them, let alone actually speak of them.

The fact that I had yet to get pregnant was concerning me to no end. But I couldn't find it in me to speak about it with anyone, not at all. I was afraid Mazen would tell me that I was being dramatic, that it was too soon to worry, and call me silly.

I couldn't tell Terri; she might think I was crazy for wanting a child this young and with everything that was going on – she simply wouldn't get it. She wouldn't understand how much I wanted this baby or how much a son was needed.

I couldn't even tell Rosanna. She was a very good friend to me, maybe even better than Terri. I loved her dearly, and I knew she would understand. But I was afraid of telling her given everything she'd gone through. I thought she might think I was a cry baby, that I had no right to be so upset about not getting pregnant after barely eleven months of trying. Especially since she had been married for years and still didn't have a baby.

So I didn't tell anyone. I kept it to myself and suffered in silence. It was better that way; no need to explain or beg for understanding, not even fear of disapproving looks.

The pregnancy test in my nightstand's drawer remained unused. My period had been a mess since I got married, not at all regular and more painful than ever. It always started a day or two early – heck, one time I got it twice in one month.

I wanted to see a doctor, but with my position now as a queen, I couldn't go to any random hospital for a checkup. And if I asked for the royal family's doctor, that meant that Mazen would know, and that put me back at the whole he'd-call-me-silly thing.

When Mazen got concerned about my constant dizziness and blackouts, he had me get so many blood tests. The doctor came and took the samples without me having to go anywhere and then we got the results later. I only needed some vitamins – not that it helped anyway, but I didn't give it much thought. It was what it was.

My point is, I assumed there was no way that all of the tests and the equipment needed to find out why I wasn't getting pregnant could be brought here. Or maybe they could bring them here, I didn't know. Mazen's father had all kinds of machines around him, after all. In both cases, it would create a huge fuss and maybe even some embarrassment that I was better off without.

My plan was to wait until after our first anniversary and then I would talk to him about it – then it wouldn't be silly anymore. I still hoped that I would be pregnant by then.

My heart ached at the thought; I really thought I would have had a baby by now. But like Mazen had said and like I also believed, it was in God's hands. We had nothing to do with it.

Inside Mazen's father's bedroom, I felt like an outsider. I felt like I shouldn't be there, witnessing this. But I reminded myself that if I wasn't here for my father-in-law, then I was here for my husband. I wanted to be there for him during such a hard time.

The doctors had told us that there was nothing more they could do for him; my father-in-law had only a little time left. Minutes, if not only counted seconds.

So I stood there in my place, watching as his soul faded away as the time passed. His wife was sitting right beside him, her hand touching his head as she looked down at him with despair in her green eyes.

On each side of him were his sons, Mazen to his right and Prince Fahd to his left. Both were holding his hands, their faces blank masks that I was sure were covering sadness and misery, as they watched their dying father taking one step after another towards death.

Janna sat behind Mazen, one of her hands covering her face as she wept for her only remaining parent taking his last breaths, while the other rested on his leg. Opposite her sat Rosanna, behind her husband, almost mirroring Janna's position and her heartbreaking sobs.

Silent tears rolled down my cheeks as I watched the scene playing out in front of me. My father-in-law was such a great guy, and while I was completely saddened by the fact that he only had minutes to live, my tears were actually for Janna. She was saying goodbye to the only form of a parent she'd ever known, and it was truly breaking my heart.

My hand rubbed Mazen's shoulder ever so slowly as I listened to his father giving him the last life lessons he would ever give him. He was struggling with his words, but he didn't stop no matter how hard it was.

He was telling him to fear God in everything he did, telling him that if he didn't do anything that would make God angry with him then he was on the right path.

He was telling him to take care of Janna and fix the matter with her husband. To treat his mother with respect and look after her. He told him to never let power control him and make his morals disappear. He warned him against arrogance and pride; he said they were the only two things that could take any man down.

Mazen was listening to him carefully, replying with a *'Yes, father,'* to everything that he was telling him.

Every now and then my father-in-law would turn his head to talk to Fahd, but his focus was mostly on Mazen. He was his firstborn after all, the king of the kingdom if nothing else. The weight on his shoulders was heavier, much heavier than anyone else's.

"*My last wish, son–*" he said breathlessly, "*You have to change your sheets.*"

My Arabic had improved a lot in the past year. There were very few words that I couldn't understand upon hearing, but there were some that simply didn't make sense to me, mostly because they were slang for something.

It was the same with those words, I couldn't understand them – what could it possibly mean for him to ask Mazen to change his sheets? Why would Mazen do that? Why was that something he chose to be his last wish? All of the questions in my head lead me to understand that his words had another meaning, rather than how they were translated in my head.

Mazen's body stiffened; it could be the only emotion he'd shown as he sat there and watched his father die. And suddenly, Mazen, Rosanna and the Mother Queen's eyes were all on me. It was brief, but it happened, and then Mazen spoke.

"*But father–*"

"*Don't argue with me again, Mazen,*" his father choked out, using his name without any title, something I'd never witnessed from him before – it only made me realize that he meant business. "*It's not an order anymore, I'm telling you this is my death wish.*"

"*Y-yes, father.*"

"*Promise me.*"

"*Fath–*"

"*Promise!*" he coughed the one-word command.

"*I ... I promise.*"

The dying man seemed to be at peace after Mazen

promised to do whatever he had asked him to do. And moments later, he was gone.

The sobs of the two young women grew louder, and my mother-in-law's eyes bled silent, heavy tears. It was odd how collected she looked to be – maybe even as good as the two men were. I knew that royalty requested just that, but c'mon! He was her husband for twenty-something years!

Mazen lifted the light sheet above his father's face, covering it, which only caused Janna to weep even harder, almost hysterically. Sweetly, Mazen turned around and took Janna in his arms, hugging her tightly and kissing her hair.

He swallowed thickly more than one time, and I knew he was holding back tears. Because Mazen simply didn't cry. He'd cried for me once, but that was it, and it only meant that his love for me topped any love he'd ever had for anyone else.

My heart ached as I saw Prince Fahd holding Rosanna and soothing her with whispered words that were meant only for her ears. It was the first time I'd ever see him this affectionate with anyone. I knew he was being the good husband that he was, to be there for his wife as she lost the man who'd been a father to her more than her real one.

Rosanna's father had been married to Jasem and Talia's mother for a few years before he had to divorce her – because she was just pure evil, as Rosanna had told me. And because Rosanna's mother was the next of the four sisters who were ready for marriage, he married her next. Just a few months later, his first wife managed to wrap around him like a snake, wanting him back. And since Islam forbade a man to have two sisters as wives at the same time, he had to divorce Rosanna's mother before she'd even realized that she was pregnant.

Mazen's father, being the king then already, had taken his cousin under his wing. He'd given her a place in the palace to live, where Rosanna was later born and raised, and she had received pretty much the same love that had been given to Janna. He'd raised her as if she was his own daughter, not just his niece.

It wasn't a strange thing for her to be this broken, and I wished there was something that I could do for both her and Janna. But sadly, there wasn't anything to be done – death never stopped for anyone. It took whomever it wanted, with no expectations.

For some odd reason that I couldn't even understand, I found my hand reaching for my mother-in-law's hand. I held it, feeling sorry for her, knowing that no matter how strong and collected she seemed to be, she surely needed to be comforted like everyone else.

When she held my hand back firmly, I knew she was telling me silently that my efforts were deeply appreciated. Our eyes couldn't meet each other's, though, not even once. And I found it easier that way.

His Royal Highness Qasem Alfaidy was buried just

mere hours after his death. In the Islamic belief, that was the only thing they could do to let him rest in peace – to rush his burial. I found it moving how he was buried with no more than a white cloth wrapped around his whole body, along with his face.

Plain white cloth, not even made of silk, was the last thing the former king wore. After wearing the most expensive clothes, his last clothes were just that – something that could barely cost twenty dollars, if not less.

And he was buried in a hole in the desert where the cemetery was – no coffin, and not even a special place for him. It was Muslims' belief that all people were equal. I was taken aback by all of this, but the meanings behind it were truly inspiring.

People came from all over the world to pay their respects and offer consolation. First families and public figures. My brother came the very next day, but I made sure that I didn't even cross paths with him. There were separate gatherings for both men and women, and it lasted for three days.

Mazen's words were always cut short, as polite as ever, but the sadness his tone held was just making my chest swell and ache. I wished I could take it all away, feeling so helpless when I realized I really couldn't.

There were people visiting around the clock, and both of us were exhausted – the same for the rest of the first royal family. I found it to be such a tiring and depressing tradition. I could see them all, tired and miserable, yet struggling to appear collected and meeting with people in formal and non-formal meetings. All they wanted was to grieve, but they weren't even given the chance for that.

Every night, we made love. Well, I couldn't really call it making love. It was sex – we just had sex, nothing more. It was as if Mazen felt like he had to do it? I didn't know. There were almost no feelings to it. There was foreplay with just the right amount to get me wet, then there was an in-and-out process. I would come, then he would come, and that was it.

His words were cut short even during that.

I could understand that he hadn't been feeling his best since his father had died, but two weeks later, I expected there would be some improvement. But nothing. There was nothing. Mazen was very depressed and I had no idea how to fix it.

He stayed up late writing on his papers furiously, almost in an angered manner. Then he would burn them ever so quickly, something that had started to annoy me. Since I could read some Arabic words now, it felt as if he was hiding it from me.

It was so silly; he'd been this way since I'd met him. His thoughts found their way onto paper whenever they were too much to stay in his mind. He always burned the papers, it wasn't because of me. But I was simply desperate to find out what was going on with him.

Prince Fahd appeared to be taking it well when we

happened to meet for whatever reason. Even Rosanna and Janna seemed to be moving on. So, why wasn't Mazen snapping out of it already? It was killing me to see him so miserable.

When more days passed and Mazen stayed the same – distant and almost cold towards me – I knew it wasn't about his father anymore. Maybe it never had been in the first place.

It was that I realized that Mazen had changed. Into someone I didn't know.

Twenty-three

A month after my father-in-law passed away, Mazen took me to the beach mansion that he had gifted to me. It was our wedding anniversary. The real one.

I had hopes that Mazen would get back to his normal self while we were there, that he would talk to me again like he used to, and that he would show me how his love for me grew with every new day – like he used to.

The only emotion I'd gotten from Mazen for the last month was the way he would cling to me so tightly while we slept, as if he was afraid he'd wake up and find me gone.

There was something huge that Mazen was holding back from telling me, and I had no idea how long it would take him to finally let it out. Who knew, maybe I could help. Or so I hoped.

The mansion was amazingly beautiful, though much smaller than the one in London with only three bedrooms, but I loved how cozy it was. It was such a great gift from my father-in-law, and I wished I had the chance to thank him for it once more.

We had only two days to spend there before we had to get back to the palace, and I was determined to make the most of it. The flight to the mansion took only half an hour, and I was happy that I was getting to see a new part of the kingdom that I hadn't seen before.

I loved seeing Mazen wearing jeans and a T-shirt, the same as he'd mostly worn when we were in London. Those days had been the start of the best days of my life, and I continued to count one new best day after another. All because they were with Mazen.

Mazen asked if I wanted to go for a swim, but I didn't know what I could wear in the water. The coast was clear as far as we could see, but we had many male guards with us. I didn't want to press any buttons or be offensive to them somehow by wearing a bikini. I wasn't much into swimming in an ocean, anyway. Joseph had made me watch Jaws when I was only four, and it had led to a bit of a phobia of open water.

Mazen was talking to me more, all smiles and kindness, but I knew better than to think that whatever was bothering him had gone away. It was still there, his eyes spoke all about it. He was depressed and anxious, but he was trying his best to hide it.

Little did he know that I'd grown to read him very well, even better than he'd thought. Most of the time, Mazen was an open book to me, despite all of his masks and blank expressions that he'd mastered so well.

I was his wife, the closest person to him, even closer to him than his mother had ever been. I knew Mazen well. But not well enough to read his mind and find out about his concerns. I wished I could, though.

"I thought we said no diamonds!" I said when Mazen handed me the small box, it looked like the ones used for jewelries.

"It's not. Open it." He smiled.

When I opened the box, I found a smaller box inside it with some papers under it. I took the little box out then I opened it.

The grin brightened up my face as I touched the golden bracelet inside. It had many charms dangling from it, and my grin grew bigger with each one my eyes caught.

One of the charms was a cross, and another one was a heart. Another was Big Ben that represented our time in London. I smiled when I saw that one of them was a horse. It was a lot similar to what I got him.

"Wow! This is amazing." I smiled brightly, "Thank you so much, angel." I hugged him tightly, loving my gift.

"I'm glad you like it." He smiled back, "There's a space left for more charms. I will bring you one of two each year, and when it can't take more, I'll get you another empty one, so we can keep filling it for as long as we live."

My lips found his, drawing my gratitude in a kiss. I couldn't help imagining ourselves as we grow old together. White hair and a dozen kids.

Kids ...

Before the thought trouble me, I took my cell phone out and tapped on the screen a few times until it showed what I wanted, then gave it to him.

"This is what I brought for you."

"Wow! A used cell phone! Thanks."

Chuckling, I punched him playfully on the shoulder. "Look at the picture, smarty pants. I couldn't bring it here."

Mazen did what I told him, and the smile on his face grew. "You made this?"

"Well, not actually engraved it, but yeah – it's custom made." I smiled.

"It's incredible." Mazen took me in his arms, and I was very happy that he liked it, I knew he would.

It was a statue, made of pure gold. But that wasn't what made it beautiful. It was that it was a horse that had a shirtless man on its back, and a woman with only a shirt sitting in front of him. It represented the night when we shared our first kiss.

"It's in the main office in the palace, so every time you look at it, you would remember me."

Mazen shook his head, "I never stop thinking about you to begin with, Princess."

It was a wonderful moment, I couldn't believe that the both of us gifted one another almost the same thing. Memories. Memories of us and our love.

"You still didn't look at your other gift."

"Oh, there's more?"

"Yes, in the box."

"It's only papers there … and a map?"

"Yes, it's the kingdom of Alfaidya." He grinned, then took out the map and gave it to me.

"Um … thanks," I spread it open on the bed where we were sitting, thinking that it might come handy someday. Maybe.

I heard Mazen chuckling, "You're so cute, Princess." He said, "Look here,"

I looked where he was pointing at on the map, frowning as I tried to understand what he was doing. My eyebrows flew to my hairline as I read the letters carefully, not believing my eyes.

'Queen Marie Archer's Square'

"You named a square after me?" I asked in disbelieve and shock, tears already glistening in my eyes.

"Well, you said no diamonds."

We made the best of the two days, spending them wrapped around each other and enjoying each other's company. I wished Mazen would open up to me about what had happened to make him like this, so different from the Mazen I knew. But he wouldn't – not that I asked, anyway. I chose to pretend that I'd ignored it.

When we made love, it felt like it had been months and months since the last time he was inside of me. It was filled with emotions, and his words of love were warmer than ever.

"You're the best thing that has ever happened to me. You know that, right?" he whispered into the quiet night. The crashing of the waves only yards away was the only sound we could hear.

My smile was my response to his words, my mind all dazzled and still fogged with my post-orgasm bliss.

"I can never let you go. I *won't* ever let you go, Princess." His voice was almost desperate, and I was confused by how passionate he was while saying those words – he already knew I wasn't going anywhere. "I can never live without you, Marie."

My hand touched his cheek. "The same as I could never live without you, angel," I told him, wondering why he seemed relieved at my statement. It felt like he didn't know it already, like he needed the reassurance.

If you'd just tell me what's going on in your head, Love ... things would be much better, for both of us.

I woke up much earlier than normal. Mazen had woken up to shower and pray at 5 AM, then he came back to bed and fell asleep again, but I couldn't get back to sleep myself, even though I hadn't left the bed.

When I was pretty sure that sleep had gone and wasn't going to come back, I got out of bed, showered and dressed in another sundress. I went to Mazen's side of the bed and kissed his cheek.

"I'm going to take a short walk and be back before you're awake."

He wanted to get up and come with me but I insisted that he go back to sleep. The poor guy hardly ever got to sleep in, and it was barely seven after all.

"Take four guards with you," he said sleepily, his eyes closed as if he was afraid that sleepiness would escape him if he opened them.

"I'm going to take two."

"Three."

"Only two, Mazen. It's enough."

He groaned, but didn't say anything. I smiled and ruffled his messy hair, then took myself downstairs.

Donia and Hana – another servant – were already in the kitchen preparing breakfast. I didn't feel like eating or drinking anything, so I decided to skip it until I got back from my walk, to eat with Mazen after he woke up.

"Did you happen to have packed any cloaks for me, Donia?" I asked.

"No, your majesty. I'm very sorry."

"Hey, it's okay. No big deal, I can wear one of yours."

"One of mine?" Her eyes widened.

"I mean, if you don't mind."

"Of course not, your majesty. It's just – it's not good enough for your majesty to wear."

I chuckled. "My majesty believes it'll be perfect." I hoped the humor in my tone would help her loosen up a bit. She sounded frightened at the idea of me wearing her clothes, but I didn't see the big deal about it.

It wasn't often that I wore cloaks, but my sundress was shorter than what I normally wore, and it was sleeveless. I knew that I most likely wouldn't meet anyone, but I still didn't want to bring attention to myself if we happened to cross paths with anybody.

Brad and Fawaz were walking right behind me as I enjoyed my walk on the almost-white sand. The feel of my bare feet sinking into the soft sand was indescribable. The crashing waves were making a low roar as the cool breeze hit my face.

I hugged myself as my mind went here and there, thinking of everything that was important and everything that wasn't. I tried to keep my thoughts happy, not wanting the bad ones to affect my good mood and my enjoyment of this beautiful day.

As I walked far from the mansion, I saw the wires that separated the area of our private beach from the rest of the shore. I was about to turn around when my eyes caught people in the water. For some reason, I stood there and watched for a few minutes, seeing that it was a man and his wife.

What made me really surprised was the fact that the woman was dressed all in black, and her face was covered. I had no clue how was she able to breathe. It was very dangerous, especially if her niqap got wet or something. And of course, her clothes were so heavy and so much.

I shook my head. *There is hardly anyone around; she should at least remove the face cover in order to enjoy it more,* I thought. But given the fact that I could see – probably Brad and Fawaz could, as well – them from a place where they couldn't see me, she was right in taking precaution. It protected something she believed should be hidden.

Without any judgment – not much, anyway – I turned around and decided to go back home. A few yards later, I heard a little voice calling *''Auntie!''* It was traditional for kids to call older women *'Auntie'* in the kingdom, and I looked back to see a little boy running my way.

I stopped in my tracks, seeing Fawaz take a few steps to stand in front of me while Brad stepped even closer to my side. The boy had very tan skin, black hair and beautiful dark eyes. I noticed that he was very skinny, his clothes were much too loose on his body.

"*Stay back, boy,*" Fawaz ordered with his gruff voice.

"Let him, it's okay." I said. Fawaz could be a little too much when it came to my protection. He was just a little kid, for God's sake.

The kid stopped in his tracks, but I took a step in his direction and motioned for him to come closer with a grin on my face, which he did with a big smile.

"*Please take some, please,*" he said, offering me some gum. I was taken aback by him wanting to give me that; I thought it was incredibly nice of him. But when I took another look at him, I saw that on his shoulder was a big plastic bag full of small boxes, which with a closer look appeared to be holding gum in them.

My smile fell and a frown appeared between my eyebrows. "*Oh!*" I paused. "*Are you selling them?*"

"*Yes, Auntie. Please, take some.*"

You've got to be kidding me!

"*How old are you, Kiddo?*" I asked after I kneeled in front of him.

The little boy adjusted the heavy bag on his shoulder, then held three fingers up to my face. "*Four,*" he said. The collar of his shirt moved slightly with the movement, revealing pale skin where the sun couldn't reach.

He'd been in the sun for too long, and too many days.

I chuckled softly, then took one of his two held-down fingers and straightened it to join the rest of his three fingers. "*This is four, sweetie.*"

"*Okay, are you going to take some gum?*"

"*Yes, I will,*" I assured him. "*Where's your father?*"

"*He's with God.*"

I swallowed thickly. "*How about your mother? Where is she?*" My hand touched his shoulder.

"*She's home with my little sister.*"

"*She doesn't have a job?*"

"*No, she's sick. How many you want?*" he asked, seeming to be getting impatient with all of my questions.

"*How much for one?*"

"*One pound.*"

"*I'll take two,*" I said with a smile and he got so excited. "Fawaz, do you have any cash on you?"

"Yes, your majesty." Fawaz put his hand in his pocket and got some bills out. He was about to pick out two pounds to give me, but instead I took them all from his hand and offered them to the little boy as he gave me the two packs of gum.

The kid looked down at the bills in his hands then looked up at me. "*That's more than two pounds.*"

"*I know that, but I want you to have it.*"

"*Why?*"

"*It'll make me happy.*"

"*I can't take it. I only want two pounds.*"

When I saw that he was pretty serious about not taking the money, I tried again, "*How about if I take everything you have in there?*"

He looked at me with wide eyes. "*All of it?*" he gasped his question.

"*Yes, sweetie. I really like gum and yours looks so good,*" I smiled.

"*Okay.*" He smiled brightly, taking the plastic bag from his shoulder and offering it to me. My heart broke a little as I saw him rubbing his shoulder where the bag had been hanging.

Brad took the heavy bag from my hand and I thanked him, then heard the little boy chuckling. "*What are you laughing at, Kiddo?*"

"*You speak funny,*"

It was my turn to laugh slightly. "*Yes, I guess I do. Can you tell me what your name is?*"

"*Mazen. But Mom calls me Mizo.*"

"*Oh! That's a beautiful name. It's so precious to me, you know? My husband's name is Mazen, as well.*" It wasn't the first time I met someone with my love's same name. It was some kind of a habit actually, for people of the kingdom to name their kids after the royal family's.

"*Really?*"

"*Yes.*"

"*But I was named after the Crown Prince,*" he said with pride in his voice.

I looked at him in awe. "*Well, he's the king now. Did you know that?*"

The little boy who was named after the man I loved the most in the whole world only shrugged in response, then told me that he had to leave.

"*Wait, do you live nearby?*"

"*I live in Manial.*"

I looked up at Fawaz, asking with my eyes if he

knew where that was, and his answer was just a nod.

"*Okay, can you tell me your father's name?*"

He shook his head and then turned his back to me and started walking away.

"*We'll meet again, sweet boy,*" I called after him, promising.

It turned out that there were laws which prevented kids under the age of twelve from working at all. But apparently, not everyone obeyed, especially in some places like the princedom where the beach mansion was located.

To a point, I understood. But not really. I knew that each country – including America – had its poor, and even some homeless, which the kingdom appeared to be lacking in, to an outsider. But with more studies and a few meetings with some of the ministers, I found out that there were lots of those in that certain princedom.

What got to me the most was the fact that this very place was ruled by Jasem.

I wouldn't put it past him to steal from the money and services that were provided to each princedom. And even if it wasn't enough, it was his job to make his area rise, not to let it get this way, where small children had to work and a mother stayed home because no proper medical care was offered to her.

I tried, a lot. But I knew that I wouldn't see results

right away. I wished there was a way to replace Jasem, but Prince Fahd told me it was only if he committed a crime or got seriously sick that we could do that.

Speaking to Mazen about it was out of question; he was already dealing with too much to bother him with things I could work out on my own. Sadly, some of the things that were on Mazen's shoulders were things I didn't even know. Because he'd never shared them with me.

A few days later, Mazen asked me to come home early because there was something he needed to talk to me about. I was anxious to find out what it was; it seemed to be pretty serious. I wondered if it was something related to the kingdom or if it was about us.

After I'd come back home and changed, we talked for a few minutes. There was so much tension in the air, and I had no idea why it was there – that almost never happened between Mazen and me.

I waited for him to bring up whatever he wanted to talk to me about, and eventually he did.

"Marie, we just celebrated our first anniversary together, and I– …" he started, but it seemed like he was at a loss for words. "I think that we should …" He stopped again, huffing while rubbing the back of his head.

"What is it, Mazen?"

"I think we should seek medical help to …"

He didn't need to continue this time for me to understand what he was getting at. Mazen wanted a child.

Twenty-four

It was stupid. *I* was being stupid. I couldn't understand why I was feeling so hurt by the fact that Mazen wanted us to seek medical help. He was right, and he was being reasonable. It had been a year, after all.

Maybe it was because whenever I was depressed and worried about not getting pregnant, even with having regular unprotected sex, Mazen had been the only one to assure me that I shouldn't be concerned.

He has always told me it was too soon to worry, always said that I was crazy for feeling sad every time I got my period. But that wasn't the case anymore. Mazen was now considering seeing a doctor about it, because *he* was concerned.

That fact made me hurt inside, because now it wasn't just worries anymore – it was *real*. Something could be wrong.

Back in London, before we got married, Mazen had

asked if I was on any birth control. Then he'd asked if I wanted to use any, once he'd learned I wasn't on anything. Back then, Mazen had wanted children, but only if I wanted them as well.

He had been thrilled when he found out that I wanted the same thing, and later on when I didn't get pregnant right away, he'd been the one to tell me there was nothing to worry about and to wait.

Now it was different, and I understood why. It wasn't about him wanting children anymore. It was about him *needing* them. One, at the very least. And it *had* to be a boy.

We were running out of time; we had less than two years left, otherwise he would lose his position as king. Not only that, but it would go to his uncle, and few years later – his cousin, Jasem.

Mazen had held my hand all the while we spoke. I was cool and collected the entire time, but I couldn't control my tears when he told me he'd had himself tested and everything was fine. That meant that something was wrong with *me*.

"Marie, it doesn't mean something is wrong with you – don't say that. We don't know anything yet," Mazen had said. "It could be that just a small pill is all we need. It could be just the stress because of the kingdom, the company and everything else. It could be that it's not the time God has chosen to bless us with a child just yet."

"But what if we weren't blessed for years? What if it more than just a small pill was needed?"

"Please, don't worry about it. We don't know what's wrong. We don't know if anything *is* wrong, in the first place," he had told me.

I disliked the fact that he'd never told me about the

sperm count test thing that he'd taken. It was something that concerned us both – he should've told me.

"I didn't want to bother you," was his excuse.

I didn't like his excuse any more than I didn't like the act itself. Still, I said nothing.

But it hurt.

That night, Mazen held me close, maybe even closer than on any other night. Sleep wouldn't consume me, concern did.

Mazen didn't tell me that he was worried, but I couldn't blame him. I didn't tell him of my worries, either. Not often, anyway.

But then again, many of his recent acts were now a bit clearer. I realized that maybe this was why he's been acting so strange lately. Maybe this was why he'd been upset. Maybe.

It didn't explain his rage that one night, though, when he'd started breaking things and wanted me to leave. It couldn't just be that he was concerned by the lack of a pregnancy. It wasn't like Mazen to act like that for just a concern.

My thoughts turned from there to doubting everything Mazen had done in the past few weeks. Thinking that maybe whenever he held me close, it was to keep me still after sex. Because I'd read somewhere that that helped a lot with conceiving.

Then I thought that maybe the times he'd fondled my breasts, he was actually examining them to see if I was ovulating, because I'd also read that breasts got bigger at that time.

I shrugged those thoughts away, trying my best not to let them disturb me to the point I believed they were real.

Mazen wouldn't do that. I refused to think that our intimate time was anything but that. I refused to think that he'd held me close for any reason other than wanting that – my closeness. Just like I adored his. I refused to think that his touch was anything but that – touching me, because he loved me and enjoyed me. Just like I enjoyed them – his touches.

I sighed, wondering what the future would hold for us. It was then that I felt Mazen's hand moving to touch my own as we spooned, tangling our fingers together and holding tight.

"I love you, Marie," he whispered, maybe knowing how much I needed to hear it. I always did. Always would.

"I love you, too, angel." I was glad that my voice didn't break as I said the words.

Rosanna could tell right away that something was wrong with me. We were sitting in my office, discussing some project that we'd started studying together right after I came back from the beach mansion, and it seemed like she had to repeat herself more than one time because I was distracted by my thoughts.

"Are you okay?" she asked.

"Huh? Yeah, I'm fine," I replied. "What were you saying about the cost, again?"

Rosanna's response was to close the folder we were looking at and put it aside. "Okay, what's going on? Did you fight with his majesty or something?" Her voice was whispered, despite the fact that we were sitting alone in my office.

She'd come to know me so well in the past year. She knew that only a fight with Mazen, or even a simple argument, could truly get to me. But that wasn't the case this time.

I shook my head 'No'.

"Is your grandmother okay? Was it because your brother was here again?" she asked. My grandmother had been fine the last time I saw her two weeks ago. And I really couldn't care less about Joseph being here. I only hoped that he'd come back – after he'd left right after paying his respects when our father-in-law died – to fix things with Janna. I learned that he'd stayed for mere hours, but I didn't know if Janna had allowed him to see little Marie yet. I hoped she had.

I shook my head again, not saying anything.

"Then what is it, Marie? You don't look so good."

"Thanks."

"I'm serious."

A sigh left my mouth. It would be the first time I'd spoken to Rosanna about my concerns about how we were having trouble conceiving. I didn't know how to begin, or if I should say anything at all, but to be honest – the idea of speaking about it to someone who wasn't Mazen sounded very appealing.

So I told her everything that I could think of about the subject. Starting from all of my hopes when my period was late after our first month of marriage, up until Mazen told me we needed to seek medical help.

At first, I was worried about talking to her about that, given her history with miscarriages and her own trouble getting pregnant. But the look in her eyes gave me all the assurance I needed. Rosanna was acting just like any best friend would – she listened, held my hand and gave me a shoulder to cry on. Not once did she give me a look that made me think I was being overly dramatic, compared to everything she'd gone through herself.

"I saw a gynecologist right after we decided we would seek help – she was wonderful."

"Dr. Hadeer?" Rosanna asked.

"No. Dr. Maya," I replied. It turned out that there was a whole center inside the palace for women's care – only for the first royal family members. I guessed that Rosanna had used it most of all, but I learned that my mother-in-law had had some problems after giving birth to Mazen that had required her to need its services, more than most women would, for a long time. Same thing for Fahd and Janna's mother, even before she gave birth to Prince Fahd. So there wasn't really any fuss about it when I visited; everything needed for the tests was already there.

"How did it go?"

"I don't really know, Rosanna. She didn't say anything was wrong, but she didn't say that things looked good either."

Some of the scans I'd had to go through were painful, but Mazen was there the whole time, holding my hand once and smoothing my hair the other time. He'd kept saying the sweetest words all the while we were there. I'd been worried, searching the doctor's face for any sign about anything, but I couldn't read anything on her face.

Now as I waited for the tests results to come back, I was worried sick.

"I mean, I have to wait – and worry – for a few more days before I know if there is anything that needs to be treated, and it's driving me insane. I can't think of anything else," I said, frustration evident in my voice. "And above all, things are very tense between Mazen and me. I can't even explain it."

"Yeah, I know how it feels," Rosanna said as she gazed somewhere over my shoulder.

That was what I'd feared the most when I started telling her about this whole thing – that I would stir up ugly or hurtful memories for her. I felt like I needed to apologize, but then again, I thought that addressing it by even apologizing could be rude, so I didn't say anything.

A few moments passed in silence before Rosanna decided to end it. "You know, Marie, whenever someone tells me of their problems, I make sure to never mention what I would've done if I were in their shoes. Because I know that I could never really know unless I was there.

"But this time, I can relate. I can relate very well. I could be in your shoes. I was. I *am*. So, I'm going to tell you what I've gained from it." She paused. "Let me cut straight to the point in just one word: Heartache."

I looked straight into her eyes, so she would know I was listening closely.

"When we first started seeing a doctor, I was just as anxious as you are about the results. And when they finally came in, I was a mess. My stress was affecting my treatment, and later on – I couldn't keep a baby inside of my stomach." Rosanna's voice broke a little, but she recovered quickly. I squeezed her hand that was already in mine.

"To this day, I keep wondering if I hadn't worried *too* much – would it be any different? Maybe I would've gotten pregnant earlier? And when I did – would I have gone through it safely? Because we never figured out why I was losing the baby every time, you know?

"I will never know the answers to that. And the guilt tried to eat me alive, consuming me every time I thought about it. But lately, I've learned not to let this all affect me." She smiled softly.

"I try to look at other people, ones who have been married for ten years and still are trying. Or those who were told they can never have a baby, no matter what. I try to see that I'm in a much better place than them, so I won't worry so much. I can just hope that God wills that I can carry a child, and someday I might go all the way with it."

"You will, Rosanna." I wished that my words held some reassurances in them.

"If God wills." She nodded with a smile, swallowing thickly. "But that's not all, Marie. Things got so bad with Fahd that I seriously started wondering if we were truly meant to be together until death do us apart, like I'd always thought."

"No!"

"Yes. Trust me, all of the stress and the thoughts of 'whose fault is it' could do that to any relationship," she said. "There was a time when I became obsessed with the thought of getting pregnant. I wouldn't allow him to touch me unless I was ovulating, no matter how much he begged me for it. It was such a hard time that now thinking back on it, I can't believe I actually did that.

"He was always moody, and I was always screaming. Sex became just a way for me to get what I wanted – it wasn't an act of love anymore. And I regret all of the days – months – that I spent away from my husband emotionally as the need to get pregnant possessed me.

"There were times I took pregnancy tests over ten times a day. I would take one in the morning and two an hour later, as if I might have got pregnant while he was at work!

"There were times I hated him for being okay, hated that nothing was wrong with him and I had to suffer alone, hated him for not taking a pill to fix something like I needed to. We went through Hell and back. Any act of kindness he showed me fell flat. It was only his fault in my head, somehow it was – or so I'd thought. It was like – if I wasn't married to him, or married at all, I wouldn't be going through all of this pain and stress. It was such a dark time.

"Back then, I couldn't understand that he was suffering with me, as well. Emotionally, if nothing else. Because he loved me, and because he wanted a baby, too. I could only thank God that I was blessed with an understanding husband who would've done anything for me to get me comfortable enough to actually live stress-free. But not all guys are the same, and I've seen marriages fail for the very same reason.

"Fahd took me away, on another honeymoon. It was there that I got pregnant for the first time. It was there when the hope started to rise. I know that there were times when it faded away, but Fahd was always there to restore it." Her smile was genuine this time.

"I'm glad to hear that. Prince Fahd is a great guy."

"He is the best," she agreed. "My point in all of this, Marie – don't let stress take away your chances of having a healthy pregnancy, or getting pregnant in the first place. That's the first step. And the most important thing – don't let worry force your love into fading away. Make this hard time into something to make your relationship even stronger – that's what will matter in the end. Because seriously, what would a child do for you when his parents have already lost each other in trying to make it?"

Of course, I knew that Rosanna knew better – she was

speaking from experience, after all. It sounded like she wanted only the best for me.

I couldn't remind her of the time frame we had, or speak to her about the fear of Mazen's uncle or his cousin taking over the title. It was her father and brother we were talking about, after all.

That was what I hated the most. We were best friends, we told each other everything, but there were things we couldn't talk about. Or maybe it was just me, to be honest. Maybe I chose to ignore those things, just to not make things awkward.

It was sad.

That night, I decided to surprise Mazen in his office, deciding I'd follow Rosanna's advice. I would live my life normally, make the best of it, love Mazen more and make our relationship even stronger. No matter what the results of the tests would be, we would get through it.

Or so I hoped …

My guards cleared the space for me from the other guards standing by Mazen's office. I met one of his private secretaries in the waiting area outside of his main office.

"Your majesty," he nodded his head.

"Hello, Yasser, how are you doing?" I smiled.

"I'm all right as long as you and his majesty are, your majesty, thank you."

"Is the king free?" I doubted it, but still asked.

"I'm afraid not, he's in a private meeting. But I'll tell him you're here."

"No, it's fine. Don't say anything. I'll just wait for him here until he's finished."

"As you please, your majesty. Can I get you anything?"

Politely, I passed on his offer and sat next to the main office's door with Brad by my side as I waited for his meeting to end.

Since work would never end, I decided to use the time replying to some e-mails. A few minutes later, Yasser had to go inside to do something, or maybe to tell Mazen some important news. The moment he spent opening the door and before he could close it behind him, I could hear the faint voice of Mazen as he spoke to whomever he was with.

"We have yet to get the reports, but what I saw on the monitor didn't look at all go–"

I frowned. What kind of conversation was that? I didn't give it much thought, deciding it was probably about the market or something like that. After all, the numbers had been crazy lately.

Yasser spent a few minutes in there, and then the door opened again as he let himself out. Once again I heard a strange line falling from Mazen's lips, but I knew then that it wasn't about scales or whatever. It was about me.

"I know it was my father's death wish, but I can't hurt my wife. I can't imagine what she would feel if she knew wh–"

The door was closed again, blocking me from hearing anything further of the conversation.

Stupid soundproof things!

I couldn't think of anything else as I sat there, while the meeting seemed to go on for days. I kept wondering what they could be talking about. And why my father-in-law's strange death wish had anything to do with me? Or why it would hurt me? I couldn't find the answers to the questions in my head.

Eventually, the meeting was over, and it turned out to be the Sheikh who'd first married us here in the kingdom. I'd learned that the word 'Sheikh' in Arabic referred to elders, or those who had great knowledge of Islam. Like 'Priest' in Christianity.

I wondered what could be going on that Mazen needed to seek religious advice about. I never got my answer.

For the rest of the day and the day that followed, my mind was completely wrapped around one thought: the death wish.

Asking Mazen about it was not an option; he had kept it away from me because he'd thought it would hurt me if I knew of it. So I didn't ask – he would find a way to get away from answering, anyway.

It was then that I remembered the looks on their faces when his father had spoken those words. Of course, it had something to do with me. How come I'd never thought of that before?

But the words he'd spoken were weird. They hadn't stuck in my mind because I didn't understand them, nor had I thought it was important for me to know, despite the fact that it'd seemed so hard for Mazen to agree to obey it.

Rosanna wouldn't tell me either. If it was indeed something that would hurt me – she wouldn't tell me.

Luckily – I guess – I had a session with my Arabic professor later that day. Her visits were now only twice a week instead of four, and we were mostly focusing on how to read letters and words. It was much more difficult than learning to speak, but I was determined to learn it.

When she was about to leave, I stopped her, "Professor Mallak?"

"Yes, your majesty?"

"I want you to tell me the meaning of something,"

"Of course, your majesty."

"I think it's slang for something, because literally it doesn't make any sense."

"I see, what is it?" she asked.

"(*Change your sheets*)" I told her.

"Oh. Well, may I ask who said it to whom?"

"Um, it was one man to another," was all I said.

She adjusted her glasses and then asked yet another question. "Is the other man married?"

"Yes." For some reason, my heart started beating fast, as if I already knew the answer.

"Well, then it means 'Take another wife', your majesty."

Twenty-five

Numbness spread all over my body. I couldn't feel my hands, couldn't feel my legs. All I could feel was my heartbeat, which seemed to be at war with itself, not merely speeding up in panic, but making my heart quake irritably inside of my ribs.

'Take another wife,' my father-in-law had said to my husband.

'I promise,' he had agreed.

I felt lightheaded, and I needed to sit down, I thought, a moment before realizing that I was already seated. I was looking at the armchair strangely, as if I were asking it where it had come from, when I heard the professor asking if I was okay.

"Huh? Oh, yes. Yes. I'm fine," I replied, not even able to form a polite smile.

"All right, I'll be going now. See you next week, your majesty."

I didn't know whether I nodded or not, or whether she left right away or maybe said something else. I didn't know how long it took Manar – my private secretary – to come back to my office and to be the second person in who-knew-how-long to ask me whether I was okay.

"Can I get you anything?" she asked when I told her that I was fine.

"No."

"Okay then. You have a meeting in thirty minutes with–"

"Cancel it."

"Pardon me, your majesty?"

"Cancel the meeting, cancel everything. I'm tired," I said as I stood up and left the office, Brad and the rest of my personal guards following right behind me.

Inside my wing, I didn't feel numb anymore, I felt empty. So empty. I was choking up, but no tears wanted to fall from my eyes. I was shaking inside, but my body was still and my steps were steady as I made my way to my bed.

I sat on the edge of the bed, took off the scarf that was lying loosely on top of my head, and threw it to the ground. My head was buried in my hands, a once familiar position that had lately become a stranger. It was something I did when I felt out of control, when I was about to have a panic attack. I'd been pleased to notice just days before that such episodes seemed to have stopped. I guess they weren't that far away, after all.

'Take another wife.'

'I promise.'

My breaths started to tangle, and I knew that very soon I would start losing control over them.

I knew that Mazen's religion allowed him to take more than one wife at a time, but I'd never once worried that he would. I thought our love was so special as to eliminate the need; I *knew* it was. I'd never thought Mazen would do that to me, I never thought he would ever force me to share him with another.

My hand touched my neck, as I started choking up more and more. My throat was closing up and my chest was heaving with my fast breaths.

The more I thought about it, the more it became clear what had been going on all of these past months. Since the anniversary of our first marriage, when Mazen was crashing glasses and seeing red.

That night he had visited his father, and of course something had happened there – that was why he was so mad. And later on when his father was dying about a month later – he'd told him it wasn't an order anymore, it was his dying wish.

'Take another wife.'

Mazen knew me well. He knew it was something I would never accept. It wasn't my religion, it wasn't my culture, it wasn't how I was raised. It wasn't how I thought humans were created to live. I was a woman who was in love with a man, and I would forever want us together. Alone. Sharing him was out of the question.

My husband had witnessed how I went crazy jealous on him when I saw a lipstick smudge on his clothes that I was sure wasn't my own. He'd seen me and known how I felt when I learned of his history with Talia.

Talia. Oh, dear God!

Of course, she would be the one to marry him; they'd been meant to be married all along. But I'd just happened to come between them and mess up all of the plans.

God, no!

I couldn't allow these thoughts to make me doubt Mazen's love for me. I knew he loved me. Mazen loved me like he'd never loved another soul that had ever lived on earth. He loved me with everything in him. And all of the rage he'd felt when his father had first ordered him to re-marry was because he knew it would kill me.

He didn't want to hurt me. I'd heard him saying it with his own tongue. It was what he'd said to the Sheikh – *'I can't hurt my wife.'* He said 'can't' not 'don't want to,' like he wasn't capable of doing it. And I already knew that so well.

It didn't get past me that his father had asked him to do that when supposedly a year had passed since we'd first gotten married, and we still didn't have a child or even a pregnancy. He needed his son to have an heir. It didn't take a genius to figure that out. It wasn't about him disliking me or anything like that, it was just that – for him – it was the right thing to do. We were running out of time, anyway.

I sensed what might have been my phone ringing beside me, but the pounding inside of my head was too loud for me to be sure whether it was the vibration of my phone, or just the sounds caused by the throbbing pain in my head.

My palms pressed tightly on my temples in an attempt to get the pain to ease a little, but it was in vain. I moved my hands to unbutton my suit jacket, then I took it off and fell back onto the bed with my legs still dangling from the side of it.

'Take another wife.'

'I promise.'

Mazen *never* broke his promises, and that alone intensified my panic attack and caused brimming tears to slide down my cheeks. How could he?

I knew that he could've said it just to please his father, but how could I be sure? I fixated on how Mazen always made a huge deal out of keeping his promises.

It was so hard for me to think straight, so hard to focus or come up with a complete thought, but I just couldn't let it go. How could I?

He hadn't mentioned it, he hadn't said anything

about. But he'd mentioned seeking medical help, and I knew that was his way to fix everything. Because of course, if I got pregnant – then it wouldn't be necessary for him to take another wife.

Right? I hoped so.

Through the time I'd spent here, I'd learned a lot about many things. Polygamy was one of them. That came by coincidence when a princess came to invite me to her own husband's wedding. Yes, she was still married to him.

She was all smiles as if she was the one who would be getting married. It was the strangest thing I'd ever seen. I'd thought she had a heart made of rock. No, I'd thought there was a real rock placed in her chest instead of a heart made of flesh and blood.

I'd had to ask her, how could you be so cold about it? It's your husband who's getting married.

She'd only smiled and told me that God had ordered her husband to be completely fair to both, that he couldn't give one of them something and not the other. She'd told me that she'd get the same amount of gold and a new house just like her husband's new wife, and he would be treating them both equally.

What I thought at the time was: Seriously? Gold and a new house? Of course I'd had to ask her whether she was jealous – she'd said not really, and seemed convinced. But I couldn't imagine that any woman who truly loved her husband could be okay with sharing him that way. This, despite her insistence that she loved him so much.

I couldn't understand it, but Mona had later told me that almost everyone in the whole kingdom had grown up with one, two or even three step-mothers. And that was just how the culture was. She'd explained that God only allowed it if there was a reason for it, and it would be a sin if a man took another wife just because.

The one major reason for the religion to allow that was if the wife couldn't provide a child.

I wasn't raised in the kingdom, and I believed that one woman belonged to one man, no more. I couldn't share him. They were okay with it and it'd become a natural thing for most of them, but not to me. It never would be.

The hope inside me kept me from breaking into a thousand pieces – hope of getting pregnant soon for all of this to go away. I knew Mazen didn't want to do it. He held me every night as if I he were afraid I would disappear, as if he knew exactly what my reaction would be.

But sadly, it wasn't just about me. It wasn't about us. It was about a whole nation.

Donia was absolutely freaked out when she found me passed out on the bed. She'd come to ask if I wished to have dinner now or would wait for Mazen. Needless to say, I couldn't find any desire to eat.

I was barely able to change my clothes, and I told Donia to tell Mazen that I was asleep when he called her to check on me, since I wasn't picking up my phone. He was worried when he learned that I'd left the office abruptly and canceled all of my meetings for the day.

When he came back later that night, I pretended to be asleep. I was curled into a ball, facing away from him, and covered my face with my arm. I didn't want to talk to him; I didn't want to talk at all.

There was a wound in my chest that I couldn't speak of or even know how to deal with. I needed to gather my thoughts before I had to speak about it. Mazen had taught me that—to think deeply before making decisions, even on the smallest of things.

Mazen placed a soft kiss on my bare shoulder before he went to sleep. The kiss alone burned where it landed, and I wished he hadn't put it there at all. It only hurt me to be reminded of how much he loved me. It took everything in me not to cry when he dropped his hand over my stomach and held me close to him as he slept.

In the morning, Mazen woke me up. I'd had a restless night and I was so tired, but the pain in my heart covered up any physical pain I was feeling, and I managed to sit up on the bed right after he started waking me up.

"Good morning, Princess," he said with the softest

of smiles on his face.

“Mornin’,” was all I said as I rubbed my eyes.

“Are you okay? I was so worried about you yesterday, but I didn’t want to wake you up to ask what was going on.”

“I’m fine,” I lied. “I was just a little tired last night.”

“Is it dizziness again?”

“Yeah, and I had a blackout.” That wasn’t a lie. I was having those at least once a day, but I never let them stop me from doing my duties or getting my job done.

“Maybe we should see another doctor. This has been going on for far too long.”

“I’m fine, I promise.” I offered him the best smile I could manage and then got up and went to the bathroom without saying anything more.

The numbness was back again. I took a shower in a haze and didn’t really think about anything as I blow dried my hair. It even took me a few moments to realize why Mazen was still there when I came out of the bathroom.

My gynecologist was supposed to visit us this morning with the reports from the scans I’d had and the results of the tests I’d taken. With everything that had happened yesterday, I’d completely forgotten about her visit.

Now that I remembered, I got even more anxious.

“Donia!” I called as soon as I came out of the

bathroom and my eyes landed on Mazen. I didn't want to leave a chance for us to talk, and the servants coming in to help me get ready for the day would be a great distraction.

I was sure that Mazen had figured out that I was ignoring him. He probably thought I was just nervous about what was to come. I didn't really want him to think otherwise, since I hated to upset him.

Dr. Maya was already in our living room when we entered it. The files that lay beside her felt like swords and guns sitting there, pointing at me and ready to get to the job of killing me. The moment's wait before the doctor started talking was already doing that, though. It was killing me slowly.

Please, let it be stress. Just stress, please, I prayed silently.

"Your majesties," she nodded in greeting with a small smile. Her smile alone had me wondering whether it had anything to do with the results, if it meant they were bad or good. I studied her expression as if it would give me answers sooner. Getting the answer a minute early felt like it would be the best thing that could happen to end my misery.

Polite greetings were exchanged, and then she started speaking. Is it so crazy to say that I barely understood a word of what she was saying? It wasn't like her accent was heavy or anything, or that she was saying a lot of alien medical words – it was understandable. But I just couldn't get it. I don't think I even heard it.

I spaced out while she spoke, right after she told us that I had problems that needed to be treated.

"Here are the reports your majesty asked to be done in London. It's the same results we have here," Dr. Maya said as she handed Mazen a pile of papers.

I glanced at Mazen as he gazed down at the papers, his blank mask set firmly on his face. A slight frown formed as he read something that of course was bad, but it was gone the same moment it was born.

The results were bad.

"I have brought you all of the medications you will need for the first course of treatment," she said as she pointed to the bag she'd put on the coffee table when she first came in. Boy, it was large. "Once we are finished with the first course, we'll start with the se–…"

"Wait," I interrupted her, probably speaking for the first time since the greetings. "How long will the first course take?"

"About three months, your majesty, and the second course the same."

"How many courses do you have in mind, exactly?" I asked.

"It's going to be three courses, and I'm sure we'll start to see real results then." She offered a small smile.

Nine months? I thought. *That's almost a year. And she says we'll start to* see *results.*

I swallowed thickly. "That's too long."

"I'm sorry, your majesty, but unfortunately, the process may take time."

My lips got sucked into my mouth and I pressed on them hard, trying to keep my face clear from any of the emotions I was feeling and not allow my tears to fall. "But – we don't have time,'' I whispered to myself.

I wasn't sure if Mazen had heard me or not, but the next thing he did was place the papers on the coffee table in front of us, next to the bag with the medications, and then he held my hand.

"It's going to be okay," he assured me in a whisper. "We have all of the time in the world."

We didn't. He *knew* we didn't.

"Can we– …" I tried, but my words came out a bit choked, so I swallowed thickly once more before speaking again. "How about in-vitro fertilization?"

I thought maybe it would give us quicker results, rather than waiting for the treatment to work, but by the look on Mazen's face when I asked, I knew it wasn't an option even before the doctor could say anything.

"You see, your majesty, the problem we're facing is that the lining of the uterus is very thin. It's even thinner than for women who take birth control pills. The lining would need to be much thicker than that for the implant to be possible. And if we tried IVF, I'm afraid it wouldn't give us good results."

I wouldn't bear the child, that was what she meant. Not even with that kind of help. She was just trying to sugar coat her words.

I nodded my understanding, a tight smile on my lips, my hand squeezing Mazen's in return as he tried to comfort me with his touch.

When the doctor left, Mazen hugged me long and warm. He whispered the sweetest of words in my ear, and tried to assure me with kindness that everything was going to be okay.

I was too upset for anything to help me through it. Not even his closeness could help me that time. Because all of the while he held me, I couldn't help but think of how I might not be able to have that again someday soon. I might lose him forever.

About an hour later, we were interrupted because Mazen had to leave. I was beyond upset that he had to leave for two days for a conference in Sweden, but at the same time – I was grateful. I honestly had nothing that I thought I could tell Mazen.

My head was filled with worries and concerns, along with so many other undesirable feelings. And almost everything I was thinking about were things that I couldn't discuss with Mazen.

So, I thought it may have been for the best that he had to leave.

He left after I managed my best to assure him that I was okay and would be fine. I had to promise him that I really didn't need him to stay, because he only needed one word from me and he would cancel everything. I didn't want that.

I sat there in the same spot for maybe hours after he left, taking out some of the medications and gazing at them. I couldn't find it in me to read the instructions the doctor had left, so I just dropped everything and sat there feeling miserable about myself and cursing my luck.

"Come in," I said after I heard the knock on the living room's door.

"Excuse me, your majesty," Donia said once she stepped inside. "Princess Rosanna's servant is asking if her highness could come over to visit with you."

Rosanna didn't visit with me much in my wing, but I'd always told her to just come in whenever she wanted to and not ask permission first. She never listened.

A few minutes passed before Rosanna came through the doors, asking why I'd canceled my meetings last night and had sent her some duties to handle today instead of me. She was worried about me and wanted to be sure I was okay.

She could tell that I wasn't, but before I could tell her anything about the doctor's visit, her eyes landed on the bottles sitting in front of me.

"Hey, who brought those in here?" she blurted out

in the middle of the conversation. “Wait, are those yours?”

The sadness in my eyes couldn’t be helped. I nodded.

“Oh, Marie. Did you hear from the doctor?”

I told her of my condition, though I wasn’t really sure why I did. But I was too freaking upset and felt as if I was on the verge of throwing up. I just wanted to tell somebody.

For some reason, Rosanna looked more nervous than upset while I spoke, and her expression made me understand it all.

If Rosanna was on the same medications I was on, that meant that she was most likely suffering from the same condition I had, or at least something similar to it. And that only confirmed my doubts that I wouldn’t get pregnant any time soon.

It could take years. And then – then if I actually got pregnant, I might have a hard time actually keeping the pregnancy. The doctor had said something like that herself.

I think I was able to hear the sound of my world crashing down, right then and there.

Twenty-six

Once, I read that loneliness is a feeling that the brain has defined in the same areas that feel physical pain. Oh, how true that was! Loneliness hurt. A lot. But being so lonely was something that I couldn't really complain about – it was my own choice.

Just a day after Mazen had left, my thoughts were killing me. I obsessed over things I imagined as well as things that had actually happened. I mulled over possibilities and all of the things I was expecting to happen. It was killing me.

The nights felt much longer when Mazen wasn't around to keep me company. Without him, there was no comfort, no warmth. And given everything that was going on – all of my surroundings seemed black. Darkness. Misery.

When I thought I couldn't handle it anymore, I thought maybe a visit to Rosanna would ease my pain a little. Maybe she could explain something that I couldn't understand, maybe she could promise me that my fears were pointless. I thought maybe she could tell me of a rule that prevented Mazen from killing me by taking another wife, like she had that time when we weren't speaking for three days. I thought maybe she could help me if I unloaded on her.

But when I learned that her sister was visiting at the same time I wanted to go see her, I finally remembered why the 'Talia' thing was one of the very few topics that I'd never discussed with Rosanna. It was her sister, after all. And I simply didn't have anything nice to say about her.

So, I decided to leave the palace, thinking that maybe changing my surroundings would help me to be able to sort out my thoughts. But the thought of going to the States wasn't very appealing to me. It had too many people I knew, and too many tasks I had to take care of. I wanted to be alone, in a place where I didn't have to split my attention.

London was where I landed, and inside the house we'd been married, I grieved. All by myself. I grieved for how fate was treating me. For how life had suddenly decided to torture me. I grieved for the fact that though I owned so much, I was being denied the only thing I really wanted – something that couldn't be bought with money.

Clarity wasn't what I'd aimed for when I came here. Clearing my mind seemed out of reach. I'd come here to make a decision. I was on my own in this; there was no one that I could think of who could give me advice on what to do or even how to think.

It was my life, after all.

Memories invaded my mind and possessed my senses once I set foot in the mansion. Memories of laughter and joy. Memories of smiles, of warm hugs and heated kisses. It was the house where I'd never experienced heartache or even one gloomy night.

I didn't expect to see Anita there; I was even more shocked when I learned that she'd hooked up with Philip and they were both living together in the cottage right beside the mansion, where Philip used to live alone.

I was happy for them, but I wasn't sure my face was able to show it. The sadness in my heart was too heavy for me to lighten my face up with even a tiny smile.

Food was not in my best interests at the time, and I guess Philip took the hint after many refusals from me for him to prepare me something, when I told him I'd let him know when I got hungry. I never did.

I spent long hours in our bedroom, staring at the ceiling sometimes, and out of the window other times. My thoughts were my only company, and what bad company they were!

They kept haunting me with everything I should

do, how I should end things and just go back to where I'd been, to *who* I'd been before Mazen happened.

But then, how could I go back to being the girl who'd judged things without knowledge, judged people before even speaking to them? How could I go back to the girl who'd lived without Mazen?

Life without Mazen was pretty much impossible in my eyes.

In the warm bathtub, my tears got mixed with the water I was soaking my body in. I was hoping for more relaxed muscles and a less foggy brain. But that didn't happen. I was very tense, and the dark images of Mazen with someone else were making my mind even busier than it already was, making my heart even heavier than it had ever been.

When I got out and put on something comfortable that wouldn't really help with any of my discomfort and heartache, I went to bed again. And just as I was hopping in, my eyes caught something that I'd already seen countless times before.

It was the wooden piece that Mazen had been crafting when I first met him here in this mansion. The same piece he'd worked on for days and days after that.

Back then, I'd only seen it as a design shaped like a water drop. I'd thought it was beautiful. But now that I looked deeply at it, I saw something entirely different.

The wooden piece was actually my name in Arabic, shaped into a tear, not a drop of water. My throat tightened as I held it in my hand and brought it closer to my heart. This was what he had been working on – even before I'd come back to him. I'd been in his thoughts, in his mind, just like he'd been in mine, despite the thousands of miles that had separated us.

It was just a reminder of how strong our love was, even at times when we hadn't really realized it or thought it could only get stronger from there.

It was a reminder of how it would break me to leave him again, and for good this time.

But how could I? He was my everything, my smiles and my sunshine. He made me see life in a brighter shade of cheerful colors and long rainbows that went on forever. He was the air I breathed and the reason why my heart beat normally. Without him, I would struggle with my breaths and my heart would simply break into pieces. He was my reason for living happily, and my reason for looking forward to living yet another day with him, every single day. He was my soul mate, my husband. He was my angel.

How could I leave?

It wasn't at all easy to make a decision. And I'd really never thought it would be. It would be a life-changing decision.

Hours passed with me lying in bed, gazing at the wooden piece that had his fingerprints all over it, that little piece that had his love for me written all over it. Just staring at it made it even harder to make up my mind.

My hand reached out to touch it as it lay beside me

on the bed, right where Mazen used to put his head. One of the images in my head was of him with a faceless woman. His hand was on her stomach as it was rounded with their child together, and the smile on his face was blinding. The image that my brain drew was like a stab that went straight to my heart.

A moment later, the faceless woman became a face that belonged to none other than his cousin: Talia.

"Oh, I intend to do just that, your majesty. For my dreams always come true."

Her words came rushing back into my mind, words that she'd said to me when I'd told her to "dream on" in response to the other awful words she'd said before that. Words that now made it seem as if this girl was able to see the future, like she'd known that Mazen was going to marry her one day, still.

"And you should be aware that when he needs an heir, it's my stomach that will bear his child, not yours. His seed will only get someone royal-born like me pregnant, not some commoner like you who only got the title four days ago."

I squeezed my eyes tightly shut, freeing more tears, gasping whispered breaths, freeing the pain that I felt in my heart, pain that filled my chest with sharp knives that were cutting at my insides with every other thought that repeated itself inside of my head, killing every last ray of hope that I still had.

It's not going to happen, Marie.

The back of my hand came to my mouth, blocking

the scream that I wanted to let go of – I didn't want to alert the guards. When I knew it was safe and the scream wasn't going to be heard – I let it drop to my stomach. But when I did, I squeezed my clothes that were covering it tightly, almost in anger.

My gasps grew and I started crying even louder cries that told of the agony which was filling me, and then… then I talked. I insanely spoke to it – to my stomach.

"Why?" I whispered my question with a voice full of hurt and desperation. "Why can't you hold a child inside of you? Why can't you hold *his* child? Why does it have to be her? Why will you let me watch my love's child growing inside of her and not inside of me? Why?"

I felt like I was not whole, not complete, like a badly manufactured human being, a broken machine that couldn't even do the simplest task all women in the world are supposed to do. Because men are supposed to seed a baby and women are supposed to carry it and give birth to a child. Why couldn't I be a normal woman?

Sleep finally took over me. It was filled with nightmares, where the images I'd imagined earlier become more real, more live and more hurtful.

Like any other time, I slept restlessly away from Mazen and away from the comfort of his arms. Add to that the awful nightmares and I could call it one of the worst nights of my life.

Sometime during the night, God put some mercy on me and I finally went into a deep sleep. My night became much calmer, as if Mazen was right there beside me.

In the morning, I was awakened by the sound of the birds singing outside. They made the most beautiful melody, and I hated that I was too depressed to actually be able to enjoy it.

Once I opened my eyes, the answer why my night had suddenly become all better so that I could actually sleep, made itself known. Mazen was lying right beside me on the bed with his hand holding my own.

At first, I thought I was imagining it – it couldn't be that he was there. And with a quick bit of math in my still-fogged head, I realized that he should've been in the kingdom by now, not here in London. Meaning he'd come straight here from Sweden and hadn't gone to the kingdom at all.

The slightest move of my head woke him up, and I was greeted by the best sight in the whole world – his eyes as they gazed back into mine.

"Hey," he whispered sleepily, a soft smile formed on his lips.

"What are you doing here?" I asked the first thing that came to my mind.

"Good morning to you, too."

"Seriously, what are you doing here?"

Mazen adjusted his head on the pillow to take a better look at my face; he looked tired but still as handsome as ever. My hands and lips yearned to touch him. I had no idea how I would ever be able to leave him, or live without him.

"The love of my life is not feeling okay. I had to be with her. That's what I'm doing here," he replied.

My chest swelled, and my eyes lowered to our joined hands that were resting between us. "I'm fine. Who said I wasn't okay?" I asked, not really looking for an answer – and not able to look into his eyes as I lied to him.

Mazen held my hand tighter and brought it up to his chest, right above his heart. "This told me, Princess."

With a heavy heart, I took my hand away from his and then got up and out of bed, leaving him there without saying another word.

My feet took me to the bathroom; I just wanted to be in another place where he wasn't. I couldn't face him, and somehow I was also delaying the talk I knew we would be having soon. It would be our last talk.

The thought had me sobbing. Inside my heart there was a war, and inside my head – my thoughts battled against each other. Thinking about what I should do, and what I truly wanted to do, was driving me insane.

After God only knows how long, I came out of the bathroom, seeing that Mazen had changed into something else and his hair was damp. *He must've used one of the other bathrooms to shower,* I realized.

The smell of coffee hit my nose, and I looked at the

side table in the corner to see that coffee and tea had been placed on it, along with a few other plates of croissants and pancakes.

Wrong, I thought. *We eat pancakes at night – that is our thing.* And then I figured, *maybe not anymore.*

Inside the walk-in closet, Mazen stood there as I picked something up from the shelves. Clothes that I'd never gotten the chance to wear before rested there. I wondered what life would've been like if we'd never had to go back to the kingdom, if we'd just stayed here in London where Mazen could've finished his training and I could've managed the London branch. I wondered what things would be like if we'd just stayed here and – loved.

Utterly easy, were the simplest words that I could think of. There would've never been heartache, only love and care and joy and happily ever after.

Mazen was leaning against the side wall, thinking that he'd be there to watch me dress. I knew what he was doing; he wanted to be playful. He wanted to make me smile and he wanted me to laugh. He thought he could take all the pain away if he tried a little bit harder.

I knew this because I knew Mazen so well, but I also knew that he couldn't help me this time. He couldn't help us. What we were dealing with wasn't going to disappear if I smiled, despite whatever Mazen was thinking.

So, I made him leave. He didn't argue much, he knew that I wasn't having it.

A sip of my coffee was tasteless on my tongue, so I refrained from having more. My stomach wouldn't bear it anyway. I kept feeling the urge to throw up over and over again as I stood there trying to think of how to start this.

"Did you see what happened yesterday at the conference?" Mazen asked, trying to make small talk, I guessed. I felt awful. He never wanted to talk about work when we were together unless it was a planned meeting that required us to discuss it together, as the rulers of the kingdom stated. But I guess I'd given him no choice.

I shook my head, not looking at him. Yesterday I was dying. And I knew that by the end of this conversation I would pretty much be dead. On the inside if not the outside.

"There was this man who asked me– …" he started, but a lone tear that was released from my eye stopped him, and he came rushing toward me. "Hey." He took me in his arms and hugged me tightly. It hurt. But only because I needed it so much and I knew that soon, I might never get the chance to do it ever again.

"I know you're sad because of what the doctor said, and I want to fix it. I'll do anything to make you smile again. But please allow me, let me in," he said softly. "What did we say about communication, Marie? I thought we were past this. Don't hold back from me. Talk to me, Princess."

The gentleness in his voice was softer than silk,

and warmer than the sun. But it only made what I was about to do harder, and for a moment, I wished he was bad or mean to me. It would've made everything easier.

I shrugged myself away from his arms, the act actually paining me, but I had to do it. "Listen to you, talking about the lack of communication and holding back. Can you tell me what have you been doing for the past three months other than that?"

Mazen's eyes lowered; he knew he'd done exactly that for the past few months. Although I understood why, I still wished he had told me earlier. Not that it would've made me change my mind, though.

"You're right," he sighed. "I'm sorry, Marie. But I've had a lot on my mind, and I didn't want to bother you with it."

"Bother me with it? Bother me? You think it's not something I should be concerned about?" I asked. Mazen looked at me closely, and I knew very well that he was trying to make out whether I knew what I was talking about or not – but not actually believing that I could've figured it out already. "When were you going to let me know? Were you going to send me your wedding invitation or wait until you had to disappear for seven days to *'get to know her'* like the rules say?"

Mazen's eyes widened and I felt sick to my stomach as I said the words. Just thinking about the possibility that I might be involved in all of this because of some sick tradition that I had yet to learn about made my heart hurt. Who knew? Maybe it was the first wife who had to cook for them for the first seven days, like his mother had done for us back then. Who knew what messed up things I would be forced to do for my husband's new wife.

"Marie …"

"There's nothing to say, Mazen. I've thought about it a lot. You have to have an heir very soon to keep your position as king. I can't provide you with that. I can't give that to you. And your religion allows you to marry another, so … I really understand. You have to do it. It was your father's death wish, after all."

"Marie, what are you saying?"

"I'm saying the right thing. You're free to take another wife. I'm just not going to stick around to watch it happen." I wiped my tears, only for more to come out a moment later.

"What?"

"You heard me. And no hard feelings, really. I know it's out of your hands," I said, my words heavy on my tongue and the whole world spinning around me. "But I'm not going to share you with another woman. I'm leaving you, Mazen."

Twenty-seven

It wasn't selfishness that had made me decide to leave, it was the fact that I knew things would only get worse if I stayed. For Mazen, for me and for the whole kingdom.

It gutted me. It tore my heart into pieces, but I had to do it.

I heard him as he inhaled a sharp breath, then he took a few moments to let what I'd just said sink in before replying. His eyes never left mine as we stood there in a tense silence after I dropped the bomb that probably hurt me more than anything else ever could.

"No hard feelings and you're leaving me? That's what you have to say, Marie?"

"What else do you expect me to say? Can you bear the thought of me with another man, Mazen?" I asked, fully aware of what the answer to that would be.

The thought of him touching her, being with her … the thought of him creating other memories with her that might would be similar to ours – it was tearing at my chest like a wild monster.

I couldn't take it. I couldn't. It was too much for my heart to handle. I'd rather him cheat on me. Can you imagine that? If he cheated – we could call it a mistake and eventually get past it, maybe. But marriage? For her to have rights to him, just like I do? For her to be treated equally and loved just the same by him?

I didn't know what would be left for me if we went through that. I didn't know what would be left *of* me if we did. I'd die slowly like an abandoned flower. He was my sunshine, and flowers can't grow without that. They'd die. Just like I would be dead from the inside if I stayed to watch him marry another.

Mazen swallowed thickly. The thought of seeing me with another pained his heart; I could see it in his eyes. "No. I wouldn't. I would kill him with my bare hands before he could touch you," he said, and I knew he was dead serious.

"Exactly. So now you know how I feel."

"You promised to never leave me again," he breathed out.

"And you promised to never let me go. But marrying another woman is not actually holding me close," I cried.

"So, you're just going to leave and make room for

me to marry another? It's that simple? You're telling me I'm not worth fighting for, Marie?"

"You're worth dying for, Mazen," I said without missing a beat. "But I'm not a doormat. I won't stand by and watch you marry another. I won't sit alone night after night knowing that you're in bed with her in the next room. I won't stand aside and watch your child growing inside of her. I won't."

Pain was written all over my face as I spoke, and the look on Mazen's face pretty much matched my own. Of course I was willing to fight for him. I'd fight for him until my last breath. But – this? … there was simply nothing else that we could do. I had to protect what was left of my dignity, what was left of my broken heart.

It was killing me to watch as we both stood there, our hearts withering in pain that only the two of us could feel. We were tied to each other with strong locks. White locks. A white lock of marriage, and a white lock of love. One was hard to break, and the other was impossible to even think of untying. Our white locks were stronger than steel, but this whole thing was out of our hands.

"And you wonder why I didn't tell you this from the beginning? I knew *exactly* how you were going to react to this," he said with a hurt voice.

"I've never doubted your love. I know you love me more than anyone ever has. And, God! I love you now more than ever and I'll love you until my last breath. I know you don't have a hand in it. But I'm doing the only right thing I could think of."

"Maybe you didn't think well enough, then."

My frown deepened – what did he mean by that? A small feather of hope touched my heart. Was it possible that there was something else I hadn't thought of? Another solution to this messed-up situation? No, there couldn't be. I doubted it.

"Mazen, I know you sought religious advice. I know you can't get out of doing it."

Mazen shook his head. "Do you really know? I asked for religious advice to learn how I could pay up for not obeying my father's death wish, Marie. That was what I was doing."

I blinked twice.

"What?"

"Even before I got my answer, I wasn't going to do it, anyway. But guess what? The Sheikh told me that I wasn't obliged to obey in the first place, therefore I didn't have to do anything to pay up for it."

"What do you mean?" My heartbeats were going a mile a minute, and I held my breath waiting for his answer.

"The Sheikh reminded me that we should never obey something which would mean committing a sin. If I followed my father's wish – I'd be a sinner. Because it would be building another house by destroying the first one, and you know how sacred and valued marriage is in Islam, Marie."

I couldn't believe my ears. Mazen had already decided he wasn't going to do it? How come? I'd never been more confused.

"You promised your father."

"Some promises are made just to be broken, Princess."

"But – I can't … I have problems and my treatment will take a long time. It'll be almost impossible for us to have a son before the two years are over."

"There's nothing that's far from God. If he wills for us to have a son soon, there's no human in the whole world who can stop it." He sounded very confident in what he was saying, and though I believed every word that he was saying – I still couldn't understand.

"But – but what if it doesn't happen?"

"Then it was never meant to be."

"Mazen, do you know what that even means?"

Mazen sighed. "I know."

I was taken aback by what he was saying. "You'd give up your title?"

"For you? I'd give up my own life. I'll forever do whatever it takes for you to stay by my side, Marie. Don't tell me you don't know that already."

"But, Mazen – that's … that's huge!" My hand came up to touch my forehead. My world was already spinning, but my head was spinning in the opposite direction. I did know that his love for me was unconditional, but to the point that he'd give up ruling a whole nation just to be with me? I was so overwhelmed by that that I was left completely speechless.

"I know that, Princess." He walked toward me and didn't stop until he was standing right in front of me. "What do you think I've been thinking about all this time? It's a big deal, but I'm selfish enough to take this road. I can't stand a life without you. It's as simple as that."

His hand touched my cheek softly, and I leaned into it, seeking comfort and desperate for the ease only he could provide me. He was seriously giving up everything for me?

No!

I snapped out of my dazzled mind that had been possessed by the idea that Mazen's love for me could reach the moon and the stars, and took a step back abruptly.

"No, Mazen. I can't let you do this. This is not just about us; this is about millions of people, a whole kingdom. I can't allow your uncle to rule then for Jasem to take over a few years later. I care for those people. I won't let him turn this kingdom into some nasty forest where women and children have to suffer the most. I can't."

"Do you think I've never thought about that? I've thought about it a lot," he said. "But you're expecting the worst to happen. We still have time. Long or short, we still have it. Many things could happen. Have you forgotten about my brother? He could have an heir soon, and then we wouldn't have to worry about that. The kingdom would be even better in his hands – even better than in my own hands, believe it or not."

The fact that Prince Fahd was still in the picture had been truly lost on me. But Rosanna had her own difficulties as well. I had no idea what her views were on her husband taking another wife, but I knew it was something I wouldn't wish on my enemy.

"What if–…"

"Stop with that, Princess," Mazen cut me off. "Stop imagining and expecting only the bad things to happen. God is the most merciful, he has a plan for everything. Whomever he chooses, he'll be the king next. Consider how I could choke and die this very moment – you'll have nothing to do then. And if the title goes to Jasem eventually, then so it be. Put your faith in God. He knows best."

Moments passed as I stood there, trying to comprehend everything he was saying. "I can't believe you're doing all of this for me." A new round of tears made an appearance in my eyes as I looked at him with longing and adoration.

"Not only for you, Princess." He shook his head then touched my face again. "I've told you before, I'm so in love with you – the thought of just touching another woman makes me sick. I'm saving myself from a wretched life where you're not right next to me."

My hand covered his as I looked deeply into his eyes, seeing the sweetest frown on his face. "I'm scared for our people." It was how I truly felt.

A soft smile played on Mazen's lips. "We'll figure it out, Marie. We'll figure it out. As long as we're together – everything is going to be okay."

I nodded, knowing that my anxiety had been holding me back from living day by day. I've always worried about the future, but now it wasn't just my own. As their queen, I wanted to do what was best for them, even if it meant me leaving the love of my life.

My lips touched his, and an apology was silently made. I knew he understood why I'd come to that decision and how I was looking at the bigger picture. But I was glad he could make me see things differently, in another way where my insecurity and anxiety weren't preventing me from seeing it.

"Now, what did we say about communication?" He was playful again, and it seemed like all he wanted was to see me smile. I chuckled, my mind not able to comprehend the strength this man had, the wisdom and loyalty. I just knew that I couldn't love him more in that moment, as my eyes looked at him with admiration and awe.

"I love you more than I can express with words. And I know that a life without you would be a living Hell," I said. "I'm sorry for being this way; I'm messed up in the head."

Mazen shook his head. "I love you just the way you are." His smile was heartwarming and soul-soothing. I wanted to hug him and never let go.

My heartache was easing with every passing second I spent in Mazen's arms. But my mind couldn't rest, and my thoughts didn't settle down or leave. Not all of them, anyway.

I was overwhelmed to learn yet again how strong our love was. How it could break all laws and cross all lines. That day was the last proof I'd needed to know that our love was unbreakable, untouchable.

That day I didn't worry about something that could break our bond someday. I knew that whatever stepped in our way, we would eventually get past it. But I was still anxious and worried about the kingdom's future.

Mazen was right, I'd been expecting the worst. But I was sure that my mind wouldn't stop working until I knew that the kingdom would be safe – even if it wasn't Mazen and I who were ruling it. But that was just me.

We came to believe that I probably wouldn't get pregnant before one full year of treatment, give or take. And our first child could be a girl, not a boy. We knew that, and Mazen helped me to accept it.

But my only fear was what if Prince Fahd didn't have a son by that time either? Jasem would eventually become the king. And that was my worst fear.

Mazen was very calm about it. I guess it was due to the months he'd spent thinking about all of the possibilities and trying to figure it out without me even knowing what was going on.

I still wished he had spoken to me about it, but I understood why he hadn't wanted me to know. He'd been trying to keep me away from all of the gut-wrenching and terrible thoughts I'd had before we figured it out together. He was protecting my heart.

But being me – I knew I wouldn't ever stop thinking about it until I found a solution where I could be completely positive that the kingdom would be in capable hands if we happened to let go of our titles.

I knew that I wouldn't stop thinking about it until I found a way to get rid of Jasem. For good.

Twenty-eight

When I was little, things had been simpler. Much simpler. There was trust and purity. Things were easy and clear. But I guess that's what we've learned over the years: that trust should be earned, and that our acts must be careful.

Life was never simple for grown-ups. In school, you learn your lessons and then take tests. But in life, you go through tests so you can learn your lessons. But life lessons were always more memorable than those you had at school.

I had vivid memories of my grandfather carrying me on his shoulders when I was barely six years old. Just the mere thought of him dropping me had never crossed my mind once. I trusted him, and I had faith that no matter what, everything would be okay.

One time Mazen wanted to do the same– to carry me on his shoulders when we were on our honeymoon, just a couple of lovebirds lost in the chaos of noises and people, without guards and cameras following each of our steps.

I never let him do it.

My trust for Mazen was unlimited; he'd earned it long ago, way before we got married. But in my mind – I couldn't trust my surroundings, the circumstances … I couldn't trust what the future held for me.

In my head, I saw myself falling off of Mazen's shoulders, him losing his balance, or even an earthquake that would knock us both to the floor. In my head, I injured myself badly, and just thinking about it made my breath hitch.

That was how my brain worked; I was forever anxious about what the future held. Mazen had tried hard to get me to think differently. It worked sometimes, but not always.

Mazen was a firm believer in living the day as it was present. He told me that dwelling over the past lead to depression, and fearing the future lead to unending anxiety. To him, there was only now. He was right, but I really couldn't help the way my mind worked things.

That was exactly the case with Jasem. I couldn't get him out of my head—couldn't stop thinking about what a future with him in the throne would mean.

I knew it was too early to think about it. I knew it was wrong to expect the worst, but I needed some peace of mind, and I was absolutely certain that I wouldn't get that until I was sure Jasem wouldn't be king one day. Not in two years, not ever.

So, I lay there in Mazen's arms in the bed where we'd made love for the first time, enjoying that one day break we'd stolen away for ourselves unexpectedly before we had to go back to the kingdom in a few hours. But my thoughts were far, far away.

My thoughts revolved around a certain awful man, and all of the things I would do to get him out of the picture, to get rid of him. But I didn't want to be unfair, so I had to find something that was legit. I couldn't just kick him out of the kingdom, though I very much could with just a mere order.

Mazen's uncle – Jasem and Talia's father – was younger than my father-in-law, and he was healthy enough to rule for years to come if – God forbid – things came to it. But even that man I couldn't trust.

How could I trust someone who'd abandoned his own child – Rosanna – and left her to be raised away from the warmth of a loving father, not to abandon the whole kingdom itself?

And for his wife – the same one Rosanna had called a snake – to be the queen? Oh, dear lord. There was no way I could let that happen. That whole family was dangerous for the kingdom, and I needed them all out of the way. Or at least, I could try.

My train of thought led me to think of something that somehow had escaped my brain, and I sat up to ask

Mazen about it.

"Hey, does Jasem even have an heir? I don't think so – that would solve everything." I asked my question, following it with the answer I thought was right. That made Mazen chuckle softly.

He moved a lock of hair out of my face. "You won't drop it until you come up with something, will you?"

I pursed my lips, then shook my head; he already knew the answer to that.

"Figured." He smiled, though he looked drained. Given everything that had happened this morning, I didn't blame him for looking exhausted. I was pretty much the same, but the wheels in my head didn't know anything about taking a rest.

"So, why have we never thought about this before?"

"About what? Him having an heir?"

I nodded.

"He has twin boys and a girl, Princess."

"What?" I frowned. "You're serious?"

Mazen nodded, his thumb touching my jawline softly.

"Darn it," I said, disappointed. "I had hopes. I guess he's bi, then."

"He's what?" Mazen laughed lightly.

"Bisexual. I thought he was gay, but that wouldn't explain the kids, so…"

Mazen's thumb over my jaw stopped moving, and

he stared into my eyes for a long time. "Marie, what are you saying? Why would you think that?"

"Uh-oh! You didn't know? He's not out of the closet yet?"

"What the hell are you even talking about?" Mazen looked completely confused.

"Mazen, Jasem is gay, or so I thought. But given he has kids – it means he's bisexual, or it's all just a cover or something, I guess," I explained.

"He's not gay, that's impossible. Why would you say that?" he asked as he sat up on the bed, looking at me with disbelief.

I rolled my eyes, then got up. I didn't know why he wasn't believing me on this – I was 99% sure of what I was saying. My legs took me to the closet and I picked up the newest shoes I could find, then came back to stand in front of him.

Mazen looked even more confused as he stared at me while I held the shoes up for him to see. "Can you tell me what these are?"

"What?"

I shook the heels in front of him. "These."

"Um… Black shoes?" he answered.

"Exactly what I mean. These are Grace sandals, 2016. If I asked Jasem the same question, he'd tell me just that. No straight guy can tell the difference between women's footwear!"

"Why would you think Jasem would know that?"

"Because that's exactly what he did that awful day

when I met him. His words were, *'I'm only interested in knowing what you are doing here with those last year's Jimmy Choos of yours,'*" I told him. "He knew exactly what kind I was wearing, and which year they were made. He only spoke to me in English after gazing down at my feet. Those were same shoes I'd worn in the wedding only four days earlier; that's how he knew it was me, not Janna. Trust me, Mazen, straight guys don't think that way or even care about those things."

Mazen gaped at me for a few long moments before he swallowed. "Wow!" was all he said before pausing again, letting everything settle in. "Why did you never tell me about that before?"

I shrugged my shoulders, dropping the sandals to the floor. "I didn't think it was such a big deal."

"Dear God!" Mazen moved both of his hands through his hair. "He *is* gay!" he said, more likely to himself than to me, seeming to have thought it through or remembered something I didn't know about Jasem that made him sure I was right with my guess.

A sigh left my mouth. "But he has an heir, so I guess it doesn't change a thing." I shook my head in disappointment, my mind all ready to start thinking about another way to get rid of Jasem. But Mazen didn't give me the chance.

"This changes everything." He got out of bed and reached for his phone, calling a number he had on Speed Dial, and after a moment he started talking. *"Prince Jasem Alfaidy's second guard, I need him in a meeting room as soon as I'm back at the palace ... No, his second guard, not the first. Yes. Good."* And then he hung up.

"Mazen, what's going on?" I asked because I was confused. Why was Mazen calling to arrange a meeting with Jasem's second guard? The second, not the first, he'd said. And as soon as we got to the palace? I couldn't understand.

"I've told you before, Princess. Royalty is a dirty game. I'm just about to play it."

All the way back home, I couldn't figure out why Mazen wanted to meet with that guard or why he'd said he was going to get his hands dirty. But later on, Mazen explained everything to me.

I was beyond shocked to learn that homosexuality was illegal in the kingdom; not only that – it actually was punishable with jail time. It was unbelievable. I mean, that was ancient. Hadn't the world already gotten over that? Long ago? Apparently not. I found out that it was the same thing in all Arab countries, and some other Western countries as well.

I had my own view on the topic, but it was nothing of importance. I'd just never really thought about it. My frame of mind was stuck on what I'd seen growing up in America – how people had fought for their right to love anyone, and how they'd eventually gotten that. I simply didn't think about whether or not it was the same or different in other countries.

This thing made me realize what Mazen had actually done with that royal guard who'd failed to protect me – when I was going to escape the palace. I'd thought he was humiliating him by dressing him like a woman, but the thing was – he was humiliating him by making him do something as gay as dressing in women's clothes. Because in the kingdom, that was the most humiliating thing you could do to a man, let alone a royal guard – to have people question their sexuality or masculinity.

I think it was all the same all over the world, though. Straight guys took offence to being called gay.

Mazen was determined to prove that Jasem was gay first, before accusing him of it based only on what I thought. And once he could prove that, Jasem would be judged as unfit to rule. And that was all we'd ever wanted.

It turned out that Jasem had had a first guard for over ten years. Mazen had always wondered why Jasem would hire him for such a sensitive job that required strength and power, when apparently he had a small, skinny body – which was not recommended when choosing a guard whose job was to protect your life.

Mazen said that if it turned out that my suspicions were true, then it would explain why Jasem had kept that man as his first guard when much stronger guards were available for the position.

When we landed, Mazen went straight to his main office, not bothering to take a one-minute break after the long trip.

The meeting took hours, but when Mazen came back to our wing, I knew he'd realized that I was right. The guard had admitted seeing the first guard spend many nights inside Jasem's bedroom. It appeared to anyone with a brain that there was much more going on between them than just a guard and the one he was working for.

Mazen told me that the guard had been too scared to out Jasem directly. Mazen had had to pressure him and use his powers over him as his king to make him speak. *It wasn't easy,* he said.

"What are we going to do now?" I asked Mazen.

"Well, at least now we know a way to get him away from the throne," Mazen grinned, seeming to be enjoying this more than I'd thought he would. Of course, I understood why the happy face was there; we were getting Jasem out of the picture, and it meant a better life for – well, everyone, since he'd be in jail. "He's already coming for a meeting next week. I'll take care of everything then."

"Next week? That's too long!"

"Why the hurry, are you expecting the worst again?"

"Mazen, he's still ruling a princedom as we speak. This is not only about the kingdom; he needs to stop ruling all together. Right now."

Mazen looked at me for a second. "So eager to get rid of him, eh?" he smiled.

"Do you blame me? Mazen, I *do* care for our people. I want to have peace of mind knowing that they won't be ruled by someone who's been stealing their money, even though he doesn't really need it in the first place!"

I was already working with Rosanna on funding a school and a hospital in that princedom. All expenses would be on me, from my own money. I wanted them to have free education and free healthcare. Anything that would make life better for them, giving them something that he couldn't steal. And I knew that once the projects started working, I'd be the happiest woman on earth. But that wasn't enough. I wanted more. For Jasem to drop everything and be put behind bars where he belonged.

Mazen took me in his arms, hugging me with no words said. Moments passed before he spoke into my hair. "All right, Princess. I'll request to see him in the morning."

"I want to be there."

It wasn't like I was seeking revenge when I wanted to see Jasem's face as Mazen told him how he would charge him himself and have judges work on finding him guilty. No, that wasn't the case.

It was only that I wanted to see it with my own eyes in order to believe that it had actually happened. That he'd no longer be in charge of anything related to ruling or controlling the kingdom or any part of it. I knew that then, I would feel the sweetest relief.

We were in one of the meetings rooms when Jasem stepped in. He knew better than to give me a look that I might not like. He kept his manners – if he had any – and greeted us with respect. I guessed that Mazen's fists had hurt him long enough for him to remember his lesson.

And then, then it happened. Mazen told him everything, and the look on his face was enough confirmation. Not like we'd needed that, anyway.

Of course he denied it, but Mazen reminded him of all of the ways the law could take to prove one guilty. Forensic science was one of them. And when he mentioned that, Jasem knew that there was no way out.

I took pleasure in telling him exactly how we'd found out about it. I loved that the stupid woman he'd thought I was had managed to get his ugly world crumbling down around his feet. And that earned me the most hateful look anyone had ever given me in my entire life. I couldn't care less.

"*It's all over, Jasem. Until the judge speaks, you won't be working on anything related to ruling Al-A'merya or managing it. Though, I'm sure it'll be permanent.*"

Jasem didn't speak for a long time, and I wondered

if he'd gone into some kind of shock and was no longer here with us. His head was probably somewhere else. But eventually he spoke; his voice was low and to a point – there was fright in it.

"*Your majesty, I'm begging your kindness not to let this get out. I swear I will leave the kingdom and will never set foot in it again. But please, don't expose me.*" He sounded like he was on the verge of crying.

True to Mazen's words, to be found guilty of homosexuality appeared to be the worst thing that you could ever be accused of. Jasem was willing to leave everything just for Mazen not to speak of it. He was giving up the power to save his reputation. It was something else.

"*I'm afraid that won't be the case, cousin. You're going down anyway.*"

"*What if– ... what if I know something you don't know? Something very important to you,*" he said, his eyes hopeful but terrified at the same time.

My confusion appeared between my eyebrows when I heard his words. What could it be that he knew and Mazen didn't? I didn't think it could be of any importance, anyway. It could be that he was just stalling.

"*You believe you know of something that I don't?*" Mazen made himself comfortable in his chair, looking all confident and unfazed. But since I could read him like an open book, I knew that he was considering whether Jasem had something to say, or was just playing games.

"*Yes, your majesty.*"

"*Let's hear it.*"

"*Not before you give me your word first, that you will never speak of– ... that matter.*" His eyes lowered to the floor before rising again, desperate to read something in Mazen's that would give him the answer even before Mazen could speak.

"*What if it's not as important as you claim?*"

"*It is. It's about your family.*" His eyes looked up at me for a mere second before moving to Mazen again.

Mazen sat up in the chair, now giving him his full attention. "*What is it?*"

"*Give me your word first,*" he insisted.

"*You have my word.*"

"*I–uh, I know why your wife can't conceive.*"

Twenty-nine

Mazen was much, much better than me at hiding his feelings. There was no way to even compare us both when it came to blank masks. I could still wear one, but not as well as he could.

When Jasem spoke that line, Mazen stayed in place, looking as calm as ever – you'd think Jasem had just told him that the sky was blue. But for me – it took me a moment to compose myself. In that moment, a gasp escaped my lips. "What?"

Because surely it didn't mean that he knew what the doctor had told us or about my condition. I knew right away that it was something entirely different. And the thought was frightening.

"Aha!" Mazen said. "Well, that's old news. We already know about that. However … I'll make sure to find out how you came to that knowledge and deal with it. Also, when you speak about my wife, you'll say 'her majesty'"

His voice was very calm as he spoke, and he looked cool and collected. Only the last two words held rage and anger, more than I'd ever heard from him. Not only that, he actually followed his words with a fist to the surface of the table in front of us.

Mazen was smart; he already knew that Jasem wasn't talking about a medical issue. But he still didn't want Jasem to get away without punishment. I understood that he was telling him it was old news just to get out of his promise to release Jasem if he had some great information to share, as he was doing now. And later, Mazen would investigate and find out what was going on.

Not only that – Mazen made it look like his anger was only due the fact that he hadn't addressed me by my title. But I knew very well that it was his way to let his anger out, without Jasem thinking that he'd gotten to him with what he'd just said.

Jasem flinched at his tone and at the sound of Mazen's fist as it met the table, and I took the time to inhale deeply before a blackout could consume me and I would end up on the floor. The questions and all the possibilities of what Jasem could be referring to were scaring the heck out of me, making my heart beat fast and my head spin.

"*My apologizes, your majesties,*" he said in a low

voice, swallowing thickly; he looked completely frightened. "*I really do know something that you don't know. And I promise you that you won't find out until I speak of it, or you hear it from* her – *and that's impossible.*"

Her? That simple word led to a hundred questions appearing in my head. What did he mean? Could it be that it was something like what I was already assuming? Who was she? Doctor Maya? The Mother Queen? Wait …!

"*Okay. Say what you know. And say it quickly. I don't have all day to spend with you!*"

"*It's – it's my sister, your majesty. She's been putting things in your– ... in her majesty's food ever since you got married to prevent her from getting pregnant.*"

In my whole short life of twenty-three years, I'd never heard silence that was this loud. Silence filled the room and lingered in the air. My eyes wouldn't leave Jasem's shaking form as he sat there with his head bent down while he looked at the floor. His eyes would rise to look at Mazen for a brief moment, only to look down again in the next one, probably searching his eyes for a reaction.

This was one of the very few times when Mazen let his guard down and couldn't control the look on his face. He was beyond shocked, completely taken by surprise. Of course, it was the last thing he'd ever think of.

I couldn't believe my ears, and it took me a moment to register what the heck Jasem had just said. His sister has been putting things in my food to prevent me from getting pregnant? How come? I could count on one hand the number of times I'd seen her in the palace. But everything else aside, she was poisoning me in that way so I wouldn't have a child? How could she?

I couldn't say that I felt betrayed. Betrayal comes only from those who you thought loved you, from people you loved back and knew they'd never hurt you. I felt something else – something beyond betrayal and far from unfaithfulness. I felt used, abused, and … misled.

This may have been the longest time Mazen had ever taken to speak after being spoken to. I understood that he was gathering his thoughts, trying to control his feelings. I knew he wanted to act like the king he was, not the deceived cousin and leader. He wanted to do the right thing, because he simply wasn't programmed to let his feelings show, not in a situation like this one.

"*Princess Rosanna would never do that*," was the first thing he said. And I was disappointed.

I was disappointed because although Mazen had taken his time before speaking, a part of him was still controlled by something else other than his mind. Mazen was not in full control of his feelings this time. I knew what he was thinking … and I didn't like it.

I'd known very well from the beginning that it wasn't Rosanna that Jasem was speaking of. I knew he was talking about his other sister – Talia. And I knew that Mazen had figured it out, but he didn't want to believe it.

The first time I'd seen Talia, I'd thought she was an angel who'd somehow managed to come to earth and live on it. Her looks, her voice … everything about her seemed angelic. It was only what she'd said to me that had made me think otherwise.

In Mazen's case, he didn't have a reason to think of her in any other way. As a matter of fact, he had every reason to think highly of her. After all, all he'd ever heard from her were words of respect and … *love*.

I was sure that she'd gotten to him, and gotten to him well. They'd thought they were going to get married up until I'd shown up. Their break-up was that they'd just stopped meeting. He didn't have a reason to hate her or even dislike her. Of course, he didn't want to believe it was her – or simply couldn't.

And it hurt.

I understood him. But it hurt.

Mazen loved me beyond words, but that love didn't mean he had to hate Talia. It also didn't mean that he loved her at all. He'd told me he never had. But he'd also said that he cared. And that 'care' part was causing all of the damage.

Mazen felt the betrayal.

"*It's not Rosanna, it's Talia,*" Jasem confirmed my thoughts, and with everything that was going on, I still couldn't stop looking at Mazen and study the look of disbelief in his eyes.

"Talia!" he breathed out her name in disbelief.

"She's been doing the same with Rosanna, as well. For years."

Dear God!

My hand came up to my cross and I held it tightly, seeking comfort that I knew would never come. Was it crazy for me to feel worse for Rosanna than I did for myself? It was just that all I could think was – how would she feel when she found out? It was her own sister! And I knew what the betrayal of a sibling felt like. This was even more than what Joseph had done to me. Much more.

Mazen spoke, "*Jasem, you're telling the truth, right now, aren't you? Because I swear to God if you're lying -...*"

"I'm telling the truth, your majesty. I'm telling you that I've known of it all along. And you know this means putting me in a deeper hole than the other matter would. But I'd still rather lose it all than to be exposed."

Mazen pressed hard on his lips, forming a thin line. "*Talia doesn't have any access to our wing or the main kitchen, so unless she was getting help from our servants, then there's no truth to your claims,*" he said through clenched teeth. A moment later, I heard him muttering in the lowest voice, "*I'll kill them with my bare hands, I swear I will.*" But something told me that he wasn't speaking of Talia when he said that.

"*She – um, she didn't have to put it directly into the food, your majesty.*"

My eyes closed and I swallowed back tears; I knew right away what he meant. I knew right away how she'd done it.

"*What?*" Mazen asked in confusion, and I was once again disappointed that he wasn't letting his mind work the way I knew it did. He was very much capable of figuring it all out. He was simply just refusing to.

"The water tank, your majesty." It took a lot of strength for me to speak; silence seemed a lot easier while I sat there listening to how a lowlife had managed so easily to put me through so much pain and disappointment. But Mazen had to hear it, and I knew it would sound more believable if I was the one to say it.

For the first time since Jasem had told us all of this, Mazen's eyes caught mine. They were blood red and rage-filled, very uncertain and disbelieving. It looked like I was staring into a completely different person, not the one I saw as the strongest man I'd ever known. The one in front of me was a man whose brain was almost paralyzed by the pain of betrayal.

Heck, I was more collected than him, and that never happened, and I mean – *never*. With all of my anxiety, phobias and mental problems, I was able to sit there and believe, even be sad and broken over what I was hearing. Mazen, on the other hand – he couldn't get to that stage just yet. He was still in the disbelieving phase.

"*That's right, your majesty,*" Jasem said, bringing Mazen's attention back to him. "*She was putting the drugs in the water. She had easy access to the water tank since you ... uh, that was how I'd found out about it all.*"

Apparently it was too much for Mazen; he was slowly losing all of his strength and power to look as composed as possible. He actually buried his head in his hands and didn't utter a word.

"*How did you find out, Prince Jasem?*" I asked, because it looked like Mazen had already left the room. I knew why. On top of betrayal, he was drowning in guilt. I knew it even before Jasem had to explain it. It was Mazen himself who'd given Talia the access to our water tank, the one that supplied water to the two wings on the second floor – mine and Rosanna's.

"*I, uh, I noticed her absence whenever we visited our sister and on whatever occasion brought us to the palace. One time I followed her and I, uh, I found her with ... um, ...*" He stopped talking. I knew what he'd found her doing and with whom. And I knew he wasn't sure if he should tell me that – not because he feared hurting my feelings. He just didn't know if Mazen would punish him for it.

"*Speak!*" I ordered.

"*She was with, uh, his majesty. And when I was about to punish her for it, she told me that she was doing it for our sakes. That Prince Mazen at the time had asked all of the guards to clear the area whenever they saw a princess up there, and to turn their backs until one of the two told them otherwise. And he'd never changed those orders after your marriages, so she kept doing it that way.*"

"*Do what?*" I asked, completely ignoring the feeling of hurt and the pang of jealousy at what Mazen had done before to secure one of their meeting places. Ignoring how I was too much of a fool not to put the fact that she was up there together with how the area was cleared of any royal guards and realize she was up to no good.

But how could I? How could I know that she was poisoning our water with God only knows what? And of course, she'd fooled Mazen as well by talking about '*pleasurable memories.*' She knew how it would affect me, and how it would affect him. She knew our minds wouldn't be thinking about why she was up there, or wondering if it was more than just roaming around.

She'd played us well. Played Mazen better. I couldn't blame him for looking as wretched as he was right now.

"*Put drugs in the water, so neither you nor Rosanna would get pregnant. So eventually the crown would go to our father, and then to me,*" he admitted.

A sneer drew itself on my lips. "*And you were fool enough to believe her? It was all for her to be the queen. Not for you to be the king! She didn't want her sister to get pregnant until* she *was married to the Crown Prince and had his heir. Then she would allow her sister to conceive. But then the Crown Prince married someone else and her plans ran into some difficulties – can't you see it? It was always about her. Not your father, and certainly not* you."

He was such an idiot, but so were all of us. A bunch of fools who'd been played by a little girl who had a master's degree in evil.

It was truly as if Jasem had just figured it all out, and I gave that girl kudos for her ability to convince others of her thoughts. She was able to convince me that she was an angel from first sight. But that had only changed because she was too bitter not to let her anger at me out, by saying awful words to make me burn with jealousy. God only knew how I would have felt about her if she hadn't said any of what she'd said to me.

I would've probably still thought well of her.

"*She was going to get rid of you, eventually, Prince Jasem,*" I told him as a matter of fact, and a second later, I spoke again, "*But I don't quite understand. Princess Rosanna got pregnant six times; if the drug was preventing her from conceiving, how come she was able to?*"

"*Um, it only happened when Rosanna was away from the kingdom, or Talia had to go back to Paris where she studies. But she always made sure to visit with her at some point and ...*"

"*What?*"

"*She mixed some pills with her medications sometimes, and other times she put them directly into her drink more than one time to cause her to miscarry the baby. She did it every time she got pregnant.*"

My hand flew to my mouth. This was beyond just giving us some sort of birth control – this was murdering innocent unborn children. My heart dropped to my feet at the sound of his words. My insides broke for my sister-in-law. I didn't think she could ever get over such a thing. It would tear her heart open. Her sister had murdered her unborn children.

"*It's the same thing she did with you when you first came back from London.*"

Thirty

All is fair in love and war. I couldn't count the number of times I'd heard those words throughout my life. It was too many, I'd say. I'd thought it was something sweet, because really, I'd never actually thought about it.

But given what I was hearing now, the words were haunting my mind.

Was it really all fair in love and war? I doubted it. Killing children in wars was never acceptable, never fair. So how come it was acceptable in love?

Was it even love? I was absolutely sure it wasn't. I'd had my doubts, but now – now I was certain.

Talia had never loved Mazen; she loved the title and the position only *he* could give her. She was dying to be a queen, and she'd done everything in her power, and even beyond that, to get what she wanted. She hadn't stopped at killing her sister's unborn children; she'd even killed mine and the man's she claimed to love.

How was that fair?

How was that even love?

It was war. Yes, war.

But still, not fair.

Well, I guess if you look at the word love as the feeling she had for herself. Because though I really didn't know her well, I knew that she had only ever loved herself. Someone that evil could never feel the warmth of love or the sweetness of passion.

She was a murderer. She'd killed my unborn child.

When Jasem said that she'd done the same thing to me, I knew right away what he was talking about. I knew what he was referring to. And suddenly, everything became clearer in my mind about days that I'd already forced myself to forget. Days that had been filled with hope that came crashing down the moment I saw the blood covering my panties – that first night when I became a queen.

Mazen, on the other hand – didn't.

His head snapped up to look at Jasem. *"What the Hell are you talking about now?"* he asked in an angry tone.

"I don't know, your majesty. I – uh, I wondered one day if her majesty had gotten pregnant in the time you two spent away from the kingdom, and Talia said

that she was and she'd taken care of it. That's all I know."

I felt sick to my stomach. She *'took care of it'*. How could they use such words to describe killing an innocent soul? How could she be so cold about it? What? Did they have a good laugh out of my pain and misery? Did she enjoy the death of a child I didn't even know I could have had?

It was all beyond my understanding.

Mazen's eyes turned to me, and a silent question was heard among the crashing of our hearts. And my answer was only a tear trailing down my face and a slight nod of my head.

I could almost see it in his eyes. I could see him trying to recall the events that had followed our arrival from London. I could see him remembering the agony I'd been in when I'd started bleeding, thinking that I had gotten my period. I could see him remembering how hurt I'd been, how depressed because of it I was. And then I saw as it all dawned on him. He realized that his unborn child had been killed that day. And my heart broke a little more seeing the misery that was showing on his face, matching how I was feeling in my chest. The pain of betrayal, and the agony of loss.

Jasem didn't need to say anything further; I doubted he had anything else to add. It was like, he'd wanted to say whatever awful things he knew just so that Mazen would keep his word toward him. It was like he'd thought that poisoning the water wasn't good enough news, he had to tell us about the abortion drugs, as well. Anything just to save his reputation.

My emotions were boiling inside of my chest as I sat there, doing my best to stay composed and not let them show.

Minutes passed before Mazen was able to stand up and call the guards to take Jasem away, announcing that he was accused by the king himself of High Treason against the first royal family members, and that he was handing it over to the High Court for investigation. He then announced the very same thing about Talia, ordering that she be arrested in less than an hour, alive or dead.

His voice held bitterness that I'd never ever heard coming out of my love's kind lips.

The second the doors to the meeting room closed and we were completely alone, I didn't wait for Mazen to speak, I did. "I didn't know that I was pregnant. Or at least, I wasn't sure." I was afraid he'd think I'd hidden it from him; I needed to tell him that I hadn't even known.

Mazen only nodded, understanding.

"I just – when I lost it, I thought that my period was late and that was all."

"Young women don't suddenly start to have irregular periods, Marie," he said in a low voice.

I felt so bad for not telling him. I thought that maybe if he'd known I was late, I would've taken the test earlier, learned that I was pregnant and been able to see the happiness in his eyes as we shared the news together.

"I wish I'd known," I choked up.

"Everything happens for a reason. We would've been so happy with the pregnancy, only for the happiness to be stolen from us a few days later," he said in the saddest voice. "Her evil hands were going to be in our business, anyway, and maybe the hurt would have been even greater."

He was right. The hurt would've been greater.

Ironically, when Jasem told us of the drugs that were put into the water, I'd been kind of relieved. Hurt, deceived … but relieved. Because I'd thought, *here's why I couldn't get pregnant, now I would.* But now knowing that there was a child that had never gotten the chance to be born – it was cutting my heart into pieces. I had no idea how Rosanna would ever be able to deal with that.

I was breaking inside, and I needed Mazen to hold me back together. I needed him closer, needed to touch him, hug him. Needed my safety and my comfort.

Without moving a step, he knew exactly what I needed, and he came rushing to me, standing right in front of me as I stood there, uncertain, lost and overwhelmed by everything that was happening, to the point I started to struggle with my thoughts and feelings.

Both of his hands touched my face, hugging it between them, his bloodshot eyes staring deep into my teary ones. "We're going to make it through this. Nothing will ever break us, Marie. Do you hear me?"

I nodded with the little space his hands left for me. Accepting. Believing. "I just want you to hold me, I want to be strong enough to get through this."

He shook his head. "Marie, I'll hold you forever if you want me to. But just to hold you, not to make you feel strong. I love you so much, and I can't tell you how much it means to me when I feel you loving me back. But I don't want your strength to come from anyone other than *yourself.* Not even me. You're strong because of you. Not because of me. Let the strength grow from inside you, not because of who's standing next to you. I know you can do it," he whispered. "You're so much stronger than you think you are. With or without me."

It was like Mazen chose this very moment to help me grow out of my feelings of strength that was mostly dependent on the power that his love gave to me. He only cared about my wellbeing and how I felt. I loved him even more for it, but it was as if he was giving me instructions on how to live my life away from him.

I was too far gone in proving to myself that our love was unbreakable to let the thought bother me. I knew with every sense in me that only death would tear us apart. So I nodded once again, promising him silently that I would get past this. That I'd get through it because of me, not just because Mazen was there to hold me close.

After all, I was born a fighter.

It was only then that he hugged me tightly, whispered that he loved me once again, and promised that we would be okay. But first, he had to take care of things.

The grieving was such a hard period for me, for us. It wasn't only an unborn child that I'd lost. It was one that had been taken away from me. Ripped from inside of me.

Within days, I learned why Mazen had told me that I was strong on my own and why he'd wanted me to believe it. Mazen was breaking from the inside, as well. And he'd doubted he could help me when he was barely able to help himself.

Those cousins of his had caused more damage than we'd thought was possible. And Mazen was taking it all on his shoulders.

I could see it, I could see it all in his eyes – those eyes that were no longer able to look straight into my own, or keep contact. I could see it in how restless his nights were, and how tasteless food became so that he wasn't eating as he used to. I could see it in the blank papers he spent hours staring at, but was never able to write a word on.

It was like his thoughts were too much for his brain to hold, but weren't even defined at the same time.

He was lost. And guilt was eating at him.

Sadly, I couldn't do anything to make him feel better. I was lost on my own, trying to get a hold on my feelings and control my emotions. We hugged long, and he let me cry on his shoulder even longer. We whispered *'I love yous'* whenever and all of the time. But the pain was too great for both of our hearts for one of us to be able to help the other out of it.

We still promised each other and ourselves that we'd get through it, though. And I was sure we would. Time was all we needed, aside from being close to each other. And we already had the latter.

The trial took less time than I'd expected, and Talia was found guilty, as was Jasem.

Talia had betrayed four members of the first royal family – two of them the king and the queen. She was accused of murdering six unborn children of Prince Fahd and Princess Rosanna, and the murder of an unborn child of King Mazen and Queen Marie.

It was in such a stupid, stupid way that she'd found out I was pregnant. But I had promised Mazen that I wouldn't dwell so much on it. Because whatever happened, it had happened already. Thinking of the past only caused sadness, and it wasn't something he wanted me to feel.

It turned out that Princess Huda had seen Mona as

she put the pregnancy test in the drawer, and she'd gotten really excited, asking Mona about it the first chance she got. And that was in the waiting room where the princesses had formed a line behind me.

Mona had refused to say anything, but apparently the look on her face and the smile on her lips had made Huda squeal in excitement, which was all of the confirmation Talia had needed as she overheard them.

Nobody had doubted her when she'd had to leave the ceremony for a few minutes and then come back later. Nobody had questioned why she'd left the gathering for dinner abruptly after she'd already been seated right beside my chair – close to my unattended drink.

They'd found the drugs she'd used in her lab, and tests had showed that she was using a mix of birth control pills and morning-after pills with some other ingredients that were there only to make the cocktail tasteless when added to water, and for their effect to last for weeks.

I didn't even know that she had been studying Pharmacy. All I'd ever known was that she studied in France, but not what her field of study was.

They'd also found a number of abortion pills that she was keeping as a … precaution, in case she needed them at any time.

It made me sick to my stomach to think of how evil this girl was, and just the sight of her was enough to make me feel dizzy with rage.

Speaking of dizziness, it was one of the side effects that the poison she'd put in the water had caused me, along with the blackouts and emotional outbursts, they said.

It all made sense with how I'd felt – dizziness – that first time I'd come to the kingdom, in the six days I'd lived here after the first wedding and before going back to America. And how I hadn't felt like that when I was in London, and only began suffering from them again after I'd settled in the palace. I'd seriously had no clue.

Apparently, Donia was suffering from the same side effects, but we just hadn't known it. I had no doubt we would have put two and two together if we had. Rosanna, on the other hand, wasn't affected that way by them. Though, she was the one who'd suffered the most with everything.

Jasem was only accused of helping his sister in her acts by remaining silent about them, after gaining knowledge of her crimes from the criminal herself.

They were both sentenced to death.

The night before the execution, I had a request to ask of Mazen, because only he could do it. "I think that you should give Jasem a Royal Pardon," I said quietly, already knowing that I might be fighting a losing battle.

"Excuse me?" He had heard me very well, but he

just couldn't believe his ears – of that, I was aware.

"Mazen, please think about it. If it wasn't for him, we would have never figured out what was happening. We might have lost another baby. He saved us from the great loss that was yet to come," I tried to explain my point, leaving out the part about my heart hurting because he had three kids who tomorrow would no longer have a father. Because if I brought that up, he would tell me that I wasn't thinking like a queen – which was true.

"He didn't save us, Marie. He saved his reputation, that's it," he said bitterly. "And he's getting what he deserves."

I still couldn't understand how Jasem could prefer death to jail time in exchange for him to not be outed. He knew that covering up for his sister was High Treason punishable by death, yet he'd chosen this over that. But it was one of the many things that I couldn't understand about the culture in the kingdom, and I really wasn't in the right mental state to think about something like that.

"It's just– …"

I wasn't able to finish my words before Mazen interrupted me. "Kindness in this matter will only lead to a disaster in the future. Be aware," he said. "Also, I'm not going to live peacefully knowing that someone as low as him is alive and happy somewhere – someone who knew his sister's unborn children were being killed one after another while he stood back and watched it happen."

He was right, but I thought I should try one last time, his kids still on my mind. "I only wanted to– …"

"Please, Marie, drop this. I'm not giving him something he doesn't deserve." he said. "And remember that if he had stopped his sister from the start, we would have had a child by now – he helped get it killed."

That was all the reminder I needed to finally drop the subject. Mazen was right, and I was thinking unreasonably.

"I'm going to the stable," were his last words before he left the room, leaving me alone with my thoughts. Thoughts of the children that never got to live.

Unshed tears burned my eyes, and the hate for that girl grew a little bit more. My mind still couldn't fathom how she was able to do every evil thing she'd done.

I started thinking about how a clinic was set up in the palace for the two wives of the former king, and how it could be possible that they had had a similar scenario to what had happened with Rosanna and me. But that was way before Talia was born, or when she was too young to do anything of the sort. This or that, it was a can of worms that I would never want to open.

The most important thing now was that we'd been able to stop it. However, there was so much rage inside of me that I couldn't help myself as my feet took me out of my wing.

I was so angry all of a sudden, and I knew I couldn't blame it on the side effects of the drugs she had put in the water. That had already been taken care of. I was mad, thinking about how she was in a cell right now but was still affecting me and my husband. Just the thought of Rosanna's face when she'd found out about her was enough to make my blood boil and my steps go faster. I was going to meet her and give her a piece of my mind.

Using a couple of secret doors which I now memorized by heart, I made it to the nearest stairs that could take me to where she was. I didn't want guards to be all around me; I suddenly couldn't think. I wanted to speak to her and this was my last chance. She would be dead in the morning.

Once I was no longer in a hidden place, I found a royal guard right in front of me.

"Your majesty," he greeted politely.

I nodded my head with a tight smile and continued on my way, only to find him right behind me. Of course.

"Look, I'm not going anywhere out of the palace. Please, don't follow me. I'll be fine," I told him, not waiting for his reply as I continued walking.

Not a minute later, I heard hurried steps that only faltered when the person got close to me. I turned around, only to find that it was Brad. And given the fact that he'd found me so soon, I knew that that guard had informed him of where I was through their contact system.

I fought the urge to roll my eyes, convincing myself that they were only doing their jobs, and then I went on with my way.

Royals were not treated the same as a regular person. They didn't go to a regular jail, they didn't stay in just any cell, they always got different treatment than other people. That was the way it was.

The ones who were found guilty of High Treason, for example, didn't get locked up anywhere, as the law stated. They stayed in a special area in the palace. I believed that law was made so the criminals couldn't find a way to escape, or help from other powerful people to deceive the king or the queen. Ironically, the ones we were dealing with didn't need any kind of help, anyway. But they were still in the palace as they waited for their deaths.

Finally, I made it to the alleyway that led to where Talia and Jasem were. Each had their own cell. The walk was long until I got to where the cells were, with guards lining the two sides of the path.

I stood a few yards away from the doors, realizing which one was her cell when I saw the four female guards standing outside one of them. *"Open the door, please,"* I asked, trying my best to keep the bitterness in my voice at bay.

"Your majesty, may I have a moment to ask the visitor she already has to leave first?"

The first thought that came to my mind was:
'It might be Mazen.'

Thirty-one

People say that when you've been betrayed more than once, you lose the ability to trust.

They are wrong.

Trust is still possible to achieve, but less simple to give, harder for others to earn yet very stronger when granted.

The thought of Mazen possibly being with Talia drove even crazier thoughts into my head, and an ache started growing in my chest at the things I was imagining.

It took me a second too long to be able to convince myself that it couldn't be him – he would've told me. And even if it *was*, I was sure he'd come here just to give her a few words on how much he hated her. That would be all, nothing more. I was sure.

Love made me trust.

"No," I said, *"I'll wait."*

And I did. I waited on a chair between the doors of two cells, guarded by Brad and a few other female guards who'd appeared out of nowhere. I counted the minutes, and the wait felt like it went on for ages. And when the doors opened, I looked up, still thinking there was a slight possibility I would see Mazen.

It wasn't him; it was his mother.

I was taken aback by her presence. First, because she wasn't allowed to leave her quarters, and second – because how could she still hold feelings for this girl? The look on her face told of misery and despair that I was sure were directed at Talia, not rage and hate as it was supposed to be. The look on her face told me exactly how the whole thing was affecting her. And it wasn't the way it should have been.

It had been months since the last time I'd seen her, but she appeared somewhat different. I thought she even looked shorter than normal. But I really wasn't in the right state of mind to pay attention to how that was even possible, so I let it go.

She didn't see me as I sat there. Her steps were heavy as she left, and I saw her put her face cover down as she walked through the alleyway. She most likely hadn't even noticed that there was a man out there already – Brad – who was standing next to me. She was so out of it.

"Your majesty?" I heard one of the female guards

calling, trying to get my attention to tell me that I could go inside if I wished.

When I stood up to take the few steps to where Talia was, I suddenly could no longer see why I was going there. I'd come here to give her a piece of my mind, to tell her exactly how I felt. I was so angry and I wanted to show her what she'd done. I wanted her to feel guilty.

But in one moment, and just when I was a step away from entering the cell, I found that I really didn't want to go. I didn't know what had come over me, but all I could think was – why would I do it? It wouldn't be good for her, nor would it be good for me.

Yelling at her, or even cursing wouldn't give me back what I'd lost. It wouldn't give me my baby back.

In the moment I stood there by her door, I realized that that girl was going to be killed tomorrow morning, mere hours from now. What else could be any worse? She was going to pay for her crimes with her life. There was no more justice than that.

Another moment passed, and I realized that a girl with her heart – who'd actually killed her sister's unborn children in cold blood – might never feel the regret or the guilt I was hoping she would feel.

It wasn't worth it. She wasn't worth it. And with that thought, I returned to my wing. My mind wasn't any more clear, nor was my heart any less heavy. I was simply miserable.

Mazen didn't came back at all that night. I couldn't understand him. We should have been together during this difficult time. We should be together always. Period. But I tried my best not to overthink it; he probably only needed to clear his mind and that was all.

Love made me more understanding.

I stayed in bed until morning, not even thinking about trying to sleep. I knew it would be impossible. And when Mazen came back, I didn't wonder if he'd gotten any sleep of his own. He looked terrible.

A tight smile was all he offered me in greeting, still not holding eye contact for longer than a moment, just as he'd been doing since we found out about everything.

I didn't leave my spot on the bed all the while Mazen took his shower – I didn't feel like it. I wanted to stay there all day long. At least, until I learned that it was all over.

After he was finished dressing, he looked at me with a frown. "You're not dressed yet," he said.

I looked down at the dress I'd been wearing since last night and then back at him. "I'm not going. I can't watch that."

Mazen's lips formed a thin line before he spoke again. "You should come. But it's as you wish." And then he left the room.

I found myself going after him, wanting to watch him a little bit longer. The sadness in his voice was hurting my soul, and I wanted to convince myself that he would be okay by watching him with others. I wanted to see him with his blank mask that he wore so well in front of anyone who wasn't me, hoping that if I saw it – I would believe that he was actually fine and not breaking inside like I was.

After he left, I stood in the foyer by the open door, gazing at nothing and almost not finding it in me to reply to Donia when she asked if I needed something.

When I was about to go back inside, the clicking of high heels on the marble floor caught my attention. I looked in the direction of where the sounds were coming from, only to see Rosanna walking with firm steps with Prince Fahd following her, the guards taking hurried steps to be able to keep up with her. She appeared to be eager to get to where she was going.

Her eyes caught mine and then they looked over me, her steps faltered and then they changed direction as she made her way to me.

"Why are you not dressed yet? We have less than two hours left," she asked.

"I'm not going," was all I said.

Rosanna didn't waste time coming inside the wing and closing the door. She then pulled her face cover down, showing me her face that was paler than normal, and the circles around her eyes that were darker than ever.

"What do you mean you're not going, Marie?"

"I can't watch that. I can't watch someone be killed that way."

"They are not going to be killed; they are only paying for their crimes." She sounded very certain of what she was saying, which was the truth. But I couldn't see how that changed anything. The beheading was too brutal for me to watch, and I wasn't willing to bring my nightmares back again.

I just shook my head, not able to reply to her. I didn't have it in me to explain how my heart couldn't bear such a sight.

"Listen to me, Marie, it'll only be when you see it happen that your pain is going to ease. Only if you watch will you get your revenge. It's only fair that we watch her be killed, just like she forced me to watch my children die one after another before they even got a chance to live. Just like she forced you to watch yours."

Rosanna might have been very good at controlling her feelings just like most of the royal family, but in that moment, she couldn't help the trembling in her lips, or the tears that sparkled in her eyes.

"It's up to you, anyway," she said a moment later. "If you'll excuse me, your majesty." And then she was gone.

Her words rang in my ears long after she'd left, words that stirred up a pain that I'd been doing my best to put to sleep. And in the heat of my feelings, my decision was made.

It was beyond shocking to learn that the executions were going to be public. I knew that was the way it was in the kingdom, but my shock was due to the fact that they were royals – maybe they would get a different treatment.

"All people are equal. They should serve as a lesson for others. The law knows no difference between a royal and a servant," Mazen had said bitterly when I voiced my surprise.

It made sense. But still … it felt – I didn't even know how it felt.

We were seated on some sort of a stage, a place that was a few inches above the sandy ground in that spot in the desert where everything was set. It somehow looked like one of those arenas you'd see in historical shows, yet not really the same.

Rosanna and I were the only two people sitting down; the rest were all standing up. I could see people gathering behind the big circle that the guards formed, and I was even more shocked by the number of them.

I guess you didn't get to watch a royal's beheading often. Or at all.

They called Talia's full name, and I assumed they were about to count her crimes before Mazen stopped them.

"*No. Jasem – son of Hamed Alfaidy first*," he called

with a voice that was louder than thunder and scarier than light. I actually flinched when I heard his 'No.'

It wasn't like he was so eager to have Jasem killed. No. I understood my husband very well. He wanted Talia to suffer a bit more. A bit longer. He couldn't let them give her peace, yet. If that was what she was going to get in the afterlife, that is.

I knew that the longer she stayed alive, the longer she would suffer as she waited for her death.

I couldn't feel sorry for her.

After the guard called his name out loud and stated his crimes and punishment, Jasem was brought out of a vehicle that was standing a bit away from where we were seated.

Jasem was wearing a white *thawp*, his hands cuffed behind his back, and his legs wrapped in chains. His steps were heavy, and I had no doubt that if it weren't for the two guys holding him by both sides – he wouldn't be standing in the first place, let alone walking.

My thoughts were solely focused on his kids, I didn't know why. I felt sorry for them, for they'd grow up without a father, and also the fact that they'd actually grow up with his shame. One who'd helped with murders and high treason. I held my cross and prayed for them silently.

My eyes stayed closed peacefully as I tried to block everything out and concentrate on my prayer. But then I squeezed them tightly shut when I heard the swooping of the sword as it cut into the air before … doing what it was supposed to do.

My heart was thumping so hard in my chest that it felt as if it wanted to burst out of my body. It was only when Mazen touched my shoulder and squeezed that I started breathing again, realizing that I had stopped doing that the moment I heard all of the gasps.

It was minutes later that I reopened my eyes. It was when I heard them calling her name again. It was the same second that Mazen's touch went away as he took a step forward so he was now standing next to my chair instead of behind me.

He wasn't the only one to react at the sound of Talia's name. Rosanna also left her seat and stood up, taking a step forward.

They both wanted a better look.

My grip on my cross grew tighter as Talia came into view. I was yards away from her, but I could see her face clearly. There were no teardrops on her cheeks. However, she couldn't take one step forward. They had to drag her all the way to where her life would end.

She didn't have her face cover on; she wasn't allowed to wear it in court, either. The Islamic laws stated so. She was wearing a white *abaya* and a white scarf, only. Just like her brother, her hands were cuffed behind her back, and her feet were trapped with chains.

The guards made her kneel. The Sheikh went to her side and started telling her to repent before going to the afterlife and all that. But I didn't think she was listening.

Her eyes were focused on the man standing next to me, the only one who could save her life. She was so scared, trembling with fear even. She didn't look at all like the girl who'd told me that one day she would carry my husband's child.

I still couldn't feel sorry for her.

My eyes turned to look at Mazen, wanting to see his reaction to the look on her face. I was almost scared of what I would see. But when I looked, I only saw hate. Pure hate was pouring out of my love's kind eyes. A look that I was sure he would never, ever give me.

I stared at him, then at her, wanting to see how that would end. Trying to listen carefully to hear what she was silently telling him with her eyes. I waited to see remorse, waited to see the guilt over what she'd done. There was none.

Then the frightened look on her face turned into a sneer, an expression that had me more shocked than I'd ever been in my life. She was pure evil. Even moments away from her death, she couldn't keep the evil smile away.

That was all the satisfaction I needed to have. It wasn't that she was taking her last breaths, no. It was to be able to see with my own eyes that Mazen didn't feel a drop of compassion for her. None.

I managed to look away just a second before the sword made contact with the back of her neck. I didn't care for her. Not even a little bit. But I still couldn't look at something like that.

However, I was glad I'd managed to be present during the whole thing without breaking all over myself. I realized then that I'd grown.

Love made me grow.

"*Good riddance*," I heard Rosanna say before she walked away, and all I could think was: Indeed.

It was almost midnight, and Mazen had yet to come back home. Our day had been cleared of any meetings or places we needed to be, other than attending the execution. But Mazen still said he had things to do.

He was such a bad liar. But I was understanding and didn't comment on it. But then, he hadn't even texted me all day long, not once. And that wasn't at all like him. I knew I had to do something.

He wanted to be alone, he was hurting – I got that. But I thought it was enough. We needed to put those people behind us, start a new and clear page with no haters clinging to our necks and trying to ruin our lives.

The first thing I did was leave the wing, spotting Mo'taz as he stood beside Brad right next to the main door of the wing.

"Hey, Mo'taz," I started, "Do you know where his majesty is?"

"Yes, your majesty, last we were informed he was at the stable."

The stable again ... I thought.

"Okay, I'm going there then. Prepare the cars and guards while I get ready."

"Yes, your majesty."

It only took me about ten minutes to change, and then I went on my way to get to Mazen. I made it all the way to Thunder's room after I went to Salma's, thinking he was most likely to be there. But he wasn't.

I sighed, my legs taking me to Thunder, and my hand rubbed his soft fur. "*Hey there, Ra'ad,*" I greeted him in Arabic, a small smile on my lips. He'd started to like me more as I grew better at pronouncing his name, though he was always Thunder in my head, not Ra'ad. "*Do you happen to know where our guy is?*" I asked.

A soft neigh was all I got in reply.

"Yeah, not very helpful." I sighed again, patting his neck and then leaving the stable.

I knew exactly where he was.

Climbing our mountain had become much easier nowadays; I'd gotten used to it. My mood was improving already as I took one step after another to reach the top of it, the spot where I knew Mazen would be.

He was sitting down and gazing at nothing, seemingly completely lost in his thoughts. His back was resting on a rock behind him, and his hand was reaching every now and then for a small rock to throw away, only to reach for another to do the same thing with it.

"Hey," I called, and he stopped mid-throw to look at me, his eyes bloodshot and surprised by my presence.

Mazen stood up right away and took a few steps in my direction, offering me his hand to help me climb the last rock.

"Princess," he breathed once I stood on the same level he was standing on, moving me a few steps away from the edge. "Are you all right?"

It was typical of Mazen to ask if I was okay. Even when he looked as miserable as he was right now, he still put me first. I was the first thing he ever got to be concerned about.

"I'm fine." I smiled, moving my hand that wasn't in his to touch his cheek softly. Mazen leaned into my touch for a brief second before he caught himself and looked away. I dropped my hand to his neck, not allowing him to deny me the feeling of touching him. "You're not," I told him.

Mazen didn't answer me, he still looked away, and I watched him swallow thickly a few times. I waited for him to speak, but he didn't, so I decided to ask him to do just that.

"Talk to me, angel."

Mazen shook his head, looking down at his feet. "I'm not an angel. I'm a monster," he said in a low, saddened voice.

"What? Why would you say that? You're so far away from that."

"You already know what I did. I don't even know how you could look at me with anything other than disgust!" he said to my shock, letting go of my hand and turning his back to me.

"Mazen, what are you talking about?"

"You know what I'm talking about. I helped her, I gave her easy access. I should've been executed today along with them."

"Don't say that! You had no idea what she was doing."

"Because I'm stupid."

"No. It's because you don't think like murderers!"

I knew Mazen was feeling guilty, but this was beyond what I'd expected. He was withering in the pain and guilt and remorse.

"All of the pain you went through, everything my brother and his wife witnessed – it was all because of me."

"You're not being reasonable, Mazen."

"It's the truth, Marie. I'm as guilty as they were."

I'd had enough of that, so I went and stood in front of him. I took his face in both of my hands and tried to force him to look at me. He was feeling so guilty to the point of embarrassment. He couldn't even look me in the eye.

"Look at me, Mazen," I said, "Please." It took him a few moments before he finally managed to look into my eyes, and his were like opened gates that leaked despair and misery. The sad frown on his forehead alone was enough to make tears tingle in my eyes.

"You didn't do anything, angel. It wasn't your fault. Maybe it was through you that she found an easy way to do it, but if it wasn't for that, she would've found another way. She would've done it anyway, no matter what. It was her goal in life to be the queen. She didn't care who she took down on her way or how she got there; she was going to do whatever it took to get it. It's not your fault. It's nobody's fault other than hers. You can't keep dwelling on it. She's gone from our lives, and it's time we leave all of this behind us," I said softly. "Please, angel, don't let her mess up our lives even after her death."

Mazen's eyes stared into my eyes for a long time; the sparkling unshed tears in them were making my heart ache for him. I didn't think I'd ever hated anything in my life as much as seeing Mazen this way.

He then dropped down on his knees, his eyes looking up at me, begging me silently even before he began speaking. "Will you ever be able to forgive me?" he pleaded.

"There's nothing to forgive, angel. Please, try to believe that," I told him. "C'mon, get up, don't kneel like this." Mazen looked so vulnerable and I couldn't watch him act this way. He was forever the strongest man I'd ever met. And he would stay that way in my eyes.

"I'm kneeling in front of you not demeaning myself, but because of my love for you." He took both of my hands and placed a kiss on the back of each one, then looked up at me again. "I'm the ruler of a large kingdom, but my heart is ruled by you. You're the only person who can turn the light on in my life, otherwise everything would be so dark. You're the only reason why I can go on, Marie."

His words were like a kiss of the sun, sending warmth straight to my heart that spread through all of my insides. It was everything I'd already known, but still wanted to hear.

I found myself kneeling in front of him, then we were hugging tightly to the point it almost hurt. The dark sky above us sparkled with the beautiful little stars. The same stars that had witnessed our first kisses, and watched as our love grew.

We hugged tightly, because we both needed it.

In that moment, everything seemed like it was going to be completely okay to the point of perfection.

Sadly, back then I didn't know how wrong I was in assuming that the worst had passed and from now on we would get to live peacefully. I didn't know that someone, somewhere was plotting revenge.

Back then, I only knew one thing: Love made us stronger.

Mazen was Love.

Teaser

Golden Chains
The Colorblind Trilogy Book Three

“Breathe! Breathe! You can’t fucking die. You can’t!”

Acknowledgments

Thank you to the following individuals who, without their contributions and support, this book could not have been written:

To Sandra, for being the best friend and the best sister, I love you more than love.
To Kholoud, for staying up all night just to talk to me whenever life wasn't bearable. Ba7ebek moot.
To Sheri, for the prayers and all of the good thoughts, for being a wonderful friend whenever I felt so lonely.
To Adriana, for knowing how to make me feel better, and driving me insane all at the same time.
To Michelle, my baby sister and sunshine.
To Wendy Mathew, for always being there when I needed you the most. I would've been a mess without you.
To Widad, Zeinab, Maheen, Susan, Terri, Sahar, Joan, Carol, Isherna, Leah, and the wonderful Tee for listening to all of my rants, and assuring me that 'It's going to be okay'. I love you girls more than I can explain, and I wouldn't know what I would've done without your constant help.
To my parents, my kids and my husband, for being my reasons for living.

About the Author

Rose is a loved mother, wife, and a stay at home lawyer. Writing is her passion, and reading is her obsession. Music is her best friend and sarcasm is her speaking trend. One of her joys is bringing happiness to others and her biggest wish is that they stay true to one another. Through her stories, she wants to spread nothing except understanding, peace and love.

Additional Works:

The Colorblind Trilogy Book #3 Golden Chains Coming 2017

Forbidden Love (Janna and Joseph Story) Coming 2018